# ALFRED HITCHCOCK'S TALES TO KEEP YOU SPELLBOUND

VOLUME 1

Edited by ELEANOR SULLIVAN

THE DIAL PRESS

DAVIS PUBLICATIONS, INC.
229 PARK AVE. SOUTH, NEW YORK, N.Y. 10003

## COPYRIGHT NOTICES AND ACKNOWLEDGMENTS

4

5

# Contents

# Introduction

Here, published the same month as the 20th Anniversary Issue of *Alfred Hitchcock's Mystery Magazine*, is the first of a new series of anthologies consisting of stories that first saw the light of day in AHMM. And a bonanza collection it is, with 30 stories by some of *Alfred Hitchcock's Mystery Magazine*'s most competent and illustrious tale-spinners, including Holly Roth, C. B. Gilford, Jean Potts, David Ely, Edward D. Hoch, Nedra Tyre, Bill Pronzini, Hillary Waugh, and Borden Deal.

Also included are 7 stories that won awards in AHMM's story contest in the '60s—Jack Ritchie's "The Third Call," Robert Bloch's "A Home Away from Home," Henry Slesar's "You Can't Blame Me," Donald Honig's "The Man We Found," Lawrence Page's "Final Arrangements," Clark Howard's "Spook House," and Gilbert Ralston's "A Very Cautious Boy."

But every story in this new anthology is prize caliber—first-rate, rewarding, spellbinding reading from the master of suspense.

# The Pursuer

## by Holly Roth

When the door of her apartment had clicked behind him, Talia got off the couch, went over to the door, and pushed up the button that engaged the double lock. Then she paused and waited for her knees to steady. When they were under control, she crossed the room and switched on a lamp. Then she went into the bedroom, turned on the overhead light, and turned off the recording machine. She walked to her bedside, forgot why she was there, and then remembered. She reached into the side compartment of the small desk that served as her bedside table and brought out the telephone. She dialed the operator, and when the voice said, "This is the operator. Can I help you?" she replied, "I want the police, please."

"What is your number, please?"

Talia held the receiver away and looked at it. Then she rehung it on its cradle.

She got the telephone book from beneath the desk and looked up the local precinct number and dialed it.

She started to speak almost before the man had finished his few words of precinct identification. "Now, listen to me," she said. "I understand that the first thing the police want is one's name and address. I'm not going to give you those, and I'm not going to stay on the phone long enough for you to trace the call. If you *can* trace dial calls." The afterthought seemed irrelevant, and for a minute her mind went blank.

"Look, lady." The voice at the other end was tired. "How about you tell me what you *are* going to tell me insteada what you're not?"

"No, I'm not going to tell this story to a dozen people a dozen times. I want someone important."

"All right! All right! But I can't give you to anyone else until I know who to give you to, can I? If I decide to plug you onto *anyone*, I gotta know which one, don't I? Different departments, different cops, different jobs. See?"

That made sense. She said, "I'm being blackmailed. That's why I don't want to tell it to everyone."

The voice turned faintly coaxing. "But how's anyone gonna come to see you if we haven't got your address?"

Talia was suddenly exhausted. She said. "I've always heard—read, understood—that the police were no help in matters of blackmail. That people either paid, or killed, or got killed. I—"

The policeman's voice turned serious. Until that moment he had been humoring her, but now something—her words? a truth?—had reached through to him. He said, "One minute, I'll connect you."

It was more than a minute. She wondered again about the tracing of calls and thought, I'll have to chance that.

The wire came alive. A new voice said, "Lieutenant Bonner speaking. What's this all about? Who's blackmailing who and why don't you behave and give us your name?"

A bully, Talia thought. Like Bart. A type she knew well. He would not be helpful. She brought her voice to a careful, unexcited monotone. If she could impress him with her steadiness, her sanity . . ."My name is Cory—"

"Well, Mrs. Cory—"

"Miss Cory. Please listen for a minute. I am being blackmailed. I was also—hit. And I was threatened with a knife. I want to tell someone about it. That's the law, isn't it?"

"Yeah, but—"

"And I don't want to tell a man at a desk, and then another man at another desk, and so on. So if you will just advise me—"

He roared. "*Wait* a minute! How can anyone—important or not —come to see you and talk to you if you won't give us your address? —What's your first name?"

"My phone is not listed. So what good would my first name do you?" But this was the police; unlisted phones wouldn't hinder them. She said, "I don't want anyone to come to see me." To come into her place, to clog her three quiet rooms, to add to the sacrilege that had already desecrated her living room . . . "I want to go there. But where do I go, whom do I ask for?"

10                                    ALFRED HITCHCOCK'S ANTHOLOGY

He grunted. "All right, all right. You can come here. Write it down." He gave her the address. "If you come over right away you can ask for me. Lieutenant Bonner. *Are* you coming over now?"

"No." She couldn't. She wouldn't be able to make it.

"When, then?"

"In the morning?"

"In the morning ask for Lieutenant Corelli."

"How early?"

"He comes on at eight."

"Thank you."

"Wait! Look, lady—Miss Cory—if this stuff is on the level, how d'ya know you're going to be okay, safe, until tomorrow?"

"I'll be all right." She looked around the small room. "I'm safe here. Thank you." She hung up.

She said to the uniformed policeman behind the big desk on the platform high above her, "May I see Lieutenant Corelli, please?"

"What about?"

"I have an appointment."

He grunted, reached for an old-fashioned telephone with a standing mouthpiece and said, "Lieutenant Corelli." After a minute he said, "Lieutenant? A lady to see you. Miss—" He raised his eyebrows at Talia and then repeated after her, "Miss Cory. . . Yeah, Lieutenant." He hung up. "Upstairs." He nodded at the stairway just outside the door to the big room. "Second floor. End of the hall. Room two-ten."

She said, "Thank you," and went out to the stairs.

The door to Room 210 was open, and a heavy-set man in shirt sleeves sat facing her across an expanse of desk, his head bent over a mass of papers. Her first thought was that the desk was too big for the room; then she noticed the walls—they hadn't been painted, she thought, in at least ten years. She stood, waiting for a second, and then she knocked on the open door.

The man looked up.

There was an empty moment, after which he registered surprise as thoroughly as an actor who had been trained for a lifetime in the art. Then, in one hasty motion, he stood up. He said, "Miss Cory?" His voice, even in those two short words, struck her as beautiful. Every consonant got equal rights, and the tone came from deep within him.

But deep wasn't far, she thought; he was only five eight or nine inches tall, a stocky man. He had a pleasant face, despite a network of wrinkles—premature wrinkles, she decided; he had reached no farther than early middle age.

"Yes. And you are Lieutenant Corelli?" He nodded. "Lieutenant Bonner told me—"

"Yes, I know. He left me a report. Come in, please. Sit down. And let me take your, ah, bag."

Reflexively, her grip tightened on the small but rather heavy box. "I'll put it right here beside the chair, thank you."

"Fine. Now will you start from the beginning? And may we have it taken down?" He added quickly, "If we decide we can help you I won't be permitted to do so until I have a statement. So it would save you from going through the explanation all over again."

She nodded. "Certainly. I've come to make a statement. And my—stubbornness on the phone was just to avoid saying it all over and over again. I had no other reason."

His mouth turned upward in a slow smile. It grew very wide and she saw then where his wrinkles had come from. His entire face took part in the smile, and the exercise had told on it through the years. He said, "I shouldn't admit it, but I think you may have been smart. You sure would have told it a few times. If it's—important." He raised his voice and called, "Sergeant!" A man in uniform, its jacket unbuttoned, came through a door opposite her. Corelli said, "A statement to be taken, Sergeant." The man disappeared into the back room, reappeared with a shorthand book, and sat behind Talia, beside the open door. Not then or ever did she hear him speak.

Corelli said, "Start with your full name and address, Miss Cory."

She gave him that. He nodded. "And your age?"

"Almost twenty-eight."

"All right. Go on."

She went on: "Four months and three days ago, on January twenty-first, I came here from my home town, Lafayette, Iowa. It's a small town, sort of a suburb of Des Moines. Before I left—on December twenty-third—I shot and killed my brother, Bartholomew Cory."

The wrinkles in Corelli's face twitched. It was too mobile a face, she thought. It would distract her. She raised her eyes and fixed them on the wall above him and to his left. She would forever afterward re-

　　　　ALFRED HITCHCOCK'S ANTHOLOGY

member the crumbling paint on the dirty green wall.

"Briefly—and there's no sense in being more than brief; if you want details you can wire Des Moines—Polk County—and they will send you records, I'm sure." On the periphery of her gaze, she saw the nod. "So, briefly, it was like this. My brother came home at three in the morning. Slightly after that, they decided. He had forgotten his keys so he climbed in through the dining-room window. He was drunk. They established that. It wouldn't matter, it wouldn't be—pertinent—except that it accounted for the odd noises he was making. Like a—an animal. Between the fact of the—the guttural noises, and the fact that he didn't sound like himself when he finally spoke, and the fact that after I warned what I thought was an intruder to stop or I'd shoot he still hurled himself through the window at me—well, I shot him. There was a—a hearing; the jury agreed it was an accident. That was—" She looked briefly back at the lieutenant and then refocused on the patch of wall. "That was that, I thought.

"But last night a man came, threatened me, hit—me, demanded money." She waited.

Corelli said gently, "Well, now you have to tell me about that, don't you?"

"No. The beginning only. He phoned me at my office, Krause & Kane, an advertising agency on Fifth Avenue. He said he knew all about me. He used my full name, Natalia Eileen Cory. He was—very threatening. He said he would come to my apartment at eight o'clock. So—"

"He asked for your address?"

She looked down at him. "No."

"But you told Lieutenant Bonner your phone is unlisted. Is that true?"

"Yes." She frowned.

"Well, we'll discuss it later. So he was going to come to your apartment at eight o'clock. And he did?"

"At five minutes' past. —Do you have an electric outlet in here?"

"An elec—" He stared at her, but only for a second. Then he stood up so that he could peer over the desk. He looked down at the box and then up at Talia. He said softly, "Well, well," and a new set of muscles came into play on the expressive face.

"Sergeant," Corelli said, and composed himself for listening.

She hadn't played the recording back the night before. She hadn't been sure of how to do so and was afraid she might accidentally reverse and erase it; she had been too tired; and she had been, before her four hours' sleep, afraid to relive the experience. Now she was relieved to find that the machine operated perfectly, and every sound came through with entire fidelity. She made her mind as blank as possible and lapsed from rigidity just twice: when she first heard her own voice she felt and showed surprise, and when the cracking sounds came she winced with each blow.

By a quarter to eight she had been ready and waiting. For the next ten minutes she sat, like a figure caught in a slip of the earth's rotation, motionless, weightless, thoughtless. The couch faced the door, and her eyes, almost unblinking, were fixed upon that door.

The downstairs door buzzer didn't sound until five minutes after eight, and as she got up to push the release button she could not have said if the period since she had assumed her vigil had been a lifetime or a second. But with the necessity of motion came thought and response. She went into the bedroom and turned the switch on the recording machine, adjusted the box behind the door so that the rear crack of the partly open door was near it, and then went and stood at her front entrance. When she heard steps in the outer hallway she opened the door without waiting for the knocker to be lifted.

The figure outside was shorter than she and very thin. That was almost all she could see at first because the only light within her apartment came from two shaded lamps and, as a result, the stronger hall lights outlined him and made details difficult to discern. But, even in that outline, there was something very odd . . .And then she realized that she had interrupted his preparations; he had a handkerchief folded into a large triangle before his face, and his arms were raised as he tried to tie it behind his head. The eyes above the handkerchief stared strainingly at her and she saw that he was shocked, probably because she had so nearly caught him undraped. She had a moment's desire to laugh—this undernourished little man was not the figure of terror her frightened imagination had conjured. And then she saw the eyes, and the menace, all the menace that had existed in her imagination—and more—was there. The eyes had enormous pupils and a peculiar lack of focus, and when he spoke his reedy, high-tenor voice did nothing to

14

lessen the threat. He said, with a flat lack of intonation that sounded particularly odd in the high voice, "Close the door. Just leave it a little open. Right away!"

She obeyed, almost as a reflex action.

The voice came around the door: "Now turn off the lights in there."

She moved across the room and switched off her lamps. The room was still surprisingly well lighted; on a spring evening, New York glows.

The door opened and quickly closed, and the latch clicked.

He said, "Sit down," and she sank onto the couch.

The small man moved with a sidling motion until he was in front of the wing chair that faced the couch; then he sat on its edge. He did not remove his hat. (It looked too large for him, Talia thought, or was it because such juvenile types usually didn't wear hats?) The two screens—the hat's broad brim and the handkerchief—combined to make an amazingly effective shield. She could see nothing but the narrow strip of face that contained the unnatural-looking eyes. His brows were in the shadow of the brim; his ears were hidden by the handkerchief; the hair at the sides of the head was identifiable as hair only because one knew it was there—but for all she could tell, it could have been purple. With only those straining, staring eyes as guide she couldn't begin to place the man. But perhaps she didn't know him.

He said, and there was venom in every high quavering note, "You're the kind that comes out on top. You always do. In every moment of your life. This time you kill a man, and what happens? You get away from everything and come out on top."

That was true enough, Talia thought numbly. Not that she had always come out on top, but that she had this one time.

He said, "So I'm going to even things a bit."

He seemed to be waiting. Talia said, "Yes?"

"I'm going to take some of your money."

"This is very foolish," Talia said evenly. "What you are discussing is called blackmail—" .

The high voice reached higher, into a kind of piercing whisper: "Don't you call me foolish, and don't you dare patronize me! Understand?" There was hate in his voice and killing in his eyes, and she realized she was terribly afraid. It was a particularly dreadful fear to be made so frightened by so inconsequential a little man.

THE PURSUER                                                                    15

She kept her voice even and tried to keep any intonation, patronizing or otherwise, out of it: "What I'm trying to say is that I *don't* understand. To be blackmailed, a person has to have a secret worth paying to keep, and the money to pay with. I haven't either."

"That's part of your arrogance. You earn a hundred and fifteen dollars a week, don't you?"

She looked at him blankly. How did he know?

"Or didn't you ever bother to figure it out? Six thousand a year is a hundred and fifteen dollars a week. So you must take home just about ninety dollars a week."

He waited. She said, "Yes."

"Well, *I* don't. So we're going to share things a little more evenly. I want thirty dollars every week. That won't bring me up to ninety, but it'll put me ahead of you, and I want to be—I *belong* ahead of you."

"But *why* should I pay you? Even a nickel?"

He laughed. The sound was somewhere between a snicker and a neigh, and she had a momentary fear that she would be sick as she saw that his eyes, luminous and staring in the room's dim light, didn't change at all, didn't get even slightly narrower. "Would you like all those innocents in—the place you work—to know that you are a murderess? To know all about you?"

"No." She swallowed and went evenly on. "No. I wouldn't. But I wouldn't pay anyone anything to keep them from knowing. I might leave my job, and just get another one. And if you told the people at the next job, then I'd get another, and so on forever. If you earn less than I, I don't see how you could afford to keep following me around. And I don't see what good it would do you."

The man got off his chair and walked unsteadily toward her. A minute later she realized she should have been afraid, but her immediate reaction was that he must have been even more frightened than she because his knees were shaking even more than hers. But as he stood over her and she looked from his legs up to his eyes, she saw that it was not fear but rage that caused his trembling. And then he slapped her. He was wearing heavy brown-leather gloves. Very unsuitable for the weather, Talia thought. And felt the pain. They heavy leather cracking across her face sounded like a shot in the quiet room. A series of shots, she thought, as his hand fanned back and forth so that first the gloved palm hit her left cheek and then the back of the hand hit

16

her right cheek, in a volley of slow, deliberate, stinging blows. Talia sat as still as the rocking blows permitted, and stubbornly refused to let herself cry. There was nothing so degrading as physical violence. That was what had made Bart so dreadful. But Bart had never hit *her*, Talia—he had never dared. This little man, half Bart's size, dared, and he got away with it. Because in his left hand, inches from her breast, he held a knife. The light gleamed off its long length in a single piercing ray, since its tiny width offered little surface for reflection; the knife had been honed until it was not much more than a stiletto.

Talia sat as still as possible. She didn't want to die. And the little man would kill her. There was no doubt at all about that.

Then his hand stopped its deliberate fanning motion and he backed slowly away, back to the wing chair, and perched on its edge once more. "Now," he said, and his voice sounded more relaxed. "You see? You mustn't be impertinent. Even if you are so bold that you don't care who knows you are a murderess, there are two other reasons to pay me. One is that I'll kill you if you don't." He paused. Then he said, "Do you understand?"

"Yes." And she believed him.

"And the other is that I know something about that murder that no one else knows. *You saw him—because the light was on.* Didn't you?"

I'm not *sure* I saw him, Talia thought. But the light *was* on.

"So I don't even have to warn you about staying away from the police. You have a lot more to fear from them than I have." He stood up. "I'll phone you. I'll tell you how to pay me the money. Exactly thirty dollars every week. In a post-office box, I think. I won't see you for awhile." He moved toward the door and put his hand on the knob. Then he turned back and faced her. "But later—after I've taught you your place—we're going to become very good friends. Intimate."

The door closed behind him. Gently.

When the recording had run its course, the sergeant had halted it, and she had refastened her eyes on the wall.

The lieutenant asked, "Those cracking sounds—is your face swollen, Miss Cory?"

"Yes."

"Um." Then the next words were snapped out. "Is that machine yours?"

Her startled eyes came down to his "No."

"Where'd you get it?"

"Borrowed it."

"Where?"

"From a neighbor."

"Name?"

"Richards. James Richards. He lives in the apartment directly below me. He also works for an ad agency, and he once told me that he sometimes taped TV and radio programs."

"He's a good friend? You told him why you wanted the machine?"

"No. He's only a—an elevator acquaintance." When she first moved in, Richards had tried to be somewhat more than that, but Talia—frozen into her solitude—had snubbed him. Last night he had been a little stiff at first, but was too nice to maintain the attitude. "I didn't tell him anything. I was going to say that I wanted it for the same reason he used it, but he asked no questions and so I didn't have to lie. He showed me how to work the machine, to run a tape, to erase. And that was all." Except that he had been very kind.

"Um. You behaved with—admirable—dispatch and forethought Miss Cory."

Was that sarcasm? She said, "I've read all the stories that everyone else has read about blackmail. This seemed the best way to handle it."

"Um." He sat back in his chair and then moved quickly forward again. She moved instinctively backward. "*Were* the lights on when you shot your brother?"

"Yes."

"And you didn't say so? To the police? To the court?"

"No one asked me."

"And you didn't volunteer the information."

It was a statement. She said nothing.

"Um. I gather that you were supposed to have shot at a prowler. *Did* you know who it was?"

No amount of rapid-fire questioning could draw a fast answer to that. She had spent hours thinking about it, and she thought again now. "No," she said at last. "Possibly—in that very last second—possibly I might have known. But it was too late then."

"Didn't you like your brother?"

Talia took a deep breath, and said, "That is beside the point, Lieuten-

18                                    ALFRED HITCHCOCK'S ANTHOLOGY

ant Corelli. Wire Lafayette if you're curious. The blackmail happened here; the—shooting—was in their—jurisdiction."

"Um." He smiled, but it was a pale, frosty imitation of its predecessors. He said, "Maybe it's foolish of me to tip you, but you seem competent enough to know where the cards lie. So . . . you tell me you were acquitted, Miss Cory. The law of the United States forbids double jeopardy. You cannot be tried twice for the same crime."

She looked at him levelly and then she too smiled. It was the first time she had smiled in that office, and a tiny reflection, a rather surprised reflection, shone back at her from the broad, dark face before her. She said, "Perhaps it's foolish of me to—to tip *you*, Lieutenant Corelli, but you look competent too. Certainly competent enough to find out the simple truth: I was *not* tried for my brother's death. Not even on a charge of manslaughter. There was merely an inquest. I could be put on trial at any time."

"I see." He stared at her with obvious curiosity. There was some other quality in his face, she thought—admiration? He said, "You realize, I imagine, that your statement here is not privileged. I am not a priest, or a lawyer, or a doctor."

"Yes, I know."

"Well, in view of that realization on your part, it was—courageous—of you to come here."

A compliment? Or a threat? She said nothing.

Corelli spoke briskly. "Now this"—he waved at the tape recorder—"this character. Description, please."

She shook her head. "Almost nothing." She explained about the hat and handkerchief. "He was short—"

"How short?"

"Perhaps five feet seven or eight."

Corelli smiled. "Everything is relative. To me that is 'average.' I am five feet eight."

"Oh. But you see, I—"

"You are taller. Yes."

"And also he seemed shorter because he was—diminutive. Thin. Slender. No shoulders to speak of."

"The voice seems very high. Is the recording sound accurate?"

"Yes."

"Um. Then could it have been a woman?"

"A woman?" It was a new thought and she gave it time. Then she shook her head. "I don't know. Perhaps. I don't think so."

"Color of eyes?"

"I don't know."

"But you saw them."

"Yes. But there were no lights on. I think they were colorless."

"Colorless usually means gray."

She shrugged helplessly.

"The same applies to the color of his hair?"

She nodded.

"But he seemed young?"

"Yes."

"His hands?"

"He wore gloves. Thick brown leather."

"You *could* see the color of those?"

She looked at him inquiringly, but the dark face was impassive. "Yes."

"Suit?"

"I don't know. I don't notice men's clothes. Men simply look well-dressed or badly dressed to me. Or gaudy or not gaudy. His suit was gray, I think. Shabby. Not well pressed." She wondered if he didn't believe in the man at all. Her description certainly wasn't very convincing. But there was that recording. . . She looked down at the box.

"I believe he exists, Miss Cory."

The mind-reading made her jump slightly.

"But it is possible," he went on, "that you could have something else—an ulterior motive—in mind. Let's suppose—just suppose—that you were to kill a short, thin man tomorrow. Or a woman. In your apartment."

It was too much to take in all at once, but she trod doggedly along his path of thought. And she got as far as an answer. "In view of my—my history, that wouldn't be very sensible of me, would it? Recording or no?"

He smiled slightly. "No, it wouldn't. But it was just one of several suppositions." He leaned forward. "Listen to me while I play it straight: If your story is the simple truth, there are several noticeable oddities." He put up a hand. "Don't interrupt. I didn't mean the oddities in *your* story; I said was playing it straight. I mean *general* od-

ALFRED HITCHCOCK'S ANTHOLOGY

dities. Let's take the matter of identification: You can't identify this person; he just seems vaguely familiar. Right? But he knows"—he ticked the points off on his fingers—"your middle name, your address—although he would not have been able to find it in the telephone book—your salary. Taking just that much into account, it sounds as if he must work with you. Does that suggest anything to you? Incidents, peculiarities?"

The idea was merely shocking. She showed it. "I am new in my job, of course. I have made no friends in the office. Friends, yes, but not—" She stopped, looked a little helpless, and he nodded to show his understanding. "My position there is—remote. Removed." She struggled to explain. To him, and to herself. "No matter how calmly I seemed to take it, the—the business of my brother's death was—shocking to me. Like in major surgery, the whole body is jolted—well, my mind was jolted. And my h.bits. My—everything." She looked up at him, and he nodded again. "So my relationships at the office are not—not quite normal. I speak to and am friendly with my superior, Mr. Long, my office mate, Janet Furman, one of the telephone operators, the office boy, one man in the art department . . . a few others." She lifted a hand and let it fall. "And it's all impersonal." She made a discovery and voiced it: "Because I am impersonal."

"I understand. But it suggests little in connection with this blackmailer. We come to the second connection: He also sounds like someone you should be able to identify from the past. He discussed your past life. What you 'always' had done. Would you necessarily know everyone in Lafayette?"

She struggled with that. Then she asked, "Are you a New Yorker, Lieutenant?"

He raised his eyebrows. "Yes."

"Then you probably don't know about small towns, and they're hard to explain. It's like— You have high schools here in New York where they have as many as ten thousand students at a time, isn't that so?"

"I went to one."

"Well, then, after fours years I imagine you know, in a way, those ten thousand people. Maybe you don't speak to them all, but years later if one becomes famous or if you find yourself with one of them at a party or on a—a committee or something, you'd both probably know you went to school together, isn't that right?"

He nodded appreciatively.

"Lafayette has about eight thousand inhabitants, and I know them all in that same way. There are people whom I do not know well enough to speak to on the streets of Lafayette, but if I passed one of them on Fifth Avenue we'd probably stop and speak. And we'd sound and feel and *be* really friendly."

"Now, that's very clear. So you rule Lafayette people neither in nor out of your speculations." He leaned across his desk. "At the end of our interview I'll take certain standard steps. For instance, I'll have a check made on possible known offenders. That will be a routine police step, and pretty damn foolish. This person is very vindictive about you, very personal. His approach and demands are those of an amateur. But still I'll make that gesture. In addition, I'll ask you to advise us of anything that occurs, any direct contact or anything merely unusual. Then, if and when the person actually approaches you again, I'll take decisive steps. If there should be an attack on you, or anything resembling it, we'll provide police protection. At the moment, there is not enough to warrant that.

"Now, these steps, until the man shows his hand more clearly, are largely defensive. But with the information I have I see no way to go out and *find* this man. Do you?"

She shook her head. He was obviously working up to something. She waited.

"But there *is* a possible way. He probably comes from, or has a connection with, Lafayette, Iowa. Enough to know details of your life. Enough to know that—the lights were on. If you will let me question you—?"

"You *have* been questioning me. I *have* let you."

"You forewarned me that the shooting that occurred in Iowa was not in my jurisdiction."

"Oh. About that. But that is irrelevant."

"I don't think so."

She felt helplessly caught. She could not live in a world in which the little man wandered freely—with a knife like a stiletto—looking for her. Neither could she relive that night before Christmas Eve, with its multiple horrors. But the lieutenant seemed to be saying, "Either you cooperate as I see fit, or I will make only routine gestures." In essence, he would do nothing unless he could put her through a hell.

Why? she wondered, and couldn't imagine an answer. What mattered was that she was caught in a classic situation—between two impossibilities. This, a choice of impossibilities, was what drove people crazy. Well . . . the years of coping, existing, enduring that had stiffened her mind stood solidly behind her and gave her the solution, the simple solution: one of the impossibilities would have to be made possible. She asked, "Ask your questions." She wondered why he was looking at her like that. Had her stiffening of will been visible to the eye?

"Right. Who was in the house that night?"

"Everybody. That is, Mollie, Bart's wife; her mother; Junie, my little niece; and my father."

"But *you* dealt with what was supposed to be an intruder?"

"Why, yes." Her surprise showed. "I dealt with everything." She paused. "That sounds disgustingly martyred. It wasn't. It was sheer sense. My father is very, very old. Mrs. Bolling, Mollie's mother, was—is—an invalid. Junie is four years old." She spread her hands.

"And your sister-in-law? The mistress of the house?"

How wonderful it would have been, how simple, if Mollie had been the mistress of the house! "Mollie is timid, nervous. Frightened."

"All right. Now, what happened?"

Just like that. "Well, we heard the noise and—"

"Who's we? Everyone?"

"Oh, no. My father is deaf. Mrs. Bolling pays no attention to things." Except her own hypochondria. "Just Mollie and I."

"It woke you?"

In Lafayette, no one had asked that question directly. She said tonelessly, "I was up."

"Were you usually up at three in the morning?"

In Lafayette, they had accepted a whole set of contradictions without mentioning their existence, to say nothing of inquiring into them. She was fully dressed—so she was up; it was three in the morning, so her senses were blurred with sleep; it was three in the morning, so of course the lights were out. In Lafayette someone had said, "Night before Christmas Eve. Must have been wrapping packages, huh?" He didn't add, "In the dark?" Whichever of the sweet people it had been—and until that Christmas, Talia had not fully realized just how many sweet people there were in Lafayette—whoever it had been had spoken with a kind of tenderness and had not waited for an answer.

The words—the lie-by-implication—that it was the night before the holiday trembled on her lips, but she did not speak them. She said woodenly, "No."

"But you were up that night."

"Yes."

"Well, Miss Cory, why?"

There was a little pause and then he said, "My God, Miss Cory, don't tell me they never asked you that question!"

"No. They didn't."

He stared at her, his face unreadable. It was a homely face, but a very nice one. He was probably a very nice man. She hoped that he would not be the one who would make her life forever unlivable. Then he said something strange: "My God," he said, "they must love you very much in Lafayette."

Yes, she thought numbly, perhaps they had. She felt the tears coming and held them back as she had before—stubbornly. "I was up," she said coldly, "until about one-thirty or two because Mollie was up. Mollie was upset. Mollie was . . ." How did one describe Mollie, who certainly wasn't crazy but whose fears and weaknesses and clingings sometimes pushed her to the border? How to describe Mollie, product of her mewling mother and vicious father, in a few well-chosen words? Talia found just one word: "Mollie was hysterical," she said frigidly.

"Why?"

"She got—get—that way. That night she had decided that because Bart was out late he was drinking and that as a result he would—hit—her when he came home."

"And would he have?"

Talia looked back into the distance and discovered something. "Because she so clearly expected him to, he probably would have."

"I see. So you were up until one-thirty or two, you said, with your sister-in-law. And then?"

"Then," Talia said woodenly, "the phone began to ring."

"In *Lafayette?*"

Talia looked at him and then accepted the humor. It even helped. "You're quite right. People do not telephone at two in the morning in Lafayette. They're asleep. In most houses."

"But not in yours?"

"He called often."

"He did?" Corelli asked. And she again thought his voice beautiful.

"Yes."

"And who was this person who called in the night?"

"I don't know."

"What did he say?"

She no longer saw Corelli. She was back in the dark, echoing hall-way, with its ceiling lost in the shadows two stories above her, with its ugly, time-blackened, cheap oak paneling; she was looking at the screeching black snake of a telephone, and listening to the whispering, insinuating voice. "I cannot tell you what he said. Unrepeatable things. Over and over. Almost every night. If I hung up, he called again, and I was afraid the ringing would wake everyone. When I left the receiver off the hook, Bart got furious. I was afraid if I did it often Bart would ask why, guess why."

"And why didn't you tell him? Tell the authorities?"

Her mind was still back in Lafayette, seeing the streets, the people on the streets, the library, the school she had gone to, the single traffic light on the corner of Oak and Third. "You don't understand small towns. My house, our household, was looked at queerly. For good reason, I suppose. We were not a—sensible group of people. And I didn't want this to be broadcast, so that people would think—"

"But these calls were *outside* you, outside your house."

"You certainly don't understand small towns," she said tonelessly. "They run on the principle that where there's smoke, there's fire. The voice talked constantly about 'my lover.' I never went out with anyone. When boys asked me, years ago, I said no. And they stopped asking. But he talked about 'my lover' and said—unrepeatable things. They would have tapped the phone. They would have heard what that voice said, and some of them would have repeated those—delicious bits of scandal, those—" She came back out of Lafayette and said, "That's why I was awake at three o'clock."

"And your sister-in-law?"

"She had been asleep for a little while. But the noise, the noise of the—prowler—woke her. She called down over the banister."

"And then went with you to investigate?"

"And then went to the third floor. After all, there was Junie. She had to protect Junie. She took Junie upstairs with her."

"I see." She thought that perhaps he *did* see. He said, "And you went into the dining room and shot the man. You thought it was the owner of the voice on the phone?"

"Yes. Exactly. That is . . . " She stopped.

"At the very last minute you saw it was your brother."

"Yes." He had a kind face, but it was also perceptive. Perhaps he was perceptive enough to understand . . . She sat very straight in her chair and looked directly at Corelli. "I tortured myself for awhile about that. But I won't permit myself to be weak and foolish and give in to imaginings like—like Mollie. Make my own purgatory. The voice had said he would come some night. And he—detailed—what he was going to do. So I was upset, very upset—and there is the whole answer. When I realized it was Bart, I was just about to fire the gun. If I had been normal, perhaps I could have stopped. I wasn't normal, I couldn't stop." She paused, and then, surprisingly, smiled faintly. "While I'm getting it all out, there is this too. You were right in your assumption that I didn't like Bart. He was a mean man, a bully. And he was largely responsible for my being—caught. In that house. In Lafayette. Bart was—well, for instance, my father wanted desperately to go into a home, an old people's home, on the other side of Des Moines. A lovely place in lovely, green grounds. Papa is eighty-two, and he wanted the companionship of people his age, and the care that he needed but didn't want to burden me with. It was an intense desire, a daily prayer, and it was pathetic that he should be denied anything so logical. But Bart wouldn't let him go. Bart said Papa would be shaming him, but what was really in Bart's mind was the house. The house was Papa's, of course, and to get into the Templeton Home everyone has to sign over his property to the Home. It makes perfect sense—they take care of you until you die. Bart said Papa should give him the house and *then* apply to Templeton for entrance. Papa wouldn't do that; he wanted to pay his way.

"Multiply Bart's treatment of Papa by a hundred other such things and you know what Bart was like."

"Um. Well, thank you, Miss Cory. This will all help—"

"I don't see how," Talia commented, out of honesty and a small bitterness at having been forced back to Lafayette.

"No?" Corelli's wrinkles cooperated to form a vivid question mark. "Well, I'll explain, then. Almost every evil springs from a preceding evil. The smallest situations find their seeds in situations that preceded them. Life, all life, is a chain. Your sister-in-law, for instance, did not spring hysterically into being. So when you came here and admitted to the past event, I found it hard to ignore what I consider the plan of life. Out of a shooting like that, such things as your current experience grow. And, incidentally, the only way to break the chain is to—break it. Not try to bury a few links."

Suddenly, surprisingly, the wrinkled face reddened. "Quite a speech for a cop, I guess. But in a way it makes sense that a cop should feel like that, because every day we see those situations growing out of others. Sometimes we come in the middle. Other times we watch the first link forged."

It did make sense for a policeman to be aware of such a "plan of life," Talia thought. But she would have been willing to bet that he was unique in his ability to see and understand it.

The wrinkles had composed themselves to impassivity. "Besides," he said, and his voice was as brusque as he could make it, "in simple police terms, there is something particularly screwy about that recording. That voice on the phone in Lafayette—was it a very high voice, Miss Cory?"

"No." She stared rigidly at him. "It was no voice. He whispered."

"So?"

"It could be." She thought about it. "But this man, yesterday, he didn't say obscene things."

"No, because now he's gone into action."

Talia felt cold.

Corelli rose. "Thank you, Miss Cory. We'll be in touch with you."

Talia stood up very slowly. She reached for the box, but he said, "May we hold onto that?"

"But I have to return it."

"Oh. Well, tell you—leave it for the day and we'll rerecord it. You can pick it up this evening. That okay?"

She nodded.

"I probably won't be here. Just ask for it at the desk downstairs."

She nodded again.

"Thank you, Miss Cory. And—try not to worry."

She was dismissed. As she walked down the stairs, she thought, Not worry?

It was only a little after ten o'clock when she rode up thirty-four stories and entered the glass box of an office that she shared with Janet Furman. She did not intend to explain her lateness, to compound small lies, but when she caught Janet looking at her swollen face she answered both unspoken questions with one explanation: "Went to the dentist this morning."

"Oh, you poor kid!" Janet's pleasant contralto was full of sympathy. "The dentist and bra copy, all in one day!"

Half an hour later, Talia struggled up out of lacy comments about the iron strength of sheer wisps of engineering steel and caught Janet's eye. The eye looked hastily away, but it had been filled with curiosity. It occurred to Talia then that one rarely came away from a dentist with *two* distended cheeks—and curiously reddened cheeks, at that.

She made no further explanations. Carl Neilson, who should have been in the art department, manufactured a reason to visit, and commented, "Gained weight, I see." Mr. Long did a doubletake. Even Billy, the office boy, on his interminable rounds of empty-the-outgoing-box and fill-the-incoming-box, looked sideways at her each time he entered their glass box.

She escaped at five minutes to five, to Janet's obvious astonishment; Talia was usually the last one out of the office. She went to the office-equipment store, gave the make and model number of Jim Richards' machine, and bought a fresh roll of tape. Then she stopped at the police station, where a different but no more cordial man sat behind the high desk and, after unnecessary and lengthy explanations on her part, searched for and relinquished the recorder. It had been leaning cozily against his foot.

Home in her apartment, she replaced the role of tape with the newly purchased one, closed and latched the machine, and carried it down a flight of stairs. But her knock on Jim Richards' door brought no response. She went down to the superintendent's apartment, explained that Mr. Richards would call for it, and left the recorder with him. She also got a scrap of paper from him and wrote a note to Richards, telling him where the recorder was and thanking him. She put the note in his mailbox and rode the squeaking elevator back to her apartment.

Then she made dinner, including soup. She drank the soup, scraped the lamb chop into the garbage, and went to bed. But, once there, she stared at the picture opposite her bed, saw the not intended patterns

28                                    ALFRED HITCHCOCK'S ANTHOLOGY

the city's glow brought to eerie life on the canvas, listened for the silent phone to ring, and slept finally at three in the morning. The experience of rigid wakefulness, the strained listening for a telephone's ring, and even the hour at which sleep became possible—none was new to her. But it had been awhile since she had suffered it.

The next morning her swollen face had subsided and her cheeks were no longer red, but the result was as unfortunate as the abnormality had been. She looked worn, thin, and tired. She shrugged at the mirror; there was simply nothing to be done about it.

She existed through the day. If her drawn face, her increased remoteness, her total silence drew surprised glances, she was almost unaware of them.

In the late afternoon she was visited by an achingly familiar sensation. In Lafayette, in the early hours of the morning, Talia had increasingly often awakened to an oppressive sense of impending horror. She had inevitably come to associate the awakenings with the whispered phone conversations that almost invariably followed. She had been astonished and frightened by what clearly seemed to be telepathy—and also irritated, since she did not believe in telepathy. But some sort of telepathic phenomenon was certainly at work, whether she believed in the theory or not. There was one occasion when she lay in bed, stiff and tense, waiting, only to have the sensation suddenly depart. And then she knew he had changed his mind.

In the office that day, the feeling came upon her with a force greater than she had ever experienced. She looked up from her papers and through the glass partitions. There was nothing to see, just the usual people and their dimly repeated images, the usual desktops, with their usual clutter.

At five, Janet's swishing departure roused her and she went home. But the feeling of dreadful expectation traveled with her through the congested streets.

In her apartment building, the self-service elevator seemed to move very slowly. She finally reached her floor, opened the door, and then stood in rapidly diminishing light as the elevator door swung automatically to, depriving the black hall of the glow from its interior.

She stood still for no more than a second, and then her mind became acutely active and aware. It was almost as if the dullness she had experienced for two days had been a resting on the part of her mind, a saving-up of its energy in order that it might deal with the emergency she had known would come. And the last hour's fright had been the immediate warning. She took three long, entirely silent sidesteps away from the elevator, moving toward the far end of the hall away from her door. Then she stood still again, breathing in slow, shallow drafts, her mouth slightly open. No sound of her breaths came to her ears. And I am nearer my breathing than he is, she thought. The thought brought a touch of hysteria, and she coldly pushed it away. She might not know where he was, but neither did he know where she was. Not yet.

She devoted a second's thought to the possibility that she was imagining danger where none existed. But the hall lights could not have burned out, because there were three of them. The odds against three bulbs burning out at once were astronomical. Could there have been a short, a blown fuse, a power failure? . . . Her knowledge of electricity died there, and anyway, she realized, it was better to feel silly later than to walk into nameless horror just to prove her bravery to herself. It— And she heard the sound.

*He* was breathing. She thought with ridiculous pride, he's not as smart as I am. But why did she hear him now when she had not heard him during the preceding moment? Perhaps the elevator's noise—no, it was because *he was coming nearer.*

The hall was in the shape of a square. At her back was the elevator door; on her left was a blank wall—another building was built flush against it. The wall facing her opened to permit the stairwell and, to the far right, her own door. The fourth wall held the doors of the two other apartments. It was from the region of that fourth wall that the sound of breathing came.

But now, in the darkness, she could see—something. For a second she peered intently toward the right, and then, quickly, she dropped her eyelids until her eyes were almost entirely shuttered. What she had seen was a reflection of the little man's eyeballs. They had seemed luminous, she remembered. And he had kept them so wide, so unblinkingly, so trainingly wide.

She moved to her left and around the inverted corner with a big, silent, careful step, a thought-out, planned step. If this went on, they could go round and round forever.

Through her slitted lids she caught repeated glimpses of his shining

ALFRED HITCHCOCK'S ANTHOLOGY

eyes, increasingly clearer, increasingly nearer. She didn't understand how she could see them. To reflect light, there had to *be* light— And then she felt a terrible, convulsive pain in her chest. My heart leaped, she thought wonderingly. Because I know now that I can't even go round and round . . . She had realized that in a minute she would come to the end of the blank wall she was inching along, using her spread fingertips as a guide, and there, on her left, would be the stairwell, and a faint, almost imperceptible glow was rising from the floor below. It was not enough to light her hallway or to define her outline when she was flat against the wall as she now was, but there was light enough so that her figure would make a greater darkness as she passed it.

But when she made the right-angled turn, before she reached that area of faint light, she would come to the up stairs. They led to the roof, and no light came from that direction. So she would climb them.

Would he know and follow? Probably, she thought, very probably. But she had to try . . .

Jim Richards' voice, funneled up the stairwell, sounded puzzled and apprehensive. He said, "Miss Cory?" There was a moment of utter silence while the man beside her—so near now—stopped the rasp in his throat, apparently stopped breathing altogether. Then Richards said more urgently and more loudly, "Miss Cory!"

She had reached the stairs leading to the roof. She put her foot on the first step and heard the cracking sound as her heel jammed against the riser, and so she gave up silence entirely. She yelled, "Go back, Jim! Go back! He has a knife!" Then, on the second step, she fell.

She hit full on her chin, and in the moment that followed she was deafened by a roaring in her ears. Then she heard the steps, the pounding footsteps of what sounded like a dozen men. And a scuffling. She tried to push herself upward—to help Richards or to run?—and as she placed her hand flat on the stairs a shoe came crushingly down on her knuckles. And through the pain she knew the answer: she was getting up to help; to catch him; to end the nightmare forever. Her other hand went out with intuitive, lightning speed and grabbed the ankle that was flashing past her.

The man fell heavily, and she was aware almost at once of her mistake. The ankle was that of a big man, the weight that fell against her was that of a big man, and above her she could hear the receding footsteps; Richards would not be the first man; he would be the pursuer. And she knew that she had tripped the wrong man.

She twisted around on the step and sat up—it was surprisingly difficult to accomplish; she must have fallen harder than she had realized. She shook off the renewed roaring and blinked away a blackness within the blackness of the hall, and said in a voice the sounded distant but almost normal, "Mr. Richards, are you hurt? I'm sorry. Are you—" She stopped and looked down at her hand. Beside her hand. There was a glow, like the glow that the little man's big eyes had given off. But this was long and even more glittering. The faint light reflected off the long knife, and Talia gave up her fight, gave in to the inner blackness.

She was lying on her couch. Her head ached. She moved it gently to the left and discovered Jim Richards sitting in the wing chair. The knife was in his right hand and his left thumb was flicking the blade.

He looked up and said, "He left us a souvenir." He waved the knife, then put it on the end table beside him and came over to the couch's side. He asked gently, "Head hurt?"

Her voice sounded strained: "I'll be fine in a minute. I think I simply knocked the breath out of myself when I fell."

"You've only been—out—a few minutes. I didn't know what to do. I was considering cold towels, doctors, smelling salts . . . but who has smelling salts anymore?"

She smiled. It was an effort. "Not I," she said.

"I guessed that without looking. By the way, I did have to look in your pocketbook. For the keys."

"Of course."

He sat on the foot of the couch. "I heard the elevator—you know that squeaking noise it makes. Then I heard the gate up here, and then the door as it closed. All this was a sort of habitual notation; I had never realized that I hear it. But I do, and that is just the beginning of the pattern. There should be two more sounds—your door closing, and one step as your heel clicks across the floor there before you step onto the rug." He pointed at the door, and Talia saw how the familiar rug ended on the familiar parquet about two feet from the door.

"Because it was all subconscious, I wasted a minute or two before I thought it out, defined the lack. I got scared then. Immediately. Because of the recording."

32

Her lashes had been lying on her cheeks. They went swiftly upward. "Recording?"

"When I picked up the machine last night, I checked it. Force of habit with mechanical gadgets. One roll was in backward. I fixed it, and then tested the machine. I heard your voice. Then I ran the tape. Forgive me—" He paused. "No, I'm glad I listened. It explains you." He smiled faintly. "Explanation was even good for my ego. I had been wondering if *anyone* could be as thoroughly repulsive as you seemed to find me."

"But I changed the tape," Talia said numbly.

"You must have changed the unused tape."

"Oh."

"What are you going to do with that—that record of viciousness?"

"I took it to the police. Yesterday morning. They made a copy."

"Good girl!" He looked astonished, but the astonishment faded slowly into something else. "Courageous," he said. "Wise."

"Courageous?" Corelli too had said she was courageous.

Color rose high on his cheekbones. He said, "Well . . ."

"You, too, interpreted the business about the 'lights being on'?"

"Too?"

"The policeman, a Lieutenant Corelli, understood it imi explained to him. Shall I explain to you?"

"Not unless you wish to." He sounded stiff.

He was a good-looking man, which was probably why she had avoided him so diligently. He was also a nice man, and it was his effort not to pry that was making him sound stiff.

"I do wish to," Talia said. She pulled herself upward against the cushions, and then she told him the story. She found it easier to tell this second time, and she told it differently, not limiting herself to the barest facts, but permitting herself some interpretation and explanation. But no apologies; what had happened had happened.

When she had finished, Richards' first comment was a repetition of Corelli's but he said it with less surprise and more warmth. "You may not realize," he said, "how revealing their treatment of you is. They did everything they could, it seems, to make it easy for you. Such a reaction doesn't spring up, all uncultivated and untended. They must have been seeing your position, sympathizing with you, for many years."

Talia had not thought that through. Now she nodded.

"And after the inquest?" he asked.

"We—cleaned up. We were not only the loose ends of a tragedy; we were the dregs of Bart's rule. We had to be—tidied up. It was surprisingly simple—each of us simply followed our wishes. Papa went into Templeton and deeded them the house, of course. They'll sell it and realize enough to make Papa feel comfortable. Mollie and Junie went to Mollie's brother and sister-in-law. Bart left seven thousand dollars' insurance; I had insisted on insurance, but he had lied to me, after all. It was supposed to be fifteen thousand. Still, in Lafayette . . . Mollie's brother and his wife are sensible, unimaginative. He owns the department store, and Mollie can be useful. I think she'll be"—she paused— "if not happy, at least content. The baby will be infinitely better off. Mollie's brother has no children, and Junie is very loveable.

"I came here. I had been a copywriter in Des Moines for the branch office of a Chicago firm. They offered me a transfer, but I wanted the break to be complete." She stared into the distance. "The only people who didn't come out well were Mrs. Bolling, Mollie's mother, and a sister of Mollie's. Mrs. Bolling went to stay with her. The sister lives in Flint, and among a whole series of terrible character traits, she's a hypochondriac. They are either going to have a commiserating good time, or, more likely, they're going to try desperately to outdo each other in rare and violent symptoms. I suppose I should feel sorry for them." Her faint smile said that she was trying and finding it difficult.

Richards asked, "And this—this 'little man,' you don't know, can't remember, who he is?"

She shook her head. "If you had asked me that question at noon today I'd have pointed out that I can't be sure there is anyone to know or remember. And I'd have said that no matter how likely it might seem there was no certainty that he did come from Lafayette. But this afternoon . . . It's hard to explain and it sounds ridiculous. Just that a feeling I used to have—a warning, almost—came back to me. That man's phone calls used to bring it on; today I was warned again. And although his voice is still not really familiar, something he said is the same. When he left here he explained he wouldn't see me soon and— and then he made some threats."

"I remember." His pleasant mouth tightened.

"Well, the man who whispered used to do that. He'd talk and talk and then he'd say he wouldn't call again soon. But he'd call very soon.

Today I began to know, without even realizing it, that it would be the same. That he'd come back right away."

Richards got up, walked over toward the wing chair, and stood, with his back to her, looking down at the knife. He said, "Well, the police are the next step. If you'll tell me where the phone is—"

"Oh, no!"

He turned around, surprised. "But—"

"No," she said. "I'm too tired, first of all. I'd have to wait for them, and talk to them. And Corelli isn't there at night, so I'd have to go all over everything again. And they'd come here. They'd invade . . ." She stopped.

There was a little silence and then Richards said, "It *is* a pleasant apartment, isn't it?" The extent of his perception surprised her. "But you *must* tell them," he commented. "That knife has to be turned over to your lieutenant."

"Yes. Of course. In the morning. I'll go over on the way to work."

"Tell you what." Richards sounded brisk. "Suppose you let me do it. They'll probably want to talk to me anyway, since I tangled with the guy. I can't tell them a helpful thing—he got away like an eel—but they'll want a report. Then I'll meet you for lunch and tell you what they say. Okay?"

"It's an imposition—"

"As long as you don't object, it's not an imposition, but a settled fact. Fine. Now, about tonight. Do your feelings of—invasion—extend to me? If not, I think I'll camp on your couch."

The feeling of invasion did *not* extend to him. She examined the realization with surprise. But it would be too much to accept. "I'll be all right," she said slowly. "There's really no need—"

"Same answer as before. As long as you don't object, it's not a matter of needs, but a settled fact." He smiled. "I'll be very comfortable. It's a surprisingly long couch for a lady's apartment. But then you're rather a long lady, aren't you?"

She slept well and immediately. When she awakened she found that she had overslept by fifteen minutes, and knew immediately that she was alone in the apartment.

The knife was gone from the end table and there was a note in its place. It started without salutation, and she wondered if he didn't know what to call her. "Miss Cory" would have seemed foolish and "Natalia" was rather overwhelming. He wrote:

"I am not at my best by the dawn's early light, and anyway I want to catch your cop before he goes out. I'll pick you up at noon at the cigarstand in the lobby of your building. I *do* mean *noon*—not five seconds later—because I know a wonderful place to eat that has two flaws—five hundred other people know it, and it has eight tables. I'll make a reservation, but they won't hold tables. Noon!

Jim

If you need me for any reason don't hesitate to call my office."

She didn't need him, but when he called a little before eleven, she was pleased.

Richards said, "Thought I'd better warn you that we're having company for lunch. Your pal."

"Lieutenant Corelli?"

"Yeah."

She said, "What are you so happy about? You sound different."

"I am, as they say in books, jubilant. Look, Natalia . . ." He paused.

"Talia."

"Ah, that's a nice name—mighty nice. Well now, look: Lieutenant Corelli is a happy man too. He's proud of himself for having done police work at a distance of about a thousand miles. It looks as if you didn't do it, you see."

Talia stared through the partitions. "Didn't do it?" she repeated.

Then her voice arose: *"Didn't shoot Bart?"*

A silence fell around her and she realized how loudly she had spoken. She turned slightly in her chair and saw through a haze that Janet and Carl and Billy were staring at her. So was Mr. Long, who was standing in the doorway.

There had been bedlam in the office, and the cessation of sound apparently became noticeable to Richards too. "What's going on there?" he asked.

As she looked at the four, they quickly went back into motion. Mr. Long continued out the door and the other three resumed their moving-day gestures, which seemed to consist largely of loud conferences.

"Desks are being moved," Talia said into the phone. "Please. What— Can you explain what—"

"I shouldn't have shocked you like that, but I didn't want you to spend even one more hour . . . Apparently they were so fond of you in Lafayette that their only idea was to get the matter over with. So, after the, ah, autopsy, they looked at the bullet and said, 'Ah, a bullet.' You said you had fired a gun, they found a hunk of lead, and that was that. But when Corelli talked to them he suggested they look around the woodwork, and they did, and what do you think they found? A bullet, neatly embedded in the windowframe. A bullet from your brother's service gun, the one you fired."

"But why"—in the unreality of the moment her mind could grasp only the simple, immediate facts. Take one thing at a time, she told herself, and started with the first: "Why would the lieutenant even think of such a thing?"

"Because the lights were on."

"The lights were on?" In her bewilderment her voice rose and she felt the little stir behind her. I must keep my voice down, she thought dimly.

"My dear, there's nothing subtle about that. Corelli saw it immediately, I saw it immediately, anyone would see it immediately. Only reason you didn't was that you were so utterly convinced that you shot your brother. But—how did the guy know about the lights *if he wasn't there*? You see? So they're going to—to find out about the angle of the bullet, and re-examine it to determine its make, things like that. No matter what, only one shot was fired from the gun you held and that was in the windowframe. See?"

No. Not quite. But enough to . . . "Oh, my," Talia said with insane inadequacy. "My," she said.

"You can say that again," Jim Richards said, still jubilant.

"Thank you." She was caught tightly in the grip of inadequacy. She tried again:

"*Thank* you."

Richards seemed to find it adequate. "We'll thank Corelli," he said. "You and I. At high noon."

Talia hung up slowly and then turned in her chair. Welling up in her was the desire to tell someone, anyone, to shout the news. She wouldn't, of course. But she substituted a smile for the unsaid words.

Janet looked at her over an armful of dusty folders "Wow!" she said simply. "That must have been quite a conversation."

Carl Neilson said, "Sure sounded like it." He looked at Talia with longing admiration.

Janet said, "Billy, wait!" The office boy was tugging at a file cabinet. "You can't budge that alone! Anyway, the telephone thing on the side of the desk is on too short a wire. We can't move the desk any farther." She let out a small wail. "All I wanted was a little light and air, just a little light and air! The world is against me!" She dropped the folders on the floor beside her desk, which had been moved just far enough to partly block the door, and slumped into her chair, looking determinedly woebegone.

"Being in a—a fishbowl like this somehow makes it worse. I *ought* to have light and air."

Talia smiled at her. "Aren't fishbowls usually round?"

"We're the exotic kind of fish in the rectangular tanks."

"Are you sure you won't change desks with me?"

Janet shook her head with exaggerated despondency. "I'd love to, but my conscience simply won't let me."

Billy said, "The telephone man is in the building., Miss Furman. I saw him. Shall I get him and bring him up here?"

Neilson said, "Good idea. And then we can move the desk and file this afternoon."

"You could do it at noon," Janet said, with a bland face and a notice-able air of innocence.

Carl Neilson examined her suspiciously. "I'll bet you and Talia are going to lunch at noon."

Janet giggled.

"Oh, no, you don't," he added. "I am making like slave labor merely for the sly purpose of enjoying you girls' company. If you're not willing to give me at the very least advice and comfort you can requisition the stockroom for help—and wait a week or two—or three—or four."

"All right," Janet said meekly. "Billy will bring the telephone man as soon as he can, and the two of you can come back after lunch."

"Sure." Neilson smiled at Talia and went out, tailed by Billy.

Janet said, "Seems unfair of *me* to take advantage of his overpower-ing passion for *you* to get *my* desk moved. But no one feels that way about me."

"Don't be silly," Talia said vaguely, and smiled brilliantly at Janet. She would like to have sung, to have danced . . . She turned back to her desk, and found that she was teaming with ideas. She picked up a pencil.

Janet said, "It's five of twelve, Talia." She was standing in the doorway.

Talia came abruptly out of her surprising absorption. "Whoops!" she said. "That gives me three seconds for lipstick."

Janet waved and left, and Talia grabbed her purse and started picking her way through the clutter toward the door. As she moved around Janet's desk the office boy appeared in the doorway. He said, "Miss Cory please, I couldn't find the telephone man."

"Well," Talia said, "that's all right, Bunny. Janet will have to— She stopped. She kept her eyes on the pile of file folders she had been about to step over, and after a controlled second she said, "I mean Billy, of course. And about the telephone—"

"It doesn't matter. That you finally recognized me. After all, you've known me all your life so I knew you might see me someday."

Talia looked up. A small boy— No, a man. He must be just about her age. But how would anyone ever guess it? She said, "Your glasses are different."

"You mean that horn-rims make such a difference? You just never would have recognized me, huh?"

"You wore—silver rims." And the pale eyes behind the thick glasses had always looked very small, looked very small now. The glass she thought numbly, must be the reducing kind. Like the wrong end of a telescope.

"I'm flattered." The sarcasm had a cruel bitterness.

"And your hair, your hair was—" How to describe Bunny Williams' hair? It had been, not blond or fair, but colorless. Colorless, and long but thin, lying limply on his head like bleached monkey fur.

"I dyed it. I don't know why I bothered. You wouldn't have seen me if I wore a placard. If I'd called myself to your attention—if I'd slapped your face from side to side. Hard." He took a step forward and she saw his mouth. She had never noticed his mouth before, but she had never really noticed him before at all, not as Bunny Williams nor as Billy, the office boy. He had a tiny round mouth, like a rosebud. "You never saw me at all, did you? Not in the sixth grade, or the seventh, or the eighth. Not at dances, not at graduation from high. Not when I made a fool of myself by asking you on the picnic."

Had he done that? She had no memory of it. "I never went out with anyone—"

"A girl like you? Don't try to give me that, I never knew who he was, your lover, but I knew I'd find him, and so I watched and waited, and then when I thought I had him—when I saw him crawling in that window, I was so *sure* I had him—and then it turned out to be that bully of a brother of yours. And the man I was waiting for got away. So I'll take you from *him*."

There must be something she could say. If she could divert him— "Then," she said, "you really shot Bart by mistake. They'll understand that it was a mistake."

"You never saw me. Never knew me. Not on the street. Not on the telephone. And when I came to your back door with groceries you said, 'Are you the new delivery boy?' and smiled. And you didn't know me at all. But you had known me all your life." The little rosebud kept opening and closing . . . She took a step backward.

He took a step forward. "Doesn't matter now, you snob. And it doesn't matter what you look like anymore. You're never going to snub people anymore. I've put it off too long; now I'm going to take care of you." He moved around Janet's desk, and Talia found herself beside her own desk, her back to the window. There were thirty-four stories of air behind her.

He said, "You have my best knife—"

She spoke quickly. "You can have it back. I'll bring it in tomorrow."

When the little rosebud smiled, it curled and opened a trifle. Talia felt her stomach turn in revulsion, and nausea rise. "No," he said. "You won't bring anything anywhere tomorrow. And anyway, I have another." And he had. He held his hand low in front of him, and there was the knife. She looked through the glass walls. Would no one see?

"It's lunch hour," Bunny Williams said. "All those high-paid snobs get out of here before twelve and they don't get back until after two. I go at exactly twelve-thirty and I get back at one-thirty, in time to punch the time clock. Did you know there is a time clock down in the stockroom?"

"No. I— You can't get away with this, Bunny. There are three girls out there. Behind you. Just look. And Mr. Long's door is open. He's still in there."

ALFRED HITCHCOCK'S ANTHOLOGY

"I'm not turning my head. It's so unusual to have you look at me—straight at me—seeing me—that I'm going to enjoy it for a minute. Then . . ." He gave the knife a tiny wave, and the rosebud mouth curled at its edges.

"But why? Why?"

"Lots of reasons. I'll remove you from *him*. Was that him in the hallway last night? . . .

"I heard you talking on the phone before. 'Didn't shoot Bart?' you said. So I know that they finally decided to stop looking at you, smiling at you, touching, patting you—everyone could always look and smile and touch and pat. Except me. But you weren't around anymore so they looked at something else. The bullets, I suppose. So now I've got another reason: No one's going to do it for me, so I've *got* to do it. And anyway, I can't let you out of this office because now you know me. *How* do you know me? What finally made you see me? Tell me. Then when you're gone and there isn't anyone alive to prove to me all the time that I'm nothing, and I start to be something, then maybe I can play up whatever it was that made you know me. What made you know me?"

Talia stared at him. He wasn't very near her yet. If she ran . . . But there was no quick way around that big desk.

"How?" he said insistently.

"How? Oh, it was just—just the way you said, 'Miss-Cory-please.' In school you used to say, 'Miss-James-please' and 'Miss-Wetzel-please' ". . .

He took a step forward and she pressed her back against the windowsill. For some reason, it had been wrong to tell him. The thin little face before her, the small staring little eyes, the horrible, curled little mouth—all had twisted with a terrible hate. "So you remember me because I was humble, is that it? Maybe if I'd crawled on my belly up your back steps with your groceries *then* you'd have known me?"

She shook her head numbly and forced her eyes away from the contorted face.

And there, as her eyes stared over the hair that now looked exactly like monkey fur, was Richards. And Corelli. They were almost up to the doorway. Corelli shook his head violently, and she looked quickly back at the face.

It was smiling.

"Don't bother," he said. "I won't look around. Why would they come? I'm just the little office boy, talking to the big lady. And when I stick this knife in your throat no one's even going to notice. Then I'll wipe it on your blouse and just walk quietly out of here. Who'll think of me? Who *ever* thinks of me? You see what you did when you made me so unimportant? You took care of *yourself.*"

He laughed, a little, high, throaty giggle.

"You see what—" He stopped and his eyes shifted to her left. Why? she wondered. There was nothing beside her but thirty-four stories of air. But . . . a window separated her and him from that air. And then she knew what he was looking at. The window was showing him a reflection—the whispery reflection of all the glass they were surrounded by; the reflection, however dim, of the two men behind him, who had reached the door . . .

He swung violently around to his right, and as his hand went out to help him keep his balance the knife in it whistled past her breast, an inch away.

There was a second of dead, motionless silence. Two men were just inside the open door, standing side by side, facing the desk. It was the same as it had been in her hall, Talia thought. They were going to run around and around the desk like—like the Marx Brothers. She felt hysteria rising . . .

Richards broke the stalemate. He leaned down and put his hand flat on the desk and then, in a flashing motion, rose into the air. The vault would bring him down within a few feet of Bunny. But as he landed, Bunny. He moved to his left. But he *can't,* Talia thought in that interminable second. The glass wall . . .

He rose in the air, only an instant after Jim had, and, like Jim, he went feet first. Through the glass wall. Jim stopped, looked at the jagged hole, and turned to Corelli. But Corelli had gone out to the door of the next glass box.

Bunny hesitated briefly, and then he rose again, and again he went through the wall. In the next box he didn't stop, didn't hesitate, didn't bother to see if Corelli was near. He just kept going, insanely, like an automaton on a pogo stick. Over the low wooden partitions, through the glass walls.

People came into view. Talia saw Mr. Long and the blank astonishment of his face, and then another of the shattering crashes exploded

42                    ALFRED HITCHCOCK'S ANTHOLOGY

into the splintering echoes of its predecessor and she thought, But how many fish tanks are there? There can't be more!

She looked again and saw the vaulting figure; it was—all red. She looked away, and realized that something like silence had come. No one spoke, and then splinters of glass detached themselves and dropped away, making a diminishing little series of tinkling sounds, as if the wind had blown across a Christmas tree and the ornaments had moved gently together.

Into the new silence came voices. Movements. A girl emitted a long delayed scream. A babble arose and through it, quite near, she heard Corelli's voice. He said, "She all right? He didn't touch her?"

Richards said, "No, he didn't. She'll be all right."

And she knew she would be.

# Final Arrangements

## by Lawrence Page

The idea had come to him suddenly, and he had been fascinated by it. At the time, it had been a ridiculous daydream—but the more he thought about it, the more sensible and imperative it became.

Early in the morning, he sat in the living room staring at the wall as was his custom. He would rise every day with the sun, make breakfast for Elsie and himself, and then sit lost in thought.

This practice of early morning meditation was a brief, daily escape from reality. For Elsie never came into the living room; she hadn't come in once in the last ten years of their married life.

She sat in a wheel chair in her bedroom. She sat silently, bitterly. Her silence was broken only when she was shrieking at him, complaining about this or that. When she wasn't upbraiding him, she habitually stared at him with contempt, reminding him that he was responsible for her condition.

For ten long years she had been impossible to live with, and so each morning Rutherford Parnell, to lessen the pain, slipped into his own peculiar euphoria.

"Rutherford!"

"Yes—yes—" Roughly her voice had jerked him back to the living room. "Yes, Elsie?"

"Well, come in here, *please!*" she shouted.

He arose with a vast weariness and walked into her room. It was dark (she never allowed him to raise the shades) and smelled faintly musty.

"This tea is weak!" she said, her voice a thin high-pitched squeal. "Weak, like you! Everything you try to do is weak, or cold or useless. But you don't have the decency to hire someone who can cook, do you?"

"Mrs. Casey will be over, as usual," Rutherford said, calmly. Mrs. Casey was the eighth in a line of women he had hired to be a companion for Elsie. "She can't be here to cook breakfast, you know."

"I know. And a sloppy breakfast *you* make. Leave me alone, now, Rutherford. Unless you'd like to take me for a drive!"

How many times in the past decade had he heard that statement: *Unless you'd like to take me for a drive.*

He closed the door and walked into the living room, stopping to look out the window. He saw Mrs. Casey coming up the front walk.

Mrs. Casey was a warm, kindly woman, and Rutherford enjoyed talking to her. The dead-weight of Elsie's personality had not thus far affected her manner.

He opened the front door. "Good morning, Mrs. Casey," he said.

She was thin and tall, with a smiling Irish face. But her Irish face wasn't smiling today. "Good morning, sir," she said. "I was wonderin' if I could talk to you, Mr. Parnell."

"Surely," Rutherford said, and felt ill at ease.

"Mr. Parnell," she said as she came into the house, "I'm afraid, sir, that I'll have to give notice. I've found a position that pays a good deal more money . . ."

"I understand, Mrs. Casey, I understand. You will be able to finish out the week, won't you?"

"Oh, surely, sir."

Rutherford would have liked to say, "It's really not more money that you want. You're leaving because you can't stand her. Isn't that the truth?" But he said nothing. Instead, he put on his hat and coat and walked out of the house.

It was a clear, sunny day. It was also the day Rutherford had picked to carry through the plan upon which he meditated morning after morning. He came to a halt at the bus stop on the corner and waited for Number 16, Downtown, as he had every weekday morning for ten years. He had sold the car, after the accident. But that hadn't removed the car or the accident from his thoughts. And Elsie never let him forget that he had been at the wheel that drizzling November night, and that it had been his error in judgment that had sentenced her to life in a wheel chair.

As he stepped into the bus, he nodded to the driver as he did every day; then he moved to the rear and took a seat by the window, as he did every day. But today, he left the bus three blocks before his regular stop.

A telephone booth stood nearby, just off the wide cement apron of a service station. He went into the booth and called his office.

"Mary?" he said. "Hello, Mary. This is Rutherford."

"Why, Rutherford—aren't you feeling well?"

"No, I'm not. That's why I called."

"You want me to tell Mr. Speaks you won't be in today? Oh, I do hope you feel better. It's not at all like you, being out for a day . . ."

The senior Krushman of Krushman and Sons, Funeral Home, adjusted the spectacles on the thin bridge of his nose. He cleared his throat, ever so gently; his smile, intended to express sympathy, suggested a slight nausea.

"May I be of help, sir?"

"I would be grateful," Rutherford said, very softly, very carefully, "if you handled all the details for me."

"Of course, of course," Krushman said. "I understand. I know this is a most trying time for you. May I please have the name of the departed one?"

"That won't be necessary," Rutherford said. "I've written the address on this slip of paper. And if you would come by this evening and—and—take the deceased."

Krushman cleared his throat, but not quite as gently this time. "It's a little irregular, I must say. And from whom, sir, will I get the necessary information?"

"When you arrive—you'll get it then. Eight o'clock tonight. Would that be all right?"

"Eight o'clock—yes, of course," Krushman said. "Now what type of funeral were you interested in?"

"The—the—"

"Departed one," Krushman put in helpfully.

"Yes," Rutherford said. "Yes, the departed one won't have many friends attending, I'm afraid."

Mrs. Casey expressed surprise that Rutherford had come home so early.

Rutherford smiled at her. "Take the rest of the day off, Mrs. Casey.

I want you to get home early too. In fact," he produced a wallet, "I'll pay you off now *and* with a little bonus."

Mrs. Casey's Irish face was somber. "I hope I didn't offend you this morning, Mr. Parnell. You do know why I'm leaving, don't you? I told an untruth this morning, that I did. It's not—"

"I know why you're leaving. It's my wife you can't stand. And I certainly understand how you feel. Oh, I don't blame you one bit, Mrs. Casey, not one bit."

Mrs. Casey fidgeted in embarrassment.

"I hate her too. I wish she'd die, so I could be free. But she won't die. That would be a courtesy to me that's beyond her. If I could only walk away from her as easily as you can, Mrs. Casey."

Mrs. Casey, at this point, mumbled a quick goodbye, and her departure was clearly an escape.

"Rutherford! Rutherford, is that you?"

The voice from the bedroom was sharp, piercing, inescapable.

"Yes, dear," he said. "And I'm coming."

He took a moment to clench his fists, to steel himself, and then he strode into the bedroom. He went immediately to the windows, yanked up both shades. Sunlight filled the room.

"Rutherford!" she screamed. "Have you gone out of your mind!"

Rutherford took the poison he'd purchased at the drug store from his pocket, extended the package toward her. "I brought something for you," he said. "A little present. Something to help you escape your constant loneliness and bitterness."

"What are you saying? Pull those blinds down. You know I can't stand bright daylight at this hour, Rutherford! Has your incompetence gotten you fired now?"

"Angel," Rutherford said. "Did I ever tell you that you're beautiful? Because if I did, I was a liar and I want you to know about it!"

"You're insane!" she shrieked.

He moved out of the bedroom quickly and into the small kitchen, where he poured a large glass of milk. He was all too aware of her voice going on endlessly in the other room, and it spurred him on. He opened the package and, with a teaspoon, dropped two helpings of the rat poison into the milk.

Then, glass in hand, he strode back into her room.

"Don't try to make up to me—I hate milk and you know it!"

"But you drink it every night," he said. "And besides, I'm not trying to make up to you. I haven't been able to make up to you in ten years!"

She burst into tears and put her head in her hands. The wheel chair creaked with her sudden movement. "You're horrible! Mother told me not to marry you! I should have listened to mother."

"Your mother never told you not to marry anybody. As soon as she saw a chance to get rid of you, she reeled me in like a prize catch. Even your father couldn't stand you!"

"Rutherford! You are horrible! Horrible!"

"Don't you want to hear the news, Elsie, about the present I bought you? Freedom. An escape for both of us. A chance to get away from each other!" He snickered. "After all, this present cost me over three thousand dollars!"

"Three thousand dollars! Where—where—"

"I cashed in my insurance, Elsie, dear. All the value of it. Three thousand, five hundred dollars and eighty-two cents. And I cancelled the term insurance. What about that!"

"Rutherford! You have gone out of your mind!"

"Just listen to me, will you? I've a proposition for you." He held the glass of milk steady, held it with both hands. "How would you like to go away to a rest home?"

"Don't be absurd," she said. "Is that your proposition?"

"That's what I thought you'd say."

He smiled—a gentle, sad smile—lifted the glass and drained it in one gulp. "You'll soon realize, Elsie dear, that things here weren't so rough for you . . ."

She didn't know what he meant—for a few minutes.

ALFRED HITCHCOCK'S ANTHOLOGY

# Countdown

## by David Ely

The meteorologists had correctly forecast fine weather; everything seemed made to order that day. The offshore winds had swept away the clouds, the sky was a clear and trackless field of blue and the sun ranged well off toward the northern horizon, as if deliberately posted where it could not interfere with the great event taking shape on the earth below.

People had come by the thousands, in cars and buses and taxis, and the sandy waste outside the high wire fence was jammed. Here and there among the vast throng were refreshment stands, and strolling salesmen hawked souvenirs, balloons and straw hats. At the very edge of the fence a few tents had been pitched by those who had arrived days in advance to be certain of getting a first-rate location. State troopers were moving among the crowd, but their primary concern was to keep the traffic lanes free, for the people were in a quiet and expectant mood. There was no disorder. Everyone was waiting patiently to see the dramatic climax of the International Space Year, a man rocketed up toward the planet Mars.

Within the fenced area, the atmosphere also was calm. Among the cluster of long low buildings were gathered the press and dignitaries, each group occupying its designated location. The television and newsreel cameras were set on a large wooden platform in the center of the asphalt square that separated the Commissary from the Project Headquarters building. In rows of chairs on one side sat the scores of newsmen and magazine writers who had come from virtually every country in Europe and from both the Americas; on the other were seated more than two hundred guests, mostly scientists and political figures. For the more important spectators, a shaded pavilion had been constructed north of the Commissary; these privileged visitors included three Chiefs of State, a dozen statesmen of ministerial rank, and a few members of royal families. Everyone remained quietly in place, anxious not to disturb the scientists and technologists who moved with sober deliberation on their final tasks.

"ZERO PLUS ONE HOUR!"

The loudspeaker system cracked out the phrase like a rifle-shot. Instantly, the crowds on both sides of the wire fence were hushed, and all heads turned east toward the giant rocket that towered on its pad, across the protective belt of sand. In the deceptive haze of reflected sunlight, the slender cone seemed to quiver, as if the initial combustive thrust were already urging it heavenward.

Security Officer Farquhar leaned against the east wall of the Commissary, his thoughts uneasily revolving around the thousand possibilities for trouble. He had been assigned to the security end of a dozen manned space shots before, yet this one was the most nerve-wracking, for not only was it of top importance, but also it was an international undertaking, involving scientists from a score of nations, who had turned the area into a babel of languages, suggestive of loose ends—even sabotage.

Officer Farquhar frowned, attempting to dismiss his fears. He had done everything possible to guard against sabotage. For many months, everyone connected with the Project, from the Director down to the restaurant bus-boys, had been rigorously investigated and kept under observation, and in the security files there was a thick dossier on each person, packed with the most intimate and revealing details. Nowhere was there the slightest hint of trouble. Farquhar's mind gradually lightened. At any rate, no one could accuse him of a lack of diligence.

"Look, sir," came the amused voice of his jeep driver nearby, "the women are starting to bawl!" The driver grinned and pointed the antenna of his walkie-talkie toward an area twenty yards north, where chairs had been set up for the convenience of the Project staff. Since the scientists were at work at the pad or in the buildings, these chairs were occupied principally by wives, children and a few service personnel not on duty.

The driver was right. Several of the woman were furtively dabbing at their eyes with handkerchiefs. Farquhar smiled tolerantly; the tension of so many months was nearing its climax. Why not tears? It might be better if the men could weep, too, for some relief.

He noticed one of the women in particular, partly because of her unusual beauty, partly because she remained standing, despite the liberal provision of chairs. He squinted against the sun to see more clearly. No, she was not actually crying. Something odd about her, he thought. She stood as stiffly as a statue, with her hands clenched at her sides, staring fixedly out across the sands toward the rocket.

Officer Farquhar recognized her then as the wife of one of the scientists, a physicist named Whitby. To look at the woman, one would think that Whitby himself were about to climb into the rocket, instead of Captain Randazzo. Farquhar shrugged. Tension had varying effects on people. Still he wondered a little . . .

In the main control room of the Project Headquarters building, Captain Miguel Randazzo sat calmly munching a chicken-salad sandwich and sipping a glass of milk, as if he were not in the least interested in what the immediate future held in store for him. Occasionally he would glance with mild amusement at the grave countenances of the top scientific staff members who were busily involved with charts and telephones and the banks of intricate machinery that covered the walls.

In any other man, Captain Randazzo's air of nonchalance would have been properly ascribed to a despairing bravado, or to drugs. But Randazzo was neither desperate nor drugged. His handsome face displayed a quiet smile; the strong and shapely hands that held the sandwich and the glass did not tremble in the slightest, and his slim but powerful legs were crossed with an elegant casualness. One would have thought that he was merely going to travel to New York, or to Rio, instead of to Mars and back again.

If he had evidenced any unease, the fact would have been instantly noted by the two renowned men of medicine who sat respectfully beside him, watching his every move. An eminent psychiatrist stood nearby, but he had nothing to note on his scratch-pad but his own nervous reactions.

Randazzo had been chosen from among some fifty volunteers with previous space-flight experience, and had subsequently confirmed the wisdom of his selection by rapidly mastering the technical skills required for the operation (and repair, if need be) of the complicated equipment in the spaceship cabin. The harsh physical trials which had eliminated so many hopefuls had not bothered him in the least, for he was well-rested from the Olympic Games, where he had won four gold medals for his proud little nation. In his spare time, Captain Randazzo pursued his hobbies—hunting kodiak bears alone and unarmed, raising prize orchids, and writing Latin verse plays. On top of these accomplishments, the Captain had an international reputation for romantic gallantry, a reputation which he had not been able to embellish during his recent weeks of semi-seclusion at the Project.

"ZERO PLUS FIFTY!" boomed the loudspeaker system. Every man in the room—save the astronaut—started in automatic alarm.

Randazzo simply smiled, and as the Project Director walked by, he hailed him jokingly in colloquial German: "Don't forget to put plenty of steak on board for me, eh?"

The Project Director smiled quietly but passed on without response. The food supply necessary for the three-month round trip consisted solely of processed concentrates, hardly more than capsules. But even this compressed nourishment occupied more space than he wanted it to have, what with the necessary protective packing and cooling mechanisms.

But the Director was more concerned with another matter at present. The cabin temperature-regulating system had indicated a faint tendency to deviate from its rigid automatic control. It was the single piece of equipment that had not performed to absolute perfection during the months of testing. True, Randazzo could make adjustments by means of the manual control, but nevertheless—

"Get me Whitby at the pad," the Director ordered his communications chief.

As he waited, he gazed through the window at the assembled dignitaries and at the sleek conical shape beyond, on which their hopes and fears were centered.

"ZERO PLUS FORTY-FIVE!"

Too many mechanical intricacies, thought the Director, touching his moist brow with a handkerchief. Too many thousands of tiny interlocking parts—something was bound to go wrong . . .

"Whitby speaking."

The Director responded more sharply than he had intended. "How's the Temp-Reg doing, eh?"

"Seems in perfect order now," Whitby replied.

"Seems!" the Director snapped. "Do you realize that if—" He caught himself. Of course Professor Whitby knew. If Temp-Reg slipped by the tiniest fraction of a degree—and if the manual failed as well—Captain Randazzo would gradually become either parboiled or frozen.

"If you have any doubts, Whitby, now's the time," the Director said, more quietly.

"In my best judgment, Temp-Reg is in proper working condition," came the thin, pedantic voice.

"Good enough," said the Director. "Every expendable in place now?"

"All except food. Wait a minute—here comes Dr. Anders with it now. That's it. We'll have everything tight in two minutes."

"Good," said the Director, and handing the receiver to the communications man, he turned thoughtfully around to survey the room. Too many parts and pieces, he thought, but as his eye fell on Randazzo he felt a heartening optimism. At least the human factor in this gigantic venture was flawless. No wonder the press referred to the fellow as "The Perfect Human."

At the launching pad, Professor Whitby ran his pencil rapidly over his final check-list.

"You're a bit late, you know, Max," he said in mild reproof to a tall, gaunt chemist who was helping two technicians load several long metal cases into the gantry elevator.

"Only eighteen seconds," Dr. Anders replied, with cool precision. He frowned in a preoccupied way at the cases, then gave the nearest one a pat of satisfaction. "All right," he told the elevator crew, "take them up."

He turned to Whitby. "That's everything, I suppose?" It was a purely rhetorical question, for both men knew to the last detail exactly what went inside the cabin and in what order.

Whitby looked up from his check-list. "Of course," he muttered. His eyes were darkly circled. "Well, we're all through now," he added. "Let's go."

The two men climbed into a waiting jeep and, with a final salute to the technicians who would remain at the pad until Zero Plus Ten, they drove across the hot sands toward the group of buildings and the crowd of watchers.

"Everything perfect for The Perfect Human, eh?" Dr. Anders said.

Whitby gave him a quick glance. "Perfect!" He wrinkled his face in distaste. "He's perfect physically, perhaps—and superior intellectually, I suppose, but . . ." His voice trailed off.

Dr. Anders raised his eyebrows inquiringly, but Whitby said no more.

"ZERO PLUS THIRTY!"

Captain Randazzo yawned and stretched. "Time to dress for dinner," he remarked, noting the approach of two Nobel Prizewinners from M.I.T. who were bringing him the space-suit they had themselves designed. "Correct that error in the third lining, gentleman?" the space-traveler inquired, with a wink.

The M.I.T. luminaries smiled back, but the hovering psychiatrist leaned forward with some interest. "If I may ask, Captain, what error?"

Randazzo feigned a look of surprise. "Why, they didn't leave enough room, that's all."

"Not enough room?"

"Room for a space-woman," declared the astronaut, in English that betrayed no trace of an accent. "Three months is a long, long time, eh?"

The M.I.T. men chuckled, but the psychiatrist made a careful note and remarked: "I suppose you will miss the companionship of women, Captain." To which the hero replied with equal gravity: "Correctly stated, sir, and if I may be allowed to abuse the convention of modesty, the reverse will also be true."

"ZERO PLUS TWENTY!"

Security Officer Farquhar winced from the loudspeaker blast as he walked along the corridor of Project Headquarters. His pace was steady but his mind was troubled by two small facts which might or might not be connected—and, even if they were, might be meaningless.

First there had been Professor Whitby's expression as the scientist left the control room after making his final report to the Director. Farquhar had caught only a glimpse of that face, but he would not soon forget its tortured look.

The Security Officer would have dismissed it as evidence of intolerable anxiety about the success of the Project, except—

Except that he still vividly recalled the beautiful young woman who had stood rigid with grief and tension in the Staff area, staring desperately at the distant rocket. Whitby's wife.

There was a third fact, too, or rather, a rumor. Captain Randazzo was said to have indulged his romantic inclinations even in the relative isolation of the Project, although this was hard to credit, for he had been so closely watched in these recent weeks.

Farquhar shivered as he heard the crowd outside break into a sudden rising babble of excitement. He glanced at his watch. Yes, by now Randazzo would have left the building and climbed into the jeep—

He felt weak under the weight of his responsibility. It would be unthinkable to approach the Project Director at this time, solely because of the facial expressions of a husband and wife. And yet he was distinctly uncomfortable about it. Already he had slipped into the security room to check the Whitbys' dossiers. No hint of discord had been inscribed there, but Farquhar had noted down the names of the couple listed under the heading, "best friends at Project," Max and Olga Anders. He needed more information—quickly, if at all. Dr. and Mrs. Anders might know something, assuming there was something to be known.

But thus far he had been balked, for he had searched through the Staff area for Mrs. Anders without success, and her husband, too, was nowhere to be found outside.

Now, reaching the end of the corridor, Farquhar came to a door marked "Nutritional Chemistry" and stepped into a laboratory lined with huge sinks and tables and cupboards. The laboratory was empty, but Farquhar called out Dr. Anders' name anyway.

"Yes?"

Dr. Anders emerged from a refrigerated room at one end of the laboratory, wiping his hands on a towel. "Oh, were you looking for me, Mr. Farquhar?" He carefully shut the cold-room door behind him. "Just cleaning up," he explained. "If you let a mess stand for a while, it's a dozen times harder—"

Farquhar interrupted him impatiently. "I'm going to ask a personal question, Dr. Anders. I hope you don't mind answering. I assure you, I have my reasons."

Dr. Anders shrugged without answering. From the corridor the loudspeaker echoed a fresh warning: ". . . PLUS TEN!"

Farquhar found he was perspiring freely. Now the astronaut would have been strapped inside the cabin . . . the hatch would be closing, the final-check crew climbing into their jeeps—and in five more minutes, the automatic controls would take charge. If there was anything to his doubts, he had better waste no time on circumlocution.

"I'm going to speak bluntly," the officer said. "You and your wife know the Whitbys better than anyone else here. Tell me frankly—do you have any reason to believe that Mrs. Whitby has been guilty of any improper relationship with Captain Randazzo?"

Dr. Anders rubbed his lean jaw reflectively, then turned toward the window and clasped his hands behind his back. "To the best of my knowledge," he said slowly, "yes."

Farquhar did not hesitate, but reached for a telephone.

"One more question," he said as he dialed. "Does Whitby know this too?"

"I'm fairly certain that he does, yes."

Farquhar muttered an oath, then barked an order into the telephone: "Farquhar speaking. Find Professor Whitby at once. Bring him to the nutritional lab—immediately."

He slammed down the phone and mopped his brow. Dr. Anders was regarding him with a curious look.

"I can't believe it," Farquhar said hoarsely. "We kept him under close surveillance. We had him watched, guarded—almost every minute—"

Dr. Anders seemed amused. "Are you really surprised, Mr. Farquhar? Don't you think The Perfect Human could have devised means. of evading your vigilance if he wanted something badly enough?" He laughed shortly. "That probably added to the fun of the thing, don't you think? Having not only to woo and win another man's wife—but also to outwit the security men assigned to protect him! What a challenge for a man who strangles bears as a diversion!"

"I can't believe it," Farquhar repeated but his words were lost as the cavernous voice of the loudspeaker cut in: ". . . PLUS FIVE!" Now the automatic controls were operating. The whole system had passed into the shadowy realm of electronics, where cold mechanical intelligences whispered millions of messages at lightning speed, causing levers to drop, gauges to quiver, and microscopic doors to slam tightly shut . . .

56                                    ALFRED HITCHCOCK'S ANTHOLOGY

Even so, it could be stopped. Farquhar knew that in the control room the Director now stood tensely watching his hand near a button marked KILL.

It could be stopped, but at a fantastic cost. Once the myriad fine-tooled parts began to move—and they were moving now—a stoppage might ruin half of the delicate equipment, would certainly delay the shot for many months, would cost millions. No, he could not ask the Director to wreck everything on a sheer hunch. He stared down furiously at his clenched fists and only slowly became aware of Dr. Anders' voice.

"You can't believe that a faithful wife could be seduced, is that it, then?" Dr. Anders asked, twisting his lips ironically. "Don't be ridiculous, Farquhar! This Randazzo is no ordinary mortal—he is perfect! And beyond that—yes, far beyond that—he is a man soon to vanish on a hero's mission into the sky, perhaps never to return!" Dr. Anders folded his long arms and cocked his head to one side. "What woman could resist the appeal of such a man, a man who comes to her in secret, a man who is already a legendary figure—"

The door swung open. Whitby strode in, his blond hair dishevelled. Behind him were two security agents.

Farquhar stood up. His whole body was trembling; he found it almost impossible to control his voice as he rasped out the brutal question.

Whitby's face colored, then paled. He glanced in bewilderment at Dr. Anders, but Anders had turned toward the window again.

"Yes or no!" snapped Farquhar.

Whitby stretched his hands apart in a despairing gesture. "Yes, it's true—she told me herself last night—but I don't see that it's any of your—"

He was choked off as Farquhar seized his shirt-front roughly with both hands.

"Tell me, Whitby—have you done anything to—to—" The Security Officer was himself almost beyond coherence.

Dr. Anders cut in dryly: "To sabotage the rocket?"

Whitby pulled loose from the hands that clutched his shirt. He staggered back. "I? Sabotage the rocket?" He sank back against a counter and his head tipped weakly against the cupboard above it.

"Sabotage it—*did you sabotage it?*" Farquhar's voice rose to a shout.

Whitby closed his eyes and feebly waved his hands. "Are you insane? You think I would destroy—" He began to laugh, his body stiffening, his head still pressed against the cupboard. "Me?" He gasped the words out through his painful hilarity. "No—no—I knew his reputation, yes—I suspected him—but with other women, other men's wives!" He laughed again. "I never thought it would be with mine!"

Dr. Anders stepped swiftly over to Farquhar. "Look here," he said softly, "the man isn't lying. The only item of importance under his direct control is the Temp-Reg system, and—"

His voice was drowned out by the sudden roar of the loudspeaker system, beginning the final sixty seconds of the countdown:

"FIFTY-NINE, FIFTY-EIGHT, FIFTY-SEVEN . . ."

Dr. Anders had to yell to make himself heard. "It's automatically monitored, Farquhar! If anything is wrong with it, the Director will know at once!"

". . . FIFTY, FORTY-NINE, FORTY-EIGHT . . ."

"There's a monitor dial for everything!" Dr. Anders shouted. "You must know that youself! Call him and check!"

Farquhar seized the telephone and dialed with shaking fingers. Dr. Anders turned abruptly away and stared at the window's square of sky and sunlight.

". . . THIRTY-ONE, THIRTY, TWENTY-NINE . . ."

Farquhar cursed the loudspeaker's enormous voice. Suppose Whitby were lying—suppose Anders were lying too. They might be in it together . . . perhaps Anders had a similar motive—

". . . NINETEEN, EIGHTEEN . . ."

His call was answered. But the communications officer refused to disturb the Director.

Farquhar swore at the man, begged him, ordered him—

"TEN . . . NINE . . ."

At last the Project Director's voice barked at him savagely from the receiver.

Farquhar screamed the words: "Do you have the Temp-Reg system under monitor?"

"Of course!"

"And is it working properly?"

". . . FIVE, FOUR . . ."

The Director's voice cracked back: "Of course!"

Farquhar dropped the receiver as though its weight had suddenly become intolerable, and as it clattered on the desk, the building trembled slightly and the crowd outside burst into a prolonged roar that seemed to grow enormously in volume, and to roll in upon the men like surf, like vast gray thunderbanks—

"It's off! It's up!"

The two security agents rushed to the window to see the slowly rising column of steel and fire and smoke.

But the other three remained where they stood; Farquhar at the desk, Anders five feet behind him, and Whitby at the counter near the wall.

"You see," said Dr. Anders, slowly, "It was all right."

Whitby's body was still stretched in painful tensity against the counter. "I thought of it, Farquhar," he whispered, "Lord knows I thought of it. But I couldn't do it—no, not even for *that*."

Then his tension broke. His body relaxed so quickly that he almost fell, and as his head flopped forward, the cupboard door against which it had been pressed swung open.

By the dozens, tiny pellets came cascading out. They rained down on Whitby's head and shoulders. and spun and rolled upon the floor. The entire room seemed covered with them, and still more rolled to the cupboard's edge and dropped down.

Wonderingly, Farquhar stooped and picked one up. It was pliable in his fingers, reminding him of a yeast tablet.

He glanced at Whitby. The man's face had gone milk-white and he was staring wide-eyed, not at Farquhar, but beyond him.

"Good Lord, Max!" he hissed.

Farquhar turned around, conscious as he did so of the increasing and triumphant cheering of the crowd, and of the loudspeaker voice that crackled now above the roar with a piercing excitement: "STAGE ONE SUCCESSFUL, STAGE ONE SUCCESSFUL . . ."

He looked at the yeasty pellet in his hand, and then at Dr. Anders. The chemist's lean face was oddly contorted; he was smiling in a quiet way, as if anticipating some subtle witticism he was about to utter.

"Was this"—Farquhar waved his hand to include the thousand pellets that lay scattered throughout the room—"was this supposed to have been in the ship?"

Dr. Anders folded his arms and inclined his head almost imperceptibly.

"You mean—you deliberately loaded empty food containers in that cabin? You mean he's off in space to starve to death?"

"Oh, no," said Dr. Anders. "He needn't starve."

Farquhar stared at the man. "But if the containers were loaded empty—"

Whitby broke in. "No! They weren't empty! They were weighed at the pad! They were fully loaded!"

Farquhar shook his head and drew his hand across his face, as if to erase some incredible idea. "Loaded? Loaded—with what?"

But Dr. Anders merely repeated, in his calm and even tones, the phrase he had just used: *"He needn't starve."*

Whitby shuffled forward with the uncertain step of a much older man until he bumped blindly into a heavy counter and could go no farther. When he spoke, his voice was but a whisper, yet the words seemed to take shape almost palpably in the air, like smoke:

"Where's Olga, Max? Where is she? Where's your wife?"

Dr. Anders made no reply. His pale eyes were fixed on the window, on the patch of blue beyond, the great skyway that opened ever wider to where the silent planets circled in the infinite and peaceful harmony of space.

ALFRED HITCHCOCK'S ANTHOLOGY

# She Is Not My Mother

## by Hilda Cushing

"**S**uppose you tell me in your own words what led up to this—this antipathy you seem to have for your mother," Dr. Willetts said gently.

Claire Tarrant pressed her lips together tightly. She thought antipathy was hardly the word but apparently it was the one used by Aunt Lucy. Dear, bewildered Aunt Lucy.

She could imagine her saying, "Her father and I just can't understand it, Doctor. She has always been reasonable beyond her years. Then right out of the blue, when everyone was so happy, this sudden antipathy for her mother!"

She could see the worried frown creasing her father's handsome face the day his sister suggested consulting a psychiatrist. Everyone said Claire looked like her father, the same intense, dark eyes, the matching wavy hair and the smooth olive skin. She was tall. Already she reached his shoulder.

But the pleasure that usually swept over her at the thought of her father was missing today. The pain she felt at hurting him was too intense. Only because she loved Aunt Lucy had she agreed to this waste of time. There was no question in her mind that it was a waste because she knew she was right. The burden of this knowledge rested heavily on her thin shoulders and sitting there in her white blouse and slim skirt she seemed much older than her twelve years.

Dr. Willetts' voice broke into her thoughts. "Just begin anywhere, Claire, anywhere. Tell me about when you were a little girl."

"I can remember we lived in San Francisco," she hesitated.

What could she say that Aunt Lucy had not already told him? Then in answer to his encouraging smile, "My mother and father met in San Francisco and were married there."

She went on to explain that her father worked for a large company that kept moving him from one plant to another. That finally he arranged to be sent back East to the area near Boston where he and Aunt Lucy had spent their childhood, to a little town where, after their parents' death, Lucy, fifteen years older, had raised her brother.

"You're so like him," Aunt Lucy once said to Claire. "Your father never really was a child. Not in the ordinary sense. From the time Carter was two his mind was years ahead of his body and he was always impatient. By the time he learned discipline he was a grown man." She smiled at the girl. "You're like him but you have more self-control than he used to have."

She had had to learn control. The years had passed so slowly, but she was impatient now. She had to go through this because they all, even Aunt Lucy, hoped it was just a childish psychosis. Then aloud, "Daddy, Aunt Lucy and I are all that are left of the Tarrants. Mother was alone, too, after her uncle died, so both she and Daddy wanted to come East to live near Aunt Lucy."

"Go on." The doctor's voice was low. She wished she knew what he was thinking. Not that it would make any difference. Nothing he could think or say would make any difference. Yet she wondered how much Aunt Lucy had told him. Had she explained that Claire's IQ was the highest anyone in her school had ever tested, and that she was now in its special class for the gifted?

If he knew this, surely he would not suspect her of trumping up a fuss to attract attention to herself, and surely he would hesitate to accept her father's unspeakable belief.

The doctor was urging her on. She caught the word "accident."

"Yes, it was a horrible accident," Claire said. "Daddy and I were lucky. We were thrown clear. I was only five years old but I remember we both had only scratches and bruises." She paused a moment. "But the other people—it was a young man and his wife—were in the other car and they were killed instantly."

"That was when you and your parents were on your way East?"

"Yes, my father had been transferred. The accident was near a small town in Ohio."

"And your mother?"

No doubt he expected she would stumble over this part of the story. But in the seven years since the accident she had become used to it. It didn't bother her because the distant rainbow had always been in sight.

ALFRED HITCHCOCK'S ANTHOLOGY

"Mother had to be dug out from under the wreckage. It was weeks before the doctors knew she would live." She thought of the long weeks that dragged into that first year. Much of that time her father spent at the hospital hundreds of miles away. She remembered her feeling of loneliness. "She was terribly disfigured," she said abruptly.

Dr. Willetts murmured, "Did that bother you—to see her that way?"

Did it? To be honest, maybe at first, but it was her own mother! Besides, there was the promise that after a few years everything would be all right again.

She had been fairly happy that first long year, as happy as she could be without a father and mother. Aunt Lucy, of course, had done everything she could to make the passing time bearable.

Her father's company had given him a temporary assignment in a section of Ohio near the town where her mother was hospitalized. The visits her father made to them, whenever he dared to leave Della, were brief and rare.

"When Mother finally came home, Daddy took the house next door to Aunt Lucy. After that, whenever Mother needed treatment or seemed overtired, Daddy would send me over to her house. That was quite often. So you see, I really had two homes."

She had two homes. One where a harassed and preoccupied father devoted his time to a wraithlike creature who flitted silently about the rooms—a house where curtains were almost always drawn against the light—a house where its woman seemed to find comfort only in the presence of her husband—and a home where Claire clung to the precious moments her father allotted her.

"How did you feel," asked the doctor, "when you knew your mother would go away again for perhaps another year?"

"I was glad. The accident had changed her so. I don't mean just her looks but her whole manner. She used to be so gay and happy. We always knew that Mother was coming into this money from her uncle when she became thirty-five. That was last year—six years after the accident." She took a deep breath and then went on. "I knew all about the plastic surgery that was going to make her look all right again. Daddy explained all it would mean to her. So, of course, we were happy when she left to get fixed up, even though it would take such a very long time."

Dr. Willetts sounded thoughtful, "Your father hadn't planned for any plastic surgery until the legacy?"

"Other things came ahead of that," she said quickly. "Learning to walk right again, to use her hands. More than just skin grafts. She was burned so badly. It couldn't be done all at once!"

"Of course," he agreed smoothly. "All that takes time."

For some reason she felt on the defensive. "Daddy used up all of his money and Aunt Lucy has only a small income." She looked at him.

"I thought possibly insurance," he mentioned mildly.

"Aunt Lucy says that was only a drop in the bucket. And that, although the other couple was speeding and it was their fault, they had nothing and there was nobody for Daddy to collect from." She took a deep breath again. "It was wonderful for Mother to come into all that money because plastic surgery is terribly expensive." She remembered the day she waited with Aunt Lucy for the return of her parents. "It was going to be so wonderful! When they came in the door and we heard laughter I was so happy. We hadn't heard Mother laugh since the accident and that was so long ago."

She rose from her chair. "I promised my aunt I would talk to you, and I have, but it doesn't make any difference. That woman is not my mother!"

Claire went back the next week because her aunt urged her to go. This time the doctor again went over her story with her and then suggested, "Perhaps if you try to look at it from your father's viewpoint."

"His point of view?" Her voice was only slightly unsteady. "He thinks I'm jealous—jealous of my mother!"

"And you think he is completely wrong." It was not a question. His voice was gentle.

She said, "I haven't had my mother, not really, for seven years. Don't you think I'd give anything to have her back as she was—my beautiful, happy, loving mother?"

"Isn't that what she is now?"

The little knot that came and went in her stomach these days tightened as she shook her head. "I'm sorry, doctor. No matter what you say, you can't make me believe she is my mother. All this—we could go on forever. It never would make any difference."

When, after a half dozen more visits it still made no difference, Lucy Tarrant told her she could stop going to Dr. Willetts.

Her father's reaction was swift. Sitting frozen and silent in a corner of Lucy's livingroom, Claire listened while he briskly told them he was taking Della to the Orient.

"When you come to your senses, Claire—" his handsome face twitched "—we'll come back. Your mother," he accented the two words, "has been through enough. She can't stand any more. Especially when it's cruel nonsense." Then in a burst of exasperation, "For heaven's sake, girl, don't you understand what it is you are doing to her?"

"Carter!" Lucy's voice was distressed.

He stood up. With some effort he softened his voice as he leaned over his daughter. "I forget how young you are, Claire." His appeal had a hint of hysteria beneath it. "Claire, a husband has ways of knowing—ways I can't expect you to understand. But you've got to believe me when I say I *know!*"

She sat there just looking at him, her face a mask, the knot in her stomach twisting and turning until Aunt Lucy rescued her with a slow, "Give her a little more time, Carter. You and Della go on your trip. It might be the best thing."

"I certainly hope so!" The look Carter gave his sister was a mixture of annoyance and doubt. "She's beyond me. I leave her to you!"

He strode from the house, his tall, lean figure taut with frustration. Claire made no move to stop him. She was completely numb. Not because her father was upset. Not because the trip had originally included her. But because there was nothing she could do about it. She was sure.

Her father's absence made her next step easier. He had reluctantly approved her aunt's wish to take her to the psychiatrist, but he never would permit this. At first Lucy Tarrant was aghast. When she finally agreed, it was obvious that she only did so because she hoped it would lead to complete and final disproof of Della as an imposter.

At the last moment she offered to accompany her. This was typical of Lucy. She easily could have let Claire go alone and have the police dismiss her as a headline-seeking delinquent. That, of course, would have ended the whole thing without solving anything.

Chief Costa, a heavy middle-aged bachelor whose work filled his life, took a while to warm up to them. His weathered face was skeptical at first, but as he listened to Aunt Lucy's concern and Claire's inflexibility his curiosity and then his interest soon became apparent.

He took the cigar from his mouth to ask Lucy, "She's pretty young, isn't she? Do you go along with her on this?"

Aunt Lucy flushed.

"No, but we've talked it over carefully. I could only agree with her that this was a place where she might find help. I was sure that, even if you refused, you would keep this a confidential matter." Then more resolutely, "Yes, she is young. She's only twelve, but a grown-up twelve. Her father was like that, too, as a boy. It makes everything more difficult as you can see." Her voice appealed to him. "Perhaps you can help her regain her peace of mind."

The chief regarded her silently and then turned to Claire, pointing his cigar at her.

"All right, then. You say she's been away in a hospital for over a year having all the plastic surgery." His face was intent. "You didn't expect her to come home looking just the way she did seven years ago, did you?"

"No, of course not," she answered patiently. "Daddy told me they couldn't make her the same even if they had more than the few snapshots they did have. I didn't expect it."

"You were only five. Do you remember at all how she looked?"

"Not too well," she admitted, "Only in a vague way."

"Then what was so wrong about her?"

Claire answered with hesitation. "Her eyes. When she came up the walk I just assumed it was Mother. It was nice to hear her laugh and hear how gay she was. She hadn't been like that since the accident." She paused. The pain was in her stomach again. "When she looked at me I saw her eyes. I knew then." Hurriedly, before Lucy could interrupt, she added, "Yes, I know, her eyes seemed like the pictures and they're blue like my mother's—but they aren't! She isn't my mother!"

"How can you be so sure?"

"We used to have a sort of game." The pain was less now. "We played it almost all the time. Daddy and Mother would say the most absurd things, make up the most fantastic stories with perfectly straight faces. Sometimes it was just between the two of them but mostly they were teasing me. The only way I could tell for sure if they were fooling

ALFRED HITCHCOCK'S ANTHOLOGY

or serious was to look right into their eyes. Then I could always tell. It's not just Mother. I would know my father's eyes, too, no matter what!"

"All right," said the chief. "Let's assume you're right. You say your mother left home a little more than a year ago with your father to enter a special hospital for plastic surgery in New York City. Did either of you visit her during the time she was there?"

"Daddy did. He said Mother didn't want anyone else until she was all better. He was the only one."

"He tried to see her every week but she wouldn't always let him," offered Lucy. "It depended on her mood, you see. Also, the doctors didn't want her disturbed too much. There was a great deal of pain, and sometimes they had to make her look worse before they could improve her."

"Then if you're right," the chief said brutally to Claire, "your father was in on it. Don't you agree?"

She stared at him, shocked.

"No!" she said.

The chief laid down his cigar with exaggerated care. "Now, my young lady, you say he took her there. You say he saw her almost every week. You say he brought her home. Now just when do you think anyone could have taken her place without his knowing it?"

Claire shook her head. "She is not my mother," she said firmly.

"Unless—" The chief pulled thoughtfully at his swarthy jaw. "Unless, of course, there was some radical surgery that completely changed her appearance overnight. Have you any recent picture of her?"

Aunt Lucy answered. "Not since the accident. No one would want—" her voice trailed off.

Claire's eyes sharpened.

"Don't they take before and after pictures in hospitals like that—perhaps even fingerprints?"

The chief looked at her for a long moment. "Maybe." Then turning to the woman, "You think she might feel better if we investigate a little?"

Aunt Lucy nodded. "I think so. We've tried everything else. It is what you want, isn't it, dear?"

As they rose to go the man put his hand gently on the girl's shoulder. His hooded eyes were deep with sympathy. "You relax, now, young lady. It may take a little while but we'll find out something for you, I'm sure."

A wave of gratitude washed over her.

"Maybe I can find some fingerprints," she offered eagerly. "May I bring them to you if I do?"

She waited while the chief turned slowly to her aunt. The woman started to protest, saw the look on Claire's face, shrugged helplessly and turned away.

Her father's house yielded no fingerprints visible to the eye that were more than a few days old. Their excellent cleaning woman had seen to that. Sergeant Keller, in charge of the fingerprint department, patiently dusted the articles Claire brought to him. Some she was sure her mother had touched; others she knew "that woman" had handled. There were no prints besides her own and Aunt Lucy's and the cleaning woman's, or they were too smudged to be of any use.

When Claire exhausted that hope the days seemed to creep by, broken only by postcards from the Philippines, Japan, Hong Kong and other parts touched by the cruise. Thrusting aside any feeling of guilt, she doggedly took them down to Sergeant Keller even though he told her it was a waste of time. The many persons who must necessarily handle the cards over the miles would ruin any identifiable prints on them.

Sometimes she stopped in at the police station without any excuse. The sergeant took the time to chat with her and explain the latest theories and developments connected with the job of identification.

Whenever Chief Costa happened to see her as she was coming in or going out of the station he would exchange a few words with her. The kindliness of the two men warmed her and made the waiting more bearable.

Finally the chief had word from the hospital in New York. He told Claire and her aunt he hardly expected anything different. "This should convince the young lady," he said heartily. "This is proof without question."

He handed the picture to Claire. "The hospital sent these copies. It isn't their policy to take fingerprints but it seems they took pictures every time they touched her. If that's her in the first one, then the others have to be too. That's for sure."

Claire looked at the pictures carefully and handed them to her aunt without comment.

"That's Della all right," said Lucy eagerly. "Surely, Claire dear, that's enough proof."

The girl was silent. She looked at the envelope she held in her hand. She felt uneasy. She changed the letter from one hand to the other.

Finally she looked at Chief Costa. "I got this letter today from her." She found it impossible to say "mother." "She wants to come home. I was going to give it to Sergeant Keller for fingerprints. I thought any inside the envelope would be protected. But I suppose you wouldn't be interested in it now."

"My dear," he said patiently as Lucy Tarrant sighed audibly, "I've just shown you proof that this woman is your mother. What more can I do?"

She was careful not to turn around or look back as she and Lucy left the office.

She could tell by the sound of crackling paper that the chief was fingering the letter she had managed to slip into his hand at the last moment.

Two days passed before Chief Costa summoned the two again to his office. He spent some time arranging their chairs just so, discussing the weather and their health, settling himself in his own seat, clearing his throat, rubbing his rough chin and then sighing heavily.

Lucy looked puzzled. Claire's wide eyes were serious.

"You've found something," she said slowly.

His eyes under the jut of his forehead were watchful. "Not exactly. But I've had time to do a lot of thinking."

He picked up an envelope and addressed Lucy. "Your niece left this with me the last time you were here. It's a mighty touching letter from a woman she thinks isn't her mother." He paused a moment and then said, "Suppose your niece has been right all along?"

"Oh, no." Lucy's hand covered her mouth. "She's Della. Even Claire has to admit that now."

"Just suppose she isn't. Suppose Della Tarrant is dead and buried."

They stared at each other. Aunt Lucy turned to take Claire's cold hand in hers.

Her niece formed the words carefully, "My mother—dead. You know that?"

He placed the envelope on the desk. "I don't know anything. I'm just supposing. By now you know how important just one clear fingerprint can be. According to Sergeant Keller you've learned a lot about his department these past weeks. So you know if there is a clear print in here we might find out a lot about it by sending it to Washington." He seemed in no hurry. He flipped the envelope onto the desk again. "You know there are several reasons Washington might have her print on file. She might have worked for the government, she might have been in the armed forces, she might even be a criminal." He hesitated, searching her face. Claire returned his gaze stolidly.

"All right—I send the print. I get an answer and suppose that answer says this print belongs to Mrs. William, or Daisy, Ambrose. What would that mean to you?"

Lucy gasped.

"I see it means something," he continued. "Wasn't she the woman who was supposed to have been killed along with her husband in that accident seven years ago? So maybe she wasn't killed. Maybe it was this young lady's mother who was the victim instead."

"But Carter," protested Lucy.

"That's right," nodded the chief. "Your brother identified the woman who was still breathing as his wife. After all, why not, even if she was Daisy Ambrose and a stranger? She was alive, wasn't she, and there was a pile of money coming to his wife in six years, wasn't there? That is, if she was still breathing in six years."

"But he didn't know this, this Mrs. Ambrose." Aunt Lucy shrank back in her chair. Claire was motionless.

"According to your story he had plenty of time to get acquainted with her after the accident. Didn't he spend weeks at her bedside even before she became fully conscious? She could have had any kind of a past. What did anybody know about William Ambrose and his wife? Nobody claimed the bodies. There were no known relatives. Her husband was killed in the accident. Why wouldn't she agree?" He nodded his head sagely.

"She would be lucky to have the same general coloring as Mrs. Tarrant and to be near the same height, wouldn't she? Who ever would discover the fraud? She was terribly mutilated and there was only a

70                    ALFRED HITCHCOCK'S ANTHOLOGY

little five-year-old girl who had known the real Della Tarrant. A little five-year-old girl could never be any danger to them—or could she?"

Claire's voice was icy. "You mean that wasn't my mother—not ever—since the accident?"

"It might not have been, young lady. Tell me, did she ever really look you straight in the eye during those years since the accident? Didn't she usually keep her head turned away so no one would see how bad she looked, and didn't she try to avoid you as much as she could—in your father's house with all the curtains drawn? Didn't your aunt have more to do with you than this woman did, ever since you were five or six years old? Am I right? If you still remember her eyes I'm willing to bet it's only from when you were very little." He waited for her answer.

She ignored his questions.

"And my father knew it?"

"Must have, if the rest is true. Those pictures from the hospital prove that there is only one time there could have been a substitution. That's right after the accident." He peered at her. "You handed me a letter. I read it. Now you tell me what you expect me to do with it. By any chance you want me to look for prints on it?"

Her eyes were steady. He kept on. "You just might be right, you know. Of course, if there has been fraud, well, the State isn't too hard on first offenders. A few years, maybe."

She clenched her fists. The pain had doubled. "You made up that whole story from one little fingerprint that might, just might, be on this letter?"

He nodded.

She took the letter from the desk and slowly tore it into small pieces. She asked quietly, the pain subsiding, "Where's the story now?"

He answered, "A real good officer of the law would probably have had the letter photostated, young lady. He might even keep it in his files for a while in case you change your mind again someday. But," he sighed, less heavily this time, "but then again maybe you've torn up all the evidence there might be."

At Logan Airport a week later, Claire waited with her Aunt Lucy for the west coast plane to touch down. As the steps were wheeled into place and the passengers began to stream from the craft, her eyes were busy searching among them.

"There they are!" Lucy cried.

There he was, Carter Tarrant, her tall, handsome father, striding confidently toward them, his hand protectively under the arm of the tanned and lovely woman who matched her steps to his.

Claire flew to her father. "Hello, pet," he laughed happily, loosening her tense grasp with some difficulty. "Take it easy! We're just as glad to see you!" He turned her to face his companion. His voice quickened. "Here's your mother. Aren't you going to say hello to her?"

There was the barest hesitation as the girl looked into Della's eyes. Then, ignoring the twisting knot in her stomach, she leaned toward the woman, kissed her quickly and said brightly, "Welcome home—Mother."

# Spook House

## by Clark Howard

I made it all the way through last season without a nickel's worth of trouble—right up until the last night, almost the last hour of the last night. And then I ran into enough trouble to make up for every minute of that peace and quiet and still last me a couple of lifetimes.

I run a little game of chance on the midway of one of the biggest amusement parks in the midwest. Got myself a nice one-man operation that I work in a seven-foot-long wooden stand with a counter in front for my wheel. Behind me, on the backboard, I've got shelves with all kinds of toasters and radios and shiny stuff like that to attract attention. It's a nice little setup, see, and I keep the place dressed up with colored banners and crepe paper to make it kind of stand out from the rest of the stalls.

My gimmick is simple. I got this wheel with twenty-one numbers on it. It's like a roulette wheel only it stands up straight. You pick a number for two-bits a chance and if your number hits, you get a coupon. Three coupons and you pick out any prize in the house.

I control the wheel, naturally. I ain't in business for my health or anything like that. But I generally give the players a fair shake. I get all the prizes at wholesale, see, and all I want to do is make a dollar or two on everything I hand out; it's just like running a store or something. Most people lay down a buck and after four turns of the wheel they only got one coupon so they quit. So I give 'em a cheap ballpoint pen or a pair of paste earrings for the coupon and I've made 85 cents. A few of them, if they're really after one of the big prizes, keep laying the money down as fast as I can pick it up. In that case, I let 'em feed me until I've got my two or three bucks' profit on the prize and then I let the wheel hit for their third coupon. They get their radio or whatever they want for a few bucks less than it would cost them in a store, and I get a coupla bucks more than it cost me in the beginning, so everybody's happy.

Like I said, it's a nice little one-man operation and I usually don't have any trouble. The season is four months' long, May to September, and I take it easy the rest of the year with what I make during the summer. My location on the midway is a choice spot, right next to the Spook House. I get the people as they're coming out, see, after they've been scared out of their pants by all those big spiders and weird faces that jump out of the walls in that place. By the time they've been through the Spook House, they're ripe for a nice, quiet little game of chance.

The park closes at midnight. It was a little after ten, the last night of the season, when these three guys came up to my stall. They were young, but all pretty big guys—the motorcycle-boots and leather-jacket types, the kind that tries to push everybody around. They looked mighty mean under the amber lights I had strung across my stall.

I went into my spiel right away and they all three started playing. I let one of them have a coupon the first time around and then passed all three of them for the next two turns. On the fourth turn I let another guy have a coupon and then let 'em all pass again for four more turns. After that, I gave the last guy his first coupon and then they all had one apiece. Each player gets a different color coupon, see, so they can't put 'em together and snag a prize before I make a profit.

They kept laying the dough down and I kept spinning the old wheel. In the next eight runs of the wheel, I gave only one of them a second coupon. The game goes pretty fast. They'd been at the counter only about five minutes and already I'd pulled in twelve bucks.

Two of the guys finally quit and each of them took a ballpoint pen. But the third guy was bound and determined to go away with one of my little pocket radios. He was the biggest and meanest-looking of the three and he got meaner-looking every time he lost. Also, he was the guy with two coupons already and he was hot after that last one.

He started playing a buck at a time, taking four numbers on the board. I kept a mental count on how much he had laid down and he was still about fifteen bucks away from that little portable. But he kept flipping those dollar bills on the counter and I kept spinning, making sure the wheel didn't hit any of his numbers.

Ten bucks later he was real mad. And he was also broke. He

ALFRED HITCHCOCK'S ANTHOLOGY

scratched around in his pockets looking for more money, but I could tell by his face he knew he didn't have any. While he was dragging everything out of his pockets, though, I saw something he did have. A long, shiny switchblade knife.

Finally, he stepped real close to the counter and pushed out his jaw at me. "I want one of them radios," he said.

I gave him my best carny smile. "Sure, friend," I said. "A few more turns of the wheel ought to do it. Your luck's bound to change."

"I ain't got any more dough," he said accusingly. "You got it all."

"Sorry, friend," I said. "If you want a radio, you gotta keep playing. Get a few bucks from your pals. Number eighteen's about due in four or five more turns." For another fin, I figured, I'd let him have the radio and be glad to get rid of him.

"I ain't borrowing any dough," he told me. "You got all you're gonna get, sharpie. Now gimme one of them little radios before I come behind there and get it!"

I stood my ground, dropping my hand down to a wooden club I kept handy under the counter. I looked at the guy and got a little scared. It wasn't hard to see he really meant what he said.

"I ain't kidding, you sharpie," he said, and started around the side of my stall. He shoved his hand in one pocket of his jacket and right away I thought of that switchblade he'd flashed.

I snatched the club out and held it up just high enough so he could see it. "Hold it!" I said, trying to sound as mean as he looked. "Don't start no trouble in here if you know what's good for you. There's cops all over this place. And all I gotta do is yell 'Hey, Rube' and there'll be fifty guys down on you before you know what's happening!"

He stopped cold and looked straight at me, his face contorting in anger. One of his pals came over quick and grabbed him by the arm. "Better not, Frankie," he warned. "We can't afford no trouble now! Don't forget, man, we're still on probation for that gang fight."

When I heard that, my mind went back to a few weeks ago when I'd read about a big teenage gang war where one kid was killed and another one lost an eye. I wondered if these were three of the guys that were in it. They sure looked the parts, all right. Not that it made any difference right then, anyway. The guy called Frankie was still watching me, still keeping one hand in his pocket, still looking like he wanted to cut me up into one-inch squares.

"Maybe you're right," he said reluctantly to his friend. But he shook the guy's hand off his arm and straightened up real tall. Then he took out the knife and very slowly and deliberately flicked it open for me to see. He stuck one arm out in front of him and shined the blade up and down his jacket sleeve.

"I'll give you one more chance to give me one of them little radios," he said. "What about it?"

I glanced over my shoulder and saw two cops walking idly toward my layout. Then I looked back to the punk and said boldly, "Nothing doing, brother!"

Frankie's eyes narrowed. He closed the knife and put it back in his pocket. He had seen the cops, too, but his face didn't soften any. No fear at all showed in his eyes.

"Okay," he said softly. "I'll be seeing you later."

He turned and walked away, followed quickly by his two pals. I watched them move off into the stretch of midway, until they were lost in the crowd, and then I put the club back under the counter. The two cops went by and I bobbed my head at them and they waved back. For a couple of minutes I just stood there watching the people, not even trying to snag a customer, and then I sat down and had a smoke.

I didn't have too many players after the three punks left, so I started getting my few personal things together. I'd sold my stock of prizes to one of the other hustlers who was going down south with a carnival. I started packing a few of the things for him.

A little after eleven, Corinne came over. She was one of the change girls at the Fascination layout; a brunette, stacked up nice, but kind of tough-looking like she'd been around—which she probably had.

"Hi, Sam," she greeted me.

"Hiya, doll. How's tricks?"

She shrugged her shoulders and came on behind the counter. "So-so," she said, sitting down on one of my camp stools. "What are you doing after we close tonight?"

"I dunno. Why?"

"Some of the gals are throwing a little party over at Rollo's. Wanna come?"

Rollo's Tap was a little place just outside the park. A lot of the last night crowd would be in there. I kept thinking about those three guys and how mean that Frankie looked.

"I don't think so, doll," I said. "I'm gonna be driving south early in the morning and I wanna get some sleep."

I had cleared nine grand that season and I was planning to take it easy for a few months down in Miami Beach. And the more I thought about those three guys, the more I was tempted to hit the highway right after I closed.

"Thanks anyway, Corry," I said. "I'll see you next season."

After she left, I shut off my banner lights and got the rest of the prizes packed. Along about midnight, all the big lights started to go out and pretty soon the midway was just about dark. The last of the people drifted toward the front gate. For some reason, I kept looking around me every couple of minutes, like I was expecting something to reach out and grab me. Those three guys were really under my skin.

The guy I sold my stuff to came over. He had his station wagon by his stall, but couldn't get it over to mine because the maintenance men were already dismantling the ferris wheel and it was laying across the drive. I helped him carry the boxes over to his place. We had to make five trips, but finally it was all packed in his wagon. He paid me and we said our goodbyes and I started back to my stall to lock up for the last time.

The midway was dark and deserted all over now. I kept glancing around with every step, keeping away from the shadows and empty stalls. I wasn't exactly scared, but I was sure uncomfortable. Frankie had really got to me with his "I'll be seeing you later" bit.

I hurried on to my stall and picked up my little canvas bag and closed the place up. Just to be on the safe side, I decided to leave by the side gate. I was halfway there when I saw a shadow looming up ahead of me, coming slowly toward me. I froze in my tracks, too startled to even run. The shadow came closer, closer, until it was right up in my face.

Then a flashlight went on and I let out a long breath and smiled. I looked down into a wizened, weather-beaten face. Old Fritz, the night watchman.

"Whatya say, Sam," he greeted me. "Calling it a season, huh?"

"Yeah, Fritzie," I said, "guess so." I pulled out a handkerchief and wiped my face. "How about you?"

"Same," he said. "Front gate's closed already. Looks like you're the last one to leave."

SPOOK HOUSE                                                    77

"Yeah, next to you."

"Well, one more time around the midway for me and then out the side gate and she's closed up for the winter."

I slapped him on the shoulder and said, "Take it easy, Fritz," and walked away. When I got close to the side gate, I looked back and saw his flashlight bobbing in the blackness far down the midway.

I pulled open the big iron gate and stepped out to the public sidewalk. The little side-street looked deserted, was dimly lit. Just as I was about to close the gate, I heard the snarling voice.

"Hello there, sharpie."

I swung around and faced Frankie. He was standing about six feet away from me, smiling coldly.

I started to step back through the gate, but two arms suddenly went around me from behind. Then I heard Frankie's laugh, low and mean, a cruel, sadistic laugh. He moved toward me slowly.

I wasn't scared now. I was terrified. These punks meant business! I realized I was going to have to fight for my life!

I don't know what made me do it—instinct, maybe, the law of survival—but all at once I was fighting like a wild man. As soon as Frankie was close enough to me, I hit him solidly in the stomach. Then I shoved backward as hard as I could and slammed the guy behind me into the iron gate. I heard his head hit the gate and felt his arms drop away from me. For a second then, I just stood there, feeling pretty damn brave over what I'd just done. Then something crashed into the side of my face and I saw stars. The third guy, I thought dumbly as I fell to the sidewalk, dropping my canvas bag, hitting the concrete solidly—I had forgotten about the third guy.

I just lay there, trying to focus my eyes and my mind, when I got caught by a hard kick in my side. I groaned, began to crawl away quickly, scrambling as best I could to my feet.

Then two of them were rushing toward me. One of them was Frankie, and he was holding the open switchblade in his hand. The guy with him was the one who had hit me from the side; light glinted off the brass knuckles on both his fists.

Desperately, I sized up the situation. I was to one side of the exit gate now and they were beyond the other. The gate still stood partway open. I sucked in a mouthful of air and ran like hell for it.

I made it about six inches ahead of the guy with the brass knuckles.

ALFRED HITCHCOCK'S ANTHOLOGY

Leaping through the gate, I swung it behind me furiously, hoping frantically that it would catch and lock them out. Instead, it hit the guy square in the face and knocked him down. Then the gate swung wide open again.

I paused long enough to see Frankie stop and drag the guy to his feet. By this time, the third guy was up again too. All three of them started through the gate. I turned and ran like hell again, down the darkened midway, and behind me I heard three pairs of feet coming after me.

I ran until my lungs were bursting and my tongue hanging out. Then I had to stop or else fall on my face. I moved into the shadows and leaned heavily against one of the stalls. My hand touched crepe paper and I looked up suddenly. It was my own stall. Or was it? I looked around quickly. The Spook House was right behind me. Yeah, it was my stall, all right.

I turned back to the Spook House. It looked funny to me. The moonlight made it look odd, but that wasn't it. It was something else. I looked closer, squinting my eyes. Then I realized what it was. The doors—that's what looked funny. During the season they were red and white and yellow, bright carnival colors. Now they were a dull gray. All of the windows were too.

Then I remembered. They were metal storm doors, put on for the winter. The windows had matching metal shutters. Sure. I had watched one of the maintenance men put them on the back windows before I opened my stall that day. They fitted the windows and doors snugly and clamped in place with snap-locks. They could be opened from the outside but not the inside, and they—

The outside but not the inside—

A sudden crazy plan began to beat in my mind. I dropped to my knees and peered around the side of the stall. I listened intently. I couldn't see Frankie and his pals, but I could hear their footsteps. They had stopped running and were moving around quickly from one place to another, looking for me. I guessed they were about a hundred feet away.

I might make it, I thought wildly, if I hurry—

I turned and crept on my hands and knees toward the Spook House. The cement was hard on my knees. I kept going. I moved quickly, as quickly and as quietly as I could.

At last I made the front of the Spook House. I stopped for a second and listened again. The footsteps were getting louder. I started crawling as fast as I could go.

I went past the front door and down to the corner of the building and around the side. At the first window I came to, I stood up, staying close to the wall. I reached up and withdrew the latch slowly and opened the metal shutters, then reached past them and pulled gently at the window. Silently, I prayed. Then the window opened. I sighed heavily.

I left them both open and began to crawl back around to the front of the building. My luck was running perfect so far. Now if only the front door was unlocked. No reason why it shouldn't be, I thought hopefully. If the window was open, then the door should be open too. What would be the sense in locking the doors and leaving the windows open? What was the sense in locking anything at all, when the park had a 10-foot fence around it with electric current at the top to stop anybody who tried to climb it? I knew in my heart the front door would be unlocked. But still I trembled at the thought it might not.

I got back around to the front and back to the door, and again I stopped and listened. The footsteps of Frankie and his pals were so loud now, I thought they were right on top of me.

I stood up quickly and threw open the four snap-locks that held the metal door in place. I didn't bother to be quiet anymore; it didn't make any difference now. They were so close to me, I knew I'd never be able to get away if they saw me. Not unless the inner door was unlocked.

I slid the metal door roughly across the concrete. It made a loud, scraping sound in the stillness. I listened for an instant and heard the footsteps stop momentarily; then they began running toward me. I turned and tried the inner door.

The door flew open. I started breathing again.

I ran in quickly and began feeling my way along the wall in the pitch darkness. I had been in the Spook House a couple of times and I tried to remember the layout. I knew I was in the first room, the one with all the scary pictures that light up all over the place. The window I had opened should be the first one along the next wall, the side wall.

I kept going, inch by inch, foot by foot, until I got to the corner. Then I heard them at the front door.

ALFRED HITCHCOCK'S ANTHOLOGY

I froze. I could barely make out their figures in the open doorway. They were standing very still. I knew they were listening for me, waiting for me to make a move, a noise. The window was only a few feet away from me. I tried to take another step sideways, but the wooden floor began to creak and I stopped the movement of my foot at once.

I began to sweat. Maybe, I thought frantically, maybe I've trapped myself!

One of the figures in the doorway moved into the room and disappeared into the darkness. I could hear him as he felt around, his hands hitting the wall, his footsteps loud in the empty room.

My heart pounded wildly. I turned my head in the direction of the open window and tried to judge how far away it was, wondering if I could make it in two or three quick steps. I looked back toward the doorway, squinting my eyes, trying to figure how much closer I was to the window than they were to me. Then I heard the guy inside the room make another noise. He sounded dangerously close to me. I expected any minute to feel his hands reach out and grab me by the throat. Suddenly, I wanted desperately to run for that window, to dive right through it. But deep down inside me I knew I would never make it. The guy in the room would take off after me as soon as I took the first step. The few seconds it would take me to scramble through the window would be all he needed to get to me. My feet probably wouldn't even touch the ground. If only they would look on the other side of the room, go the other way—

Then I got a brainstorm. Quickly, I unbuckled my belt and slipped it off my trousers. I wrapped it around my trembling hand, then took it off and pulled it into a tight ball. I fingered it anxiously, hoping it would be heavy enough.

Holding my breath, I raised the belt above my head and tossed it lightly across the room. It seemed like twenty minutes before it landed. Then it hit and hit perfectly. It sounded exactly like a clumsy footstep. I braced myself and got ready to move.

The two figures disappeared from the doorway and moved across the room, away from me. I heard the guy that was already in the room run toward the noise.

Then I moved. I hurried along the side wall, not caring about the noise I made, knowing the sound of my footsteps would be silenced by the noise of their own.

I groped ahead of myself in the blackness until my hand found the empty space of the window. I threw a leg over the ledge and got out fast.

I paused for a split-second outside the window, listening to the movements inside. Then, leaving the window open, I slammed the steel shutters closed and quickly shoved the latch in place. I pulled at them twice to make sure they were shut good and tight, then turned and started for the front door.

All the panic and tension and fear began to take hold of me then. I was panting for breath, shaking all over; my side burned like fire, where I had been kicked, and my cheek was numb with pain where the brass knuckles had smashed against my jaw; my mouth was dry, my tongue swollen, and my eyes blurred with sudden tears. I ran like a drunk man, tripping twice, falling to my sore knees once, groping along the side of the building blindly. And all the time a single thought in my mind, screaming at me: The door—the door—run—run—run—

I made the corner of the building and hurried along the front. I stumbled again and almost fell a second time, clutched at the wall to keep my balance. I cursed. I sobbed. But I kept moving. And I made it to the door.

From inside I could hear a mutter of voices. I dragged the heavy metal door forward. It came toward me noisily in jerky, broken motions that matched my rising and falling strength.

In an instant of silence, from inside again, I heard loud, echoing footsteps running toward me. I heard Frankie curse. The sounds grew louder, nearer. I dragged the door closer, then stepped behind it and braced my body against it. I got a last burst of strength from somewhere and pushed for all I was worth.

The door would have closed all the way with the last push, but just before it slammed shut, an arm shot through the opening and stopped it. The heavy steel edge smashed into the arm and I heard a sharp, sickening crack. From within, echoing loudly but muffled by the almost closed door, came an agonizing scream. I leaned my weight against the door and, in the dim moonlight, I watched the protruding fist writhe and twist. And then the fingers opened and stiffened, and then went limp, and as they did, I heard something fall to the concrete at my feet. It was the switchblade knife. I stared at it dumbly. The hand obviously belonged to Frankie.

ALFRED HITCHCOCK'S ANTHOLOGY

I let up the pressure against the door just a little, and the arm fell back inside. I slammed the door fully closed then and braced myself against it heavily as I groped with the snap-locks. Heavy fists pounded and heavy feet kicked at the door from the inside. But it did no good. The fourth snap-lock fell in place and the big door was tight.

I heard them yelling as I walked slowly away, down past my old stall, on down the darkened midway. Before I had gone far, I stopped to rest, to listen. I couldn't hear them anymore. It's them doors, I thought. Them heavy metal doors. They keep all the noise inside.

I went on back to the side gate. From there I could see the bobbing white spot of old Fritz's flashlight as he came down the side-street of the midway. It was two-and-a-half miles around the park and Fritz looked like he was still a quarter of a mile away. I didn't wait for him, but picked up my bag where it had dropped and walked on out of the park.

At the corner I stepped into a phone booth. Digging a dime from my pocket, I dropped it in the slot and dialed the operator. She answered right away.

"Give—give me the police," I said softly.

I could hear her making the connection. My face was throbbing in pain. I reached up and touched it gently with one finger. It was tender, swollen, crusted with dried blood. I felt my side then, where I had been kicked. When my hand touched one spot, I had to moan in agony. My ribs, I thought, must be broken.

I was hurt, trembling, crying again—and mad. They were dirty hoodlums. Rotten, good-for-nothing, punk hoodlums.

So what now? The cops come and get them and lock them up for a few days and then some judge has to turn them loose again because they're under age? Just kids, is that it? Teenagers? A little wild, somebody will say, but not really bad kids. And then they'd be back on the streets again.

I shook my head slowly. No, not this time. Not these three. Not if I could help it.

I hung up the phone, got my dime back and stepped out of the booth. As I walked slowly down the street, I thought: It's going to be a long cold winter in that Spook House, boys.

# Second Chance

## by Robert Cenedella

It was on his sixty-fifth birthday that Oscar Brown killed his wife by pushing her down the cellar stairs.

In all probability, he would not have done this had he not come across a dusty ancient book when (at his wife's insistence) he had been cleaning out the attic the day before. The book was called, intriguingly: *Magique Potions & Spelles; or, Ye Compleat Sorcerer;* and when Oscar turned its brittle pages one heading caught his eye: *Ye Potion Extraordinaire, The Which Changeth Dreary Lives in Wondrous Wayes.* Beneath this rather fulsome title was a recipe which surprised Oscar since all its ingredients could be found in any pantry. And below the recipe was an important instruction: "Do not drink of ye potion until thou hast firstly rid thyself of whatsoever or whosoever hast caused thee discomfort. Onlie then shouldst thou mix and drink. Great wonders shall follow, and thou shalt have what thou deservest from Life."

In this instruction, Oscar thought he perceived a joker: if you had rid yourself of whatsoever or whosoever had caused you discomfort, why should you need the potion? Still, remembering that the old house he and his wife inhabited was said once to have been owned by a crone who had been hanged for witchcraft, Oscar felt that he should ponder the words, "Great wonders will follow . . ."

He might have put the matter from his mind had he not wandered into the park the next day. It was his birthday. He was sixty-five years old, nearly old enough to die; and there in the park he sadly watched lovers strolling in the sunlight, the young men's arms about the young girls' slim waists; and he heard the provocative feminine laughter which preceded the stolen kisses.

The contrast between his wife and these young girls in the park was almost too much for him to contemplate. Nadine had always worn bombazine dresses with high choker collars. At night in their bedroom, while still fully clothed, she always put on a long flannel nightgown; leaving the sleeves empty, and from under this virtuous covering she removed her clothes without contortions—an exhibition of body control quite as remarkable though not as interesting as a tassel dancer's. She greeted each day half an hour before it arrived, shook Oscar awake, and began a filibuster against sin which lasted until it lulled him to sleep at nine P.M. She kept their house spotless, and saw to it that he helped her do so. She was especially maniacal about dusting keyholes. In this, Oscar detected a symbolism which depressed him.

And so, sitting in the park watching the young lovers, Oscar felt his eyes watering with self-pity as he realized that his youth was past. There had been, or should have been, girls for him: soft-fleshed girls whose convulsive embraces he had never experienced and whose desperate glad nightcries of passion he had never heard—and all because when he was twenty-five years old, he had married Nadine for her money.

And so he walked home finally, an old man whose mind writhed with secret voluptuosities, and he pushed his wife down the cellar stairs.

Then, before going to tell a policeman that his wife had had an accident, he carefully mixed the potion described in the ancient book, and drank it. It was quite salty.

At first, no great wonders followed at all, except that he did find himself rich.

There was, to start with, the original fortune for which he had married Nadine only to find that she guarded it as righteously as though it had been her body. There was in addition seventy-five percent of what Oscar himself had earned in forty years of toil. Nadine had taken this from him, and had saved it. She had taken the other twenty-five percent too; but this she had squandered on stew meat, dark green shapeless drapes, turnips (her favorite vegetable), contributions to missionaries engaged in clothing heathens, rice pudding (her favorite sweet), WCTU dues, and (for Oscar) a bicycle to pedal to work. But there was plenty of money left—more than a million dollars, in fact.

For a whole month it seemed that the money was all that Oscar would get for his pains.

But then the great wonders commenced.

His hair started to turn slowly from gray to brown. His limbs began to feel looser. His digestion became increasingly better. The glasses he wore began to make things blur in front of him until his eye man recommended that he take them off. He did this, and discovered that he had regained the good vision of his younger days.

It was hard to down the wild stallion of hope that made antic leaps within him, but he waited, trembling, until his third teeth began to push his upper plate right out of his mouth—and then he let the stallion beat its front hooves against his ribcage.

He was growing younger!

This of course posed a problem for him, but he had heard of more unpleasant ones. He discreetly moved from his home town before anyone could notice how he was changing, and after ten minutes of cerebration in a hotel room some five hundred miles away, he developed a plan from which he never thereafter swerved.

He had lived through forty years of Nadine's strident respectability, and he now proposed to wipe those forty years out, to grow backwards until he reached the age of twenty-five again, and then to find or buy an empty-headed, rattle-brained platinum blonde and to start having fun with her.

He would have to marry the girl, for he knew that by no other course could he gain her exclusive services; but marriage, he reflected, was not so bad provided one married a mistress rather than a wife—and, besides, in his unique situation it would be well to have a legal claim on the young lady until he had passed from puberty to mumbledypeg and no longer cared for her.

But he must avoid discovery. If the world learned that he was getting a year younger every six months, it might take an interest in him. The government might surround him with a house and the house with a barbed-wire fence suitable for imprisoning natural resources, until no platinum blonde would be able to see him unless she bought a ticket to see him. And of course no blonde in all the land would be empty-headed and rattle-brained enough to open her arms to him if she knew that before their silver wedding anniversary, she would be changing his diapers.

And so Oscar moved every six months, transferring his fortune from bank to bank.

He was lonely, but surely not for the sound of Nadine's voice, and in each of the quiet rooms in which he lived while he grew from sixty-five to sixty to fifty-five to fifty and so backward and backward, he sat smiling—and, sometimes, I am afraid, drooling—at what would happen when he could once again be twenty-five.

As he approached thirty, he found it quite difficult to keep from winking at girls; and when he passed thirty and entered his twenties, the devil kept whispering to him that starting a few years earlier would really make little difference. But Oscar Brown knew that a man, even a young man, would not forever be able to hold to the standard of conduct he had in mind, and having by this time read Mr. Kinsey on the subject of seventeen-year-olds, he wanted to be certain that he would be neither jaded nor indifferent when he reached that energetic age.

So, austerely as any monk, he saved himself for earthly heaven.

When he was twenty-six minus one-half, he hastened to New York, took an apartment on Park Avenue, and before he had even unpacked, set out in the Manhattan twilight to let the town know that curfew would not ring tonight.

Most young men of twenty-six avid for a sensual pleasure are likely to place reliance on the hackneyed maxim that all the world loves a lover; but this is because few young men of twenty-six have studied human nature for eighty-five years. Oscar Brown knew well that all the world is pretty bored with a lover unless he spends his money.

So for six months Oscar spent his money. He spent it in night clubs and in certain exclusive dress shops. He spent it on exotic food and bubbly drink and costly raiment for costly brunettes.

The brunettes were to rehearse with, for his twenty-fifth birthday was fast approaching now.

When finally he went searching for his empty-headed, rattle-brained platinum blonde, he found her waiting for him in the chorus line of the Wayfarers' Club. Gloria, her name was, and she fell in love with him at first sight of his wallet.

She had had the usual hard life. Her father had been the usual drunkard. Her mother had taken in the usual washings and lovers. She had the usual sniveling brothers and sisters in the usual profusion, and the respectable people of her small home town had inflicted the usual snubs on her.

"I guess I was always a dreamer," she said. "I wanted to improve myself."

And so she had hitch-hiked to New York.

"I wanted to find something better than I'd been used to," she said.

And from what Oscar could observe, she had indeed found it, in the world of frenzied dances, spendthrift men, late parties—the world of the lifted glass and the torn dress and the music that never stopped.

Oscar had never met anyone who knew better than Gloria how to please a man who had no old age to worry about.

And so on his twenty-fifth birthday, Oscar married her.

The following morning, she gave him the shock of his one hundred and five years.

She tinted her hair to its natural mouse-brown.

"At last," she said, "I can be respectable."

She brought forth from her hope chest a wardrobe of severely plain and frumpy clothes.

She set a bedtime of nine P.M. and barred strong drink from their home.

She went over his books and declared she would handle the money from now on.

She told him he must get a good job and work hard at it. "I know you're rich, but you don't want to waste your life," was the way she put it.

When he suggested divorce, she said it was not respectable and he might as well put it out of his mind, because she would never give him cause for divorce, she was not that kind of a girl now.

And from the day he married her, Oscar started growing older again, like everyone else.

The formula, as promised, had given him what he deserved.

He was in for another forty years with Gloria.

ALFRED HITCHCOCK'S ANTHOLOGY

# The Last Witness

## by Robert Colby

I was waiting on the courthouse steps when Norma Krueger, my stepmother, and Russ Tyson, her lover, came out of the building into the harsh November sunlight of Los Angeles.

In a hushed courtroom of breathless spectators and reporters, their jury had just brought in an astonishing verdict—"Not guilty!" Sickened, raging because the man I knew they had murdered was my father, I had hurried from the room. Even the smoggy exhaust-tainted air of L.A. was sweeter than the stench of injustice.

Norma, wearing a plain powder-blue dress with a plain white collar which conspired to make her seem demure, paused dramatically at the top of the steps. Surrounded by a frantic huddle of clamorous reporters and dancing photographers, she took a deep breath and embraced the city with a sweeping gaze of triumph.

Although my father, Rudolph Krueger, had been sixty-five when he was murdered, Norma was now only thirty-seven. Her youthful figure, everything about her, was frankly sensual, yet during the trial she had toned herself down to a shy whisper, an intriguing mystery to that all-male jury.

She had gleaming chestnut hair and small brittle features underlined by a mouth which twisted into a variety of studied smiles. It was the only part of her face that did smile, for her eyes were the coolest emeralds and her thrusting little chin was relentless as a cocked gun.

Norma turned, and with a saccharine smile said something inaudible to the reporters. Then she moved briskly, grandly down the steps. Tyson, freed by the same jury, followed meekly behind her, a mascot trailing on an invisible leash.

When Norma came abreast of me she paused with the first hint of uncertainty. Though we had not exchanged a word since the day she and Tyson were arrested, she was aware that I loathed the very sight of her. I had told her with silence, and how many times had my eyes impaled her?

"Congratulations, Norma," I said icily.

Her darting glance searched the skeptical faces of the reporters. She spoke carefully, as if examining every word under the scope of their cynicism. "Thank you, Carl," she said in a syrupy voice. "How very nice. But of course I had great faith in our system of justice. I never doubted the verdict."

"Norma, I was not congratulating you on the verdict. You've been terribly clever—and lucky, so far."

"So far?" With a slight turn of her head so that she was in profile to the reporters, she gave me her secret ace—bold-eyed, smirking. "When the game is over the losers weep and the winners count their chips," she told me under her breath.

For just a moment I thought seriously of belting her right on the point of her arrogantly tilted chin.

"Mr. Krueger," called one of the photographers, "would you be willing to pose beside your stepmother?"

"Sure," I answered, "but I'll need a prop. You got a long, sharp knife?"

After a tense silence, Norma said in her on-stage voice, "Dear Carl, it's been a dreadful ordeal and your viewpoint has become distorted. I think it's perfectly natural under the circumstances, and I don't blame you in the least." She paused. "Well, I'll be seeing you, dear. Won't I?"

"I don't see how you can avoid me, because unless you're moving out, we'll be living in the same house."

Norma clamped her lips tightly and turned away. Staring at the back of her head I could almost see the sharp little gears of her mind grindingly halted.

"Mrs. Krueger," said a girl reporter with a mannish figure and impudently disdainful eyes, "do you plan to marry Russ Tyson in the near future?"

Norma's head swiveled toward Tyson. She inspected him as if he were some forgotten piece of an incompleted puzzle. Ironically, Russ Tyson was almost exactly my age, three years younger than Norma. He was a big, lazy-smiling, deceptively amiable puppy dog of a man with

90                                ALFRED HITCHCOCK'S ANTHOLOGY

thick tawny hair, a meaty, placid face, brown eyes and a heavy mouth.

Norma, turning back to the manly girl reporter, said cautiously, "I think it would be in very bad taste to discuss marriage at this time. Sorry—no comment."

Pleased with herself, she went striding off, trailed by Tyson, flanked by the unbelievers of the press.

When they had gone, escaping in separate cabs, I exorcised my fury with a rapid hike to the nearest bar. I drank four martinis while examining the still smoking ruins of the past for a clue to some future revenge.

The trial had lasted a little over six weeks. Since Tyson's defense was the key to Norma's own freedom, she had hired Maxwell Davis to defend him. His brilliant theatrics had returned more killers to an ungrateful society than any other living attorney. It was his unsmiling boast that he could free a man who shot his own mother in the squad room of Homicide.

Norma's lawyer had only a slightly less enviable record of acquittals. Norma paid all the bills.

The case had been largely circumstantial, but the circumstances were so unshakably accusing that any law school student should have been able to nail Norma and her lover to the cross of justice.

Rudolph Krueger is a familiar name in the movie industry. My father was perhaps the greatest of the old-line producer-directors. He had been shot dead in the livingroom of his own mansion, supposedly during the course of a burglary. The state contended that the burglary was contrived by my stepmother and Tyson to cover his murder.

Norma, the prosecution insisted, had gone to our place at Lake Arrowhead to establish her innocence. While she lavishly entertained her half dozen alibis, Tyson coolly, deliberately shot my father, grabbed his wallet, a diamond ring and other valuables, staging a messy display of overturned tables, broken lamps and rifled drawers before he vanished.

The police were at first puzzled, then suspicious. It was obvious that Rudolph Krueger had been sitting in a chair, reading. The first bullet had entered the back of his head at close range, the second, as he slumped forward, had splintered his spine.

Since it was a sneaky surprise killing, why the shambles of lamps and tables, simulating a fight? Would any respectable house burglar risk such a killing unless he were cornered? Unlikely.

Burglars do not usually carry guns. Even so, would a burglar be apt to arm himself with a bulky, long-barreled German Luger? The spent bullets said he did in this case. Was it a coincidence that my father owned a Luger? Another coincidence that the gun was missing?

The police did not think so. A quiet, plodding investigation caught up with Tyson and tied him to Norma. A damaging note written by Norma to Tyson had been found in Tyson's apartment. The note was not specific but it did express Norma's wish to be at Lake Arrowhead ". . . during that crucial period which we discussed."

Finally, Tyson's fingerprints were lifted from one of the overturned tables, and an hour before the murder he had been observed close to the scene.

Maxwell Davis shot holes in the state's evidence with sneering contempt. Of course Tyson's fingerprints were on that livingroom table. As the family broker he was often in the house on business. Even if he came expressly to visit Norma, that did not make him a murderer. The jury must remember that the defendants were not on trial for adultery.

As for the Luger, probably the burglar discovered it where it was kept in a desk drawer of the study, and took it away with him after the killing. If not, where was it? Could the state produce it? Could the state prove that my father was killed by his own gun?

The note, Davis said, was too vague to be considered as evidence of a crime plot. It implied nothing sinister in any case. Rudolph Krueger had grown suspicious. He hired a detective to watch Norma while he was in Europe. Aware of the detective, Norma wanted to be at Arrowhead when her husband returned because she knew the detective would report her affair with Tyson, and she was afraid. This was the "crucial period" to which she referred in the note.

"Not guilty!" said the jury, and freed them both.

As you might imagine, there was a great deal of money at stake. Had the jury convicted Norma, she would have lost her right to inherit my father's estate and the money would have gone to me.

Although my father had left me a small portion of his cash holdings, fifty percent of the Beverly Hills mansion and other properties, the bulk of his money was willed to me in trust, with the interest going to Norma for the considerable remainder of her life. Nothing short of her conviction or her death could release the money to me.

My father had earned enormous sums and he was a shrewd investor, never a spendthrift. There were over seven millions, of which greedy Norma got "only" a million in cash. But the yearly interest on six million bucks is a staggering amount, any way you look at it.

I don't suppose I should have resented the fact that my father did not leave me his money outright, for I had failed miserably in several enterprises which he had financed. But I was of his flesh and blood, the money belonged to me! I could not bear the thought that he had more faith in Norma, that scheming, murdering tramp, than he did in his own son.

My mother had been dead many years when my father married Norma. She'd had a small part in a low-budget picture which my father was backing. A lousy actress, her one great performance took place on the witness stand in the courtroom of her trial.

Norma's physical attributes were obvious, though, and she was a superbly talented flatterer. Always the opportunist, she saw that my father's ego had been destroyed when the new realistic world of pictures had refused to accept him. A stubborn, inflexible man who simply would not adapt speedily to change, he had been discarded and scorned by the very leaders in the industry who had praised him most.

Publicly, ostentatiously, Norma boosted his stock. Privately, she pretended to worship his forgotten genius. For hours she would sit with him in the darkness of that monstrous antique mansion, applauding his pathetic trophies of the past—those ridiculous, maudlin melodramas which he had produced and directed.

Norma had married Rudolph Krueger's money, and he had married the exalted reflection of himself in Norma's phony mirror.

My father was not an easy man to like. He was precise as a stopwatch, formal as a dress shirt—and just as stiff. Though he was tall and imposing, he was otherwise not much to look at. He was bald and had large protruding ears. His stern features were usually naked of expression.

He did have another side, a lighter, gayer side, but apparently it had died with his fame. He was a vindictive man who never forgot his enemies, a willful man who intended to recover his place at any cost, but when he produced his first picture in many a year it limped badly at the box office, and he was again consigned to oblivion.

While Norma flattered and humored to keep her throne, their marriage was not always peaceful. Aware that he was hardly a woman's dream, knowing that Norma was nearly half his age, my father was perpetually jealous. Suspecting her infidelity, he spent much time and fat chunks of money on elaborate schemes to trap her.

He would pretend to take a long trip, then return suddenly. Or in his absence, he would hire detectives to watch her. Once he had the phones tapped, another time he paid a handsome out-of-work actor to bait her, but Norma was on guard and all of his devices failed. The private detective who finally caught her with Tyson never had a chance to make his report before my father was killed.

The house in which my father lived was a gloomy monument to his past. I despised it. Therefore I had taken an apartment in Brentwood, but when my father was murdered and the two lovers were arrested, I moved back to the mansion. My one driving motive was to comb the house for evidence.

I had every advantage. My father did not keep servants on the premises because he said they were spies who reported every word and action to the flunkies of our neighbors and the tradespeople. Although my father's peculiar logic escaped me, the servants came by day, and at night I had a free hand. I hoped to be able to turn up the sort of concrete evidence a detective could miss.

Lieutenant Wenstrom, who had charge of the case, was amused at my promise to succeed where he had failed, but he was willing enough to let me try.

What I wanted most to locate was the gun—the Luger—and the prints it might hold. Wenstrom told me I was wasting my time. People did not leave murder weapons around to accuse them; the gun would never be found.

I could not tell him why I thought the gun was hidden right there in the house because I didn't know why myself. It was only a hunch. Yet it was so strong a hunch that I could close my eyes and *see* that Luger resting in some dark, secret cache, waiting for me to discover it.

When I had done everything to find the gun, short of tearing down the walls, I began to believe Wenstrom was right—it just wasn't there in the house. Nor could I uncover so much as a scrap of paper, a piece of clothing, a bloodstain, a hair that could be used to rope and drop Norma and Tyson.

As the last days of the trial faded I became so frantic that I would lie in bed dreaming of ways to manufacture evidence against them. Then,

ALFRED HITCHCOCK'S ANTHOLOGY

abruptly, it was over. They were beyond justice, safe from legal vengeance forever. I could almost hear them laughing.

It was dusk when I left the bar. I had remained long enough to build the foundation of a plan. It was a dangerous all-or-nothing plan, but if I could bring it off, the prize would include both revenge and money.

The mansion, square and ugly as some ancient museum, squatted on a hill overlooking Sunset Boulevard. I could see its lights at the crest of that long, upward sweeping, tree-studded lawn as I turned off the boulevard and climbed toward it.

I was surprised to find that Norma was completely alone in the house. She was seated behind my father's desk in the study, going over accounts, writing checks. She had changed into a turquoise sheath which hid few of her assets; her hair had been rearranged, her makeup restored. The person she had pretended to be in that courtroom farce now seemed comparatively like a shy, pallid nun.

"Welcome home, Norma." I had entered silently and when she looked up her expression was startled, though I could see no fear in her eyes. Well, I thought, she always had more guts than brains. "Adding up the take, Norma? Counting the spoils?"

Her narrow smile flickered and went out. "Sit down, Carl," she said coolly. "I've been expecting you."

"Expecting me?" I sank into a chair.

"Of course. You live here, don't you?" she asked sarcastically.

"How true," I answered. "I hope you won't find it inconvenient to have me around."

"I suppose you'll always hate me and you'll always think the worst. Carl, you're just like one of those bitter, self-righteous reporters, ready to condemn the slightest appearance of evil on the theory that where there's smoke, there's got to be fire. If twelve intelligent men found me innocent, why can't you at least give me the benefit of the doubt?"

"Because," I said, aiming a finger, "*you* know, and *I* know, that you murdered my father!"

"I don't know any such thing!" she answered, her face livid.

"Tyson held the gun," I continued, "but as far as I'm concerned, you pulled the trigger."

"Carl," she said weakly, "I—I loved your father. Can't you realize—"

"Don't give me that, Norma! You didn't love him any more than I did," I lied. "He was a wicked old creep out of the dark ages, a silly unbending dictator who never thought of anyone but himself and his idiot ego. He was a toy Hitler in a toy empire. Don't kid me, Norma—we both hated his guts!"

There was a shade of truth in that fabrication and I was convincing. I figured it to be the exaggerated picture which Norma had of my father when she rationalized his murder.

"Why, Carl!" she exclaimed with real amazement. "I'm shocked! And I—I think you're dreadfully ungrateful. Your father helped you in many wonderful ways."

"Norma," I said, "your hypocrisy is showing, don't you think?" Winking, I gave her a conspiratorial look.

A faint smile touched the corner of her lovely mouth. "Maybe," she admitted. "Maybe just a little. Really, Carl, I had no idea—I mean, if you had so little use for your father, you certainly put on a fine show. In all these years you never said a word to me against him."

"Just this once," I said, "let's be honest with each other. We were enemies, Norma. No, not enemies—competitors. If I had told you what I really thought of the old man, you'd have carried it right back to him. You'd have crucified me. Am I right?"

Norma settled more comfortably in her chair and lit a cigarette. "No comment," she answered, though her twist of smile was a confirmation. "You certainly are a contradiction," she went on. "If you hated your father so much, why all this animosity toward me?"

"Haven't you guessed? I have nothing against you personally, Norma. But I love money, especially money that rightfully belongs to me. Truthfully, I was praying for that jury to toss you to the wolves."

"My, my," she said, "you *are* savage, aren't you?"

"No, but I'm a nasty loser."

"You don't care that your father was murdered?"

"Do you see me weeping? I care about losing the dough. Happiness is a thing called money. But I'll tell you this, Norma: Tyson bungled the whole business from the opening gun—no pun intended. He was about as subtle and believable as a rhino in a china shop. If you'd had *me* on your team there would have been no jury. There wouldn't have been any case to take to a jury!"

96

Her face was a stone but her eyes scooped me up. I hurried on. "Listen, Norma, if you hadn't been smart enough to hire Maxwell Davis, Tyson would have fallen right off the mountain and he'd have taken you down with him. Have to hand it to old Davis—he can talk circles around the slickest politician who ever lived!"

Norma chuckled agreeably and I laughed with her.

"Yeah, that old guy is an artist," I said, shaking my head in admiration. "He's got real talent! He can take a piece of evidence and turn it around until you see only the side he *wants* you to see. For instance, that bit about the table. Tyson puts his big clumsy paw on it and you think he's a dead duck. But Maxwell Davis tells us his prints *belong* on that livingroom table. Tyson comes here all the time as an invited guest and he just naturally is gonna put his hand on a table if he's sitting beside it." I sighed. "But how stupid! Why didn't he wear gloves?"

"Well, he did!" said Norma defensively. "But then he had to take them off for a minute because—" Her mouth gaped, her wide-eyed expression begged for my untroubled reaction—a smile of resignation, a shrug of indifference.

I stood. "Thanks a lot, Norma," I snarled. "That's all I wanted to know!"

Trembling with the need to feel my hands closing around her neck, I moved toward her.

Instantly she reached into a desk drawer which stood partly open. I stared into the long-barreled, awesome mouth of a Luger pistol.

"I told you, Carl," she said evenly, "I was expecting you."

"My father's gun!"

"Russ was afraid to leave with it," she said. "If by some chance he got caught with this gun before he could dispose of it, we were finished. So he hid it in the house."

"Where? I couldn't find it, and I know this place."

For a moment I thought she was going to giggle. "Did you try the freezer?"

I nodded. "Not bad for a couple of amateur killers. I can't wait to see Wenstrom's face when he hears the story."

She sat back, holding the gun casually but steadily. "I suppose you expect Lieutenant Wenstrom to hop right over and arrest me," she said scornfully. "But of course, he can't."

"No, he can't," I agreed. "I know all about the law of double jeopardy. So what will you do now—shoot me?"

"Don't be silly, Carl. I'm not dumb enough to push my luck that far. Just go away and leave me. If you'll sell your share of the house, I'll give you a great deal more than it's worth."

"I'll think about it," I said. "I'll let you know. Now give me that gun. If you don't, I might have to mess up your pretty face when I take it away from you."

She hesitated, then handed it across to me. I tucked it under my belt and left. The plan was going better than I expected.

In the morning I told Norma that just the sight of her made me retch. Then I gathered my belongings and moved back to Brentwood. I spent another two days working out my plan to the smallest detail. Then I phoned her.

"I've decided to sell my interest in the house," I told her. "And I'm going to hold you to your promise to buy at more than it's worth. You can afford it, Norma."

"The house is a white elephant," she said cagily. "People just won't buy these huge old relics today. They tell me I'll be lucky to get seventy-five thousand for it. So I'll be generous—I'll give you fifty for your share."

"The house isn't much," I admitted, "but there's almost an acre of grounds and I know what the whole package is worth because I checked. You'll give me a hundred thousand."

"I will?"

"Yes, you will. And I'll want it in cash." I didn't need the payoff in cash but I had my reasons.

"Why cash?" she asked irritably. "That's an absurd demand."

"You'd better hurry off to the bank," I said, "because I'll be over to pick up the money at eight tomorrow night. Have Tyson bring a quit-claim deed for me to sign. He can act as witness."

"Now listen here, Carl, you can't dictate—"

"Oh yes, I can. And don't interrupt, because I have a few other items here. Tell Tyson to bring a complete list of my father's stock holdings along with their estimated value as of tomorrow's closing prices. From you I want an accurate accounting of the cash value of the remainder of the estate after debts and taxes."

"I won't do it!" she snapped. "None of those things concern you and I won't be blackmailed. I don't give a damn if you think it would be fun to expose the truth. Nothing can touch us now."

"You're wrong," I said. "They can't try you again for the same crime, but they can easily convict you of another one. Did you know that lying on the witness stand constitutes perjury? They would send you and Tyson to prison for about two years, and they'd do it with the greatest of pleasure, I assure you."

There was an electric silence. "All right," she said quietly, "I'll do what you ask. But don't come here thinking that I'm going to hand over your father's estate under threat, because I'd rather go to prison."

"Don't worry, Norma. All I want is that hundred thousand—in cash."

"Besides," she continued, her mind clicking again, "I'm pretty sure Max Davis could quash that perjury charge without too much trouble."

I didn't say so, but I rather agreed with her. I had met Maxwell Davis as I was leaving for Brentwood two days before. He had come to see Norma about something or other and paused on the steps of the house to shake hands with me.

"No hard feelings, son," he had said. "I was just earning my fee, you understand."

A big, hearty man with a merry twinkle in his eye, he had a mild Southern drawl, and the courtly manner of Old South aristocracy. I thought it childish to resent him because he had done his job all too well, so I shook hands with him and told him that regardless of my personal feelings, I thought he was probably the most gifted defender in the world today.

Now Norma was saying, "I don't like the idea of having Russ come over. Because of the sordid publicity, we decided not to see each other for a while."

"How touching," I replied. "I want Tyson there—period. If you'll tell him to keep his mouth shut and sneak over after dark, there won't *be* any publicity."

"Very well," she agreed.

"And tell Tyson that if he wants to save himself some grief he'd better be on time, not a minute late!"

I hung up.

At six forty-five the next evening I stood at the box office of a small independent theater in Westwood, chatting with Dorry, the ginger-haired cashier. I had chosen this particular theater because my father had bought an interest in it just a few months before his death. Consequently, I knew the staff and, more important, they knew me.

The first feature of a double-header went on at seven. I had seen both pictures shortly after they had been released. Together they would consume three hours and fifty-seven minutes.

In the lobby I spied Bill Steinmetz, the manager, wisecracking with the candy girl. I spent about five minutes making small talk with him before I went inside and took a seat next to a fire exit. The ticket man played usher on those rare occasions when he was needed, but most of the time he was out by the door.

At fifteen minutes before eight I glanced around. A handful of customers in the center section watched the picture with rapt attention. None of the staff was about.

Soft as a shadow I melted away, out the fire exit door. From my pocket I took a small wedge of cardboard, inserting it so that the door was ajar just enough to insure reentry.

Norma and Russ Tyson were waiting in the livingroom. Tyson appeared to be extremely edgy. He kept glancing at me nervously, checking my face as if it were a barometer.

Norma was cool, withdrawn. I signed the quit-claim, Tyson signed as witness. Norma handed me a briefcase bulging with currency. I didn't bother to count it.

Tyson delivered a list of securities with their market values; Norma handed me a few clipped sheets of paper, the accounting I demanded. I glanced at these briefly before folding them neatly into a pocket of my suit. I could have dug up the information myself with a little effort, but I wanted to keep those two preoccupied so they would not guess my real purpose.

"And now I've got something for *you*," I announced. "You might say it's a reward for, uh, services rendered."

In my lap I unwrapped a box I had taken from the trunk of my car before entering. It contained the Luger pistol. I held it toward Norma. "Would you like to have it back, Norma?" I asked.

"You know very well that I would," she answered, standing tentatively and smiling for the first time.

100                               ALFRED HITCHCOCK'S ANTHOLOGY

I said, "When you smile, Norma, you're quite a beautiful woman, in an evil sort of way." And she was.

As she moved toward me, still smiling, I reversed the gun and pulled the trigger. I shot her carefully three more times. She staggered back, recoiling as if she were being struck by some giant invisible fist. She was still sagging to the floor when I turned the gun on Tyson.

I have never see anyone so frightened. His eyes were hugely dilated, he trembled like a wet puppy.

"Tyson," I said, "take a good look at her. You don't want to die like that, do you?"

His eyes flicked down to the body. He couldn't seem to voice an answer but he shook his head violently to indicate that he was far from prepared to die.

I said, "You'll be dead in one minute if you don't do exactly as I tell you, Tyson."

"Anything," he sobbed. "Anything you want."

"It was Norma who really killed my father," I said soothingly. "You were just her tool. She simply used you—isn't that right?"

"That's right," he said tremulously. "She used me. I—I didn't know what I was doing. I couldn't resist her."

"Exactly. And for that reason I'm going to give you a break. I'm going to let you write a note admitting that you killed my father—and Norma. Then you can take this hundred thousand—I'll hardly miss it now—and get out of the country as fast as you can run with your tail between your legs. If you get caught, you're on your own. I'll deny you, the note will condemn you. But at least you'll have a chance to survive. Fair enough?"

He nodded furiously. "Perfectly fair."

I marched him to the desk in the living room and made him open the drawer himself and take out a piece of my father's stationery. I went around to the other side of the desk and held the gun an inch from his temple.

"Pick up that pen and write," I ordered, "word for word what I tell you." I began to dictate slowly:

"I had to punish Norma because she made me kill Rudolph Krueger. She had a strange power over me that I could not resist. Her voice was in my head, whispering for me to kill. I had to stop that voice—God help me!"

"That's a nutty kind of note," I said, "just right for this. If you get caught, you can always plead insanity. Now sign it!"

The instant he had signed, I shoved the barrel against his right temple and fired. I wiped the gun clean and got his prints on it. Then, holding the gun with a pencil in the barrel, I dropped it just beneath his dangling right hand.

Carrying the hundred thousand dollar briefcase now containing the quit-claim and the box which had enclosed the gun, I went out to my car and drove off without lights.

I had no trouble getting back inside the theater unobserved. On the way out I spent another few minutes with Steinmetz, remarking on the merits of the two features, gravely accepting his repeated sympathy over my father's death.

As a final touch I put a finger in Dotty's back and faked a holdup of the night's receipts.

Chuckling, I departed.

These complex arrangements for an alibi were wasted. I was never once suspected. I was widely congratulated on the ironic twist of events.

It was my turn to count the chips and I was still counting a few days later when I got a phone call from Lieutenant Wenstrom.

"You goofed," he said.

"What do you mean by that?" I asked, feeling the breath of an icy wind across my back.

"When you raked through your father's house you missed the most fantastic piece of evidence on record. If you'd found it in time, a jury would have convicted that gruesome twosome without leaving their chairs. Well, it doesn't matter now. But I just thought you might get a kick out of it, Mr. Krueger."

"What sort of evidence, Lieutenant?"

"Listen, Mr. Krueger, I don't wanna spoil it for you. You've got to *see* it to believe it. You got a few minutes to come down here?"

"Why not?" I said quickly, though a police station was the last place I wanted to visit.

Wenstrom, so tickled he seemed on the verge of riotous laughter, took me to a bleak interrogation room, sparsely furnished—just a few chairs and a table. The blinds had been drawn and lights glared from overhead fixtures.

On the table was a black box or case. A uniformed officer stood beside it in an attitude of patient waiting. Also in the room was a Sergeant Stansbury of Homicide, whom I had met before.

All seemed in a jovial mood, and for a couple of minutes we nothing-talked before Wenstrom's smile slowly faded and he began to ask questions about my father's career as he moved up from film cutter to become a top cameraman, a director and then a producer.

Suddenly Wenstrom turned to me and barked, "Did you know that your father was extremely jealous of your stepmother?"

"Yes. No doubt about that."

"He went to a lot of trouble, spent a lot of money to trap her, didn't he?"

"Yes."

He grinned. "Well, I won't keep you guessing. I'll just go ahead and tell you how he caught your stepmother's boy Tyson in the act of killing him and made a pictorial record of it for the jury."

"What!"

Still grinning, he nodded. "We didn't find those hidden cameras until yesterday when we dug a bullet out of the wall in the livingroom right beside a beautifully camouflaged camera lens. Once we got the idea, we discovered a whole battery of them. He must have spent a fortune on that setup.

"The way it worked, the cameras were activated by sounds in the room at a certain level—voices, movements, and so on. They would cut off automatically after a silence of three minutes. They worked in relays. When one camera ran out of film, another took up the job. He had sound cameras all over the place.

"He had just returned from Europe when he was killed, so probably he hadn't got around to turning the cameras off. They went right on spinning while Tyson murdered him. Hell, I'll let you see for yourself. Nate, why don't you roll that thing for the man!"

I looked back and saw that the case had been removed to reveal a projector loaded with film. Quickly, Sergeant Stansbury set up a folding screen. Then the lights were doused and there was the stuttering sound of the machine, the cone of light, the picture.

At first I was confused. It was a livingroom scene in which Norma and Tyson were the players. They appeared to be listless, waiting. Then I heard Norma mention my name, and I saw myself entering the room.

"Damn!" cried Wenstrom, "You got the wrong reel, Nate! Oh well, let's look at this one first. Okay, Mr. Krueger?"

I didn't answer. His voice came to me distantly, as if he spoke from the far end of a tunnel. I was watching myself unwrap a box, then my hand was extending the Luger. "Would you like to have it back, Norma? . . . When you smile, Norma, you're quite a beautiful woman, in an evil sort of way."

The gun leaped in my hand, the sounds crashing in a series of telescoping echoes as Norma recoiled, sagged to the floor . . .

Light splashed over the interrogation room and there was an immense silence.

"Well, Krueger, what do you think?" boomed Wenstrom's voice. "Would you like to tell us anything we can't see for ourselves?"

I considered the question for a long moment. "I think it would be best for me to call a lawyer," I answered. "Until then, I have nothing to say."

"A lawyer!" Wenstrom mocked. "Listen to the man. A lawyer! Save your money, Krueger. You don't need a lawyer with this kind of evidence. Plead guilty, get down on your knees before the judge and beg for mercy. Come to think of it, a case like this, what could a judge do for you? Better just pray, that's all you've got left."

I said, "No offense, Lieutenant, but I'm not much on praying—I'm a little out of touch. If you'll just get me to a phone, I'll take my chances on Maxwell Davis."

ALFRED HITCHCOCK'S ANTHOLOGY

# Death à la Newburgh

## by Libby MacCall

**I** know exactly when the idea first occurred to me.

One morning my mother-in-law and I were sitting at the dining room table, darning damask table napkins. I loathe darning. In this case, it was a thoroughly useless occupation, because the attic is full of napkins from her trousseau that have never been removed from the pink tissue paper in which they were delivered from the monogram-maker. But my mother-in-law was a string-saver, not to mention a napkin-mender, so there we sat on this glorious summer morning, darning away as though these were the last squares of damask left in America.

Paper napkins? That idea was entirely alien to our household. Only common people use such shortcuts. The fine old families must preserve the gracious way of life which is so rapidly disappearing from America today.

In order to prevent another disquisition on this subject, one to which I had listened for years *ad nauseam,* I had switched on the radio for the ten o'clock news.

"We bring you an announcement of urgent importance," said the newscaster. I wondered, with the frivolity that was viewed with such contempt in our gracious but humorless home, whether the men from Mars had finally landed. But no, it was nothing of that kind. "A defective shipment of tuna fish has been delivered to many stores in the metropolitan area. Several proven cases of botulism, some fatal, have resulted. All merchandise still on the shelves has been returned to the canner. However, some cans have already been sold. We urge all housewives to check their stocks of canned goods immediately for cans of tuna fish bearing the brand label Ocean Wave. Defective cans are imprinted with the serial number W357. Return the fish to the store where it was purchased and you will receive a refund. We repeat, do not use cans of Ocean Wave tuna, serial number W357."

What a nuisance! I always bought Ocean Wave brand; it was much the best. Now I'd have to go check all the serial numbers. I must have had a dozen cans of the stuff.

"Dorothy," said my mother-in-law, in her well-modulated voice, "is it possible that some of those poisoned cans might be reposing on our pantry shelves? I suggest you go at once to investigate."

I gladly seized the opportunity to escape from the darning and went out to the kitchen, where Willimae, the incumbent of the moment (they changed frequently), was polishing silver. Sure enough, I found three of the cans on the shelf bore the incriminating number.

"These will have to go back to the supermarket, Willimae," I said. "You'd better look at home and be sure you don't have any." I told her what I had just learned.

"I never buy that kind," she replied. "It's too expensive. Here, I'll give you a bag to put them in."

I dropped the three cans into the paper bag and started back through the swinging door to the dining room. It was then that the unthinkable idea entered my hitherto innocent mind.

Suppose, just suppose, I hadn't heard that broadcast. Suppose one of us had happened to eat the tuna fish. What a shattering thought! And then I took that one further step. Suppose my mother-in-law had been the only one to eat it. How many times, when she went out for her daily drive, I had imagined the accident that might take place. In my fantasies, she had fallen downstairs, suffered a heart attack, contracted a virulent infection. But never before had it occurred to me that I might be the active agent. Now, here in my hand I held the means to dispatch my enemy.

I had shocked myself. I didn't realize I could be so cold-blooded. It was one thing to dream dreams of how wonderful life might be without her presence; it was quite another to take a positive role in removing her from the scene. No, it was utterly inconceivable that I, Dorothy Jamison, a decent, God-fearing woman, could ever—unthinkable! Nonetheless, I did not return the three cans of tuna fish to the shop. Instead, I removed the labels and wrapped the cans in a lacy nylon gown I had once purchased in one of my brief moments of madness. I had never suffered a recurrence of the particular impulse, and so had

106                    ALFRED HITCHCOCK'S ANTHOLOGY

never worn the gown. There lay the unlabeled cans, enfolded in mint-green nylon lace, in the back of my drawer. It gave me a sensation of power to know they were there. Naturally, I hadn't the slightest intention of doing anything further about them. One day, I'd tidy the drawer, shake my head over my temporary aberration, and throw them into the garbage can. It pleased me to think that, if she knew about it, Mrs. Jamison would be highly indignant at the waste of the dollar-nineteen I had forfeited by my failure to return the spoiled fish.

People who knew Mrs. Jamison casually would have been at a loss to understand why I should feel anything but the greatest admiration for her. I myself, when I first met her, had thought her a beautiful and charming lady. It was at a concert of organ music, presented to raise funds for missionary work in Africa that we were introduced by the aunt I was visiting during Thanksgiving vacation, because I couldn't afford the fare for the trip home from college.

"May I present my niece, Dorothy Hunt-Morrison. Mrs. Randolph Jamison, Dorothy, my dear."

Auntie's voice indicated that I was being granted a rare privilege. Mrs. Jamison wore a smart hat atop a stylish and becoming hairdo. Her complexion was a tribute to some very talented facial expert. She had obviously been a beauty as a young girl, and was sparing no expense to remain one as long as possible.

We talked of the concert, then of my college, and eventually Auntie managed to mention—most casually, of course, and in a very well-bred manner—that my mother, her sister, had contrived to marry one of THE Hunt-Morrisons. She did not bother to add that poor old Daddy was still an assistant professor in a third-rate college.

Mrs. Randolph Jamison invited us to dinner the following evening. She said that her son, Randolph Jamison the Fourth, was also at home for the Thanksgiving holiday. I accepted the invitation with alacrity. Future holidays would be greatly enlivened by the addition of a date. Besides, judging by his mother, this boy could easily be a thing of beauty.

He wasn't. He took after his father, whose picture hung in the drawingroom. That's what Mrs. Jamison called it: the drawingroom. And if he wasn't handsome at least he was tall, moderately presentable, and very intelligent. The two ladies gossiped about the minister, the organist, the menu for the next church supper. They made it painfully obvious that we were being given a clear field to conduct a tête-à-tête.

Randolph Jamison the Fourth seemed to me to be rather awkward and lacking in poise for a young man of his obvious advantages, probably the result of his having been brought up in a fatherless household, I decided. I learned that he liked to read, and hoped to travel abroad next summer. When I called him "Randy" he lowered his voice and said earnestly that nicknames upset his mother. Everyone addressed him as Randolph.

"Even the guys at school?" I asked.

He just smiled and began to talk about a paper he was writing on the philosophy of Santayana. It was a long time before I learned that the guys at school didn't bother to call him anything at all.

The story of our courtship and subsequent marriage is soon told. Mrs. Jamison apparently decided I was the pretty, sweet, well-mannered, and presumably docile daughter-in-law she wanted. And, of course, I was a Hunt-Morrison. Auntie had always been enormously impressed by the Jamison wealth and prestige. A few days after my graduation I was married, in the same church where I had first met Mrs. Jamison. Auntie gave me my wedding. Daddy was certainly in no position to stage the kind of show that would have pleased Mrs. Jamison. Randolph and I were too busy with final exams and planning our honeymoon abroad to care, so we let them arrange things to suit themselves.

Our European trip was perfect. Paris was everything we had expected. We spent many delightful hours debating our respective tastes in art. Randolph tended to prefer the old masters, while I championed the moderns, especially Picasso. It was my contention that he only needed to become more familiar with the new painters in order to love them as I did. We did visit the Louvre, but spent most of our time at the Modern Museum. Since I'd had several excellent Fine Arts courses at college, I was able to point out to Randolph how one should look at a modern painting.

We were very happy. We hated to have the trip end, but we couldn't remain perpetual honeymooners. Randolph was to go into the family business, and I would learn to be a housewife.

Mrs. Jamison met us at the dock. Our room was all ready for us, she said. She listened with the greatest interest to our accounts of all that we had seen and done. I felt like a princess in a fairy tale. After all the years of making-do and doing-without, it was marvelous to be living in this large, beautiful house, with nothing demanded of me except to behave like a lady. But I soon tired of being a guest, and began to talk about looking for a small place of our own.

"But, how ridiculous!" said Randolph's mother, with her girlish tinkle of laughter. Originally, I had thought that silvery giggle quite charming. It was beginning to annoy me. After 'all, she could scarcely be considered a girl any more.

"Why should you bother with a pokey little house, when there is all this room here? And you know nothing of housekeeping, Dorothy, my dear. Stay at least until I have taught you the rudiments of cooking and how to manage servants. Randolph is accustomed to being very comfortable. I feel certain he would prefer to remain here until you become proficient."

I looked at Randolph, waiting for him to say he'd be glad to put up with my newlywed burnt biscuits for the sake of the privacy and fun we'd enjoyed in Paris and Florence. He didn't say it. He avoided my eyes. Later, when we were alone in our room, I suggested we'd better begin house hunting tomorrow.

"Mother's probably right," he said. "It would be better to stay here until you learn to keep house."

He seemed different, diminished, when with his mother, but I couldn't very well tell him that. If he himself didn't feel the subtle difference in our relationship, well then, I'd learn to keep house in a hurry, that was all.

I learned. Gradually, the dealings with cook and painter, the preparation of meals on cook's night out, devolved upon me. Once or twice I invited another young couple to dine with us, but the evenings were not a success. I couldn't very well tell Mrs. Jamison she wasn't welcome at dinner at her own table in her own home, but her presence did not encourage youthful gaiety. I pointed this fact out to Randolph.

"It's time I went to see Hunter & Connolly. A small house will do. Is there any particular section of town that you'd prefer?"

Randolph gave me an apprehensive look. "I'm afraid Mother's grown used to having us here. She'll probably be very upset."

"Nonsense! After all, we're not moving out of town. We'll see her often."

About two weeks later, Hunter & Connolly showed me a nice little bungalow. At dinner, I described it. Mrs. Jamison produced a delicate handkerchief and began to weep, very discreetly, taking care not to smear her carefully applied cosmetics.

"I had thought you were so happy here," she said.

"Why we are, Mother, we are," Randolph said.

"Then why do you want to leave me?"

I tried to explain why a young couple should live by themselves, especially during the first few years of marriage. Mrs. Jamison continued to weep. That's a Victorian verb, I know, but I can't help it. She didn't cry or sob. She wept, gracefully, to an accompaniment of gentle dabbings with the lacy handkerchief.

"It isn't as if I ever interfered."

"Oh no, Mother, of course not. You'd never do that."

"Really, I cannot bear the thought of being all alone in this great house."

Randolph succumbed to her act. He ended by assuring her we would give up the idea of buying the bungalow on Elm Street. When we had retired for the night, I tried a little act of my own, but it didn't work. I was an amateur and no match for Mrs. Jamison. I couldn't weep. I cried, and my nose and eyes grew red.

I gave in, for the moment. At any rate, I decided to redecorate our bedroom to suit our own tastes, since we were to be here for some time. It was quite charming when I had finished. The lovely little Picasso drawings I had acquired so inexpensively in Paris were the perfect final touch. Randolph continued to prefer his old masters, but I felt certain the constant exposure would eventually convert him. And I consoled myself with the thought that it wouldn't be for long. Surely, when a baby arrived, Mrs. Jamison would soon tire of being awakened at night. But no baby arrived. I suggested adoption. My mother-in-law was horrified.

"How can you possibly suggest giving an adopted child the Jamison name?" she said. "How can you?"

That night I really staged a scene for Randolph. "Can't you see that she's living our lives for us?" I screamed. "We have to get out of here. I'd rather live in a slum, if only I could have you all to myself."

Poor Randolph, pulled in two directions by the two women he loved; but I lost every round. My mother-in-law had too long a headstart and was much too skillful at playing on his feelings. I began to picture her as a monster in disguise. I spent hours dreaming about what I'd do when at last she died, but she continued in the best of health.

Then came the announcement about the fish. It amused me to toy with the idea of using it someday. It would have to be very skillfully done, of course. I certainly wouldn't want Randolph or me to get some by mistake. How would I manage it, IF, of course, I should ever decide to do it—which I never would. There would have to be individual portions, and then there was always the possibility they might become mixed on their way from kitchen to dining room. How did people in detective stories manage these things? Murderers? Often they didn't and the wrong person was killed, thus confusing the detective. Anyway, the whole thing was ridiculous. I was no murderer.

If it hadn't been for the livingroom curtains, I probably would never have done more than think about it. After twenty years, the curtains wore out, and were returned from the cleaner in truly sad shape, with gaping holes. New ones must be purchased. I suggested one of the new fabrics that resisted dust and didn't need to be ironed.

"And perhaps we might try a print for a change. I saw some lovely ones in Hofstetter's window last week."

Mrs. Jamison was aghast. "This room was planned with the aid of a very famous decorator," she reminded me. "I wouldn't think of making any change in his scheme. It would destroy the entire effect."

"I don't believe they make that material any more."

"Well, you must go to all the best shops. I'm sure it is possible to replace the drawingroom curtains with some that will be identical.

I spent a day in the city—a delightful day; four hours at the museum, where they were having a special art exhibit, two hours lunching with an old school friend. Just before I caught the train back, I stopped at a department store and picked up a swatch of an off-white fiberglass, identical in color with the worn-out curtains.

"See how similar this is," I said, "and how practical. Nobody carries that old-fashioned stuff any more."

Mrs. Jamison gave one hostile glance at my swatch. "It's out of the question. You must try again at other shops."

That did it. After all the patient years, suddenly I'd had it. There had been far more major disagreements, but somehow this unyielding stand on such a small matter as those curtains was the final straw. I determined to get this old woman of the sea off my back. With her out of the way, perhaps I could recover my husband, who had gradually withdrawn into a little world of his own. He had become sweetly remote, never quarreling with me, but rarely speaking unless he needed to ask the whereabouts of his clean shirts. In the evenings, he read. At table, he replied to direct questions, but usually remained aloof from all conversations. Tonight was no exception.

Mrs. Jamison expatiated at some length on the rash which she said had appeared on her back as the result of the shrimps upon which we had dined the previous evening. Suddenly, I saw my opportunity.

"Yes," I said, "I think you are absolutely right. You ought to avoid eating shrimps from now on. I'll make sure there's something special prepared for you when I plan shrimps for dinner."

The following Thursday evening was Maruska's night out. (Maruska had replaced Willimae, who had departed in a huff, after Mrs. Jamison had criticized the way in which her toilet articles had been dusted.) The only witness to the fish episode had been disposed of—by the victim herself. How ironic!

On Thursday evening, I prepared Shrimp Newburgh for dinner. I used individual ramekins, one for Randolph, one for me, and in Mrs. Jamison's dish I placed a serving of tuna fish, covering it with the Newburgh Sauce. There was no possibility of confusing the dishes. The curled-up shrimp could be discerned plainly.

My heart pounded as I bore the dinner to the table.

"How kind of you to remember that I am now unable to eat shrimp." Mrs. Jamison spoke graciously, favoring me with a slight smile and inclination of the head, just as though I were the housekeeper—unpaid, of course.

I have no idea how I managed to get through the meal, nor what we talked about. All that night I lay awake, wondering how botulism manifested itself. How long would it be before she began to feel ill? Would she be able to call for help? Would she die quickly, or linger for days?

By breakfast time, there had been no sound from Mrs. Jamison's room. I passed her closed door and hurried downstairs to put on the coffee. At the usual hour, I heard Randolph enter the dining room. I came in, coffeepot in hand, in time to see him draw out his mother's chair so she could seat herself. She was wearing her lavender-velvet negligee.

I nearly dropped the coffeepot.

112

What could have gone wrong? The next time I went to the city, about a week later, I betook myself to the library to see what I could learn about botulism. I hadn't dared look it up in our local library.

"An acute intoxication, manifested by neuromuscular disturbances, following the ingestion of food containing a toxin elaborated by Clostridium botulinum," the book said.

Much to my surprise, I learned that the disease does not develop for eighteen to thirty-six hours after the contaminated food has been eaten. Botulism is often difficult to diagnose, I read, unless more than one person becomes ill from the food. It can take the form of "aspiration pneumonia" due to difficulty in swallowing, and is often incorrectly diagnosed as pneumonia. Botulism is caused by improperly preserved food, but every can or jar in a batch does not necessarily contain the organism.

Now I knew what had happened. My can of tuna did not harbor any of the dear little germs. Did either of the other two? We would see.

I waited six weeks before trying again; no sense in arousing suspicion. For the second time, I prepared a Newburgh Sauce, lacing it liberally with sherry. It was delicious. Both Mrs. Jamison and Randolph complimented me on it. This time I did not lie awake during the night, since I knew it would be hours before any symptoms appeared. Actually, it was closer to two days.

"I don't know what's the matter with me," Mrs. Jamison said, looking up from the book she was reading. "I can't seem to focus my eyes on the print. I think I had better go and lie down."

Mrs. Jamison never got up again. The doctor (I'd been telling her for years he was incompetent) made out the death certificate, putting "pneumonia" as the cause of death. Everyone in town who was anybody attended the funeral. Randolph and I spent an entire week receiving a stream of callers bearing condolences, before we had a chance to speak to each other in private. At last people returned to their own affairs and left us in peace.

The first night we were alone, I said, "Dear, don't you think it would be a good idea if we went away for a little while? Tell your office you'll be gone for a few weeks. We might go to Paris and have a second honeymoon. Then, when we get back, I'm going to do over the whole house. These rooms need more color. First of all, I intend to get rid of those gloomy old oil paintings. I haven't decided whether I should stick to Picasso and Chagall, or whether some of the new abstractions mightn't be more effective. We can shop around in Paris and see what's available."

"I have already notified the office that I am going away," said Randolph, "but I would prefer to travel by myself, Dorothy. And I wouldn't plan to do anything to this house, if I were you. I have turned it over to Hunter & Connolly, to be sold. I shall make you a liberal allowance. You can hang any kind of painting you wish on the walls of whatever home you select."

"Randolph!"

I was utterly unable to do more than gasp out his name. Did he suspect what I had done? But how could he have found out? Had he seen those cans in my drawer?

"I'm sorry, but I feel that it's now or never. For years I've dreamed of what I'd do if I were free from Mother's domination. Now that I am, I have no intention of letting it be replaced by that of another woman."

"I only did it for you," I sobbed, "so we could have a life together. I don't want to dominate you, only to be happy with you, as we used to be."

Randolph gave me a long, penetrating look. Then he smiled slightly and handed me his clean handkerchief.

"You ought never to cry, you know. It makes you look most unattractive."

# A Cold Day in November

## by Bill Pronzini

Bodega Bay is a small fishing village on the Northern California coast, some sixty-five miles above San Francisco. The village, the good-sized inlet of the same name, and a complex of several buildings called The Tides, achieved somewhat of a national prominence a few years ago when Alfred Hitchcock filmed his suspense movie, *The Birds*, there. Since then, they get a good deal of tourist business in the spring and summer months—sightseers, vacationers, visitors from the outlying towns, self-styled fishermen who boast to the bored party-boat captains about the record king salmon they are going to catch but never do—but during the winter, the natives usually have the place pretty much to themselves, and it takes on, falsely, the atmosphere of a staid, aloof New England seacoast hamlet.

There were only three cars parked in the lot around which The Tides is built when I pulled in there on a cold, gray Monday morning in mid-November. The fog, which perpetually shrouds Bodega Bay this time of year, was almost like rain.

I parked in one of the diagonal slots at the far end, directly in front of the Wharf Bar and Restaurant. A chill wind, laced with wet needles of fog, stung my face when I stepped out, and I turned the collar on my overcoat up against it and pulled the brim of my hat lower. I stood there for a moment, shivering, then looked in through the windows at the interior of the restaurant. Only two of the burnished copper-topped tables were occupied, and there was no one at the short bar. I wondered if they made enough during the winter to warrant staying open, but then I supposed they did or they would have closed.

Just past the windows, an open archway led inside the building. I went through it, moving past the round cement tanks, empty now, in which shellfish are kept fresh, and stepped into a long warehouse area to the left. Wooden tables used for cleaning and packaging took up the length of the wall along one side; the rest of the oblong expanse was cluttered with large squarish carts with oversized metal wheels, small dollies, stacks of wooden pallets, rows of storage lockers, two large refrigerator units, a large scale, and a lot of exposed, white-painted water piping. The odor of fish and salt water hung heavily.

At the far end, a young man wearing sneakers, a pair of faded dungarees, and a well-worn sweatshirt was washing down the concrete floor with a hose. I went down to him. As I approached, he turned, releasing the hand shut-off on the hose. He had brown eyes and a shock of brown hair combed down low over his forehead in the current collegiate fashion. Across the front of his sweatshirt, in cardinal-red lettering, was printed *Stanford.*

The description I had been given matched him well enough, and the sweatshirt made it fairly conclusive. Timothy Culhane had told me the week before that his son, Mark, and Steve Litchik had attended Stanford University in Palo Alto together, and a mutual acquaintance of theirs I had found in San Francisco had told me that the two of them had come up here to Bodega Bay to work the salmon boats.

I stopped and said, "Steve Litchik?"

He gave me an appraising look. His brown eyes were slightly wary, as if he thought I was going to try to sell him insurance. "That's right."

I gave my name and what I did, and then I said, "I understand you're a friend of Mark Culhane."

A frown knit his eyebrows. "Yes?"

"Can you tell me where Mark is?"

"What do you want with him?"

"His parents would like to know his whereabouts," I said. "It seems they haven't heard from him since August, when he told them he was coming north with you."

The frown deepened. "That's kind of odd," he said. "Mark was always pretty close to his family. He used to contact them about once a month or so."

"Uh huh," I said. "Now, can you tell me where I might find him?"

"I don't know where he is."

"He's not here in Bodega Bay now?"

Litchik shook his head. "He left about a month and a half ago."

"He didn't tell you where he was going?"

"No."

"Why not?"

"He left sort of suddenly."

"How do you mean?"

"Well, he was here one day and then the next he was gone," Litchik said.

"Did you talk to him at all prior to his leaving?"

"The afternoon before. We had a beer together."

"And he didn't say anything about it to you?"

"No, nothing."

"Didn't that strike you as being a little strange when you found out he'd gone?" I asked. "You were friends, after all."

"A little, I guess," Litchik answered. "But Mark was sort of impulsive, you know? If he got something into his head about taking off, then he'd just do it. That was the way he was about things."

I nodded. "How did he seem to you that previous afternoon? Was he excited? Nervous? Anything that might have indicated he was expecting to leave?"

"No. He was the way he always was."

I lighted a cigarette, put the match in my pocket. "What about his belongings?" I asked. "Did he take them all with him?"

"I don't know."

"You didn't room together?"

"No," Litchik said. "We did for a while when we first got here, in August. But then Mark sort of took up with this Sherry Davidian and he moved up there."

I thought that over. "He was living with a girl?"

"No, no," Litchik said. "I didn't mean that. Sherry's parents own a boardinghouse up on the hill. They had a room vacant, and I guess Mark wanted to be near her. He spent all of his free time with her."

"I see," I said. "Why is it you didn't move with him, Steve?"

"The rooms up there are only big enough for one," Litchik said, "and they just had a single vacancy."

"How did you feel about Mark's moving?"

He shrugged. "It didn't matter to me one way or the other."

"Did you and Mark share expenses before?"

"Yes."

"Well, didn't that put an extra burden on you, paying full rent?"

"Oh, I guess it did, somewhat," Litchik answered. "But they don't charge you much for rent up here, and food is reasonable."

"Did the two of you still pal around together after he moved into the boardinghouse?"

"When he wasn't with Sherry," Litchik said, a hint of annoyance touching his eyes. "Listen, what are you getting at?"

I decided to drop it. "Nothing," I said. I looked around for a place to put out my cigarette. I didn't want to use the floor after he had just finished hosing it down.

Litchik saw that, and a faint smile lifted the corners of his mouth. "Go ahead," he said. "I've got to go over it again anyway."

I returned his smile, dropped it. When I looked up, I saw that the trace of annoyance had disappeared from his eyes. I asked, "Can you tell me where Mark worked, Steve?"

"When we first got here, he hired on as a deckhand on one of the commercial salmon trollers."

"Which one?"

"The *Kingfisher*," Litchik said. "Andy Michaelis' boat."

"Where can I find this Michaelis?"

"Over at the slips on the other side of the bay. He's usually tied up there, and one of the fellows told me earlier that he'd seen Michaelis over there, making repairs. There's a road a few miles up that swings around to Bodega Head."

I nodded. "How long did Mark work for Michaelis?"

"Just until the end of the season."

"And then?"

"He did odd jobs for Guido Rigazzo, at the Rigazzo Fish Company."

"Where's that?"

"About a mile this side of the end of the bay," Litchik said. "You'll see it as you go up the highway."

I chewed thoughtfully at my lower lip. "Did you ask any of the people you mentioned if they knew where Mark had gone?"

"Sure," he answered, "as soon as I found out he'd left. But none of them knew, either."

"How did you find out, by the way?"

"Mr. Rigazzo called me here on the morning after Mark left. He wanted to know if I knew where he was, because he hadn't reported to work."

118                     ALFRED HITCHCOCK'S ANTHOLOGY

"How did Sherry Davidian take Mark's going away?"

"She was pretty shook up," he said. "I think she was in love with Mark, and it hurt her that he went off the way he did."

"Was Mark in love with Sherry, do you think? Really in love?"

"From the way he acted, I thought he was. But I guess he couldn't have been, could he?"

"That's a good question."

I asked Steve directions to the Davidian boardinghouse, and thanked him for his time. Just before I turned to go, he said, "Listen, you don't think anything's happened to Mark, do you? I mean, I didn't think too much about his leaving so unexpectedly at the time, even though I was a little pushed. But now that you've told me Mark hasn't been in touch with his folks since then . . ."

There was what I was sure was genuine concern in his eyes. I tried a reassuring smile. "Let's hope not, Steve."

"Will you let me know if you find out anything?"

"Count on it."

"Thanks." He moistened his lips and I thought he was going to say something else, but he just opened the shut-off on the hose and began to spray the floor again. I wasn't sure, but I thought his shoulders had a slight slump to them that had not been in evidence when I first approached.

I left him and walked over to the warehouse entrance to the bar-and-restaurant. My feet felt as if I had been walking in wet snow for some time, and I could feel a chill across my neck, even with the heavy overcoat. I had not eaten breakfast before driving up from San Francisco, and a cup of hot coffee and a sandwich seemed a very good idea at the moment. It was almost noon by my watch.

I sat at one of the tables inside and ordered a grilled ham-and-cheese and black coffee from an elderly, smiling waitress. She brought the coffee right away and I sipped at it and smoked a cigarette and did a little thinking. I didn't resolve much.

The sandwich came and I ate it and drank a refill on the coffee. My feet had warmed up some, and the chill was gone from my neck. I left a fifty-cent tip for the waitress and paid the tired-looking bartender for my lunch, then went out and got into my car again.

I started it up and sat there for a moment, then drove through the lot, up onto Highway 29, and turned north.

The Rigazzo Fish Company was a long, narrow, red-roofed building that extended out a good distance into the bay. A weathered gray sign confirmed the name, and that Guido Rigazzo was owner and proprietor. There were a couple of ancient, corroded hoists off to one side of the gravel parking lot, two well-traveled pickups angled in beside them, and a dusty green sedan, vintage 1950, parked nearest the highway.

I parked my car and went up to the building. I tried the door but found it was locked so I went around to the side where there was a narrow catwalk that followed the side of the building. I walked along there, looking down at the gray water churning against the pilings, and came out onto a flat dock. A short wooden pier in pretty bad disrepair was attached to it, jutting sixty or seventy yards into the bay. A lone salmon troller was tied up at the end of it.

A tall, blond-haired kid in a plaid jacket and rubber boots was doing something to a fisherman's net near the open entrance to the red-roofed building. I crossed to him and asked where I might find Guido Rigazzo.

"In his office, probably."

"Where's that?"

"Inside. On your left."

"Thanks," I said. I went in through the open corrugated doors. The warehouse was cluttered with much of the same as I had seen at The Tides, except that there was more of it. A bank of machinery, with a crisscross of conveyor belts, took up a portion of one wall at the upper end, and there was a large wire cage with a padlock on its wood-framed door that had a lot of crates stacked inside. On my left was an enclosure that would be the office.

I knocked on the door, and a hoarse voice asked, "What is it?"

I opened the door and looked in. A short, bearish man in a tan windbreaker sat behind a paper-cluttered desk, an open ledger in front of him and a pencil hooked over his right ear. He was thick-featured and olive-complected, and his blue-black hair was a snarl of pomaded ringlets. He looked up at me with eyes that were sea green, flecked with bits of yellow; they had an almost electric quality to them and I had the foolish thought that when he was angry, sparks would fly from them like an exposed high-tension wire.

I said, "Mr. Rigazzo?"

120

"Yeah?"

"I wonder if I could speak to you for a moment."

"What about?"

"One of your former employees."

"Which one?"

"Mark Culhane," I said.

He closed the ledger, leaning back in his chair. "What's your interest in him?"

"I've been hired to find him. I'm a licensed private investigator," I said, and told him my name, and where I was from.

He said, "Who was it hired you?"

I didn't particularly care for his questioning attitude. "Does that really matter, Mr. Rigazzo?"

"No, no, it don't matter," he said quickly and gave me a half-apologetic smile. "Just wondering is all. Is the kid in some kind of trouble?"

"Not that I know of," I said. I couldn't see any harm in telling him who my clients were. "Mark's parents retained me to look for him. They haven't heard from him in over three months, and they're naturally pretty worried."

"Oh. Well, yeah, I can understand that."

"I'd appreciate any help you could give me."

"There ain't much I can tell you."

"You don't have any idea where he might have gone?"

He moved his heavy shoulders. "Where do kids go these days? They spend a little time someplace, and then they move on like—what do you call them?"

"Nomads," I·said.

"Yeah, like nomads."

"When was the last time you saw Mark, Mr. Rigazzo?"

"Second of last month, I think it was. When he quit for the day."

I thought about that. I took my wallet from the inside pocket of my suit coat, opened it and looked at the pocket calendar I keep in one of the plastic inserts. "The second was a Wednesday," I said.

"That's right. On a Wednesday."

"Uh huh." I shifted my feet. "How often do you pay your employees, Mr. Rigazzo?"

That got a frown out of him.

"Once a week," he said. "Why?"

"What day?"

"Friday."

"Then Mark had three days' pay coming for that week. Did he ask you for it Wednesday night?"

"No," Rigazzo said. "Why should he have?"

"It stands to reason that if he was planning to leave that night he'd want his money, don't you think?"

Rigazzo licked at his lips. "I never thought about that." He took a short, greenish-colored cigar from inside his desk somewhere and began to unwrap it slowly. "Maybe he hadn't decided to leave when I last seen him. Maybe he got in into his head later on."

"Maybe," I said. "Did Mark do or say anything that day to indicate he was going away?"

"No," Rigazzo said. "I was kind of surprised when he didn't come in Thursday morning, because he always got here right on time. I called that friend of his, Steve something, works down at The Tides. He didn't know where the Culhane kid had got off to either."

"What did you do then?"

"What could I do? When he didn't show up Friday, either, I figured he'd taken off the way they do, and that was the end of it."

I nodded. "How long did Mark work for you, Mr. Rigazzo?"

"About three weeks."

"Would you mind telling me what his duties were?"

"Cleaning up, running errands, things like that."

"You were satisfied with his work, I take it?"

"Sure," Rigazzo said. "He done a good job."

"He liked being around boats, I understand."

"That's what he told me when I put him on."

"Did he appear to be happy here, then?"

"I guess he did, yeah."

"Then there weren't any difficulties here that might have influenced him to leave? At least, none that you know about?"

He shook his head. "We got along just fine."

"All right, Mr. Rigazzo," I said. "I appreciate your time, and I won't take up any more of it."

He got on his feet and put out his hand. I took it. He said, "Listen, I hope you find him all right."

"So do I, Mr. Rigazzo."

"Anything else I can do, you let me know."

"Thank you, I'll do that."

I went out into the warehouse again, and through the corrugated iron doors onto the dock. The blond-haired kid was still fiddling with the fisherman's net. I walked around to the catwalk and along it to the gravel lot in front.

The sky was very black now, and the wind was up. It wouldn't be long before the rains came.

The road that wound around the northern lip of the bay to Bodega Head was relatively new and in good condition, but I drove slowly; the fog was thicker on this side and visibility was not good.

When I came abreast of the boat slips I pulled my car off onto the shoulder, got out and crossed over there. I stepped up onto the ramp leading out, walking with my head bowed and my hands thrust deep into the pockets of my overcoat, feeling the icy wind numb my cheeks. My eyes began to water, and I had to stop once and clear them with a hankerchief.

There were only a couple of commercial boats anchored in the slips; the sound of them rubbing and banging against the board floats was almost lost in the sibilant howl of the wind. It didn't look like anyone was around, and I wondered if maybe Steve Litchik had been mistaken about this fellow Michaelis being here. It seemed to me to be a very bad day for making repairs of any kind.

I had almost reached the end of the ramp when I noticed movement on one of the boats in an end slip on my right. I moved to the edge and squinted there, shielding my eyes against the probing wind; I could just make out the markings on the starboard gunwale of the troller—*Kingfisher*, and below that, *Bodega Bay*.

I climbed a short metal ladder onto the swaying float and made my way carefully to the end slip. A tall, well-muscled guy, wearing only a thin T-shirt and denim trousers, was kneeling on the troller's deck; his too-long hair fanned out in the wind behind him like a horse's mane at full gallop. He had the engine housing up, and there was an open tool box beside him with an assortment of wrenches laid out on a strip of canvas. I had a view of the engine but I couldn't see what he was doing to it. I stepped up close to the stern. "Ahoy!" I shouted, trying to make myself heard above the wind. "Ahoy, there!"

He came around quickly, a box wrench he had been using held in one hand. There were smudges of grease and oil over the front of his shirt and on his hands and arms. He had one of those boyishly handsome faces that women seem to find appealing, but his lips—a dark, almost purplish color from the cold—were skinned back with annoyance, spoiling the image. I wondered what he was trying to prove by not wearing a coat of some kind.

He said, "What the hell do you want?"

"Are you Andy Michaelis?"

"Who wants to know?"

I called out my name. "Can I come aboard?"

"What for?"

"I'd like to talk to you."

"I ain't got time to talk now."

"It'll only take a minute."

"I'm busy, friend,"

"This is kind of important . . ."

"Some other time," he said. "Breeze off, friend."

He was beginning to irritate me; I didn't like his impoliteness, or his insolent tone, or his manner. "Look, *friend*," I said, and there was an edge to my voice, "I'm trying to do a job. All I'm asking is a couple of minutes of your time. After that, you can get back to whatever you're doing and I'll be on my way. That will make us both happy."

His eyes narrowed. "Just who the hell are you?"

"I'm a private investigator," I told him. "I'm attempting to locate Mark Culhane, and I was told he worked for you as a deckhand for a while in September. Now—"

He got up onto his feet in a single motion, balancing himself on the rolling deck of the troller with his legs spread. Something dark and indefinable had passed across his face at my mention of Mark Culhane. His teeth were gritted together, and his free hand was balled into a white-knuckled fist at his side. "You got about thirty seconds to get the hell away from here," he said.

I tasted the sourness of rising anger in the back of my throat. "And then what happens?"

"You want to know that? Stick around."

I stood there, not moving. Our eyes were locked together. He had twenty years and about thirty pounds on me, but I doubted he had my knowledge of basic judo. I had an idea I would be able to take him, but I couldn't see any point in it.

In a controlled voice I said, "I'll be seeing you around again, Michaelis."

"Don't plan on it."

I turned my back on him and walked slowly along the float toward the ramp. I did not give him the satisfaction of looking back.

The boardinghouse where Mark Culhane had lived was a two-storied building on a road that wound upward along the face of the hill overlooking Bodega Bay. There was a fine view of the harbor and Bodega Head and the Pacific Ocean beyond—or at least there would have been on a clear day. Now, the ebbing gray tendrils of fog allowed vision of little more than vague, surrealistic outlines, the way background is seen in a dream. The wind, oddly, was not as strong up here as it had been at the boat slips.

I parked my car in front and followed a crushed-shell path that led through a shimmering sea of vermilion and pink and lavender ice plants. As I neared the railed front porch, a girl about twenty or so came around from the rear of the house.

She was about five-eight, very slender, finely-boned, and she wore a pair of men's blue jeans and a heavy jacket with a fur collar. She had short flaxen hair, with a bright green scarf over it to keep it from tangling in the wind. Her cheeks were flushed from the cold, giving her a healthy, effulgent look. In her right hand she carried a pail.

She stopped when she saw me and set down the pail and stood waiting. She was smiling; it was a nice smile, friendly, contagious. "Hello, there," she said when I came up to her.

I smiled, too, genuinely. "Hi."

"If you're looking for a room, I'm afraid you're going to be disappointed. We haven't a single vacancy."

"No, I'm not looking for a room."

"Well, I hope you're not selling anything. My folks don't allow solicitors." Her tone was apologetic.

I shook my head. "As a matter of fact, I came to see you. That is, if you're Sherry Davidian."

"Guilty," she said lightly. "But why do you want to see me?"

I introduced myself. "I'd like to talk to you about Mark Culhane."

Her smile went away. Her mouth compressed in a hard, determined line, but her eyes held an open kind of sad and painful hurt. I believed the eyes. "I don't have anything to say about him," she said.

I felt uncomfortable. "Would you have any idea where he might be now?"

"No, and I don't care."

"He's missing, you know."

A frown corrugated her forehead. "Missing?"

"No one seems to have an inkling where he is."

"Why are you trying to find him?"

"I'm a detective, from San Francisco," I told her. "Mark's family hired me to find him. He hasn't been in touch with them for three months now."

"But I thought . . ." Her voice trailed off.

"You thought what, Sherry?"

She took a breath. "I thought that was where Mark had gone."

"Home, you mean?"

"Yes."

"Why did you think that?"

"I don't know," Sherry said. She averted her eyes for a moment. "No, that's not right. I thought he went home because of me."

"Why would he do that?"

Her eyes flashed defiantly, returning to mine. "Because I loved him! Because I wanted him to marry me!"

I looked out over the ice plants, shuffling my feet on the shell path. "Did Mark want to marry you, Sherry?"

"He said he did," she answered. "But he wanted to wait for a couple of years, until we were older. But it was all right with him if we—"

I cleared my throat and said quickly, "Did you argue about getting married? Have a fight?"

"We argued about it."

"Often?"

"A couple of times."

"When was the last time you saw Mark, Sherry?"

"The night before he—well, left."

"Wednesday night? October second?"

"Yes."

"Did you have an argument that night?"

"No. No, not really."

"Then why did you think he'd gone home because of the marriage question?"

"I—I just did, that's all. Why else would he have left so suddenly?"

"Tell me about that last time you saw him," I said. "Did Mark say anything to intimate he was planning to leave?"

"No."

"Would you mind telling me what you talked about?"

"The swimming party, mostly."

"Swimming party?"

"We were going over to Rio Nido, on the Russian River," Sherry said. "I know a bunch of kids there, and Mark and I were invited to this swimming party one of them was having. The weather was still pretty warm then."

I nodded. "Anything else?"

"A lot of little things, I guess," she said. "We went for a ride up to Jenner and back, because it was a nice night, and we just talked the way you do when you're out driving."

I frowned slightly. "I was told Mark didn't have a car."

"We borrowed my parents'," Sherry said. "They liked Mark, and—" She broke off, her slim throat working.

I said, "Did you come back here after your drive?"

"Yes."

"What time was it when you arrived?"

"About ten-thirty or so."

"Did you go right in?"

"Well, I did, yes."

"Mark didn't?"

"No. He went to see Mr. Rigazzo."

I had been getting a cigarette out of my overcoat pocket. My hand froze around the pack. "What did you say?"

"Mark went to see Mr. Rigazzo," she repeated. "He lives up in Carmet-by-the-Sea. We had stopped by there on our way back from Jenner but he wasn't home, and Mark thought he might have been working after hours at the fish company. We were going to stop there first, before coming home, but it was getting pretty late and Mark said he didn't mind walking down there later on, because it was such a nice night."

I moistened my lips slowly. "Why did Mark want to see Rigazzo?"

"To ask him for Thursday off," Sherry said, "so he could go to the swimming party in Rio Nido with me. I had just found out about it that night, you see, and I hadn't had the opportunity to tell Mark. He was sure Mr. Rigazzo wouldn't mind giving him the day off to go."

"And that was the last time you saw Mark, when he left to go down to the fish company?"

"Yes."

"One last thing, Sherry," I said. "Were Mark's belongings gone when you checked his room?"

"He didn't have much, really. Just a couple of changes of clothes and an old suit and some toilet articles."

"Then he didn't take them?"

"No," she answered. "That's another reason why I thought he went home. He told me once that he had a lot of things there, from when he was going to college."

I was silent for a moment, and then I said, "Okay, Sherry. You've been a great help and I appreciate it."

She put her hand on my arm. Her eyes were worried now. "You—don't think that . . ."

I knew what she was going to say. "Don't worry," I said in what I hoped was an encouraging tone. "Mark's all right. I'll turn him up before long."

"But you seem so grim now . . ."

I smiled and patted her shoulder. "I'll be in touch with you as soon as I learn anything."

"Would you do that, please?"

"Of course."

I turned to go. Sherry said softly, "Then, goodbye."

"Goodbye," I answered. "And don't worry." It sounded lame this time, and I thought I had best get out of there as quickly as possible.

When I reached my car I paused before getting in, to look back. Sherry Davidian was still standing where I had left her, a very small and very sad statue in the polychromatic splendor of the flowering ice plants.

The Rigazzo Fish Company was closed when I got down there a few minutes later; one of the pickups and the green car were gone. I parked and went around to the dock in the rear, but the corrugated doors were locked securely.

I went back to my car and drove up along Highway 29 for a couple of miles until I spotted a public telephone booth at one of those roadside stands that sold fresh crabs in season. It was boarded up now, for the winter.

I dialed the operator and asked for Bodega Bay information; there was no directory in the booth. They had a listing for a Guido Rigazzo in Carmet-by-the-Sea. I wrote down the number in my notebook, and then thanked the operator and waited for my dime to come back. When it did, I dialed Rigazzo's number and let it ring fifteen times, counting, but there was no answer. I hung up then, retrieved my dime, and returned to my car.

I sat there for a time. Now what? I wanted to talk to Rigazzo before I did anything else; I had a supposition—a hunch, if you will—that was nagging the back of my mind. But it was only that, and without anything substantial I would have been foolish to act on it.

There was another thing holding me back too—the fervent hope that I was wrong.

I started the car and pulled out onto the highway again. Darkness was coming on now, with that quick deceptiveness you only seem to find during the winter, and I had to put on my headlights. The fog was thick and roiling still, but the velocity of the wind seemed to have lessened considerably; I wondered if it would rain after all. I looked at my watch and saw that it was almost five.

Even though I had not gotten an answer on the telephone, I decided I would drive up to Carmet anyway. I didn't have the vaguest idea where else to look for Rigazzo.

I reached Carmet-by-the-Sea—a spread-out, rather affluent community, comprised mostly of retirement people—some twenty minutes later, but when I finally found the address in a phone book and located Rigazzo's cabin-style home, I found it dark and deserted. The attached garage was open, and a car, this year's model, was inside. I rang the doorbell a couple of times and got no answer; Rigazzo, wherever he was, probably had one of the pickups I had seen at the fish company earlier.

I drove back to Bodega Bay. It was fully dark when I arrived, and I stopped at an all-night cafe a couple of miles north of The Tides and ordered something to eat. I had thought, while driving, that I was hungry, but when the food came I found I had difficulty getting it down. I left the cafe and went down to The Tides Motel and took a room.

Once inside, I lay down on the bed and smoked a cigarette. Then I got up and began to pace the room. I was restless. I should go looking for Rigazzo, I should start asking questions of people; somebody had to know where he was.

There was a free coffee dispenser in the room and I made myself a cup and drank it. I lay back on the bed and thought it all out again carefully. I still came up with the same possibilities. If only I could . . .

I sat up. An idea had got into my head. I didn't have to talk to Rigazzo at all; if I was right I wouldn't get anything out of him anyway. There was another way, a simpler way, to prove or disprove my hunch.

I put my overcoat on and took my keys off the nightstand. I knew full well that if I dwelled on the implications, gave them attentive consideration, I would not go through with it—and I had to know.

I looked at my watch. It was ten-thirty. I went out to my car.

The Rigazzo Fish Company lay enshrouded in fog. The trailing gray wisps gave the building an almost ethereal quality in the darkness, and my footfalls on the gravel parking lot rang unnaturally loud in a stillness otherwise marred only by the bay water breaking against the wooden pilings below. I had left my car five hundred yards up the highway, and had made my way here slowly and with a surreptitiousness that was distinctly alien to me.

I reached the front of the building and stood in the shadows. I was chilled. I was nervous. I had been a cop once; I had a healthy respect for the law. Breaking and entering is a felony, and as such carried with it a stiff prison sentence. If I were caught . . .

Well, all right. I put that thought out of my mind and turned to the door and tested the knob. It was still locked, but then I had expected that. If I were going to get in at all, it would have to be at the rear.

I went along the front of the building, staying in the shadows, and stepped up onto the catwalk. I moved deliberately, watching my footing on the damp wood, mindful of the black water below. I came out onto the dock and stood with my back against the warehouse wall for a

ALFRED HITCHCOCK'S ANTHOLOGY

moment. I could make out the pier through the fog; there were two fishing boats tied up at the end of it now.

My heart had begun an irregular thumping in my chest. In spite of the cold, I could feel perspiration on my body; the palms of my hands were moist and sticky. I advanced to the corrugated doors, bending to examine the lock. I pushed gently at them, just above the lock; there was a faint rattling sound. I straightened. I couldn't get in through there without waking half of Bodega Bay in the process.

I walked to the opposite side of the building; no more doors, and no windows at all. I retraced my path back to the corrugated doors and stood there and took a couple of deep breaths. It was no good. I was kidding myself; I had been all along. The thing for me to do was to get the hell out of here, go back to my motel room, and wait it out until morning. I could talk to Rigazzo then, see what I could get out of him, and then if—

The sound of the pickup truck turning off the highway, then onto the parking lot in front, was distinct and unmistakable.

I froze, listening. There was the squeal of worn brake lining as the pickup came to a halt. Two doors slammed, almost simultaneously.

I looked around, wildly, but there was no way I could get off the dock without being seen—unless I wanted to go over into the icy bay water, and I ruled that out immediately. I could hear the heavy tread of boots on the catwalk now. A few feet to my left were several stacks of crab pots similar to those I had seen at The Tides. I jumped there, my heart flailing violently, and crouched down behind them.

The sound of voices carried to me almost immediately, drifting on the night wind. They were disembodied, unintelligible at first, but as whoever it was drew nearer on the catwalk I could make out the words.

". . . just don't like it, I tell you."

"So you don't like it. You heard the weather report. The storm won't break until morning."

"To hell with the weather report. It'll be plenty rough once we hit open water."

The two of them came into view, dark shadows at first, around the side of the building. They paused there. I couldn't see either of their faces, but I didn't need that to identify them; their voices were enough—Guido Rigazzo and Andy Michaelis.

Rigazzo said, "How's she running now? Okay?"

"I spent the whole damned day working on her, didn't I?"

"What's got you so jumpy tonight?"

"I don't think we ought to make the run, that's all."

"I told you what Bannister said on the phone. They're bringing in a hundred cases. What are they going to do with them if we don't pick them up?"

"I don't care what they do with them."

There was a silence for a moment, and then Rigazzo said, "Listen, you're not worried about that private dick?"

"I don't like him snooping around here."

"He's not going to catch onto anything."

"That's what you say, Rigazzo."

"What can he find out?"

"What happened to the Cullhane kid, that's what he can find out."

"Keep your mouth shut about that," Rigazzo said sharply. "The kid just took off. That's all anybody knows."

"Well, I still don't like it," Michaelis said.

"You're not starting to punk out on me, are you?"

"Is that what you think, Rigazzo?"

". . .what it sounds like to . . ."

They were moving along the pier now, and I couldn't understand any more, but I had heard enough. Crouching there behind the crab pots and listening, an insane impulse to go after them took hold of me, but I forced myself to remain still, watching the two of them move along the pier. I saw them, dimly, approach one of the boats tied up at the end and board her. It would be Michaelis' troller, the *Kingfisher*.

After a few moments, I heard the throb of the diesel. The *Kingfisher* edged away from the pier, out into the bay; it looked like one of those eerie, phantom ships you hear about in seafaring legends as it moved off through the fog. They were running without lights.

I came out from behind the crab pots and ran along the catwalk and then through the gravel lot, up onto the highway. I had my keys in my hand before I reached my car. I slid in under the wheel, turned over the engine and took it out of there, tires wailing on the damp pavement.

I drove fast and hard, my eyes fastened on the white dividing line and my hands tight on the wheel. It took me ten minutes to reach

ALFRED HITCHCOCK'S ANTHOLOGY

the entrance to Doran Park, and another fifteen to wend my way along the narrow, sand-dune-bordered road to where the Bodega Bay Coast Guard Station was situated.

I parked in front of the entrance and went inside and pushed my license photostat at the surprised seaman on office duty. I did a lot of fast talking, and that got me, finally, in to see the night commander—a young, sandy-haired, sleepy-eyed guy named Fitzpatrick.

I told him my story—what I had heard, what I had found out, what I suspected. He didn't look quite as sleepy anymore. He made me tell it another time, studying my identification while I did, interrupting periodically with questions. When he had apparently satisfied himself that I wasn't a crank of some kind, he told me to stay where I was and hurried out of there.

I paced his office, smoking, until he came back a few minutes later. He sat on a corner of his desk and told me what was being done, and that he had called the county sheriff's office to have a deputy sent over, and that there wasn't much for us to do now except wait.

We talked it out in detail again, and then one of the men brought us some coffee. I smoked until I ran out of cigarettes, and then I borrowed a pack from Fitzpatrick. I kept looking at the clock. Time crawled with a merciless slowness.

It was past one-thirty when the call came in.

I was there when Fitzpatrick took it in the radio room. One of the two patrol boats he had dispatched had picked up the *Kingfisher* only minutes before, about five miles up the coast. They had presumably been headed back for Bodega Bay.

The men from the patrol boat had boarded her there and had taken Rigazzo and Michaelis into custody. Michaelis had put up something of a fight, and they'd had to subdue him. The reporting officer didn't say what kind of fight, or how they had subdued him.

He did say this: in the troller's hold his men had found one hundred cases of bootleg Canadian whiskey.

Fitzpatrick, a moon-faced guy named Cooper who was the deputy county sheriff, and I were waiting when they brought Rigazzo and Michaelis in. Michaelis had a strip of adhesive tape on his right cheek, and a lot of foul words for me on his lips. Rigazzo was sullen and silent, but his green-and-yellow eyes were sparking.

They were ushered into another part of the building, and Fitzpatrick and Cooper went there with them. I didn't ask to sit in on the questioning, and I wasn't invited. I waited in Fitzpatrick's office.

It was past four when Fitzpatrick returned. I was dozing in a chair; I had been too keyed up before to realize just how tired I was, but the apprehension of Rigazzo and Michaelis had released all of my pent-up tension and left me feeling drained.

It had taken them a while, Fitzpatrick said, but they had gotten a confession finally. They had concentrated on Michaelis—Rigazzo was uncommunicative and refused to say anything without his lawyer present—and under pressure, Michaelis had told them everything.

It was just about the way I had figured it, though of course I did not know the details until Fitzpatrick filled me in.

The way it was, Rigazzo and Michaelis had been part of a small-scale organization involved in the smuggling of "moon" whiskey from somewhere up in Canada. They would go out in Michaelis' troller at variable intervals—usually once a month—and meet some kind of vessel and make the cargo transfer at sea. Then they would bring the stuff back to Rigazzo's fish company, where it would be stored for a day or two—as short a time as possible to eliminate risk. Then it would be shipped out by truck to various distributors in the northern California area.

Michaelis had given Cooper and Fitzpatrick the name of their contact man—a Canadian named Bannister—and a pretty good idea of how the thing worked. Fitzpatrick had sent the other patrol cutter he had out to search for the other vessel, but they hadn't found it. Fitzpatrick didn't seem particularly worried about that. He had enough information now to break the back of the organization, and when that happened they would get them too.

Everything had gone along smoothly for Rigazzo and Michaelis until the second of October. They had a run set up that night, and they were at the fish company when Mark Culhane came along to ask permission of Rigazzo for the following day off to attend the swimming party with Sherry Davidian.

Mark had, apparently, overheard a portion of their conversation. He had panicked and tried to run, and Rigazzo and Michaelis had seen him. Rigazzo caught him and there was a scuffle, and Mark Culhane had been thrown to the concrete floor of the warehouse. He hadn't moved. When they checked him, they had found blood on the back of

134

his head from where it had hit the concrete. He was dead.

Rigazzo had calmed Michaelis down—he had been badly shaken, he said—and they had talked it over. Rigazzo said that the only thing for them to do would be to get rid of the remains, and then play it as if Mark had simply run off. They took his body out to sea that night and weighted it down and put it overboard.

The idea had worked well for them until I came along, digging. There were a lot of things, I found, that didn't coincide, and when I had put all of those things together I had come up with the possibility of the smuggling angle.

It was almost six when I left the Coast Guard Station. I did not want to see Steve Litchik and I did not want to see Sherry Davidian; and most of all, I did not want to drive back to San Francisco and see Mr. and Mrs. Timothy Culhane—but I would.

I would see them, all of them, and I would tell them what had happened to a nice young fellow named Mark Culhane who had been in the wrong place at the wrong time.

# A Degree of Innocence

## by Helen Nielsen

The office of the president of Baker, Benson and Company was on the thirteenth floor. Clint Dodson wasn't consciously aware of that fact when he closed the gold-lettered door behind him and walked slowly toward the tall windows overlooking a sweltering city. He wasn't consciously aware of anything at that moment, except a kind of mental numbness through which memory was beginning to filter like light through a fog. The memory was being formed about Sheila, because nothing important had ever happened to him before Sheila.

"Mr. Dodson, aren't you feeling well?"

Clint Dodson heard the receptionist's voice as if it were an echo. He turned his head toward the sound of the echo. He was a gray-faced, pudgy little man of forty-six, his dark hair receding in a ridiculously deep widow's peak, his eyes lost behind the glittering lens of rimless spectacles.

"I'm all right," he said. "I just wanted to get some air. It seems stuffy."

"It is stuffy. I'll certainly be glad when they get the air-conditioning repaired. Did Mr. Benson see you?"

"Yes, Miss Carlisle. He saw me. Thank you."

The receptionist went back to something she was typing, and Clint turned back to the window. Pretty girl, Miss Carlisle, but not half so pretty as Sheila had been the day he came in off the road and saw her for the first time.

What Clint Dodson never understood was how he could have been so lucky in love. It wasn't his appearance, surely. It wasn't his aggressiveness, or brilliance, or charm. Those words were for Roger Benson, the junior partner, who was younger, handsomer, and a dedicated

136

bachelor. The peculiar thing was how Clint had thought Sheila was Roger's girl in the beginning. The office gossips were responsible for that.

"Make no passes at the blonde bombshell," they warned him. "She's got her cap set for brass. You won't get a tumble."

They were kidding him, of course. Clint never had the nerve to make a pass at any of the office girls, least of all one as attractive as Sheila. She had been hired while he was on the road. She smiled politely when they were introduced, and then went back to taking Roger's dictation. She and Roger lunched together, dined together, went to the office party at the country club together, and then one day Sheila was back at a typist's desk and a newly hired brunette was taking her place in all capacities. The grape-vine buzzed. And Sheila, more lovely than ever with sadness in her eyes, remained silent. It was probably the sad eyes that moved Clint to action; that's how he'd come by his cocker spaniel. He mustered up enough courage to invite her to lunch and, much to his surprise, she accepted. After the dashing Roger Benson, a mild-mannered, middle-aged man was probably a relief to the nervous system. They began to get acquainted, and it didn't take long for Clint to realize how wrong the gossips had been about this girl. Sheila was really shy and sweet. Without actually putting it into words, she soon communicated what had happened with Roger Benson. Roger was ambitious. He had time for romance, but not for marriage, and Sheila wanted a home and a family—something steady and permanent. Clint mulled that thought over for the duration of a very lonely road trip, and then returned and proposed to Sheila. She accepted and they went to Las Vegas for the weekend and returned man and wife. It was the luckiest break of Clint's life.

Sheila quit her job immediately.

"A woman's place is in the home backing up her man," she declared. "I'm going to make you the most wonderful wife in the world!"

"I don't deserve you," Clint said.

She wrinkled her nose at him. Such a pretty nose.

"Clinton Dodson," she scolded, "I love you dearly, but you do have one terrible fault. You must stop belittling yourself. You're an intelligent man—" She pulled her arms from about his neck and began straightening his tie. "And a handsome man." She must have been in love to say that. "And you can be a successful man if you believe in yourself. What's Roger Benson got that you haven't?"

Then she looked straight into his eyes and Clint's nerves began to jingle like Christmas bells. Roger Benson, vice-president of Baker, Benson and Company, hot-shot operator, human dynamo, living Apollo—but who had married Sheila?

"Nothing!" Clint answered. "Nothing, nothing, absolutely nothing!"

And then he had to stop, because they were both laughing from sheer happiness. It was from that point that everything in Clint's life began to change.

On their first wedding anniversary, the Dodsons celebrated the occasion by moving into a house in a new subdivision near the country club. The down payment was covered by Clint's Christmas bonus, based on a percentage of his yearly sales—the top sales record in the office. Under the mistletoe, which Sheila had thoughtfully hung in numerous and strategic spots throughout the house, she suggested that it would be fitting to entertain the Bakers, of Baker, Benson and Company, as their first dinner guests.

"Who needs guests?" Clint wanted to know.

"Silly, the honeymoon is over."

"Why? Why can't we have a re-run, like a television movie?"

"We can, darling. We can have the longest honeymoon in history, but it's still good policy to invite the boss to dinner. I heard you mention last week that McDougal was transferring to the San Francisco office. Now you know that I don't know a thing about business, but even a mere housewife can deduce from that information that Baker, Benson will need a new sales manager. And who has the best sales record of the year?"

It was a thought. Under the mistletoe it didn't seem too important, but later it returned, and the more Clint considered the suggestion, the better it seemed.

Arnold Baker was an elderly man, rather pompous, much too fat. Clint had met his wife at the country club office parties—the president of Baker, Benson was automatically elected to the country club board. Mrs. Baker was a battle-ax and a bore. Clint really didn't expect his invitation to be accepted, but when he mentioned that it was his wife's idea to invite the Bakers as their first guests in their new home, something in old Baker's ego was touched and he accepted.

Sheila did herself—and Clint—proud. The table was a masterpiece, the dinner a delight. As for Sheila, a dream in a white dinner gown purchased especially for the occasion, she could have charmed the basket from under the cobra.

"I've been going over your record, Dodson," Baker announced over demi-tasse, "and it's amazing how your sales have gone up since your marriage. Now I understand the reason."

"Really, Mr. Baker, you give me too much credit," Sheila demurred. "But I do think a wife is good for a businessman. It makes him more stable and gives him something to really work for. If I were an executive—" Sheila paused and then laughed brightly. "Imagine, me an executive! But if I were, Mr. Baker, I'd make certain that all of my top officers were happily married men."

Mrs. Baker beamed. Mr. Baker nodded. And not until they had gone home and Clint was making a mental recapitulation of the evening did he realize the implications of Sheila's words. He spoke to her about it rather sharply, and then regretted having spoken to her in that way, for she appeared stunned.

"Oh, I see what you mean, dear. Roger, of course! That was stupid of me, wasn't it? But I just wasn't thinking, darling, at least, not in that direction. I had in mind the sales manager opening. Naturally, Mr. Baker would never replace Roger Benson."

Sheila was right. Mr. Baker never replaced anyone; he didn't even name the new sales manager. Two days after the dinner party, he suffered a stroke during the entertainment at a businessman's convention party and died three hours later. Roger Benson became president of Baker, Benson and Company.

Sheila was shocked at the news.

"Oh, how terrible!"

"He was an old man, honey."

"But to go like that—so soon."

"It's the best way to go."

"Oh, I know that! What I meant—" She stopped abruptly, then continued in another vein. "We'll have to go to the funeral."

"It's to be private, Sheila."

"Send flowers, then. . . Clint, who steps into Roger's place?"

"Sam Moorhouse," Clint said.

"That crude man? He doesn't have half your ability!"

"He has half again my seniority. Baker, Benson and Company operates strictly on the seniority system. That's why my job was waiting for me after the war."

"I think that's ridiculous. A company functions on ability, not sentiment." Then Sheila saw him frowning at her and softened. "It's just that I'm so proud of you," she said, "and I want others to see what I see in you. But I am terribly sorry about Mr. Baker—and for Mrs. Baker. It's much worse for her. I think I'll write her a little note."

Sheila did write a wonderful warm note. Clint never saw it, but he heard about it the day Moorhouse called him into his office to break the news about Clint's promotion to sales manager.

"It was the old lady's personal request," Moorhouse said. "She has faith in you, Dodson. She said she would have to have faith in anyone who has such an understanding wife."

Clint had a lump in his throat when he went home that night. It was amazing how a man's life could change at a woman's touch.

On their second anniversary, the Dodsons and the Moorhouses dined together at the country club. By this time the Dodsons were members in good standing, due to Sam's sponsorship. That had come about as a result of Sheila's suggestion that Clint wasn't getting enough exercise and, after all, she didn't want her husband turned into a money machine. Sam was a great sportsman—golf, tennis, swimming. It was exhausting to try to keep up with him, and a relief to be able to merely sit at a table and let Sam, a genial, self-made man, pour the story of his life into Sheila's appreciative ears. Sam's wife, a rugged, outdoorsy matron, who wore a dinner gown as if it was a burlap kimono, contributed to the legend at the infrequent intervals when Sam was silent.

". . . and we were so broke after the crash, Sam had to pawn my engagement ring. 'Mother,' he said, 'someday I'll buy you the biggest diamond west of Texas!'. . ."

She was wearing it, a huge, square stone that blazed like a beacon. Clint turned his head to avoid the glare, and that's when he saw Roger Benson coming toward them across the dance floor. Handsome Roger in a tuxedo that squared his shoulders and hugged his boxer-slim waistline.

He had a girl on his arm, as usual. A redhead this time, but he seemed to forget all about her as soon as he reached the table.

"The headwaiter told me there was an anniversary party in progress over here. I want to offer my congratulations—"

And then Roger stopped talking and stared at Sheila as if she'd just been carried in on a pàpier-maché cake. She was gorgeous. She kept up with the styles in clothes, coiffure, and cosmetics. She made every woman in the room look as drab as a kulak.

Sam read Roger's mind in the unexpurgated edition.

"Can you believe this beautiful girl is the wife of old Clint Dodson?" he asked. "Two years tonight, for better or for worse."

"Why, it's Sheila," Roger said. "Of course! You look wonderful!"

"I feel wonderful," Sheila said. "Marriage does that for one."

"I can't believe it, looking at you. This calls for champagne. Waiter—!"

"Way ahead of you," Sam said. "We're already on the second bottle."

"A dance, then. How about it, Sheila? For old times' sake."

Sheila might have made an excuse. If she had, it would have been all right. Instead, she looked at Clint as if to ask his advice or permission; and Clint hesitated, just long enough to make his silence seem affirmation. After all, it was a gala night and a crowded floor, and Roger was the president of Baker, Benson and Company. Later, when Clint analyzed his reasoning that night, it was the last thought that haunted him. He should have realized then that he was heading for trouble.

Sam Moorhouse was a difficult man to work under. He was blunt, honest, and straightforward; but once a man had tasted of ambition, he chafed at the reins of restriction, and Sam, in addition to the aforementioned traits, was a stodgy old fool.

"I could have closed the deal with Amalgamated this afternoon if Sam had been on the ball," Clint complained, "but I just couldn't get to him. 'Baker, Benson and Company has honored its contracts and always will honor them while I'm in this office!' " Clint's voice took on the tone of Sam's nasal drawl. Sheila listened with half-closed eyes. She was fondling the ears of Slugger, the half-grown boxer who'd replaced Clint's cocker spaniel on his last birthday. "Honor its contracts! That's a fine excuse for letting $50,000 worth of business slip through our hands! Amalgamated would have paid a bonus for that shipment. We could have put off Standard for another six months. Business is business. If trimming sail a bit gets you over the finish line ahead of the competition, what's wrong with that?"

"That reminds me," Sheila said. "Roger Benson's invited us to spend the weekend on his yacht. He's planning to entertain the whole executive staff as a summer treat."

"Roger? When did you see Roger?"

"Today—at lunch."

"Where at lunch?"

She opened her eyes wider now.

"Downtown," she said. "I came down to have lunch with my husband, but he was all tied up with Sam Moorhouse and Roger wasn't. Jealous?"

Clint was still thinking of the commission he'd missed because of Sam's ridiculous morals. His frown was for Sam, but it carried over when he looked at Sheila.

Sheila smiled at him.

"I'm not sure," Clint said. "Maybe I am."

"Wonderful! There's nothing that boosts a wife's ego as much as a jealous husband. I'll have to make a practice of lunching with Roger."

"No!"

Clint's sharpness surprised even himself. He'd never quite forgotten his feelings that night at the country club. There was a sense of being pulled in two directions at once, and a subconscious anger at the direction in which he was moving.

"Why, Clint, you really are jealous!" Sheila's smile faded. "Do you want to know what we talked about all during lunch? About you, darling. About the wonderful job you're doing as sales manager, and how much more you could do if you had the authority."

"No, Sheila! Not that!"

The hurt sprang into her eyes, and he was sorry at once that he'd spoken so harshly; but he had to interfere.

"I know how much you like to help my career along," he said, "but you're not going to do it by talking to Roger behind Sam's back. Roger's a young man, but he learned the business from Baker and respects the old man's methods. Among other things that means loyalty to the seniority system. Unless Sam could be caught with his hand in the till, and you know as well as I do that won't happen, he's vice-president and will remain vice-president until the day he retires or drops dead—and Sam's healthy as a prize Percheron."

Sheila didn't answer, and Clint said nothing more. They sat through a long silence with that last thought hanging like a ghost between them.

Roger Benson's yacht was a floating paradise: a thoroughly stocked bar, a perpetual buffet, taped music for the languid, swimming and skin-diving off the sides, and fishing off the afterdeck. Sheila was among the languid, beautifully dressed for the occasion. It made Clint proud just to watch her, graceful and. feminine. Not another man on the staff had a wife to compare with her, certainly not Sam Moorhouse. Sam's muscular mate manipulated the fishing pole, while Sam—as if to show the younger men his contempt for his own graying hairs—went in for the more rugged skin diving. Clint's athletics went as far as donning trunks and sport shirt and sunning himself on the deck until Mrs. Moorhouse made a strike which stirred up a lot of excitement. It was a big fish and a fighter. With a cry, Mrs. Moorhouse was dragged from the bucket seat and pulled against the rail. Clint scrambled to his feet. Sam, momentarily out of the water, raced toward her.

"Drop the pole!" he shouted.

"Don't be an idiot!" she gasped. "The hard ones to land are the only catches worthwhile!"

If it had been wholly up to human strength, Mrs. Moorhouse might have landed a whale; but mechanical devices have a load limit. When the line snapped, the force of that occurrence ripped the pole from her hands. At the same instant, Clint saw something flash through the air and bounce across the deck to his feet. He looked down. The big, square diamond blinked up at him like a winking eye. He stooped and picked it up. He was holding it in his hand when Mrs. Moorhouse became aware of her loss.

"Sam, my diamond! It's gone!"

"Must have caught on the pole and gone overboard," Sam said. "I'll have a look."

Sam's dive was beautiful. Sam was in condition. Sam feared nothing; he had been enthroned in the vice-president's office and would live forever. All of these thoughts flashed through Clint's mind with the brilliance of the diamond in his hand, and then he acted. He dropped the stone to the deck and hurriedly, furtively, shoved it to one side, toward the cabin, with his foot.

"Gangway!" Clint shouted. "I'm going to help Sam!"

He caught a blurred glimpse of Sheila's face as he ran to the rail—white, startled, incredibly lovely. For Sheila he could do anything—even murder.

He plunged over the side and down deep into the green depths. He was awkward. He was pudgy. He was short of breath before he began, but he knew that down underneath the ship somewhere, Sam Moorhouse was on a dare-devil stunt that would cost him his life. Clint's lungs were almost bursting before he found him; but hatred and desire had breath of their own. And by the time his hands gripped the back of Sam's trunks, Clint hated Sam Moorhouse with all of his strength, and all of his strength was as much as it took to drive Sam's body, head first, like a squirming battering ram, against the submerged hull of the yacht. It was done so quickly, Sam never even saw who had had hold of him.

When Clint surfaced seconds later, his lungs were bursting. He had to be dragged aboard, gasping and sobbing. As soon as he had a voice, he called for Roger.

"Sam—down below—hurt—needs help."

Then Clint closed his eyes and let the darkness blot out the rest.

It was three days after Sam Moorhouse's funeral that Clint was called into Roger Benson's office. The interview was a formality, Clint knew that. Baker, Benson and Company operated strictly on the seniority system and he was the next in line. Even so, Clint was nervous. His hands were damp and his mouth was dry.

"Sit down, Clint," Roger said.

Clint was only too willing to sit down. In the chair, he felt better. Leather. Soft. Luxurious. There was a chair exactly like it in the vice-president's office.

"I suppose you know why I called you in today," Roger said. He looked grave, but that was only natural under the circumstances.

"I can imagine," Clint said.

Roger's eyes brightened momentarily.

"Yes, you really can imagine, can't you, Clint? Strange. I never realized that quality in you back in the old days. As a matter of fact, I always thought you extremely dull. Marrying Sheila must have made all the difference."

"All the difference," Clint agreed.

"She's a wonderful woman, Clint. I can see how a man would do almost anything for such a woman. I might have done almost anything for her myself, had she been my wife. But not this—"

Roger had kept one hand under the desk. Now he brought it up, opened it over the desk, and then took the hand away. Mrs. Moorhouse's diamond glittered in the light. The eye didn't wink now; it accused. Clint couldn't look away from it and he couldn't speak.

"This was mailed to me in a small box," Roger said, "and. folded up inside the box was this note."

He took a small square of white paper from his pocket, unfolded it, and read aloud, "Dear Mr. Benson. Before you promote Clint Dodson to the position of vice-president in your company, ask him why he concealed Mrs. Moorhouse's diamond on the deck of your yacht before leaping overboard to presumably help Sam Moorhouse search for it under water."

That was all. Roger Benson sat back in his chair and waited.

Memories, filtering like light through a fog, and all of the memories formed about Sheila because nothing important had ever happened to him before her. Clint stared out of the window with unseeing eyes, and let his mind luxuriate in the fullness of her—her beauty, her love, her faith, and loyalty. He hadn't confessed to killing Sam. Roger would never get that out of him, and he couldn't possibly prove anything without a confession. But the career of Clint Dodson was finished. There was only one thing he could do for Sheila now.

Miss Carlisle completed the letter she'd been typing for Mr. Benson and started toward his door. She hesitated as she passed the open window. Something seemed wrong. Mr. Dodson—when had he gone out? She stepped closer to the window and looked down—and then she screamed.

Roger Benson was beside Sheila all through the funeral. Afterwards he drove her home and went with her into the house. This was the difficult time, and he groped for words.

"I just can't help feeling guilty, Sheila. I should have realized Clint wasn't well."

"No, Roger. You mustn't blame yourself. You've been wonderful."

"I want to be wonderful, Sheila. I want to make it up to you for my carelessness and my stupidity. I know this is no time to talk about it, but ever since that night at the country club I've known what a fool I was to let you get away from me. Ambitious men make mistakes, Sheila. Clint wasn't the only man guilty of that error."

Sheila swayed a little on her feet, and Roger's arm steadied her. Such a young, strong arm. She looked up at him with sad, understanding eyes.

"You haven't been too ambitious, Roger. A man's work is his life. You'll go far, very far. There's just no limit to what you can do if you put your mind to it."

Sheila knew. She'd always known. Mrs. Moorhouse was right—the hard ones to land were the only catches worthwhile, and all she'd invested were a few years with that old fool, Clint Dodson, and the diamond she'd seen him pick up and then drop to the deck of the boat.

# The Man We Found

## by Donald Honig

**N**ow that I've retired from the interesting business of scooping people up and hustling them off to remote cabins and deciding how much they're worth in, to use that very crude word, ransom (my own personal expression is "reimbursement"), I feel less inhibited about recounting some of my experiences. I believe that every man who has at least an ounce of boldness will be sure to gather tons of success, and I believe that these men should record their adventures for the edification of those yet unborn generations who, because of the increasing stagnation of our society, will have to seek inspiration from the past rather than from the dukes and dudes around them.

So I'm telling this bizarre little tale because I believe its moral justifies it, and because I would like to explain one of the reasons why I finally retired from a profession where I was the acknowledged master.

There are many uncertainties and impulses inherent in all trades and professions. Uncertainties were the daily hazard with me and my associates, but impulses were to be resisted, fought, thwarted, impeded, strangled and shipped south as soon as they achieved maturity. The following will elucidate that somewhat extreme view.

We were on Park Avenue one evening, Jack and Buck and myself, cruising about looking for some mischief. We hadn't scooped up anyone in a long time and there was a general restiveness beginning to brood over the clubhouse.

"Look at that guy," Jack said, pointing.

We looked. Strolling along on the other side of the street was an admirably dressed, distinguished-looking gentleman. He was strutting along like Prince Caviar himself, tapping the sidewalk with a swinging walking-stick. A homburg big as a roaster sat his head as if set down there by the Archbishop of Canterbury. White-haired gentleman, maybe sixty, air of pleasure and distinction, like a diplomat who has just helped carve up three small republics.

"A real nabob," said Jack.

"Should be worth fifty grand if a penny," I said.

"We're short of cash, Bush," said Buck's beery back seat voice.

Even as I was deciding, Jack was making the U-turn. That was one of the things I liked about our little organization, one of the prime reasons for our enviable success—our minds anticipated each other. Intellectual conjunction. Team work. Rapport. Without it you can't have successful wars, politics, dramatics, acrobatics or double plays.

"The next street looks good," Jack said. "We'll net him there."

"You ready, Buck?" I asked. He was always ready. The brawn of the outfit. You've got to have a man like that, able to feed a protesting citizen into the back seat of a car as easily as a stoker levels a stream of coal into a furnace.

We cruised slowly, passing the nabob to have a good look, to make sure he wasn't a wandering stage prop. But to my eye he had that serenely ravenous look of the rich. And the way he was popping along with that stick flicking and his belly round and firm as a July melon, you could tell he was the top shelf.

"Wall Street," I said.

"Manufacturing," said Jack.

We passed him up and stood on the corner. Best place to park. Gives you terrific mobility. You've got the straightaway or the quick turn at your discretion, depending on the look of the situation. Buck and I slid over and released the doors, leaving them slightly ajar. Jack kept the motor purring.

We heard him coming on. Never look back. Just sit still like you're thinking about your traffic violations. We heard his stick. Click click click. Then he became a spot in the corner of my eye. Then we opened the doors. Perfect timing. That's what I was talking about. When Buck and I got out, the nabob was between us. I stepped up to him and took the ends of his homburg and pulled down as hard as I could. Strategy. Do that to a man, that above all, and he'll not shout out, not immediately anyway, and that's all you want, that one split second of peaceful maneuverability. The nabob's face reddened with rage as the hat bulged down and made his ears flap over. Then Buck got him from behind, under the arms, lifted him right off the sidewalk and I gathered him at the ankles and we hustled him right into the back seat. This was a beauty, a classic, because he didn't utter a peep, sputter, gasp or shout until he was rolled onto the floor. Then he said, "What—" and Buck said, "Shut up."

The car was running then. Jack turned at the corner and we went into Madison and continued on crosstown, cruising with the innocence of the elect.

"Just maintain your peace down there," I said.

"This is an outrage," said the nabob.

"From your point of view, yes," I said. "But from our point of view it's a business arrangement. You look as if you're familiar with the world of commerce, of supply and demand, have and hold, negotiation and liquidation. So you ought to understand what it's all about."

"You're abducting me, going to hold me for ransom," he said.

"We're speculating on you and then placing you on the open market," I said. "Please appreciate our position."

"You won't get away with this," he said. They always say that. It's like a reflex, like saying Not Guilty. We let them utter their stock phrases: "What is the meaning of this?" and, "What do you think you're doing?" and one or two others just to show we're not absolute barbarians and believe in freedom of speech even for suppressed people. Then we put our finger against our lips, and they cease.

The nabob resigned himself soon to things evil and insurmountable and lay there with the homburg on his chest and the stick at his side and his face fixed with static anger that gradually relaxed into submission and acceptance.

Once he said, "Where are you taking me?"

"To the country," I told him, truthfully. "You can rest assured that we treat all our clients with utmost deference, commensurate with their positions in life. My staff has instructions to that effect."

It was a balmy autumn night and the ride was very pleasant. We took the West Side Drive uptown and then the Washington Bridge across the dark old Hudson. The boys were quite relaxed and content, looking forward to the events of the new situation. We were working again, and until you've been away from it for a while you just don't know how good it is.

We had a brand-new cottage to break in too. I had rented it a few months before. It was waiting for us, cupboard stocked with food, beds turned down. I always made sure that we had a new place ready. It was on a back road, very secluded and just right for our purposes.

In a little while we pulled into the driveway. Jack turned off the motor and the headlights melted into the dark. The brisk night air rang with crickets.

"You can get up now," I said to our prone passenger.

He made a gruff, opulent grunt and sat up. I helped him to his feet and showed him into the cottage. There we endeavored to make our guest comfortable.

"As far as we're concerned," I told him, "you are a guest here (and ultimately a well-paying one, I might add) and we'll be at your beck and call. Any reasonable request, for a hot-water bag to the morning paper will be granted with alacrity. But let me also impress upon you that while you will be treated with all due respect and consideration, that any attempt on your part to either run away, tunnel out, whistle, howl, send up flares, lecture us or otherwise give us a hard time will be met with firm retaliation."

He regarded us coolly. Substantial-looking man, I thought. Whisky tint to his cheeks, bit of water in his eyes, double chin. Fine gentlemanly bearing. Poised. Not in the least flustered, and I was grateful for it. The nervous and hysterical ones are the worst. (The overly hysterical ones, we generally send right back.)

"All right," he said, voice quiet, refined. "Who is your cook?"

"Jack," I said. "Very adept at scrambling eggs. Wizard at taking the pink out of lamb chops. His coffee smiles and says good morning to you."

"I'm very fussy about my eggs," he said. "About all my meals. I have a nervous stomach, and I'm sure this experience isn't going to help it any. For breakfast I have poached eggs and two slices of buttered toast. And strong coffee. I'm accustomed to porterhouse steaks at one o'clock and at six, promptly. I'll give you instructions later about the vegetables."

"Yes, sir," I said. "We'll remember that. I'll send Jack down to the town first thing in the morning to get some choice cuts."

"And caviar," he said.

"Caviar? Sure."

"And I enjoy a nip of brandy before going to bed. Brandy from the heart of the cellar, mind you."

"We'll lay in a supply," I said.

Then we showed him to his room. He jabbed the mattress with his stick.

"I generally rise at seven," he said. "But under these circumstances, I'll sleep till ten."

"Fine," I said. "I'll see to it you're not disturbed. Now, about our end of the arrangement. Let me say that scooping you up was an impromptu sort of thing, so we really don't know too much about you. Give us your dossier, so we can put a tag on you."

He removed his hat and coat.

"My name is Oscar Sigmund," he said. "My residence is on Park Avenue. My business is investments."

"Doing well, are you?" I asked.

"Quite," he said.

"Good fellow. Whom do we contact?"

"My wife."

Oscar Sigmund retired at about eleven and then we got together around the kitchen table to make our plans.

"Fifty thousand, at least," Jack said.

"Maybe even seventy-five," said Buck.

"A hundred," I said. "This guy has cream in his blood. Don't you fellows know yet, after all I have taught you, that the less concerned a client is about his situation the more digits he has in his bank account? Only a very, very wealthy man behaves with the aplomb he has demonstrated here tonight. One hundred thousand."

"Maybe we ought to ask more," Jack said. Rambunctious youth.

"Jack, Jack," I said. "Please. It's not how much you ask, it's how much you get. To ask for more than a hundred thousand, no matter who the client is, is to look for trouble. The world never takes an extravagant person seriously. One hundred thousand," I said. "And then we incorporate ourselves."

I let two days pass before making the call. From conversations I had with Sigmund, I gathered the fact that he wasn't on particularly amicable terms with his wife and that his disappearing for a day or two would not be alarming at all. So I let two full days pass. I might have let it be three, but he was getting to be a nuisance. Jack had to go into New York to buy him a special cushion to sit on because he had boils. And Sigmund was driving us crazy with his meals. Everything had to be absolutely correct. Fork on the left, napkins, all that. And a new set of dishes and new silverware too. Then the meals had to be done just right or else he sent them back. We had to make and remake his bed until it was just right, and we had to buy him a pair of silk pajamas because he refused to sleep in his drawers. And buy him also a box of dollar cigars. But he was a big fish and we were only too happy to do it all.

Then on the morning of the third day I made the call, from a phone booth in mid-Manhattan.

"Mrs. Sigmund?" I said to the woman's voice that answered.

"Yes," she said. "Who is that?" A Viennese clip to her voice. Irritating, like a pin in the ear. I could see why the old boy cut out from time to time.

"Listen, and listen carefully now. We have your husband. If you want to see him again, keep this strictly to yourself. Get a valise and fill it with one hundred thousand dollars in tens, twenties, fifties and hundreds." She started to interrupt, a note of hysteria wiping off some of that continental accent, which I had figured was affected anyway, but I told her to shut up. "You do this by four o'clock this afternoon and I'll call back with further instructions. Remember: secrecy is your only hope."

Then I hung up on her and went out in the lovely sunshine. Mingled in the crowds. Crowds are the most democratic organizations in the world; every man has his place. I took a subway uptown, met Jack with the car and we had a leisurely drive back to the cottage, where we found Oscar Sigmund patiently explaining to Buck via pencil and diagram the difference between polo and croquet.

That was the morning. At lunch I received a stern lecture from Sigmund about my eating habits. It was snobbish, but constructive. Two more bottles of brandy (when he nipped he really nipped) pushed the expenses over a hundred dollars, a new record. Then it was four o'clock and I was in a phone booth in a nearby town.

"Mrs. Sigmund?"

"Yes," she said. "I take it you're the scoundrel that called this morning."

"Yes, I am that scoundrel. Did you do as I asked?"

"Of course not."

"You didn't?"

"I think it's a bluff."

"Have you looked around for your husband recently?"

"I still think it's a bluff," she said. "And I'm going to call tn⌐ ⌐ If you're some crank who thinks he can extort a lot of money from innocent people—"

I hung up. Back to the cottage for some profound discussion. Sigmund was part of the council.

"Mr. Sigmund," I said, "your wife is treating this very lightly. She thinks it is all a bluff. Now, since it is your well-being that is involved here, perhaps you can tell us how we can—"

"I'm sorry, Mr. Bushel," he interrupted, glancing down at his watch, "but it is time for my aperitif."

Conversation suspended while Jack got up, washed his hands, put on his jacket and brought Mr. Sigmund a glass of brandy. We watched silently as he sniffed, savored, sipped and contemplated it before finally finishing it. Ten-minute operation. Then I was allowed to renew the conversation.

"Mr. Sigmund, this is quite serious, I assure you."

He folded his hands on the edge of the table and regarded me as if I were someone trying to sell him an encyclopedia written in a dead language.

"Quite serious," I restated, emphatically.

"I understand, Mr. Bushel," he said.

"*How* can we convince your wife?"

"She's a terribly difficult person. Very stubborn. I'm afraid that once she's made up her mind, well, it's made up, and that's all there is to it."

"Have you ever been away from home this long?"

"No."

"So she should be alarmed by now."

"If I know her," he said, "she's already spoken to the police and the newspapers. She's not a woman to be trifled with."

Spoken to the newspapers was right. The next morning it was on the front pages. Oscar Sigmund had been kidnaped, it said. Well, we knew that much. Now, it is always a sticky situation when the police come into the thing. The most successful deals are those that are consummated without the story ever getting out. Often, once the police and newspapers get the story, I prefer to let the client go. There are always thousands of potential clients, the way I look at it, and dismally little advancement in jail.

But I figured I'd have one more go at Mrs. Sigmund. This time from a phone booth in lower Manhattan. Had to make it short and sweet, for the police were sure to be on the wire.

Two rings and then a man's voice, annoyed.

"Hello?" I said.

"Hello?" he said.

"Hello?" I said again.

"Who is this?" he demanded, the irritation growing in his voice changing it like discoloration.

"Who is this?" I asked him right back. I wasn't going to hang on for much more. They could trace the call and be sitting in my lap in five minutes.

"This," he said slowly with measured emphasis, "is Mr. Sigmund."

That was all. I hung up and walked out of the booth. Not a thought in my head. Perfectly calm. I believe in poise at crucial moments.

I waited around for the afternoon papers. When they hit the stands, I picked one up and looked at it like a man looking to see if the date of his execution has been scheduled yet. The story was front page. Hoax, it said. Oscar Sigmund had turned up at his home early today. He had been off on a hunting trip in the Adirondacks and had been inaccessible until last night. And there was his picture. The face was not familiar.

When I got back to the cottage I handed the paper to our guest, with my other snatching the aperitif from his fingers as I told Jack to take off his serving jacket and spit on the floor.

"Who the fritz are you?" I asked him.

"My name is Skindig," he said. "I'm a gentleman's gentleman."

"I take it the gentleman to whom you belong is Oscar Sigmund."

"That is correct," he said. Dignity unruffled. Nose cool as ice.

"I say we hang him," said Buck.

"By the neck," said Jack.

"Can you explain this, Skindig?" I asked.

"Yes, sir," he said. "First of all, if you remember correctly, it was you who pulled me into your car and brought me here."

"But you claimed you were Sigmund."

"I confess to that one lone indiscretion," he said with some contrition. "I knew that Mr. Sigmund was going off for a week's shooting. So, as was my custom in these instances, I borrowed one of his suits, his hat and his stick and was on my way to a Third Avenue pub for an evening's relaxation when you swept me into your car. Once I caught onto your game, I felt the opportunity was too great to be missed."

"What opportunity?" I asked.

"To have other people, for once, fawn over me. After all these years you don't know what it meant to me. Hang me if you wish. It will have been well worth it."

No, we didn't hang him. The vote was three to none in favor, but we granted him amnesty. We even drove him back to the house and left him to make his own explanations. (He promised not to inform on us and, being a gentleman, he never did.) Later we totaled up everything and it came out that we lost $158.75 on the deal. This hurt almost as much as not getting the hundred thousand, in our current financial state. Somehow a man's mistakes have more sting to them than his successes have satisfaction.

# Night on the Beach

## by Wenzell Brown

George and Betty Warshop is city folks who come up to Cripple's Bend nigh every summer. Ain't nothin' wrong with George 'cept'n he's on the stiff side, what Maw calls a boiled shirt. As for Betty, she's cute as a cat's eyeball and lively as a bear pup. Never could see how she hitched up with a sobersides like George. But then there's a lot of marriages I could never figger. Seems like the most unlikely couples hit it off sweet as taffy and vice versy.

Now don't get me wrong. George is a real fine feller, the kind I'd trust with my last ten dollars. It's just that an evenin' with George lasts a sight longer than one spent playin' a hand or two of poker or just settin' around the general store chewin' the fat.

Summer before last the Warshops didn't show up in Cripple's Bend. Seems like they spent their vacation at Spruce Beach, way down the coast across the state line. Betty told Maw that's where she and George got engaged and the place had romantic memories for her. Seems sort of queer to me but Maw says I ain't got no sentiment and that ain't something I care to argue about with her.

Anyway, come June this year and up pop the Warshops, George and Betty and the two little girls, aged eight and six or thereabouts. Right off the bat I can see there's a change in George. It's like somebody's took the starch out of him and left him all wilted and droopy. He walks around with his hands in his pockets hardly lookin' where he's goin'. The only time he really limbers up is when he's with the young 'uns.

Maw's got a way with folks with a problem and pretty soon I see her and Betty in a huddle. I get the news from Maw second-hand but without no details missin'. Seems like George's trouble started in Spruce Beach the summer afore and Betty's eatin' her heart out tryin' to reckon out what's wrong.

156                    ALFRED HITCHCOCK'S ANTHOLOGY

'Twarn't long after that when George comes moseyin' around one afternoon when I'm a-mowin' the lawn. I go and set on the porch with him for awhile. It's easy to see he wants to open up and tell me somethin' but he plumb can't get started. He hems and haws around like he's got a mouthful of molasses.

Finally he blurts out, "Tell me somethin', Sheriff. Should a man destroy his happiness for the sake of abstract justice?"

"Look, George," I says. "Nobody can answer a question like that. Not without a bill of particulars."

I waited then, sort of expectant. But George mutters, "I guess that's right." Then he clams up and after awhile he walks away.

The next day he's back again, more jittery than ever. He's got another stickler this time. "If I told you about a crime would you be bound to report it?"

"Mebbe yes. Mebbe no. Makes a difference a lot of things. Whether it's in my jurisdiction. The seriousness of the offense. Stuff like that."

"It's murder."

I give him a quick look and he flushes, knowin' what's flashin' through my mind.

"Not me," he says real quick. "I wouldn't know how to kill anyone even if I wanted to."

I feel a sigh comin' from my throat. He's right, of course. He ain't the type for violence. Though I've learned in thirty-three years as a law officer that you can't always tell. 'Specially about the quiet ones like George.

I got a hunch he's ready to break down and spill the beans, and I must admit I was right curious. So I go around to the kitchen and fill up a couple of mugs with apple cider to wet his whistle and get him in the mood to start conversin'.

Mebbe it's the cider or mebbe he's just been holdin' in so long he's ready to bust, but it ain't long afore he's talkin' lickety-split, like he can't stop until he gets it all off his chest.

His story starts way back eleven years ago when he's a-courtin' Betty. He'd known her even longer than that, when they was high school kids together. He'd put her on a pedestal and worshipped her but he was too shy to do much more. Once he'd boosted up enough courage to ask her for a date but she'd turned him down flat. He'd been so cut up about it, he'd kept his distance from then on.

But this summer he was twenty-two and just passed his exams as a Certified Public Accountant. He had a good job a-waitin' for him in Boston in the fall and a couple months to kill afore he started. So what's more natural than to go up to Spruce Beach where his folks have rented a cottage?

Spruce Beach is one of them resort towns that's hoppin' like crazy in the hot weather and deader'n last year's fishin' license as soon as it turns cool. There's a boardwalk stretchin' along the waterfront for a mile or two, and an amusement center with a merry-go-round, a fun house, a ferris wheel and such. Besides that, there's a pier pokin' way out into the ocean with a penny arcade and dance hall at the end.

George is gettin' bored with it all when who does he bump into but Betty? To his surprise she greets him like a long-lost friend. What's more it turns out that she's stayin' with her widowed Mom at the Panther Inn. Betty don't know no one in Spruce Beach and she ain't the kind to go in for easy pick-ups so I guess George's comin' along seemed a godsend.

Anyway, it ain't no time at all afore they're seein' each other most every day. They go in swimmin', stroll along the boardwalk, or go for long walks on the beach. Or mebbe they just sit and sip lemonade on the veranda of the Panther Inn.

Right from the start George knows that Betty is the girl for him. But every time he feels himself ready to pop the question he gets so scared he's tongue-tied. The same with kissin' her. He manages a goodnight peck off and on, but Betty always turns her face so that all she gets is a little smooch on the cheek.

George is half crazy with lovin' her and seein' her slip through his fingers, so one night he decides, come hell or high water, he's goin' to propose.

His words come out all stiff and formal, and all he can do while he's waitin' for the answer is to scuff up the sand with his shoe.

Betty lets him down as easy as she can. She says, "I like you a lot, George. But I don't want to think about marriage. Not yet anyway."

George wants to throw himself at her feet and plead his case but he just ain't built that way. Instead he mumbles some platitudes and don't even try to kiss her when he leaves her.

Toward the end of the summer the weather turns chill and damp. The crowd stops comin' up from Boston and the regulars pack up and

158                                        ALFRED HITCHCOCK'S ANTHOLOGY

go home. The pier closes down and so do most of the concessions. The beach that's been swarmin' with bathers and picnickers is wind-swept and deserted.

Betty don't mind. She loves the storms and the white-crested breakers smashin' up against the boulders around Hurricane Point. No matter how wild the night is, she wants to go out into it. And George don't make no objections as long as he's with her. All the same, he knows that what she's doin' is dangerous. There's been reports over the radio of rollin's and muggin's in lonely spots around Spruce Beach.

Time's a-runnin' out for George. Finally, it's the last night afore he's got to leave for Boston and his job. There's a no'wester blowin' and it's kickin' up a heavy surf. When George calls for Betty she's all set and waitin' for him on the veranda, dressed up in a yeller slicker.

The night's so dark and stormy they can hardly see their way along the beach to Hurricane Point. But when they get there the rain slacks off real sudden-like, and the moon comes out from behind the clouds. The breakers are still slammin' against the rocks but the beach is all smooth and silvery.

They spread the slicker out in the lee of a pile o' rocks and sit down. George is gettin' set to make a last try at breakin' Betty down and persuadin'er to marry him. But, like always, he's havin' a hard time gettin' started.

That's when he sees this young feller comin' along the beach, hands in his pockets, whistlin' tonelessly. He's wearin' a cap with a broken visor and a leather jacket. He's cocky and swaggerin' but there's somethin' furtive about the way he's lookin' from side to side that telegraphs a warnin' signal to George. He passes not more'n a dozen feet away, his steps soundless on the moist sand. He don't spot George and Betty in the deep shadders, but George gets a good look at him. He's not much more'n a boy, nineteen or twenty at the outside.

George watches his back as he moves away. Then he glances at Betty. She's got her knees drawn up under her chin and her fingers looped around her ankles. She's starin' out over the formin' breakers and it's obvious she ain't noticed a thing.

George's hand closes over hers but he don't get no response. Her skin is cool to the touch and she keeps on gazin' straight out to sea.

George looks back at the boy who's quite a spell down the beach by now. Suddenly he comes to an abrupt stop. He freezes into position for a minute or two. Then he streaks like a black cat toward a rottin' old rowboat that's been pulled up high on the shore. He crouches there for awhile, then melts into the shadders that the boat throws, like he's hidin'.

Only then does George notice the second figger on the beach. He's comin' from the town, a man below medium height, roly-poly and obviously drunk. He's staggerin' along, weavin' from side to side, jerkin' himself upright every few steps, then lurchin' on through the sand.

George strains his eyes lookin' at the rowboat and tryin' to find the boy. But he can't see no trace of him. There's bushes behind the boat and a narrer road. Beyond that's a straggly stand o' pine trees. George reckons that mebbe the man's somebody the boy knows and don't want to meet up with, so he's just pulled stakes and scuttled out o' there.

The man comes stumblin' on. George gets the idea he's singin' but he can't be sure. The wind and the roar of the surf is drownin' out all other sounds. As he draws close to the boat, George glimpses the boy again. He's kneelin' by the prow, his body all coiled up like an animal waitin' to pounce on its prey. George sees somethin' else too, a glint of metal in his hand that could be a knife or mebbe a revolver.

George knows he should o' shouted then but he hesitates 'til it's too late. The boy darts out from behind the boat and launches himself at the man. Seem's like the man must've heard him at the last moment 'cause he swings around drunkenly and reels back a few steps. The man and the boy stand there facin' each other. Then the man lurches forward, his arms stretched in front o' him.

There's a single sharp flat crack that George could hardly hear above the rollin' crash of a breaker. The man straightens up, then crumples in a heap and lies still. The boy bends over him, turnin' his pockets inside out.

George's fingers clasp hard on Betty's wrist. She gives a gasp of pain and twists her head around, her mouth open to speak. She's had her back to the whole scene and don't know nothin's wrong. All of a sudden George realizes that's the way it's got to stay. Betty ain't built cautious like him. If she sees the muggin' she'll rush out to help the stricken man.

George is plumb scared. The boy's shot once so it ain't likely he'll hesitate to shoot again. George is shakin' all over. He's got to keep Betty quiet at all costs. Her life and perhaps his own depend on it.

She says, "George, what on earth?"

There ain't no time to think. George grabs her in his arms and presses her back on the sand. His mouth clamps over her lips to still her voice and he falls flat on top of her. Betty's strugglin' like crazy but he won't let her go. He just holds her tighter 'n tighter. Her teeth bite into his lips and he's pressin' so hard he can taste the salty tang of blood.

She flails out at him, scratchin' his face with her fingernails. Then she gets both palms beneath his chest tryin' to pry him loose. George just bears down harder 'n ever, half smotherin' her.

Then she ain't strugglin' no more. Instead she's all limp and trembly. Her arms circle him, holdin' him close, while her fingers dig into his back and her lips turn soft and pliant.

Time loses all meanin' for George. Mebbe they lie like that for a minute, mebbe ten. He can't be sure. When he does raise his head, he looks down the beach. There's a black mound near the rowboat where the man's sprawled on the sand. But there ain't nary a sign of the boy.

George lifts himself on one knee. And then he sees the boy, dangerously close, the moon shinin' full on his face. George gets just one quick look. But that's enough so he reckons the picture'll stay with him the rest of his life. The boy's like a fox, with reddish hair, eyes that have a yeller sheen to them, small sharp features and pointed lobeless ears. The gun's still in his hand.

"George?"

It seems to him that Betty's whisper must carry to the boy, even though they're down wind and the surf's still poundin' on the Point.

In a panic, he pounces again. But this time she's ready for him and rolls away. They scuffle on the wet sand until she breaks free. Her hand lashes across his cheek so hard it snaps his head back, and before he can pull himself together she's on her feet and runnin'.

George scrambles up and stares around sort of wild, but the boy ain't nowhere in sight. As for Betty, she's racin' lickety-split along the packed sand by the water's edge.

He scoops up the slicker and takes off after her. But she's got a head start and he ain't exactly the athlete type. 'Tain't long before he's puffin' like a grampus and his knees is all wobbly.

He never does catch up with her but she's waitin' for him on the veranda of the Panther Inn.

He's pantin' so he can hardly speak. But he manages to gasp, "Betty, let me explain."

She tosses her head and says real lofty, "You don't need to."

"I didn't mean to hurt you."

She don't say nothin' at all, so he tries again. "Darling, you don't know what was happening back there. It was awful."

Then, though he can hardly believe it, she's laughin', and she throws herself into his arms.

She says, "George, I didn't know you could be so passionate. You always seemed so cold. I guess every girl wants a man who'll lose his head over her sometimes. Oh, George, I do love you. I know it now."

She breaks away and runs into the inn, slammin' the door after her.

George stands there in a daze, not darin' to believe in his good luck. But finally he perks himself up and realizes he can't leave the man on the beach dead, or mebbe dyin'. He's got to get in touch with the police. But there ain't no phone in his cottage and the inn's all dark. He heads for the center of the town. He don't rightly know where the police station is but he reckons he'll find someone to tell him.

But when he reaches the main street there ain't a light on anywhere and not a soul in sight. He looks at his watch. It's close to two A.M. and the town's shut down tighter'n a drum.

While he's ponderin' his next move, a police car careens out of a side street and whizzes past him. He tries to signal it but the cops pay him no mind. Then there's another car, and a third, all streakin' along the road toward Hurricane Point. 'Tain't hard to work out the score. Either someone's discovered the fat man's body, or he ain't been hurt so bad that he can't summon help.

George starts trudgin' along the road after the cars. He's dog tired, but all the same he's walkin' on air 'cause o' Betty. He wipes his face with his hand and feels somethin' sticky. It's blood where Betty's scratched him. 'Til now he ain't been doin' much thinkin'. But it hits him all of a heap that he's in a pickle.

He's witnessed a crime and ain't made no attempt to stop it. Worse'n that, if he talks now, how's he goin' to explain him and Betty lyin' together on the beach long after midnight? If the paper prints that it ain't goin' to look good. He's in danger of losin' Betty just when it looks like he's won her.

Besides, supposin' the cops don't believe his story. Betty can't back

ALFRED HITCHCOCK'S ANTHOLOGY

him up 'cause he's sure she ain't seen a thing. With his face bloody, and sand all over his clothes, the cops might even hold him for questionin'. And if he's takin' that job in Boston, he's got to catch the noon bus tomorrow without fail.

By the time he sees the beach near the Point all lit up with the headlights of cars, he's worked himself into a lather. The way it always is when there's an accident or a killin', people seemed to've popped out of nowhere and there's quite a mess of 'em standin' round. One of the police cars is pullin' away, its siren screamin'.

George sidles up to where a cluster of men is talkin'. One of 'em is sayin', "Old Paddy Quinn got it, I hear."

"Yeah, and they caught the punk who done it. Grabbed him red-handed with the gun in his pocket. Some kid who busted out of the reformatory."

"I hope he gets the chair. Paddy was a right guy."

There was more but George wasn't listenin'. He's feelin' like he's got a reprieve from the death house. The victim has been found and the murderer apprehended without his comin' into the picture. He don't see no reason for gettin' himself mixed up in the crime or draggin' Betty in neither. So he lights out o' there and heads for home.

He's shavin' about nine o'clock in the mornin' when the news comes over the radio. Patrick Quinn, age sixty-two, has been slain with a single bullet. Caught near the death scene was Richard Pine, age nineteen, an escapee from Fremont Reformatory. In his possession at the time of the arrest was a recently fired .32 automatic revolver and Quinn's wallet. The police call it "an open and shut case."

So there it is all wrapped up in a neat package with a pink ribbon tied about it. George can't see no reason for not wipin' the whole thing out of his mind.

He spends the last couple o' hours in Spruce Beach with Betty. She agrees, as soon as he's settled down in Boston, she'll join him and they'll get hitched.

George keeps a sharp eye out for news about the murder but the Boston papers is pretty skimpy about what they carry. There's a squib sayin' the ballistic experts have proven the bullet was fired from Pine's gun and that bloody fingerprints found on the wallet is his. Mebbe a week later there's a follow-up story. Pine's managed to hang himself in his cell. That marks finish to the case as far as the police is concerned.

George has got plenty of other things on his mind. The outfit he's joined is called the Markham Leather Company. With luck and hard work and Betty helpin' him all the time, he's climbin' the ladder fast. Before ten years is up. he's become their vice president.

Takin' it by and large, his marriage with Betty is a happy one. Her only complaint is that sometimes he's too preoccupied with business and neglects her.

When that happens, she teases him. "Remember that night on the beach. You weren't so cold then."

The funny thing is, whenever she says it, he gets all trembly with a-wantin' her and the fear o' losin' her. He grips her tight like he'll never let go, and the blood starts poundin' in his ears and his breath a-comin' in gasps.

He's always a-wonderin' what'll happen if she ever learns the truth about that night, that it was panic, not passion, that first made him take her in his arms.

'Most every summer Betty suggests they spend their vacation in Spruce Beach, but George always finds a way of puttin' her off and comin' to Cripple's Bend instead.

Then last summer he gives in.

They stay at the Panther Inn. The children love it. They can't get enough of surf-bathin' and ridin' the whip and visitin' the fun house.

The boardwalk with all its concessions is a fairy wonderland and they never tire of it. They stuff themselves with frozen custard, salt water taffy, foam candy, and pizza, and none of it ever makes 'em sick. That's youth for you.

But it's the pizza they love best.

'Tain't long afore they discover a shop in a side street where a man stands in the winder dressed in a white chef's cap and fancy apron, tossin' the white dough in the air, kneadin' it, moldin' it and puttin' it in the oven.

Every day they beg, "Please, Daddy. Please let's go for pizza."

But when they get to the shop they want to linger outside to watch "the funny man" performin' his tricks of magic.

And George can't bear to look at the man. You see, he's got a narrer fox face, reddish hair, and tiny pointed lobeless ears.

George keeps a-tellin' himself this can't be the man who killed Paddy Quinn. It just ain't possible. Dick Pine committed suicide ten

ALFRED HITCHCOCK'S ANTHOLOGY

years ago. So mebbe this is a younger brother or mebbe a double. Such things do occur. All the same he knows he's deludin' himself. Every time he goes up to that winder he's sure as shootin' that he's a-facin' the boy on the beach.

He starts askin' questions around. This man's name is Sam Murphy, and he's a heap older'n he looks. He's been in trouble off and on but never nothin' very serious. Fightin', drinkin' and disorderly conduct. That's about all.

Then George gets a bright idea. He visits the morgue of the local newspaper and digs up the issues that are ten years old. Sure enough, there's a picture of Dick Pine starin' at him right on the front page. And he warn't the boy on the beach at all. This Pine was a blond, heavy-set kid with broad cheekbones and pale eyes set wide apart.

He reads the story beneath the picture. Pine was protestin' his innocence right to the end. He claims he saw another boy runnin' past him on the beach, tossin' somethin' away on the sand. So he goes to take a look and finds the gun and the wallet. He picks 'em up and it ain't long after that when the cops land on him.

One thing that backs up his story is that he ain't got a penny to bless himself with when he's arrested. But the cops say that don't mean much. Paddy was always a-cadgin' drinks. Like as not he was dead broke that night.

Nobody had believed Dick Pine's story.

But George knows it's true.

George's conscience won't give him no rest. If he'd a done what he should have and gone to the cops right away, Dick Pine would still be alive and Sam Murphy behind bars. But who's goin' to believe him now? Even if the cops take him serious, it ain't goin' to bring Dick Pine back to life. He'll have to admit his cowardice, and there's like to be some newspaper publicity that won't do him no good.

But that don't worry him much. It's Betty he's thinkin' about. He's been livin' a lie for ten years. Betty'll forgive him. Perhaps she'll laugh. But things ain't never goin' to be the same between them. Every time he takes her in his arms they'll both be rememberin' the counterfeit passion that linked them together for so long.

So George just lets sleepin' dogs lie. He don't do a thing. But he can't rest at night. He's tossin' and turnin' all the time and blamin' himself for bein' a coward. Betty knows there's somethin' wrong and tries to get him to tell her, but he won't. He never tells nobody until he spills it all to me.

He ends up by sayin', "Well, Sheriff, you're a man of the law. You tell me what to do and I'll abide by it."

I sort of shake my head. "There's a lot of angles on this, George. I got to think 'em over."

He says, "I'll be waitin' to hear from you." He gets up and walks away, holdin' himself straight and proud like I ain't seen him do all summer.

So I got George's problem in my lap. And Betty's too. Accordin' to the book there ain't no two ways about it. I got to drive down to Spruce Beach and try to clear Dick Pine's name and see to it that a murderer's not on the loose.

But then I get to thinkin' about it the way the cops down there will. Just how good is George's evidence? Mebbe over the years he's built up a picture in his mind that ain't true after all. As for Dick Pine, he's got a bad record, and suicide while awaitin' trial is usually taken as a confession of guilt. The cops in Spruce Beach ain't goin' to want to rake up muddy water, especially on a tale that's ten years old, with nothin' to support it but George's word. And George could be mistaken. After all, if Sam Murphy's a dangerous person, he's managed to keep out of serious trouble 'til now.

First I work it out one way, then the other. I don't eat much supper, even though Maw's servin' clam fritters and corn on the cob and blueberry pie. After I go to bed I'm restless as a hound dog and can't get to sleep nohow.

Maw waits 'til mornin' afore she starts needlin' me. There ain't much sense tryin' to keep anything from Maw once she's made up her mind she's goin' to dig it out. She's got more tricks than a trained monkey and it don't do no good to lie 'cause she can read me like she does the Bible, as always.

Pretty soon she's wormed the whole story out o' me. She just sits a-lookin' at me for awhile, then she says, "What you goin' to do, Paw?"

"Reckon I'll get the car out and head for Spruce Beach."

"You ain't a-doin' nothin' of the kind," she snaps. "Listen to me, Paw. I been a-talkin' with Betty. She told me 'bout that night on the beach, leastwise what she thinks happened. She reckons George lost

    ALFRED HITCHCOCK'S ANTHOLOGY

his head over her and went half crazy with wantin' her. Now you take that away from Betty and what's she got to go on with? Their marriage'll bust up, sure as God made sour apples."

"I'm a law man," I says stubbornly.

"Fiddle-faddle!" Maw gets up, comes over to me and flounces down on my lap. She's sort o' generously built, a-pushin' the two-hundred-pound mark these days. All the same it feels good a-havin' her there.

Mebbe I'm wrong and mebbe I'm not actin' the way a law man should. But I don't aim to have no ruckus with Maw. There's one thing I learned in more'n thirty years of wedlock and that is there's plenty a-times when there's nothin' for a man to do but keep his mouth shut.

# Scott Free

## by Miriam Lynch

Henry Tolman got away with murder—he loved that phrase and often turned it over in his mind, gloating. True, it had become cheapened through everyday use, but it had a special, delightful meaning for him because he actually had killed a man and the killing had gone undetected. The fact of it set him apart, raised him above other men, put him in a select circle of brotherhood with the craftiest and cleverest of criminals—the undiscovered murderers.

Only one person knew. Louise, his wife, had been in the livingroom that night. The two shadowy figures on the terrace had been in her direct line of vision. Two figures at first. And then one.

It was on account of Louise that he had killed.

Immediately after he had pushed Scott Lansing over the low terrace wall, he had been afraid that he would not be able to handle Louise. Women were emotional, she more so than most, perhaps because of her theatrical background. For a little while, she had been like someone in a bad second act. She went through the whole bit—the horror-stricken gaze, the numbed movements, the attitudes of shock.

But by the time the police arrived, Henry had her under control. It was simple, really. Whatever she knew, he pointed out, she could not prove. And she would not want a scandal, her pictures on the front pages, the story of her affair with Scott Lansing gobbled up by a cityful of greedy-eyed readers. Besides, there was her mother. The old lady was in her seventies and her heart was bad. Louise wouldn't want to do anything which might cause her mother to have a fatal seizure, would she?

So, in the end, Louise had proved an asset. Still dazed, she had answered the questions honestly because they had turned out to be the right sort of questions for Henry.

168                                          ALFRED HITCHCOCK'S ANTHOLOGY

She said that, yes, Scott had seemed depressed that night. He hadn't worked for a long time, not even in a TV shot. There had been a number of drinks, before and during the dinner; and other people, in the course of affairs, verified the fact that Scott had been drinking more and more recently.

The analysis had proved that the consumption of liquor had been heavy that evening—everything went Henry's way.

Louise could say honestly that Scott had been moody and depressed. Again, there were his closest friends who could attest to his low spirits, his desperation. Finally she had described the man's movements before he wandered restlessly out onto the terrace alone. She did not volunteer the information that Henry had followed him out there.

Nor was anything said about the photograph.

That was what had started it all, put the spark to the suspicions which were to flame into murderous purpose.

The picture was nothing, Louise had insisted, except what Henry had made of it in his jealousy-tortured mind. It was a glossy print of Scott, full-face, smiling in a way calculated to charm agents and casting directors. It was inscribed in the extravagant manner of show people: "To my leading lady—in all respects—forever and ever and ever yours, Slave."

Louise could protest until her voice gave out. She could try to explain to Henry how little the silly nickname meant, that all actors said and wrote things like that without there being a trace of real feeling in the words, that there had been only that one season when she had played in summer stock with Scott, a few suppers together, a superficial sort of friendship between them.

But Henry could remember the onstage love scenes, how he had squirmed through them on the hot, uncomfortable night he had seen the play. And Louise had hesitated about marrying him—because of an involvement with Scott? Then after the wedding, Scott "dropped in" too frequently. Louise could talk all she wanted to about his liking the food and the free drinks. Jealousy and suspicion were a cancerous gnawing which spread until Henry could scarcely stand the pain.

Then when he found the picture in her dresser drawer, the picture of the smiling face and its sickening inscription, he knew that he would have to kill Scott Lansing.

Because he could not escape that face, sleeping or waking. It seemed to be everywhere, superimposed on the faces of people in a crowd, staring out of a television screen at him, following him into his dreams. It grew larger all the time, pushing into his life and polluting it until there was nothing left for him to do except destroy its owner. Then there would be no more face to torment him.

The day the police left for the last time, he felt like a man whose cancer had been cut out by its roots. He cried to Louise, "It's gone forever! I've destroyed Scott Lansing as thoroughly as though he never lived. I'll never have to see him or think about him again! I'm Scott free. Get it?"

She looked at him full in the face for the first time since she had discovered he was a murderer. Her quiet eyes told him nothing. He knew she was still shocked. Perhaps her feeling for him was frozen right now. But that would change. He would make it change. Now that Scott was gone, they would achieve a closeness, the oneness he had always ached for.

She asked, with nothing except curiosity in her voice, "Do you really believe that? Can you go on as though this had never happened? There has to be some sort of punishment. Even for you, Henry."

It angered him that she was trying to tarnish his golden moment of triumph. He felt like striking her.

"Spare me the Sunday School lecture," he snarled. "I killed your lover. Like I'd kill any ravaging animal that was threatening us. It's what any man would do—the oldest law there is. So what's the talk about punishment?"

That was the last time she tried to convince him that Scott Lansing had been only a friend, one of dozens she had had before her marriage; the only one who had held onto her friendship, through some sort of emotional or physical need, in the face of her husband's surliness and rudeness. Henry had closed out everyone else in his compulsion to possess her completely.

Henry discovered that the face did not go away, even after the murder. He had thought that after the funeral was over (they sent flowers and sat on a hard pew through the services like two silent, bereaved mourners) the haunting features would be exorcised.

But they kept coming back and back; and he began to fear there

170                    ALFRED HITCHCOCK'S ANTHOLOGY

might be some trace, some evil talisman, that remained of Scott. He searched through Louise's things. He pawed through her old souvenirs and the mementos of her acting days and burned whatever he found. The picture was not among them.

It drove him frantic when he could not find the picture. He finally demanded of Louise that she tell him where it was and she replied calmly that she had destroyed it. He had a few hours of peace after that, and then the haunting face appeared again.

Was it the apartment then that held the restless ghost of the man he had killed? The terrace where he had pointed without apparent guile to something twelve stories below and then shoved Scott to his death? The livingroom where Louise had watched that drama of horror?

The idea of getting out of there began to possess him. In unfamiliar surroundings, both he and Louise could forget what had taken place that night. She was still shrinking from him. She had not let him make love to her since he had killed Scott Lansing, seeming to freeze with loathing when he touched her. She was spending more and more time with her mother, as though in the woman's presence she could return, for a little while, to the untroubled days of her girlhood.

Far away, he thought. If I can only get her far enough away so that the face cannot follow us.

The opportunity came so swiftly, so fortuitously, that it seemed as though a happy fate was working for Henry. He was offered a promotion, the position of district manager of his firm's middle west branch. It would mean a move to Chicago, more responsibility, a great deal more money.

Louise, of course, protested against the move at first. She did not want to leave her mother, what few friends she still had in New York; she hated the thought of a new city and its strangeness.

Henry drew on the best argument he knew.

"Your dear, gray-haired old mother!" he sneered. "The steel wire apron strings!"

"It's just that she's not well," Louise pleaded. "I have to think of that. I can't leave her all alone."

"Go on and think. Remember your lover and what led me to kill him. You want to tell her about that? If you don't, I'd be glad to. We'll see what that does to her health."

He could see in her eyes the reflection of what she was thinking. Stricken, she was realizing that he would go to any measures if she tried to thwart his proposed plans.

"Then what is there to say?" she asked hopelessly. "But promise me I can come back often to see her."

He promised, but they were empty, meaningless words which he spoke. They both knew that she would never return, that this was the beginning of a life in which there would be nobody except the two of them.

They left New York on the first day of spring in a raw, slashing rainstorm. Henry was a careful driver and the car, its back seat piled with the small articles Louise would not trust to the moving van, threaded through the rain-veiled traffic.

"Once the weather clears, we'll be able to see something of the countryside," Henry said, after they had crossed the George Washington Bridge. "We'll take our time. I don't have to report for a week yet. We'll stop when we feel like it, eat where we please. It'll be like a second honeymoon, just you and I together. This is the way I've always wanted it."

She shivered and shrank further into her heavy coat and did not answer him. He had to give her time, he realized. She'd come around gradually. Then he'd have it all—the money, the success, his wife all to himself. And nothing, nothing, nothing remained of Scott Lansing now. Truly and completely, he would be Scott free at last.

It was still raining by late afternoon. The poor visibility and wet-slicked roads made driving slow and difficult. Henry turned off the main highway in search of a motel. On that secondary road, they had to inch along in back of a lumbering truck. For miles the car remained blocked by that monstrous, slow-moving hulk in front of them.

Henry grew impatient. He swore under his breath, beat nervously on his horn. The truck finally drew over further to the side of the road and slowed down a little. With his foot on the gas pedal, Henry pulled out beyond the white line and they shot ahead toward a curve.

A twin dazzle of blinding brightness came rushing toward them at that moment. The oncoming car, traveling in the other direction, loomed directly in their path.

It was all over in a minute—the too-late shrieking of the brakes, the

172

crashing of steel and glass, the sickening impact which sent Henry hurtling through the windshield.

But he did not die. He exulted in that fact. When Louise, who had suffered only a few superficial injuries, came to his bedside, his first words were: "You and your talk about punishment! I guess, according to your standards of justice, this should have killed me. Well, I'm going to live. The doctor said so."

He could scarcely hear his own voice through the muffling of the bandages. But it was true. The doctor's words had been like the sweetest sort of music.

"It's a miracle, Mr. Tolman, but you will recover. We'll have you fixed up as good as new before too long."

Henry had to repeat that to Louise, even as difficult as it was for him to speak at all. "A miracle, that's what he said. It's supposed to be a word for saints and not for sinners!" he crowed.

She insisted that he stop talking then. Later, when she was spending more and more time in his room, she was gentle and quiet. As though, he told himself joyfully, she realized now how much he meant to her, having almost lost him.

Of course there was the irritating confinement of the hospital. The weeks spent in bed irked him and he was often testy with the nurses, sharp-tongued with the doctors. They seemed to be deliberately prolonging his stay, keeping him from his wife.

His doctor, the one who had been on his case since the accident, told him finally that the end was in sight. "It won't be too long before you're out of here. So what are you worrying about? Your job is safe, your wife took care of that. You have your health insurance to settle the bills. In any case, you couldn't return to work the way you are. We'll have to do something about your facial injuries," he said almost too casually.

That was how Henry learned that his face had been almost completely destroyed the night of the accident. And that plastic surgery would be necessary if he were not to be something people shuddered and ran from.

It was the only hope there was for him.

They all tried to reassure him, told him what wonders were being done these days in that field, that there would be no pain, no scars, and that he would look exactly as he always had when it was over.

Perhaps they thought he was afraid, the doctors and the solicitous nurses and even Louise, the silent, faithful one. He was not afraid of the knife. He had come to think of himself as a favorite of the gods, one of the charmed circle. He had got away with murder. He had come out of a horrifying car accident alive. Why should he be afraid of a little plastic surgery on his face?

He mumbled that to Louise, shortly after he'd had his pre-op medication, while he was waiting for them to take him upstairs.

"What's happened to your sweet little theory about crime and punishment?"

Then he clamped his teeth together tightly, resolved not to speak again until he came out of the anesthesia. That was the only thing which made him uneasy—worry that he might say something inadvertently while he was in the grip of a drug.

When it was over, the first thing he asked the nurse was if he had spoken while he was under anesthesia.

"Not a word," she assured him. "You were a doll, an ideal patient."

So there was that. His last vague worry had drifted away. . .

Louise was with him when they took off the bandages. She had brought along a hand mirror so that he could see the results of the surgery. She put it into his hand as he sat up in bed while the doctor and nurses stepped back to admire the surgeon's handiwork.

Henry put up a tentative hand to feel the soft, new skin. The doctor was instructing him about the application of a certain ointment until the skin became what he called "weathered."

"Because this is it now," he said. "Your face can't be worked on again, you know."

Henry muttered impatiently and lifted the mirror. And then he looked at his new face.

In that nightmarish moment, when the scream exploded from his throat, he knew. The realization burst in his inflamed brain. Louise had kept the photograph of Scott Lansing hidden all these months.

It was that picture the surgeons had worked from when they were building him a new face upstairs in the operating room.

It was Scott Lansing's face which stared back at Henry from the mirror.

# A Very Cautious Boy

## By Gilbert Ralston

Rosetti's Restaurant is tucked away in a remodeled brownstone on New York's 46th Street, close enough to Park Avenue to be considered a good address. Once, in the days of the Charleston and the blind pig, it was one of the town's plushier speakeasies. Now it has become one of the string of expensive character restaurants which dot the East Side.

Lee Costa took a moment to remember it as it was in the old days when Fat Joe Waxman owned it, keeping a fatherly eye out for the welfare of the young tenement boys who ran his less dubious errands, with particular solicitude for the developing skills of the brightest of these, one of whom was Costa.

His faith was not misplaced. Lee Costa had turned out well. Fat Joe would have been proud of him on this August night as he stood, a compact, ruggedly powerful man, amusing himself with nostalgic thoughts, quietly watching a group of opulent-looking customers enter the refurbished establishment.

Costa took another moment to look it over after he made his way past the door. The layout of the place was as he remembered it: a long bar running the length of one wall opposite a row of booths, a dining area, a check room at his right.

He stood for a moment in the entranceway near the reservation desk, pausing while a headwaiter made his way out of the gloom.

"I'm looking for Joe Rosetti," Costa said.

"Who shall I say is calling?"

"Tell him the insurance man is here."

"No name?"

"Just tell him. He'll know."

"You may wait in the bar, if you wish."

Costa crossed to the check room to leave his coat. As he turned to go toward the bar, he found his way blocked by the hulking form of one of the waiters. "C'mon," he said. "I'll take you up." He jerked a thumb at an ancient elevator in the corner of the room.

The Rosetti apartment was the only one on the fourth floor, the lock on the door opening with a muted buzz after the guide had pressed the doorbell. They entered a living room which spread across a large part of the side of the building, furnished simply and well, a group of heavy antiques giving it a comfortable feeling of old-fashioned luxury.

A rotund little man stood in the doorway of the room, examining Costa with a quizzical eye. "I'm Joe Rosetti," he said, his accent betraying his Italian parentage. He made no move to take Costa's hand, simply stood and looked at him, his head cocked a little to one side, a tiny frown of concentration on his forehead.

"You're smaller than I thought you'd be," he said. "Come in. Sit. You too, Ziggy." He held the door of the interior room open as Costa and his guide passed through. "Meet Lee Costa, Mama," he said. Across the room a tiny, dark woman raised her head, holding Costa's eyes with her own, searching his face. She sighed, the sound making a little explosive punctuation in the still room. "This is him?" she said.

Rosetti nodded his head.

She stared at Costa as she gathered up her knitting. "Take care of your business, Papa. After, we will eat." She left the room.

Ziggy stood up, looking down at Costa. "This guy bringing you some trouble?" he asked Rosetti.

Rosetti shook his head.

Costa's cold blue eyes were suddenly alert. "If I was bringing trouble, what would you do?"

"Throw you away somewhere," the big man said, taking a step toward him.

Costa turned to Rosetti. "Better chain up your ape." He turned a bland face to the standing man. "Back off, fat boy," he said calmly.

The man started for him, hands reaching for his lapels. As he bent over, Costa's foot shot out, catching him squarely in the midriff. He doubled over with an agonized gasp. Costa went to him, flipping him to the floor with a crash. "Sorry, Mr. Rosetti," Costa said. "He asked for it."

Rosetti leaned across his desk to look at the prone man writhing on the floor. "So fast," he said. "Like a snake."

"You're good at your job, Mr. Rosetti, I'm good at mine."

"He'll kill you," Rosetti said.

Costa shook his head. "No, he won't, Mr. Rosetti. He'll go downstairs and take care of the drunks. Won't you, Ziggy?"

On the floor, the man gasped for breath, turning his head like a wounded turtle. His eyes went to Costa's smiling face.

"Next time," Costa said, "I won't treat you so gently."

With an inarticulate grunt, the man staggered to his feet and out of the room.

"Why was Ziggy here, Mr. Rosetti?" Costa asked.

"I was afraid."

"Of me? You don't have to be. I'm a professional. I do what I'm paid for, nothing more."

Rosetti settled back in his chair, nervously.

"Go ahead, tell me about it," Costa said. "Our mutual friend said you had a problem."

"I have a problem. That's why I sent for you."

"Tell me the name of the problem, Mr. Rosetti."

"His name is Baxter. Roy Baxter."

"No other way to handle it?"

"I could pay."

"That doesn't usually work with a blackmailer," Costa said.

"You know about it?"

"Only what our friend told me. He said that someone was trying to shake you down."

Rosetti hesitated.

"Go ahead, Mr. Rosetti. You can trust me."

Rosetti looked away, his face working. "It was a long time ago. I killed a man. Baxter found out about it. He wants money. I know him. He won't stop. He'll never stop, if I pay. So I called our friend. I did him a favor once. A big one. Now he pays me back. With you."

"Have you told your wife?"

"She knows. But she don't talk."

"Anybody else know about me?"

"No. Just me, Mama and our friend." Rosetti reached into the drawer of his desk. "Here's the addresses for Baxter. His house. His business. A picture."

Costa glanced at the addresses. "What's his business?"

"He's a lawyer. Or says he is. I don't know how he makes his money. He's supposed to have some."

"Why does he want yours, then?"

"I don't know. Maybe he's got expenses."

"Expenses. I have them too," Costa said.

"I know. I can pay."

"Our friend said to give you the wholesale rate." Costa smiled at him again. "Could you afford five thousand?"

"Yes. What Baxter wants makes that sound like a bargain."

"How much time did he give you?"

"He said he would give me two weeks to raise twenty-five-thousand dollars. Then he goes to the police."

Costa stood, carefully tucking the papers into his pocket. "I'll look the situation over. Let you know."

Rosetti looked at him, his hands working. "Please," he said.

"I'm a very cautious boy, Mr. Rosetti. I'll check it out. Let you know." Costa let his eyes wander to the mounted tarpon over the mantel. "You're jumpy," he said. "Why don't you go fishing for a few days?"

Rosetti made a little wry grimace. "Me?" he said. "Every weekend I fish. All summer. Mama and I. Every weekend. We have a little boat. We live quiet. Run the restaurant. Fish. All of a sudden, I get a call from that Baxter. I don't fish. I don't run the restaurant. Just worry."

"I'll do what I can, Mr. Rosetti. Maybe you'll be fishing again soon."

Costa left the room, nodding pleasantly to Mama Rosetti as he passed her in the livingroom. She looked up, her sad little face following him. "You have your dinner?" she asked.

"Not yet."

"Come downstairs. We'll eat." She crossed to the door. "Coming, Papa?"

He appeared in the doorway. "Go eat," he said. "While I sleep."

"Cover up good, Papa," she said.

They sat in one of the booths in the restaurant, the little woman saying only a few words while they ate. Finally, after the coffee was served, she looked up at him.

"It is a sad thing," she said. "Papa is so afraid."

**ALFRED HITCHCOCK'S ANTHOLOGY**

"Are you?" Costa asked.

"Me? No, I am not afraid. What must be done, must be done. There is no other way. Always must a person fight. All his life. I know this."

"Don't worry about it. I will be very careful."

"Careful. Yes. I too am careful. You must be very sure."

"Don't worry, Mama Rosetti."

He rose to leave.

"You have a coat?"

"Yes. In the check room."

"Wrap up good," she said. "Don't catch cold."

Her black eyes followed him as he left the restaurant.

He made a routine check of the job the next morning. Baxter's office was on the West Side in a building on 56th Street. Costa arrived there a little before nine o'clock, losing himself in the crowd of incoming office employees, waiting at the end of the hall on the eleventh floor where he could see the entrance to Baxter's office. He was not pleased with the area. It was awkwardly arranged for a killing, with its manned elevators, people coming and going and too many late-hour businesses.

Baxter entered his office at nine-thirty, a dapper, squat individual, with the stub of a cigar clamped in his jaws. Costa waited another fifteen minutes in the hall, then entered the office, handing Baxter's secretary a card showing him to be the salesman for an office-supply company. He politely accepted the secretary's statement that Mr. Baxter was happy with his present supplier, and left, after a photographic glance at the interior of the office. He shook his head in dissatisfaction as he rode down in the elevator.

That afternoon he drove to Connecticut in a rented car, stopping at a real-estate agent's office close to the second address that Rosetti had given him for Baxter. The agent obligingly drove him through the area, rattling off the virtues of life in Connecticut as she did so. His examination of the Baxter house was made easier by the presence of a vacant house a few doors away, in which he indicated great interest. At his request, the agent drove him down the street while he examined the homes of his potential neighbors. Baxter's house was the last one in a group of six, an ostentatious modern facing the Sound, enclosed by a high brick wall. Costa stopped for a moment to study it.

The entrance was barred by an ornamental iron gate, a large "Beware of the Dog" sign across the corner of it . In the yard beyond the gate, a large boxer set up a frantic clamor at their approach.

Costa spent the rest of the afternoon as a prospective customer, thoroughly convincing the receptive agent that he was a transplanted executive named Zweller from a small business in Ohio, that his wife would arrive shortly, and that he would be back with her to buy a house. In the process, he was given a gratuitous rundown on the goings and comings of the local homeowners, including Baxter, who was known as a widower of quiet habits, currently living along, cared for by a Swedish couple who slept in town.

At six o'clock he was back at the Rosettis', seated in their living-room. Rosetti was planted in the chair behind his desk, Mama Rosetti across the room with her knitting.

Costa looked at the woman, then back to Rosetti. "I wanted to talk to you together," he said. "The job is possible. Only one thing about it I don't like."

"What don't you like?"

"I need a little insurance," Costa said.

Rosetti leaned toward him. "You mean you won't do it?"

"I mean I won't do it without help. I'll need you both."

Mama Rosetti folded her hands into her lap. "Make me understand," she said.

"I don't like his office for the job. Too busy. It'll have to be the house. And I won't drive to it."

He paused.

"So?" Rosetti said.

"So we go fishing this weekend. All three of us. I'll take care of the assignment while we're there. That will make you both accessories before and after the fact. Makes for a nice silent relationship in the future."

Rosetti turned to the woman. "Mama?" he said.

She looked at Costa for a long moment. Then she sighed, nodding her head slowly. "I think it is all right, Papa," she said. "It is a thing we have to do. I do not blame him for his caution."

Rosetti turned to Costa. "We will do it," he said. "We have no choice."

"We have a deal," Lee Costa said.

"What must we do?" Rosetti asked.

"Pick me up Saturday morning at the gas dock at City Island. Gas the boat. I'll come aboard while the attendant's busy." Costa rose to leave. "After that, I'll tell you where to go. Leave the rest to me."

"Wrap up good," Mama Rosetti said. "Don't catch cold."

Lost in a crowd of yachtsmen and guests, Costa was an unobtrusive figure as he waited on the public dock the following Saturday. He watched quietly while the Rosettis arrived on a small cruiser, edging to the dock. Then he worked his way through a crowd of noisy fishermen and stepped aboard, moving into the cabin while Rosetti kept the harassed attendant busy. Minutes later, they were moving toward the Connecticut shore, Rosetti at the wheel, Costa beside him, Mama Rosetti at her endless knitting in a wicker chair.

Early in the afternoon, they anchored the boat in the sheltered area around the point of the peninsula on which the Baxter house rested.

"What now?" Rosetti asked nervously.

"Eat. Fish. Be a playboy," Costa said.

"You hungry?" Mama Rosetti asked.

"A little."

"All right, I make dinner. Now, you fish with Papa."

At six o'clock she called to them from the cabin door. "Come downstairs," she called. "We'll eat."

"Below, Mama," Rosetti said. "Not downstairs."

"Downstairs," she said. "You're the sailor. I'm the cook."

It was a tense meal, Rosetti stopping to look nervously at Costa, Mama Rosetti silent and occupied with serving them from the galley stove.

Costa rested on one of the bunks for half an hour afterwards, arising to find the questioning eyes of the Rosettis on him again. "I'm going for a little swim," he said.

Mama Rosetti reached out a small brown hand, patted his arm. "Be careful," she said.

He smiled down at her. "I'm always careful," he said. "I'm a very cautious boy."

He disappeared into the cabin, appearing a few minutes later in swimming trunks and the top half of a skindiver's wet suit. He stood for a moment near the stern, placed a black rubber hood on his head, flippers on his feet, worked mask and snorkel into place and dropped softly into the water. He checked the collar of his wet suit to be sure that the small plastic bag he had tucked there was still in place, felt for the rubber gloves attached to his belt and swam slowly toward the shore, slipping smoothly through the black water, the rubber suit and flippers giving him enough buoyancy to conserve his strength.

A half-hour later, he stopped a few feet away from the end of the Baxter dock, then drifted in until he could rest his weight on the bottom. He reached again under the collar of his suit, pulled out the bag, opened it, carefully keeping the piece of meat it contained out of the water. He gave a low whistle, waiting while the dog's feet made a rhythmic thumping on the dock. He threw the meat almost at the feet of the dog, whose barking echoed along the quiet beach. Then he slipped back to deep water again, floating, head low in the water, breathing through his snorkel, head down, virtually invisible from the shore. The barking grew louder.

A moment later, the robed figure of Baxter came out onto the upstairs porch, flashlight in hand. After a careful examination of the yard, he called down to silence the dog. Costa waited.

After Baxter returned to his room, the dog nosed around the end of the dock restlessly, then turned to give his attention to the meat. Costa could see the outline of the animal as he nuzzled it, hear the ugly little sounds as he gulped it down. He waited while an agonized whine came from the dog, his frantic feet drumming on the dock. When the sound stopped, Costa floated in again, gave another low whistle. There was no reaction from the dog. Costa stuck his head up cautiously. The animal was lying near the edge of the dock. Costa pulled off the mask and flippers, then pulled the body of the dog into the shadow cast by the boathouse. A tiny portion of the meat was still on the wooden floor of the dock. Carefully, he picked it up and threw it into the sea, returning to the shadowed area to wait patiently for a long half-hour, pleased when the servants appeared at the back door on schedule to climb into a station wagon. They drove away, the gate closing automatically after them.

Costa let the sound of the disappearing car die out before he got out of his swimming gear and moved to the balustrade of the porch. Slowly, he snaked up it, slipping over the edge of the upstairs rail

ALFRED HITCHCOCK'S ANTHOLOGY

soundlessly, lying on the floor of the porch a good ten munutes before he moved again. On his belly, he slipped the gloves on his hands, after which he wormed his way to the edge of the French windows. They were open. Two minutes later, he was standing over the sleeping form of Roy Baxter. Costa braced his feet. His hands fastened to the throat of the sleeping man. Costa held on for a long time, then stripped the glove from his right hand to check the pulse of the body in the bed. Satisfied that Baxter was dead, he placed the glove on his hand again and left the way he had come.

At the dock, he replaced the swimming gear, pulled the dog's body to the edge of the dock and dropped with it into the water. He stopped to estimate the direction of the Rosetti boat before he towed the dog's body well out into the Sound, releasing it where the outgoing tide would carry it away. He worked his way slowly and easily back to the boat, letting the tide aid him in the long swim. As he approached it, he could see the Rosettis sitting in the stern cockpit.

"Costa?" Rosetti called.

"Coming in," Costa said. He handed them the flippers and the mask, climbing over the edge of the cockpit almost at the feet of the Rosettis. "It's done," he said.

Mama Rosetti looked at him, her black eyes inscrutable in the soft light.

"No trouble."

"No trouble."

"Take off those wet clothes. You'll freeze to death."

Costa went into the cabin, peeled out of the rubber jacket, dried his head, put on slacks and a sweater and returned to the Rosettis.

Mama Rosetti was back in her wicker chair, her hands busy again with the knitting. From somewhere Papa Rosetti had pulled out a bottle of wine.

"Here," he said to Costa. "Drink." He poured three glasses.

They drank. For a long time Mama Rosetti studied Costa's face. "Everything all right, huh?" she said.

"Worked fine," Lee Costa said. "Nobody saw me. Nobody knows I'm here. Nobody knows what happened. Except you and me."

"You shoot him?" Rosetti asked.

"I don't use guns," Costa said. "These are good enough." He held up a hard hand, pointed to the rim of calluses on the edge of his palm.

Rosetti stood and went to the cabin door. "I'm tired, Mama."

She looked over at him, her face warm with concern. "Cover up good, Papa. Sleep well." She turned to Costa. "You too, Mr. Costa. You need to go to bed."

Costa rose, standing on the deck of the boat to stretch. "Nice night, isn't it?" he said, smiling down at her.

"Yes," she said, pulling an ugly little automatic out from under her knitting. "A very nice night." She shot him, twice, over the heart. Costa's body was thrown backwards, hitting the water with a soft splash. Mama Rosetti leaned over the rail of the boat, the pistol in her hand, while she watched the body sink, as it slowly moved away with the tide.

"What now, Mama?" Rosetti's head was sticking out of the cabin door.

She turned to him gravely. "Nothing more." She threw the pistol over the side. "Cover up good, Papa. Don't catch cold."

ALFRED HITCHCOCK'S ANTHOLOGY

# A Try for the Big Prize

### by Borden Deal

Blake was a cop. He had been a cop for a very long time. He had forgotten how to quit being a cop and so he worked at the job twenty-four hours of every day. Even now, relaxed in front of the TV set on his day off, a glass of beer at his side, somewhere far back under his conscious mind a desk sergeant toiled, a mug man flipped pictures, a traffic cop ticked off license plates. So Blake recognized the man on the TV screen.

Blake had felt himself lucky that the pro championship game was coming on his day off—and that it was being televised at all, instead of blacked out locally. He had missed a lot of the football games, of course, and he had half-expected to miss this one. But he hadn't known just how lucky he was going to be.

It had been a good game, tight all the way, with the kind of thumping line play that Blake particularly liked to watch. The lead had changed hands a couple of times and now it was all tied up again. The camera swung down over the crowd and the announcer said, "And here's part of the vast turn-out for this great game." It was then that Blake saw him.

Blake was a big man, cop-size, with a shambling walk and bulky shoulders. He had played football himself, in high school, though he hadn't been able to go on to college like he had wanted to. There weren't as many football scholarships in those days. He had always thought of going on to college and then into the pros, where the real football playing took place, where you had to be a man to stay in that line. But it hadn't worked out that way; Blake had become a cop instead.

He had been a good cop. He had started out on the traffic detail. In those days, he had made a habit of scanning the lists of stolen cars—

their makes, models and license number—each morning before reporting for duty. In his rookie year, he had spotted and turned in more stolen cars than any other man on the force.

He had a trick memory for names, numbers and faces. He still remembered the telephone number of the first girl he had ever dated, his serial number during the war, the face of the first criminal he had ever arrested. Later, after he was off traffic, he began spending time in the mug room, looking at pictures. As he had worked his way up the ladder of promotion, as the years slowly bruised his big frame, as the old dream of football glory faded into an avid spectator-interest in the sport, he had several times a year spotted a wanted man—on the street, in a crowd, on a circus lot, serving hot dogs, running an elevator. He had never been wrong; and so this time he was also sure.

Blake was a gray man with a heavy pale-gray face. He had never married; he had always lived alone. And his associates had for a long time been wary and respectful of his self-contained silences, of his fabled memory for the face of a criminal, of the man himself in all his totality. For years now he had been a full detective, having gone as far as a man with his education and attainments could hope to go.

Blake stood up out of the chair. Automatically his mind had noted the exit ramp near the man he had seen, so that he would know where he was seated in the stands. FF. Out of the hole into the football sunshine, turn to the left, and there he would be—if he was still there—if the game was not already over.

The game was coming close to an end now. As he put on his shoes and stood up, strapping on his shoulder holster, Blake considered the problem. He couldn't possibly make it to the stadium if the game ended on schedule. There would have to be a tie and a sudden death play-off to give him a chance at all. His best bet would be to call the precinct, report the presence of the wanted man, let them stake out the stadium and pick him up.

His lips tightened. Blake knew the man, knew his whole history, though he had seen only a snapshot taken through a telephoto lens. He would take a chance on the sudden death playoff. This one was for Blake, not for the force. Blake had always been a loner and he would play this one alone. If the game ended and the man was gone . . . He shrugged his shoulders. It was a chance he would have to take—and he would know to keep looking for him, know he was still in town.

186

He was going out of the door of his two-room apartment by the time the thinking was ending, leaving the television set on behind him. He went down and got into his car, immediately switching the radio to the ball game. He backed out into the street and headed across town toward the football stadium. He fought the traffic with a steady remorseless determination to arrive before the game ended. The plan of the city was firm in his mind, too, and he worked his way through the fastest routes, the least traffic, that he could find.

On the radio, the game was going on, drawing towards its close, and it was still tied. The sound of the crowd in the speaker was tense and thrilling and Blake wondered if the man was yelling with them. Or had he felt panic, with the deep criminal instinct of his kind, had he already left the game? No, he would not want to leave except in the cloaking of the crowd. And, besides, he must be a good fan himself.

Blake was caught by a traffic light, eased to a stop. He heard the roar of the crowd, the excited voice of the announcer. A long pass had been thrown, a football hero had galloped with the ball to a touchdown, and one of the teams was leading. Not Blake's team —the other. Blake gritted his teeth. Come on, boys, he said in his mind. Get it back. Tie it up. Put it into overtime.

He lurched into speed as the light changed, listening to the crowd, listening to the chanting of the announcer. There was the kickoff and he leaned forward, praying for a long runback. But the man was smeared on the fifteen-yard line as he fumbled the ball and then fell on it. Blake cursed. There was only a minute left in the game and he was not going to be in time.

The minute ticked on. There was an incomplete pass, a time out, another incomplete pass. Then the quarterback completed a pass and the receiver stepped out of bounds, stopping the clock. Time for one more play, two at the most. Blake gripped his hands on the steering wheel.

He should have phoned in, instead of taking it on himself. He slid through an amber light just before it changed to red, felt the caress of luck in his mind. Then the quarterback was fading, they were after him, they were red-dogging him. He almost fell down, he ran out of the pocket, he threw long . . . long . . . he'd got it . . . he was over for a touchdown! The extra-point kick and then the whistle blew, ending the game.

Blake leaned back, pursing his lips and whistling through them. It was his now. Just as he had felt in the instant of seeing the man's face he had seen only once before, in a telephoto snapshot—this one belonged to Blake.

He relaxed, driving on to the stadium. There was time now. A few minutes before the play-off started. He could think beyond arriving, beyond spotting the man in the flesh. The whole eastern seaboard, if not the whole country, had been looking for him for six weeks, with only a telephoto snapshot to go on. No wonder he had been cool enough, sure enough, to take his pleasure at a championship football game. Blake, the first time he had studied the single blurred picture, had known that this man was not in any mug book he had ever studied. He was the hardest of all to catch, a freelance criminal who had never fallen, never served time, never been mugged and fingerprinted. He had either been very, very lucky or he had planned the one big caper for his first and last venture.

Blake had had to admire the operation. The kidnap victim had been a man with plenty of money, who would not be likely to cooperate with the police, a man who wouldn't want the police or the FBI prying too closely into his own affairs. Not a wanted man, only a dubious man who operated close to the fringe of the law. The pickup had been executed smoothly, the ransom arranged quickly, the victim released even before the ransom was paid, turned loose in a wooded countryside miles from any communication. The kidnaper had gotten his money and made a clean getaway. The only thing the police had on him was the telephoto shot taken at the moment of payoff. Blake had a taste for neat, clean operations and this was one of the finest of its type. He had gotten away with it. The case was dying now, six weeks after the payoff and not a sign of the kidnaper, nothing for the police to go on. But the kidnaper had not figured on Blake's memory for names and figures and faces.

Blake stopped the car in the stadium parking lot, got out, and hurried to the exit. He flashed his badge and went inside, trudging up the long ramp to entrance FF. He did not even glance at the uniformed policeman on duty at the entrance of the ramp. He was breathing hard by the time he reached the tunnel opening and the sights and sounds of football smote on his ears like a blow. They were playing again and the crowd was standing on its feet, wild with excitement.

　　　　　　　　　　　　　　ALFRED HITCHCOCK'S ANTHOLOGY

Blake waited until a couple of vendors exited from the tunnel; then he followed them out. He turned to the left, climbed the stairs a step or two, stopped and looked at the field. There were no empty seats, so he stood close to a row of seats to blend with the crowd. A player was running with the football. Then he was tackled, swarmed over as he tried to get around the end.

Blake turned his head, looking for the man. The sight of him was a shock, even to Blake's hardened nerves. Blake let his eyes drift on over him, before he looked again at the football field. Now he knew the man, in every detail.

He was young, not over thirty-five. He had a compact, muscular body, a face that was very ordinary, a good kind of face for a criminal to own. He was wearing a blue overcoat, in the medium price range, and under it a blue suit. Blake suspected there was a gun in the armpit, though he couldn't be sure because of the overcoat. The man had tan gloves on his hands and he was very excited with the ball game. He looked as though he had once played football himself.

The game went on in the sudden death play-off. But Blake had lost interest. He only wanted it to end now. He was engaged in a greater game than even football could be. He was surprised to find that feeling inside himself. He had never before felt that way. But now, suddenly, he did, and he knew why. There was a great deep calmness inside him, a sureness of the chances.

There was a long surging roar as a man sprinted for the goal line, breaking out of the ruck of blocking and tackling with an almost miraculous ease, and the game was over. The crowd whooped and yelled and threw things onto the field. Out of the corner of his eye, Blake saw his man begin edging toward the exit.

Blake went down the steps, got into the exit ahead of him. He went on down the ramp in the first jostling fringe of the throng without looking over his shoulder, knowing there was no other way out, and got outside the gate. He found his car quickly; then he turned his head, scanning the crowd, watching for his man. There he was, walking quickly into the parking area. Blake leaned over his wheel and started the motor. This was going to be the difficult part, with the crowd and the traffic. If he could keep from losing him here . . .

The man got into a compact car and pulled out into the exit lane just in front of Blake. That was lucky. There was nothing between them.

Blake was riding his luck today; it was deep and calm and certain inside him. For the first time in his life, he felt absolutely and completely right.

It had been so long in coming. First there had been football, the tedious and painful learning and then the sudden ending of playing the game after high school. He had started all over again on the police force, the slow and tedious learning, the grinding single-minded application, the slow, slow climb toward the top with the years moving just as slowly over him. He had reached the limit on the force also without reaching the peak, and now the years were ending on him. He had known for a long time that he had gone as far as he could go, just as he had known it about football. It was only three months until mandatory retirement age.

He was swinging smoothly behind the compact car as it threaded into the city. The man was driving sedately. He was a loner, as Blake was a loner. Loner pitted against loner. The payoff would be . . .?

It was a nice, quiet residential area where the man stopped the car. This was intelligent too. The man obviously didn't associate on the criminal level. That was why he had never been mugged, why his caper had been so spectacularly successful. He had not tried to skip after the ransom payoff, but had stayed quietly in his snug deceptive covering.

The man stopped the car before a medium-sized apartment house. Blake parked down the street from him, got out, and began walking toward the man, looking at the fronts of the apartment houses as though searching for a number. The man was locking his car carefully, meticulously, checking the windows to be sure they were all up. Blake was opposite him as the man came around to the sidewalk.

Blake, in a sudden movement, crowded him against the side of the car. "All right," he said. "You're under arrest."

The man tried to whirl away, but Blake jabbed the gun into his ribs, gripped his arm with the other hand.

"Hold it," he said. "Or I'll splatter you all over the sidewalk."

The man was pale. Blake looked around quickly. Their little flurry had not been noted on the quiet street.

"Quick," Blake said. "Into the building."

They walked quickly into the lobby, Blake holding the man's arm tightly in his big hand.

"Which floor do you live on?"

"Fifth," the man said.

They got into the self-service elevator and Blake punched the fifth-floor button. The door slid closed and the elevator whined slightly as it began to rise. Blake crowded the man against the elevator wall, slipped his hand inside the man's coat. He took out the thirty-two, looked at it, put it into his overcoat pocket. The man leaned against the elevator wall. Their breathing was loud in the quietness.

"Are you a cop?" the man said.

"Yes," Blake said. "I'm a cop."

The elevator door slid open and they stepped out into the hall.

"Which door?"

"Number seven."

They went down the carpeted hall. The building murmured with people, but the hall was empty. They stopped in front of number seven.

"Anybody in there?" Blake said.

The man shook his head.

"If there is, you're dead," Blake said. "Remember that. Now I'll ask you again."

"I live alone," the man said. "The place's empty."

"Open it."

The man reached slowly into his pocket for the key, opened the door, and they went inside. The man tried to swing the door against Blake and Blake slugged him, sending him to the floor. The man rolled, moaning, then sat up.

"Say, what is this?" he said.

Blake ignored him. "Get the coat off."

The man struggled out of the overcoat and Blake kicked it to one side. He leaned down, lifted the man, and shook him down thoroughly. He took out the handcuffs, snapped them on. Then he stepped back, looking the man full in the face.

"Where's the money?" Blake said.

"Look," the man said, his voice rising, "you're not acting like any cop I ever heard of. Are you—?"

"Yes," Blake said calmly. "I am. I've been a cop for thirty years. But I'm not taking you in."

Blake was as startled by his words as the other man was. They had sprung out of his depths, where they had been building slowly, inevitably, from the moment he had recognized the man on television.

Blake stood still, examining what he had said, and he knew that it was the truth. All of his life he had been looking for the big one. First, he had thought to find it in football. Then he had thought to find it, somehow, on the force. But over the years, the thought and the desire had submerged itself in the day-to-day routine, in the pride of being a good cop, in his own special talent for recognition and remembering. But all the time it had been there.

A man can surprise himself any day of his life. Blake had thought the old ambition was gone, bruised out of him by event and circumstance, sublimated as his desire to play championship football had been sublimated. Just as he liked to watch football, so too did he like to read about the big scores: the baseball player getting the top salary for the year, the financier cleaning up through a control fight for a big company. For days, weeks, he had been as excited by the Brinks robbery as another man might be by a woman.

The man drew a long ragged breath. His face had changed, his whole posture. "I see," he said slowly. "I see." They were no longer facing each other as cop and criminal; there was a sudden subtle alteration in their relationship, so that they were man and man, equal in their common hunger.

Blake smiled. "That was a pretty cute operation you pulled," he said. "Waited a long time for it, didn't you? Worked it out as careful as a football play. No known criminal record—striking for the top money the first time, instead of starting out on peanuts like most guys do. I've got to admire you."

"Thanks," the man said drily.

"Now I want the money."

There was no doubt of it. There had not been any doubt of it since he had strapped on his gun and started out of the apartment. Mentally, Blake stood back and admired himself. He felt, suddenly, twenty years younger, bigger than himself. He had thought that the old lust had ebbed out of him. But he was not finished yet, as they all thought he was finished. When he retired in three months, he would retire full of the secret knowledge of his victory over them all, over all the years, all the disappointments, all the men who had climbed past him to greater heights.

192                                 ALFRED HITCHCOCK'S ANTHOLOGY

The man shook his head. Blake slapped him in the face with his hard, jarring palm.

"Don't talk back to me, son," he said in a low, hard voice. "I've waited a long time too. Longer than you have."

"What kind of cop are you, anyway?"

"I'm a good cop," Blake said. "I've been a good cop ever since I've been on the force. I've kept clean. I've never taken a bribe. I've never looked the other way. I've gone through more investigations and shake-ups then you can dream of, and they've never had a chance to lay a finger on me."

The man nodded. "Now you're going for the big one."

Blake nodded too. "Just like you, buddy-boy," he said. "I'm going for the two hundred thousand you took Johnny Roth for."

"Look," the man said. "I worked for the money. Five years I planned and watched. When Johnny Roth got into that congressional investigation bind so he couldn't kick too much, I went after him. I earned that money."

"I've waited too," Blake said. "Waited longer than you can even think of. I've put in the time. I've turned down a thousand small chances, waiting for the big one. We're just alike, buddy-boy. Except I've got the handcuffs on you, now, like you had them on Johnny Roth. Where's the money?"

The man shook his head. Blake pushed him down into a chair, leaned over him. "What's your name?"

The man glared up at him. Blake caught his coat, looked inside at the label. Then he picked up the overcoat, looked at it. He prowled the apartment, found a desk, opened it and picked up an address book, looking inside the cover. Then he looked at the man.

"Ronald O'Steen," he said. "Say, didn't you play football?"

O'Steen didn't move.

"Sure," Blake said. "You played left half for Midwestern a few years ago. Did pretty good too." He stopped looking at O'Steen. "I played a little football in my time."

O'Steen looked up at him. He shrugged his shoulders. "Sure," he said. "I played out there."

Blake studied him. "Didn't football pay off for you, either?" he said. "You did better than I did. I didn't even get to college."

O'Steen's mouth twisted. "I was too light for the pros," he said. "I tried out, the year I finished, but they dropped me."

"So you went for the big one."

"Yes. I went for the big one."

"Where is it?"

"I'm not going to tell you."

"Yes," Blake said quietly. "You're going to tell me. Is it here in the apartment?"

O'Steen did not answer. Blake waited.

"All right," he said. "I'm going to try to make it light on you. If I can find it by myself, okay. If I can't, I'm going to lean on you until you tell me where it is."

He unlocked one of the handcuffs, pulled O'Steen to his feet. He led him to the bed, pushed him over backward, and snapped the handcuff around the bedpost. He left him there and began methodically tearing up the apartment.

He worked silently for a long time, with O'Steen watching him. When he was through, the apartment was a shambles. But he hadn't uncovered the money. He pulled O'Steen off the bed and took that apart, too, before he stopped, panting.

"All right," he said at last. "I guess it's going to be the hard way." O'Steen looked up at him, his face flinching. "Don't think you can hold out," Blake said. "I'm an expert, O'Steen. And I'll kill you with my bare hands for that money. You know that. Because you'd kill me for it."

"Look," O'Steen said. "Why don't you just be a hero and take me in? That ought to be enough for you."

Blake shook his head. "Not any more," he said. "I'm too old now. I'm coming up for mandatory retirement in three months. If I was a younger man . . . but I'm not." He advanced on O'Steen. "All right," he said. "Here we go."

He worked as diligently as he had worked in tearing up the apartment. O'Steen whimpered and grunted with the pain, his teeth tightly clenched. Blake remembered that he might have to take O'Steen out of the apartment to get the money, so he stayed away from the face. He stopped when O'Steen passed out. He went into the bathroom. He drank a glass of water, brought back a full glass and threw it into O'Steen's face. O'Steen moaned, coming out of it.

Blake stared down at him. O'Steen was a tough one, all right. Blake

194                                    ALFRED HITCHCOCK'S ANTHOLOGY

had not seen many men who could take what Blake had just given him.

"You're a pretty good boy," Blake said.

O'Steen's mouth twisted wryly. "Thanks a lot."

"What are you holding out for?" Blake said. "You know I can keep this up all night if necessary."

O'Steen began levering himself up off the floor, his face wincing with the pain of his body. He sat down in the chair and looked at Blake across the two feet of space that separated them.

"I'm not going to give it all up," he said. "You can kill me before I'll give it all up. I worked too hard. I wanted it too much . . ."

Blake recognized the truth in this. "All right," he said "I'll split it with you. One hundred thousand for each of us. Half is enough for me, if it's enough for you."

They stared at each other. Their relationship was changing again. It had shifted subtly, constantly, since the moment of their meeting. First, briefly, it had been cop and criminal; then it had been man and man; then torturer and tortured. Now it was becoming something neither of them could immediately define.

Blake saw the sudden decision come into O'Steen's face.

"All right," O'Steen said. "I know when to cut the take. We'll split it fifty-fifty." He tried to smile again, but it was not much of a smile. "I just wish you'd made your proposition before working me over."

"I had to see whether you'd hold together or not," Blake said coldly. "Just like you had to see whether I'd hold together for it too. We couldn't have made the deal before."

O'Steen nodded his head. They understood each other. All the way through, all the way down.

"Where is it?" Blake said.

"In a safety deposit box."

"Where's the key? I was looking for a key."

O'Steen smiled. "It's in the envelope," he said. "In my mail slot downstairs."

"Then we can't get the money until tomorrow," Blake said. "The bank's closed now."

"That's right."

"We'll wait."

"Can you stay awake all night?" O'Steen said. "I'll kill you if I get a chance. You know that."

"I can stay awake," Blake said stolidly.

The long night passed slowly in the ripped-apart apartment. Blake sat in a chair, watching O'Steen in the other chair. For awhile, desultorily, they talked, and O'Steen told how he had planned to wait six months, then take a Far Eastern cruise on a tourist ship. In the Far East, it would be easy to make a deal on the hot money.

"You can still do that," Blake said. "With your half."

"If you let me," O'Steen said wearily.

"I don't care what you do afterward," Blake said. "In fact, I'll help you when it's time to go. I don't want you caught, either."

Blake did not call in the next morning, though he was on duty for the day. The captain was used to Blake failing to call in or come in, occasionally; he would assume that Blake had a live one. The captain had implicit faith in Blake and his abilities, though he had never understood him.

When it was time to go, Blake took the handcuffs off, waited while O'Steen put on his overcoat.

"Remember," Blake said, "if you make a break, I'll shoot you down. I can always claim I was making an arrest. You don't have an out, except dividing the money."

"I know that," O'Steen said. He looked at Blake. "I'd just like to know how you caught me."

Blake smiled. "I've got a talent," he said. "I never forget a face. They got a snap of you on the payoff. I was watching television yesterday and I saw you in the crowd."

O'Steen took a deep breath. "A long chance like that," he said. "I lost on a chance like that."

"If you hadn't been a fool about football, I wouldn't have caught you," Blake said. "If I hadn't been a fool about football too."

O'Steen shrugged. "I should have got you on the operation from the start," he said. "We'd operate well together."

"Yes," Blake said. "Too bad it didn't work out that way."

They went out the door, down the elevator, and got into Blake's car. Blake made O'Steen drive the short way to the bank. They went inside the bank, shoulder to shoulder, and Blake watched O'Steen sign the register. They went together into the vault and Blake waited while O'Steen and the bank clerk unlocked the box. Then the bank clerk went away and O'Steen pulled the deep box out. Blake watched hungrily as he reached inside and pulled out the thick pad of bills. O'Steen handed them to Blake who put them into an airline satchel they had brought along from the apartment. It was the same satchel that had shown in the photograph of O'Steen taking the payoff.

Then they locked the safety deposit box, went side by side out of the bank and sat in the car. It had gone as smoothly as a well-executed draw play and Blake wondered why both of them were sweating so hard.

"Back to the apartment," he said.

They returned by another route, at circumspect speed, and parked the car. They got out and went upstairs, both of them breathing with relief as the door closed behind them. They felt almost partners in danger, instead of antagonists.

"Well, we made it," O'Steen said. "You still going to split with me?"

"Sure," Blake said.

He put the satchel on the chair, unzipped the zipper. He stared at the money, his breath caught. It was the big payoff he had been looking for all his life. Only now, in the last days of his long police service, had it come to him. It had been a sudden death play-off for sure.

He caught a flicker of movement out of the corner of his eye. He whirled, but it was too late. O'Steen had tackled him low and hard. The gun flew out of Blake's hand and he crashed to the floor, O'Steen on top of him. Blake slugged at O'Steen with one hand, whirled him over on the bottom. O'Steen was too light to resist the bulk and weight of Blake. He hit O'Steen again, felt O'Steen's fist smash into his face. He bore down with his greater weight as O'Steen's body surged against him, leaning on his struggling violence, and the thinking was clear and sharp in his mind, as though he were talking to O'Steen aloud.

I was going to kill you when we got the money. Then I decided not to. Because you're me, and I'm you. But now I know I've got to kill you. For that same reason. Because you're me. You'd come after me and the money.

It was clear and loud and hard in his mind and he turned his head so he wouldn't see what his hands were doing. He stood up at last from the limp body and his breath was a long hard sob of sound when it caught again. He was weeping. Blake had never wept in his adult life;

not since he had broken his collarbone in a football game.

He looked dully at the money, knowing it was all his. He took a long slow step towards it, reaching for it with both hands.

There was a burst of sound at the door and he whirled around. The door was splintering off its hinges as men's shoulders slammed against it and Blake reached for the gun that wasn't there. Then he recognized the men. They were precinct men, and behind them was the captain. Blake stood still, watching them as they swarmed into the room.

"We heard you fighting," the captain told Blake. "We got in here as soon as we could. Why didn't you tell me you had a lead on this case?"

"Heard us fighting?" Blake said dully. His mind moved sluggishly, frozenly. "You had the place staked out all the time?"

The captain laughed. "The FBI got us onto him. They did it the hard way. They decided he looked like an athlete, so they started checking newspaper pictures for boxers and football players about the time he would've been playing. We just started the stake-out yesterday, hoping he'd lead us to the money. Looks like we'd have had a long wait without you."

Blake watched the young dapper stranger, who surely was the FBI agent, examine the money satchel. The FBI agent gestured to one of the policemen. "Take charge of this money," he said. He turned, looked at Blake. He had cold, suspicious eyes. "It was quite a surprise when you checked into the apartment with him," he said. "But the captain insisted you had to have a chance to make your play."

Blake looked at the money the FBI man was holding in the zipper bag. He put his hand into his coat and then he remembered that the gun was on the floor.

The captain chuckled. "You played it smart," he said. "You made him think you were just after the money. You let him think it was a heist instead of an arrest. Smart, Blake, damned smart."

Blake stared at him, not understanding the words.

The captain jerked a thumb at the agent. "This FBI guy here thought you were serious about the money," he said. "He wanted to come on in, but I wouldn't let him. Hell, I knew you knew what you were doing. He'd never have told where the money was otherwise. He was too tough. I told this guy we could depend on you."

Blake stood stunned in the middle of the room. The precinct men swarmed around him, busy with their duties of tidying up the case, nailing it down.

"We tailed you to the bank this morning," the FBI agent said. His eyes were still cold, hard, intent. "When we saw you didn't head for the precinct station straight from the bank, we couldn't figure it. But your captain just kept on waiting for you. Why did you come back here, anyway?"

Blake was too stunned to grasp the danger. He merely shook his head, mumbling the words. "I had to make sure of the money," he said. "I had to be sure it was all there." He turned his head, looked at the dead man. "I didn't want to kill him."

The captain slapped him on the shoulder. "Always tying down the details," he said. "Take-no-chances-Blake, that's you. Snap out of it, man. Too bad you had to kill him when he went for you. Why, you'll be a hero now. There'll be newspaper guys at the precinct, photographers, the whole works. Why, it's your greatest case, Blake. That's why I let you take the play all the way, so you wouldn't lose any of the glory. How does it feel to be a hero?"

"Great," Blake said. "Just great." He looked at the FBI agent, recognized the residual suspicion. But there was no danger there. It was only a suspicion and the agent could never make more of it than that in the midst of the captain's faith. Blake smiled a weak smile. "When I retire," he said, "I can sit and read all my clippings. Over and over and over again."

He went on out of the apartment. He would go home now, and sleep. He needed sleep. Tomorrow there would be reporters and excitement at the precinct station and he would have to live through it all. But now he only wanted sleep. He was an old man and he needed all the sleep that he had missed.

# Killed by Kindness

## by Nedra Tyre

John Johnson knew that he must murder his wife. He had to. It was the only decent thing he could do. He owed her that much consideration.

Divorce was out of the question. He had no grounds. Mary was kind and pretty and pleasant company and hadn't ever glanced at another man. Not once in their marriage had she nagged him. She was a marvelous cook and an excellent bridge player. No hostess in town was more popular.

It seemed a pity that he would have to kill her. But he certainly wasn't going to shame her by telling her he was leaving her; not when they'd just celebrated their twentieth anniversary two months before and had congratulated each other on being the happiest married couple in the whole world. With pink champagne, and in front of dozens of admiring friends, they had pledged undying love. They had said they hoped fate would be kind and would allow them to die together. After all that John couldn't just toss Mary aside. Such a trick would be the action of a cad.

Without him Mary would have no life at all. Of course she would have her shop, which had done well since she had opened it, but she wasn't a real career woman. Opening the shop had been a kind of lark when the Greer house, next door to them in a row of town houses, had been put up for sale. No renovation or remodeling had been done except to knock down part of a wall so that the two houses could be connected by a door. The furniture shop was only something to occupy her time, Mary said, while her sweet husband worked. It didn't mean anything to her, though she had a good business sense. John seldom went in the shop. Come to think of it, it was a jumble. It made him a little uneasy; everything in it seemed so crowded and precarious.

Yes, Mary's interest was in him; it wasn't in the shop. She'd have to have something besides the shop to have any meaningful existence

If he divorced her she'd have no one to take her to concer.s   d plays. Dinner parties, her favorite recreation, would be out. None of their friends would invite her to come without him. Alone and divorced, she would be shunted into the miserable category of spinsters and widows who had to be invited to lunch instead of dinner.

He couldn't relegate Mary to such a life, though he felt sure that if he asked her for a divorce she'd give him one. She was so acquiescent and accommodating.

No, he wasn't going to humiliate her by asking for a divorce. She deserved something better from him than that.

If only he hadn't met Lettice on that business trip to Lexington. But how could he regret such a miracle? He had come alive only in the six weeks since he'd known Lettice. Life with Mary was ashes in comparison. Since he'd met Lettice he felt like a blind man who had been given sight. He might have been deaf all his life and was hearing for the first time. And the marvel was that Lettice loved him and was eager to marry him, and free to marry him.

And waiting.

And insisting.

He must concentrate on putting Mary out of the way. Surely a little accident could be arranged without too much trouble. The shop ought to be an ideal place, there in all that crowded junk. Among those heavy marble busts and chandeliers and andirons something from above or below could be used to dispatch his dear Mary to her celestial reward.

"Darling, you must tell your wife," Lettice urged when they next met at their favorite hotel in Lexington. "You've got to arrange for a divorce. You have to. You've got to tell her about us." Lettice's voice was so low and musical that John felt hypnotized.

But how could he tell Mary about Lettice?

John couldn't even rationalize Lettice's appeal to himself.

Instead of Mary's graciousness, Lettice had elegance. Lettice wasn't as pretty or as charming as Mary. But he couldn't resist her. In her presence he was an ardent, masterful lover; in Mary's presence he was a thoughtful, complaisant husband. With Lettice life would always be lived at the highest peak; nothing in his long years with Mary could approach the wonder he had known during his few meetings with Lettice. Lettice was earth, air, fire and water, the four elements; Mary was—no, he couldn't compare them. Anyway, what good was it to set their attractions off against each other?

Then, just as he was about to suggest to Lettice that they go to the bar, he saw Chet Fleming enter the hotel and walk across the lobby toward the desk. What was Chet Fleming doing in Lexington? But then anyone could be anywhere. That was the humiliating risk illicit lovers faced. They might be discovered anywhere, anytime. No place was secure for them. But Chet Fleming was the one person he wanted least to see, and the one who would make the most of encountering John with another woman. That blabbermouth would tell his wife and friends, his doctor, his grocer, his banker, his lawyer. Word would get back to Mary. Her heart would be broken. She deserved better than that.

John cowered beside Lettice. Chet dawdled at the desk. John couldn't be exposed like that any longer, a single glance around and Chet would see him and Lettice. John made an incoherent excuse, then sidled over to the newsstand where he hid behind a magazine until Chet had registered and had taken an elevator upstairs.

Anyway, they had escaped, but only barely.

John couldn't risk cheapening their attachment. He had to do something to make it permanent right away, but at the same time he didn't want to hurt Mary.

Thousands of people in the United States had gotten up that morning who would be dead before nightfall. Why couldn't his dear Mary be among them? Why couldn't she die without having to be murdered?

When John rejoined Lettice and tried to explain his panic, she was composed but concerned and emphatic.

"Darling, this incident only proves what I've been insisting. I said you'd have to tell your wife at once. We can't go on like this. Surely you understand."

"Yes, dear, you're quite right. I'll do something as soon as I can."

"You must do something immediately, darling."

Oddly enough, Mary Johnson was in the same predicament as John Johnson. She had had no intention of falling in love. In fact, she

ALFRED HITCHCOCK'S ANTHOLOGY

thought she was in love with her husband. How naive she'd been before Kenneth came into her shop that morning asking whether she had a bust of Mozart. Of course she had a bust of Mozart; she had several busts of Mozart, not to mention Bach, Beethoven, Victor Hugo, Balzac, Shakespeare, George Washington and Goethe, in assorted sizes.

He had introduced himself. Customers didn't ordinarily introduce themselves, and she gave him her name in return, and then realized that he was the outstanding interior designer in town.

"Quite frankly," he said, "I wouldn't be caught dead with this bust of Mozart and it will ruin the room, but my client insists on having it. Do you mind if I see what else you have?"

She showed him all over the shop. Later she tried to recall the exact moment when they had fallen in love. He had spent all that first morning there; toward noon he seemed especially attracted to a small back room cluttered and crowded with chests of drawers. He reached for a drawer pull that came off in his hands, then he reached for her.

"What do you think you're doing?" she said. "Goodness, suppose some customers come in."

"Let them browse," he said.

She couldn't believe that it had happened, but it had. Afterward, instead of being lonely when John went out of town on occasional business trips, she yearned for the time when he gave her his antiseptic peck of a kiss and told her he would be gone overnight.

The small back room jammed with the chests of drawers became Mary's and Kenneth's discreet rendezvous. They added a chaise longe.

One day a voice reached them there. They had been too engrossed to notice that anyone had approached.

"Mrs. Johnson, where are you? I'd like some service, please."

Mary stumbled out from the dark to greet the customer. She tried to smooth her mussed hair. She knew that her lipstick was smeared.

The customer was Mrs. Bryan, the most accomplished gossip in town. Mrs. Bryan would get word around that Mary Johnson was carrying on scandalously in her shop. John was sure to find out now.

Fortunately, Mrs. Bryan was preoccupied. She was in a Pennsylvania Dutch mood and wanted to see butter molds and dower chests.

It was a lucky escape, as Mary later told Kenneth. Kenneth refused to be reassured.

"I love you deeply," he said. "And honorably. I've reason to know you love me too. I'm damned tired of sneaking around. I'm not going to put up with it any longer. Do you understand? We've got to get married. Tell your husband you want a divorce."

Kenneth kept talking about a divorce, as if a divorce was nothing at all—not harder to arrange than a dental appointment. How could she divorce a man who had been affectionate and kind and faithful for twenty years? How could she snatch happiness from him?

If only John would die. Why couldn't he have a heart attack? Every day thousands of men died from heart attacks. Why couldn't her darling John just drop dead? It would simplify everything.

Even the ringing of the telephone sounded angry, and when Mary answered it Kenneth, at the other end of the line, was in a rage.

"Damn it, Mary, this afternoon was ridiculous. It was insulting. I'm not skulking any more. I'm not hiding behind doors while you grapple around for butter molds to show customers. We've got to be married right away."

"Yes, darling. Do be patient."

"I've already been too patient. I'm not waiting any longer."

She knew that he meant it. If she lost Kenneth life would end for her. She hadn't ever felt this way about John.

Dear John. How could she toss him aside? He was in the prime of life, he could live decades longer. All his existence was centered on her. He lived to give her pleasure. They had no friends except other married people. John would have to lead a solitary life if she left him. He'd be odd man out without her; their friends would invite him to their homes because they were sorry for him. Poor, miserable John was what everyone would call him. He'd be better off dead, they'd say. He would neglect himself; he wouldn't eat regularly; he would have to live alone in some wretched furnished apartment. No, she mustn't condemn him to an existence like that.

Why had this madness with Kenneth started? Why had that foolish woman insisted on having a bust of Mozart in her music room? Why had Kenneth come to her shop in search of it when busts of Mozart were in every second-hand store on Broad Street and at much cheaper prices?

Yet she wouldn't have changed anything. Seconds with Kenneth were worth lifetimes with John.

204

Only one end was possible. She would have to think of a nice, quick, efficient, unmessy way to get rid of John. And soon.

John had never seen Mary look as lovely as she did that night when he got home from his business trip. For one flicker of a second, life with her seemed enough. Then he thought of Lettice, and the thought stunned him into the belief that no act that brought them together could be criminal. He must get on with what he had to do. He must murder Mary in as gentlemanly a way as possible, and he must do it that very night. Meantime he would enjoy the wonderful dinner Mary had prepared for him. Common politeness demanded it, and anyhow he was ravenous.

Yet, he must get on with the murder just as soon as he finished eating. It seemed a little heartless to be contriving a woman's death even as he ate her cheese cake, but he certainly didn't mean to be callous.

He didn't know just how he would murder Mary. Perhaps if he could get her into her shop, there in that corner where all the statuary was, he could manage something.

Mary smiled at him and handed him a cup of coffee.

"I thought you'd need lots of coffee, darling, after such a long drive."

"Yes, dear, I do. Thank you."

Just as he began to sip from his cup he glanced across the table at Mary. Her face had a peculiar expression. John was puzzled by it. They had been so close for so many years that she must be reading his mind. She must know what he was planning. Then she smiled; it was the glorious smile she had bestowed on him ever since their honeymoon. Everything was all right.

"Darling, excuse me for a minute," she said. "I just remembered something in the shop that I must see to. I'll be right back."

She walked quickly out of the dining room and across the hall into the shop.

But she didn't come back right away as she'd promised. If she didn't return soon John's coffee would be cold. He took a sip or two, then decided to go to the shop to see what had delayed her.

She didn't hear him enter. He found her in the middle room where the chandeliers were blazing. Her back was turned toward him and she was sitting on an Empire sofa close to the statues on their stands. She was ambushed by the statues.

Good lord, it was as he had suspected. She had been reading his thoughts. Her shoulders heaved. She was sobbing. She knew that their life together was ending. Then he decided that she might be laughing. Her shoulders would be shaking like that if she were laughing to herself. Whatever she was doing, whether she sobbed or laughed, it was no time for him to speculate on her mood. This was too good a chance to miss. With her head bent over she would be directly in the path of the bust of Victor Hugo or Benjamin Franklin or whoever it was towering above her. John would have to topple it only slightly and it would hit her skull. It needed only the gentlest shove.

He shoved.

It was so simple.

Poor darling girl. Poor Mary.

But it was all for the best and he wouldn't ever blame himself for what he'd done. Still, he was startled that it had been so easy, and it had taken no time at all. He would have tried it weeks before if he had known that it could be done with so little trouble.

John was quite composed. He took one last affectionate glance at Mary and then went back to the dining room. He would drink his coffee and then telephone the doctor. No doubt the doctor would offer to notify the police since it was an accidental death. John wouldn't need to lie about anything except for one slight detail. He would have to say that some movement of Mary's must have caused the bust to fall.

His coffee was still warm. He drank it unhurriedly. He thought of Lettice. He ached for the luxury of telephoning her that their life together was now assured and that after a discreet interval they could be married. But he decided he had better not take any chances. He would delay calling Lettice.

He felt joyful yet calm. He couldn't remember having felt so relaxed. No doubt it came from the relief of having done what had to be done. He was even sleepy. He was sleepier than he had ever been. He must lie down on the livingroom couch. That was more urgent even than telephoning the doctor. But he couldn't wait to get to the couch. He laid his head on the dining table. His arms dangled.

None of Mary's and John's friends had any doubt about how the double tragedy had occurred. When they came to think of it, the shop had always been a booby trap, and that night Mary had tripped or

ALFRED HITCHCOCK'S ANTHOLOGY

stumbled and had toppled the statue onto her head. Then John had found her and grief had overwhelmed him. He realized he couldn't live without Mary, and his desperate sense of loss had driven him to dissolve enough sleeping tablets in his coffee to kill himself.

They all remembered so well how, in the middle of their last anniversary celebration, Mary and John had said they hoped they could die together. They really were the most devoted couple any of them had ever known. You could get sentimental just thinking about Mary and John, and to see them together was an inspiration. In a world of insecurity nothing was so heartening as their deep, steadfast love. It was sweet and touching that they had died on the same night, and exactly as they both had wanted.

# Just a Minor Offense

## by John Suter

They must have come up with their lights cut off, because I didn't know they were there until one of them shone his flash right behind me and said, "All right. What seems to be the trouble?"

He caught me standing there like a knucklehead, with the spring-leaf in my hand, staring at the coins spilling out of the pay phone. There was silver all over the floor of the booth and the shelf under the phone. A coin or two hung pinched in the twisted metal.

I didn't turn around. I figured the flashlight would be right in my eyes, and I didn't want things to be worse than they were going to be. I just stood still, watching his big arm go up and his big hand tighten the light bulb overhead. He crowded into the phone booth, ramming me against the wall while he shut the door. The light came on.

He grunted as though he'd seen what he expected to see. "Jackpot, huh? All right, kid, let's get outside and talk a little."

He opened the door, and the light went out. I started to turn, when his flash came on again.

"Hold it. Don't move or do a thing." He raised his voice. "Andy, take that hamburger out of the bag and bring the bag over here."

In a few seconds, I heard the car door slam and the other cop came up. The one who was keeping me pinned said to his buddy, "Thanks. Junior, here, is gonna clean up his mess for the phone company." He spoke to me. "Turn around. Okay. Now, hand over that hunk of steel. Lay it here."

A big hand came out in front of me, a handkerchief spread across the palm.

I laid the spring-leaf on the handkerchief. My prints would be on the metal. They sure had me cold.

"Look," I said, "I didn't do this. I just came in to phone, and—"

ALFRED HITCHCOCK'S ANTHOLOGY

"Sure," he said. His outline was big and bulky against the street-light. "They never do, not even when you catch 'em red-handed."

"If you'll listen a minute—"

"The only thing I'll listen to is that money jingling in the bag. Get to it."

I'd always been told that you don't argue with cops, and there were two of them, one of them bigger than I am. I closed up and began scooping up the nickels, dimes, and quarters. I took care not to miss any, not even a dime in a far corner, not even the stuff still hanging in the coin box itself.

Finally, I straightened and turned around, passing over the bag.

"All right, officer," I said, as evenly as I could. "I've done what you wanted me to. If you'll listen a minute, I'll tell you something that'll prove I didn't do it."

"You tryin' to tell me I didn't see what I saw?"

The other cop, the one he'd called Andy, cut in. His tone was a little quieter. "Let's give him a minute, Mike. It looks better when we come in with all the angles accounted for. We don't want something flying up and hitting us in the face later."

The big one was quiet for a second. "Okay," he said finally. "Let's hear it."

"It's this way," I said, trying to keep the relief out of my voice. "I've been out with three other guys. I'll give you their names—"

"Later."

"I'd just taken the last one home, and I started across the park, when the car pooped out on me. Right around the bend up there. It's my Dad's car. I can't get it started—acts like there's dirt in the needle-valve. Well, you know what happens if you leave a car on the street, especially in the park. It gets hauled in, and it costs you to bail it out. So I thought I'd better phone Dad, then call Brown's Garage."

"And you didn't have the change, so you thought you'd just help yourself to some—"

This Andy cut in again. "If he'd done that, it might knock out the phone, Mike. Let him finish."

I went on: "When I came in sight of the booth, I thought I saw somebody step out and disappear, but I wasn't sure. And when I got here, it was the way you saw it. The spring-leaf was on the shelf. Like a meathead, I picked it up. Then you came along. And that's it."

The other cop said, "It wouldn't hurt to check out this thing about the car. Only take a few minutes. Which way is it, kid?"

I pointed. "Over that way, half a block. It's a '57 Chevvy."

The big one took me by the arm.

"Let's go."

I walked out to the cruiser with them. They put me in front beside Andy, the driver. Mike got in behind me. As we came out under the streetlight, I saw that he had a sort of blocky face, pitted here and there. His buddy was shorter, thinner, with sandy eyebrows and a sharp nose.

We were over by the Chevvy almost before I got settled. We pulled up alongside. Andy held out a hand. "The keys."

I gave them to him. "To start it, you—"

"I know," he said, slipping from behind the wheel.

He went and turned the starter of the Chevvy over two or three times, then got out and lifted the hood. He flashed his light at the motor for a minute, then closed the hood and came back.

"It's like he says." He returned the keys.

I felt better. I was pretty sure they'd check me, but you can't count on dirt. Sometimes it works loose in a valve when you don't think it can.

Mike cleared his throat. "So how does this let him off the hook?"

Andy drummed on the wheel. "He'd never use that buggy for a getaway the way it is. Incidentally, what's your name, kid?"

"David Carey."

"Your father's name?"

"Samuel E. Carey."

Andy nodded. "The registration was in that name. Let me see your driver's license."

I handed it over. He glanced at it and gave it back. "It checks."

"Sure," I said. "It's on the level, all the way. Look, I've given it to you straight. Why don't you let me go, then hunt for this other guy? I still have to call home, and I'd better phone the garage."

Mike hefted the bag of money. "How do we know you're not in Sergeant Jensen's file on a couple of counts already?"

"I'm not. I've never been in trouble in my life. I'm not wanting to start now."

Andy said, "I'm not out to make it rough for anybody, kid. Neither

ALFRED HITCHCOCK'S ANTHOLOGY

one of us is. But we'd be pretty poor cops if we didn't take you in. They probably won't do a thing, but they like to be the ones to make the decisions."

"But the car—"

"Don't worry about the car. If you're clean, we'll see you don't get bit for something you couldn't help."

He moved the stick over to *Drive,* and we took off.

We were at the station in less than ten minutes. They took me into a room with several straightback chairs around the walls, a worn hardwood floor, and a cop behind a desk who seemed to match the room. He had thin brown hair and a hatchet face. I found out that he was the night sergeant, Driscoll.

He stared at me poker-faced and pulled out some kind of form, then started asking questions. When he got to my age and I said, "Sixteen," he looked at Mike.

Then he said, "Better call his family and get 'em down here. What's he done?"

"Looks like he smashed a pay phone for the chicken feed. Here." Mike plunked down the bag.

Driscoll's face didn't change a bit. "They won't need a lawyer, then. His old man'll be enough."

Mike picked up the phone. "What's the number, kid?"

I turned to Sergeant Driscoll. "You're going to book me?"

"It has to go on the record, son. They brought you in. I haven't heard it all yet. But whatever comes in here, it goes down on the sheet."

I didn't say anything, trying to figure a way to keep my name clean. Driscoll prodded me again. "If you didn't do it, it can't count against you. You're sixteen. We're not in the habit of blabbing all over town who the kids are who come in here. Now let's get on with this. There's enough other things to keep me more than busy."

Andy, who was standing beside me, dropped a match into an ashtray on the desk. "What's going on?"

"Some kind of fight started five minutes ago," Sergeant Driscoll said, "over near Locust and Third. And some girl's family called in around that same time to say their kid's overdue getting home—not with her friends, not in the hospital. Out parked somewhere, probably." He looked at me. "Her name's Joyce Reynolds. Know her?"

"I know who she is. She's a year ahead of me in school."

"Who's she go with?"

"I hear she goes steady with Herb Blackwood."

He looked at a note pad. "That one hasn't seen her—he says."

Andy asked idly, "Any of these kid gangs breaking and entering tonight?"

"No reports. Well—back to business." He looked at Andy, then at Mike. "Tell me about this one."

In about half an hour, Dad came down. He didn't storm in, like some of the old boys you see on TV, and he didn't come in, hat in hand, to let them walk all over him. He just looked at me, then at Driscoll (the other two had gone back to work) and said, "The officer who called said Dave was caught breaking into a pay phone."

The sergeant tapped the paper with his pen. "That's the way it looks, Mr. Carey. There's some business about your car that might be in his favor."

"What do you want us to do?"

*Us.*

The sergeant was matter-of-fact. "We'll turn this report over to Sergeant Jensen, of Juvenile, and let him check it out. Right now, we'll release the boy in your custody. I suggest that he come back here tomorrow to talk to Sergeant Jensen."

"He'll be here. What time?"

Driscoll considered. "It'll take a little time. No sense in making him miss school. Say, about four o'clock."

"He'll be here at four. Shall I come too?"

"As you like. Jensen doesn't chew 'em up and spit 'em out in little pieces. Sometimes it works out better when the kid's alone. Why not leave it to him?"

"All right." Dad turned and looked at me. "Well—you don't seem to be the worse for wear. But your mother's liable to say something about the dirt on your knees. How'd that happen?"

I brushed at my pants. It didn't brush off too well. "I guess I got it kneeling in that booth picking up the money."

Driscoll had a faint frown on his face. His voice had a slight rasp. "He wasn't roughed up, if that's what you're getting at." He made a note on the paper in front of him.

Dad seems pretty average sometimes, but he wasn't so average just

ALFRED HITCHCOCK'S ANTHOLOGY

then. His eyes glinted, and I almost thought his hair bristled. "Nobody *will* bring it up if it's not necessary. But *somebody* will drag it out into the open if it *is* necessary."

He turned back to me. "Now, let's hear about the car, so we can straighten that part out and go home."

In the morning, school was about as usual, but toward the end of lunch period Jack Burton stopped me in the hall. He halfway hung that head of his with the peroxided widow's peak, so that he was looking up, a habit of his. His eyes looked a little worried.

"I'm glad you called me, even if it was awful early in the morning. The cops talked to me, the way you said they would."

I kept up a front of confidence. Better not scare my best witness. "You told 'em straight about what time I left you, I hope? You live right by the park, and they'll be able to figure that I was telling the whole truth about the car and all."

He stuck his thumbs in the corners of his pants pockets. "Sure. We gotta stick together. I know that. Look, Dave, when you let me out, did you see any sign of Joyce Reynolds?"

"Joyce Reynolds? No. How come?"

"She lives the second house from me, remember? She's missing."

"I heard them mention it last night. What's this got to do with you?"

"She was out with Tom Fisher. Mad at Herb Blackwood, I hear, and had this date with Tom, instead. Tom says he brought her home around 12:15, close to the time you let me out. He didn't see her to the door—what a birdbrain!—and he doesn't know whether she got in or not. She didn't. So where'd she get to? The cops asked me, did I see her? I had to tell 'em no."

"Well, I didn't either," I said. "I have enough to do, trying to get out from under this phone business. You'll stick with me?"

He grinned quickly. "Beat the phony rap? I'll do what I can."

"Stick to the truth, that's all. Stick to the truth."

I went down alone to Police Headquarters to see Sergeant Jensen at four o'clock, the time they'd set. Mom tried to get Dad to go along, but he thought it over and said I'd have to learn to face things alone more often now. He'd checked on Jensen and thought I'd get a fair break.

Jensen's office wasn't much more than a desk, three chairs, and a lot of filing cabinets. The sergeant was a short cop, looking something like Franchot Tone, with a good bit of gray in his hair. He seemed sort of good-natured, but when he looked at me with those hazel eyes of his, I felt he'd known me all of my life, that he knew everything about me.

He waved me to a chair beside his desk and sat looking at me without talking for a minute or two. Finally, he decided to open up.

"David Carey. I've never run into you before, Dave."

"It's not my fault that you have this time, Sergeant."

"I wonder how you mean that," he said quietly.

This put me off-balance a little. Getting double meanings out of what I'd said, when I'd hardly opened my mouth.

"All I mean is I've always tried to keep out of things that cause trouble. And here things have turned on me, and I get pulled in for something I didn't do."

"There're a lot of kids breaking and entering these days who aren't getting pulled in. For all we know, you might be a member of one gang we're after. You see?" Jensen fingered some papers. "I have a number of reports on you, Dave. Good reports. That's in your favor. Of course," he said with a little more bite in his tone, "we had a kid in here about three months ago just your age. What they called a 'model boy.' He decided to steal a car and did—but he was caught."

I kept quiet.

"That boy, and these vandals we haven't caught yet, think that they don't amount to anything if they're being normal citizens. If they're not leaders, or something, they have to prove themselves some other way. Maybe that could be you. Could it?"

I tried to figure out what to say.

He studied me. "Dave, if you have anything at all to say about this affair that you haven't told us, I'd advise you to tell us now. It'll make things a lot easier if we decide to carry this further."

"Sergeant, I don't know what you want me to say, but all I can tell you is I didn't do it. It doesn't matter how bad it looks."

He shrugged. "All right." He looked at those papers again. "Against you is the fact that you were caught in a phone booth with the box pried open and money all over the place. You had an automobile spring-leaf in your hand. Your fingerprints were on the metal. *They were also on the phone box.* What about that?"

In spite of myself, I began to sweat some. "I put my hands on the box when they asked me to gather up all the money. Some of it was still in the box. I couldn't help it. Did they mention that?"

He made a note. "No. I'll verify it."

"Did you find any other prints on that spring-leaf?"

"Yes, but they weren't any good. Yours blurred them."

"Isn't that in my favor?"

He compressed his lips briefly. "It could be. It could also be that you just picked up that hunk of steel somewhere, knowing that somebody else's prints would be on it."

"Sergeant," I said, trying to get through to him, "if that's the case, why'd I be fool enough to use the thing barehanded? Why should I want to put my own prints on it?"

His answer was mild. "It doesn't add up. Now—in your favor. Your story about the boys you were out with checks. We talked to them all, and you did just what you said. You did seem to be heading back across the park after you let the Burton kid out."

"And the car—doesn't that help?"

He nodded. "The car. Yes. We called the garage. There was dirt in the needle-valve as you guessed. The officers who brought you in verify that it wouldn't start. All of this, plus good character references, add up in your favor. The question now is, do these things weigh more than our finding you practically in the act?"

"But, Sergeant," I said, "the phone company didn't lose any money. All they have to do is fix the phone. It means a lot to me to keep my name clean. Why don't you give me the benefit of the doubt?"

His eyes became cold all of a sudden. "The phone company helps to pay my salary, the same as everybody else does. Any decisions I make had better be good ones, no matter who's involved."

He just sat there and let me fidget. Finally, he spoke in a mild voice again.

"Let's talk about something else for a minute. Do you know a Joyce Reynolds?"

"Some. I see her around school. She's a Senior, I'm a Junior."

"See her last night?"

"No, I hear she's missing."

He looked at me directly again. "Yes. You could have seen her." It was a flat statement, but it sounded almost accusing.

He had me worried. "She lives near Jack Burton," I said, "sure, but I didn't see her last night."

He turned his attention to the tips of his fingers. "What's she like?"

"I don't know too much about her, except in a general way. About five feet four, real black hair, not built quite as much as some—but you might look twice. She's been steadying with Herb Blackwood, but maybe that's over. I hear she was out with Tom Fisher last night."

He said casually, "I understand you're a little interested yourself."

I got sort of hot. Jack Burton must have— "Who says?"

"Somebody."

"Well, you tell somebody he doesn't know what he's talking about! Look, she's a Senior, and Senior girls hardly even look at Junior boys. Besides, she's going steady."

"You go steady?"

"No."

He considered his notes. "You're what? Sixteen? Then it may be understandable that you don't go steady. Run around with three or four other boys, no girls? The way it was last night?"

"Usually."

"But Joyce Reynolds— Did you ever make any passes?"

I felt like squirming, but I sat still. "She's about a year older than I am. Why should I?"

"Why not?"

"I'd seem like a kid to her. Don't you get it?"

He shrugged. "I didn't say she'd reciprocate—though that's not impossible, either."

I imagine he could tell that I was simmering, the way my voice must have sounded. "Sergeant, why're we beating in time on this? What's it got to do with a busted pay phone?"

He was stiff-faced when he answered. "They found Joyce Reynolds' body this morning. In the park, in a crevice under some big rocks. Not too far from that phone booth where they picked you up."

I couldn't say a thing.

"She was strangled and beaten," he went on. "Maybe somebody made a pass and got mad when he didn't get anywhere. Maybe it was somebody she looked on as sort of a kid. Maybe she even laughed at him when he got serious. *How about it?*"

I finally found my voice. "Me? First you say I wreck a pay phone,

ALFRED HITCHCOCK'S ANTHOLOGY

then you say I killed Joyce Reynolds. What am I supposed to be—a one-man crime wave?"

"It's not so crazy as you might think, boy."

"Me? Why me?" I almost yelled. "How do you know Herb Blackwood wasn't hanging around waiting for her when Tom Fisher brought her home? How do you know Tom even brought her home? How about Jack Burton? All that stuff you said about me you could say it about him—and he lives close to her house. How do you know he didn't walk her over to the park after I left him? What time was she killed, anyway?"

Jensen looked away. "This much I'll give you: we don't know yet."

"Then—"

He stared coldly at me. "I'll tell you what could have happened in your case. Not Fisher's, Blackwood's or Burton's case. Yours. You pick up this girl and drive to the park. You make a pass, but you get nowhere. You get mad and slug her, then you strangle her. You try to hide the body—temporarily, anyway. Then you go to leave—and you can't start the car. You begin to sweat. That car is close to the body. It can tie you to what you've done. So you decide to fake a smash on that pay phone, maybe you even hang around until you're sure of being picked up. This is to fix our attention on you for a minor offense, instead of murder. Who'd be robbing a phone if he'd just committed murder? A neat trick, if somebody doesn't see through it. Now that's the case we can build against you. *Can you prove otherwise?*"

My brain had been busy while he was piling things on. "Sergeant, you'd better be thinking about those others. Listen, if I did what you just said, where'd that spring-leaf come from? The one that was used on the phone?"

"How should I know?"

"If I smashed that phone to draw attention away from Joyce, I'd have to get that hunk of steel in a hurry, wouldn't I? You know how clean they keep the park. Where'd that leaf come from?"

"Out of the trunk of your car. Where else?"

I snorted. "Are you kidding? You take a look in that trunk, the way Dad keeps it. You could eat off the floor. All that're in it are the spare tire, jack, and lug wrench. Chains in the winter, not now."

Jensen looked thoughtful. "What kind of tires have you?"

"Tubeless."

"Okay. With inner tubes, a lot of drivers used to carry a spring-leaf to pry the tire off the rim if they fixed a flat themselves. That doesn't sound likely here."

He shut up and thought. Then he said, "All the same, I'm going to check with your Dad about that spring-leaf. In the meantime, I guess we'd better have you tell me about this Jack Burton."

He pulled some papers over in front of him.

"Where shall I start?" I asked, feeling easier.

He didn't answer. He was staring at two papers lying next to each other. He studied one, then the other. Finally, he looked up.

"You and Jack Burton run around with several other boys quite a bit?"

"That's right."

"Sort of a gang?"

"I wouldn't call it that, Sergeant. You know how that sounds nowadays. Why do you always—"

"Look on the bad side? I'll tell you why, Carey. You don't drive your Dad's car every night. I don't think he'd let you. So, if he keeps the trunk so clean, the spring-leaf wouldn't be in it all the time. Why not? You know—a spring-leaf makes a pretty good jimmy, especially if the end's filed down. I'll have to look at your little toy to see about that. Now, if your gang had been breaking and entering, you'd have a spring-leaf with you on certain nights, all right."

I pointed to the papers on his desk. "I suppose it says so in there."

He tapped them. "Oh, no. It doesn't say a word about that. But one of them says that whoever tried to shove Joyce Reynolds' body under those rocks had to kneel to do it. The other report has a note on it that your father was concerned about some dirt on the knees of your pants when they brought you in last night."

He stood up suddenly. "Now, I wonder if we went out to your house and brought back those pants for the lab to test, would they find the same kind of dirt as that by the rocks?"

I couldn't say a thing. The pants hadn't gone to the cleaner's. And I knew where the dirt on the knees came from.

# The Long Terrible Day

## by Charlotte Edwards

The long terrible day started at exactly eight o'clock. The siren hooted from the paper mill and the chimes of the church on Main Street clanged in the steeple, telling the time as they always did.

Ernie's chair scraped as he pushed it back. Clearing his throat, he said, "Time to be off," which he announced every workday morning.

I sat at the table in the breakfast nook, a cup of coffee halfway to my lips. The paper was spread before me, but my eyes were on my husband.

What I had just seen in the middle of the front page formed an after-image that fitted over his features; fitted perfectly, neatly, in every detail—except the mustache, crewcut and twenty extra pounds.

Ernie leaned across the table and patted four-year-old Steve on the head. "Mind Mama," he commanded.

Steve nodded, his mouth too full to answer.

Ernie walked around in back of me, his steps heavy and sure, to the high chair. "Daddy's girl be good today," he coaxed.

Liz chortled and offered him a spoon of oatmeal from which the overload dropped rhythmically.

"Some kid," Ernie gloated, then moved behind my chair. His hand lay, heavy as his footsteps, warm and sure, on my shoulder. "You're going to spill your coffee." Large, broad-shouldered, powerful, he looked down at me.

I smiled up at him.

Eyes, amber, green-flecked. Small scar dividing the right eyebrow, tilting it up.

I lowered my gaze, set the coffee cup back in the saucer, picked up the paper. "Ernie," I said, "there's the craziest thing here—"

He didn't look, but bent to kiss me. His lips were warm and gentle.

His mustache tickled a moment against my mouth and was gone—the red mustache, small, neatly clipped, almost rusty; grown the first year of our marriage.

"Gotta rush, kid," he said. "Big day. Save it, eh?"

"But it will only take—"

He rumpled my hair, then he was gone.

I was alone in the house with my children. The long terrible day was fifteen minutes' old—only I didn't know it was going to be a long terrible day, not then.

He'd have gotten a bounce out of it. Ernie could take a joke, even when it was on him—if he wasn't upset, wasn't angry, wasn't hurt.

I stood up abruptly. Maybe he was still upset about last night. Maybe that's why he wanted to hurry. I shook my head. Ernie didn't have to have a reason for rushing to work, for cat's sake. He did that often.

I began to clear the table, ignoring the paper, awkwardly folded there beside my plate. I rinsed the dishes carefully and wiped around Steve's comic book, around the *Daily Express*, leaving them like two puddles to be mopped up later. I pulled Liz from the high chair, washed the accumulated debris from around the smiling mouth, and carried her into the livingroom, setting her carefully in the playpen, handing her an assortment of soft toys.

For a moment then, I stood still, as if waiting for something. As if it needed only physical quiet to start it in motion, a hammer, a deep, slow, heavy-swinging hammer, started pounding inside the cave of my left ribs. Thud, bong, thud, boom, it picked up tempo faster and faster, heavier, louder. When it filled my ears, filled the neat small room, the word came out, sharp, sudden. "No!"

The hammer slowed almost to a stop. "All I have to do," I said to myself, "is go back to the kitchen and pick up the paper. Look at the drawing again, carefully, don't snatch impressions."

Shame began to crawl through me. I hated women who checked for lipstick, notes, phone numbers; suspicious, untrusting wives.

With sudden determination I walked briskly to the kitchen, but instead of picking up the paper, I found myself washing the dishes. Sounds came remotely: Liz gibbering, Steve rumbling, the roar of cars on the freeway.

"I *will* look." I went to the table, propelled by my own loud words.

The headline was louder than my voice in its grim declaration:

GIRL FOUND BLUDGEONED TO DEATH ON GOLF COURSE
"The body of Marylee Adams, 18, was discovered early this morning, head gashed by repeated heavy blows, in bushes by the 16th hole of the Arnaughton Golf Course. There was no sign of the murder weapon.

Miss Adams, who lived at 1617 Central Street with her mother, had many suitors, according to the information so far obtained.

Police Chief J. Hampton Jones remarked upon the similarity of this crime and that of the killing of one Sandra Hims, also 18, on a public golf course in Kansas City about five years ago. At that time the murder weapon was found, a heavy car jack.

The drawing (at right) was forwarded from that city, and is based on a witness' description of the suspect, the man with whom Miss Hims was last seen leaving a Kansas City bar."

My eyes pulled from the words, fastened on the four-column picture centered on the page. The hammering started again.

I began at the wavy hair, growing clean and straight above the broad forehead, followed the line of the nose with its rounded tip, the cheeks that hollowed in a little just above the square chin. I traced the thin, determined curves of the mouth.

Heat rose in me until I was scorched with panic. I stared, horror blazing through me, at the face of Ernie, my husband, staring back at me from the printed page of the *Daily Express*. Except for the mustache, the crewcut, and the twenty extra pounds, it was Ernie as I first knew him, when I first met him.

The chimes from the church on Main Street spoke out nine times.

I stared out of the window at the two orange trees showing in the yard. Ernie took good care of the trees.

The picture was a thing to laugh at, and over, with Ernie, a product of an artist's imagination five years ago. So what? Nobody else would notice except a fantasy-ridden, silly wife. Ernie'd had a mustache ever since we came here, and extra flesh and short hair. Talk about lipstick-crazy wives!

"You done any killin' lately?" I could hear Jim, Ernie's boss, roar;

Jim, who wouldn't take a mint from Ernie.

Everybody loves Ernie—kids, dogs, men, old ladies, neighbors. No one would believe it for a moment.

I love him and I don't believe it for a moment, either. You don't love a man who could smash a girl to death. You'd know about a thing like that. It wouldn't be in a gentle, quiet man like Ernie. When things close in on him, he just gets up and walks out. A couple hours of walking around and he's back—sweet, trouble forgotten—like last night.

I closed my eyes and leaned forward. The chair squeaked, like the squeak I'd heard during the night and had just barely roused to notice.

When was that? What hour? What time?

Eighteen is just beginning to live. Was Marylee Adams blonde? Was her hair freshly set in rollers and pin curls, the way kids go around, and a scarf?

Eighteen—I was eighteen five years ago when I first met Ernie, first saw his hands, square and strong and clean. He didn't work in a garage then. He was dapper and a bachelor, and he came to the door of my mother's house selling appliances.

Mama liked him at once, and when Papa came home from his sales trip, he and Ernie talked half the night and ate nearly a whole cake, baked by me with love. Yes, it was love, even that first week.

Every weekend for over two months he came to the white house in the small town, and Sunday evening came too soon.

"I don't like to say goodbye to you. I don't like going back to the city anymore," Ernie would say.

Then one Saturday he came, breathless in his quiet way. "This man in California advertised in the city paper, a good steady job in a garage. I wrote him, and he called clear across country—and hired me!"

That week we were married. On the train, Ernie was already sprouting the mustache above his firm upper lip.

Eighteen—five years ago—the white house was left behind, the city left behind. The city; what city?

Did she have rollers, and pin curls? Oh, it would hurt worse with pin curls, all those little steel clips ground into the bones of her head . . .

Like the lost morning hour, I had no recollection of leaving the house, of starting the old jalopy which ran like new because of Ernie's

222                                   ALFRED HITCHCOCK'S ANTHOLOGY

skill. Liz was beside me. Steve stood in back, eager, talking. I started to make a grocery list in my mind.

Bread, margarine, the city, eggs, cereal, what city, shortening, Kansas City. That's the city. Kansas City, sugar—twenty-five miles from the white house and Mama and Papa—

Steve began to count the bongs in the steeple. Ten o'clock, two hours since eight. "Eight—nine—ten," Steve said it for me.

The doors of the supermarket flashed open in that miraculous way that intrigued Steve.

I walked through, lopsided, to hold Liz's hand. The store was so bright I felt as if I'd emerged from a tunnel. The normalcy, the bustle, the clang of registers and rustle of bags slowly oozed into me.

Sorting, pricing, watching the basket pile high behind Liz, the displays were walls protecting me from the morning, the paper awkwardly folded over on the kitchen table.

There was a bad moment at the meat counter.

"Round for Swiss?" I asked.

The butcher nodded. "Okay, Mrs. Cochran. Pounded like usual?"

"Like usual."

I stared into the big mirror lining the wall behind the butcher: like usual, short brown hair, brown, seemingly untroubled eyes; typical young mother, typical week's shopping.

Then, beside my reflection an arm rose. In the hand was a hammer-hatchet. It went up. It came down with a dull thud. Up, down, up, down—BLUDGEON.

"That's enough, Peppy," I called sharply.

The arm stopped. "Heck, it ain't pounded half as much—" He shrugged, wrapped the gummy red meat in thick white paper, wrote red numerals on it, and shoved it toward me.

It took all my self-control to pick up the package.

At the cheese case Jim's wife called to me. "See you tonight."

"Tonight, Eloise?"

"Pot luck, remember?"

Every other Friday we got together with seven other couples. Eloise's house was the meeting place this time.

"I'm not sure. Baby-sitter trouble—"

"Bring 'em along. Tuck 'em in."

I moved toward the checkout counter. "Ernie wouldn't like—"

Eloise laughed. "Ernie likes whatever you want."

I swallowed. It hurt. The truth hurts.

What he couldn't buy, Ernie made up for in effort, like feeding the kids on Sunday, emptying the rubbish, scrubbing the kitchen. And bigger things, like not being a bachelor in a good-looking suit anymore, but wearing coveralls, for all the greasy dirty work he did. And the hard work was for me, wasn't it?

Or was it—my mind talked straight at me—because a well-dressed salesman with amber eyes and curly hair couldn't be so easily traced if he were a garage mechanic in a city a couple of thousand miles away?

I looked for Steve at the checkout. He was sitting on the magazines, doubled over a comic book. My eyes slid from him and lighted on the paper stand.

BLUDGEON yammered out at me, Ernie's five-years-ago face yammered out at me, the cashiers, Eloise—I gripped the counter edge.

Eloise's arm went around me. "Kid, you're white. What's the matter? You scared?" She laughed. "That guy's five hundred miles away by this time, honey."

I pulled myself together, said, "I'm all right. It's really nothing."

I followed the boy with the carry-out basket. The sun hit me without heat. Funny, the market had seemed so bright. Now the market was a tunnel, and the outdoors brazen.

"You want these in the trunk, ma'am?"

I nodded.

"Then I gotta have the keys."

I pulled out my case and walked to the back of the car. I inserted the round key, noticing impersonally that my hand shook. I turned the key. The boy reached over to lift the trunk lid, then transferred the cartons. I lifted my arm to bring the trunk lid down.

Suddenly, my hand was halted. My heart was halted. Even with the cartons, the trunk looked—different, not right.

I stared at the boxes, at the spare tire, waiting for it to hit me, to know what was missing from the rear trunk of the jalopy.

I stared, seeing where it should be. I tried desperately to see it there. I leaned forward, finally, and pushed the heavy cartons aside, one knee on the back bumper to put myself closer. I peered into the corners and felt behind the spare.

224

The car jack was gone! The heavy, solid old jack that Ernie insisted should be there because the tires were recapped was gone.

Roars hit against me, bruising and sharp. Eleven of them bounced and hurt before they faded. I was pulling into our driveway before I realized they weren't roars at all, but the chimes in the church steeple striking the hour before noon.

All right, so the morning was almost gone. See, world? I'd washed the dishes and done the shopping. Now I'd burn the rubbish. The *Daily Express* on the table would catch quickly, burn the crazy ideas, the weird wicked thoughts; ashes and dust—and Marylee Adams was pretty as a picture.

I got my scissors from the sink drawer and sat down at the kitchen table. Carefully I cut out the front piece from the *Express*, picked up my purse from the drainboard, folded the clipping into a tidy square and tucked it into the zippered compartment. Then I crunched up the paper, put it in the top of the wastebasket and carried it to the back of the yard. I emptied the basket and struck a match. I was right. The *Daily Express* burned fast and set everything else on fire—but it burned away no evil thoughts.

As I went through the kitchen door the phone rang.

"Hello." I heard a tinny voice but a close voice. "That you, Sara?"

For a moment too sheer to hold, comfort oozed into me. "Ernie?"

"I been ringing all morning." He sounded worried.

"I went shopping."

"Oh. You still mad? About last night?"

That depends, I thought calmly, on what happened last night. "No. Why?"

He hesitated. "You seemed so—kind of funny this morning."

"Funny?"

"You still seem funny." He sounded strange this time; on guard, yet prying.

"I'm all right."

"Look, Sara," he spurted, "I took a walk is all. Got that? Sure, I was sore. So I took a walk."

I held up my hand and studied it. "A long walk?"

I could hear him breathe before his answer. "Pretty long. You were asleep when—"

"I know."

"Weren't you?"

I thought about that. "Sort of—dozing."

"Oh, I wish—"

"Why?"

"Never mind. You still sound funny. Look, I forgot my lunch. I have to work right through. I'm—I'm doing a paint job on old Tinsdale's car—"

"I'm sorry." I was. "I forgot to fix your lunch." There *was* an hour then, before eight o'clock. "Then I sat down to look at the paper—" I bit my lip, hard.

"What was that about the paper?" His voice was harsh, louder.

"Nothing."

"Jim just rolled a cart through here. What was—"

"I'm sorry—"

"Well, look, could you bring it down to me? Like I said—"

"I heard you."

Could I bring it down? Could I talk to him, with the square of paper in my purse and mind, and sound like Sara Cochran, the mother of his children, the wife of his bosom?

"Something is the matter." He slowed his words. "I think you better come on down here."

"The kids—"

"I want to see you, Sara." Ernie had never spoken like that; flat, in command.

I hung up slowly, slowly, cutting off his tone.

The phone rang again instantly.

"You hung up. Why?"

I grabbed for breath. "Because I wanted to fix your lunch, silly."

He grunted. "Well, say, the other thing. Last night—you know when I took that walk—I, well, I stopped in here. Thought I'd maybe try to mix the paint for Tinsdale—"

"Yes?" Oh please, no, not that!

"Well, I got a few spots on my gray slacks. Jim's all set for the shindig." He made a funny sound. "You know me. One-pants Cochran. Be a good kid and clean those spots out for me, will you?"

"All right."

"And, Sara—"

"Yes?"

"If it's too much trouble—I'll ask somebody to bring me a hamburg."

"You sure that's all right?" Calm and easy now. Get ready for the question. "I've got a washing started—" That sounds good, Sara.

"Sure, it's okay. Just that you were—"

"Funny, I know. Well, I'm not now."

"Good. I'll see you tonight. And remember the gray pants, eh?"

"I'll remember, Ernie." Now! Ask it now and fast. "Ernie?"

"Yes?"

"Old Man Tinsdale? What color's he having you paint his car?"

Ernie did laugh this time, short. "Bright red. Isn't that a howl?" He hung up.

I walked steadily back into the bedroom and opened the closet door. Ernie's slacks were on a hanger. I carried them, not glancing down, into the kitchen, to the window, to the brightest light. I held them out, letting the sun touch them shrewdly to be certain.

They were spotted all right, small spots, but a lot of them. Maybe Old Man Tinsdale's car was supposed to be bright red—but the paint didn't hold up on flannel. All those little spots were brown, rusty brown.

All hell broke loose suddenly, inside and outside of me. The noon whistle shrieked. Liz began to cry. Steve slammed into the house. The room, the house, reverberated with the noise.

But the biggest sound, the loudest yell, the highest whistle, came from inside myself, a noise that grew and grew and tore me apart.

Ernie Cochran, my husband, was a murderer!

When you are afraid something is true and you fight off the knowledge with everything in you, and when at last the proof of the truth seems indisputable, a stillness comes. I knew that stillness. It lasted until I had the kids in for their naps and bent to kiss them.

That was a mistake. That pushed the first tickle of the knife into the shock. These wonderful children—with a murderer for a father?

*If* he is, part of me staunchly cried. *If*. *If*.

I shut the door and went into the livingroom to the little desk. The morning, I decided, was one segment of a continued play. The new hours, they would be the next installment.

What then?

I unzipped the compartment of my purse in the kitchen and pulled out the clipping.

How could I doubt it? There before my eyes?

I was, I knew, dodging a decision. "Accessory after the fact," came neatly to my mind. What do you do when you believe your husband is a murderer and nobody else suspects it?

Suppose nobody ever suspects it? My heart leaped with a strange looseness, a relief. Suppose you just go on, and every morning he leaves and every night he comes home to you and nobody ever dreams that Ernie Cochran has battered and crumpled and shattered and crushed—everybody loves Ernie.

The looseness tightened into a sudden knot. What if he does it again?

I went to the phone, compelled. I dialed quickly. After what seemed hours the voice came, heavy and remote.

"Police department."

"Homicide," I heard.

The voice lost its casualness. "Homicide? Lady, you mean murder?"

"I mean murder." Who said that in that strange easy way? Not Mrs. Cochran. Not about Mr. Cochran.

"Just a minute."

In an office somewhere in the heart of the city men were moving and stirring, maybe pounding from door to door, asking and demanding, trying to get a clue.

My eyes landed on the gray flannel slacks, folded over the back of the kitchen chair. Come to the phone and I'll give you a clue, I thought, a little wild now with the waiting, the hum in the line going right into my ear and brain.

"Sergeant Anderson speaking." It was a new intense voice. "Homicide."

"I—" I began. "I—" I swallowed. I lifted my head from the dial that seemed to be going around and around of its own free will. "I want—" I swung my glance toward the door.

Ernie stood there. His shoulders seemed to fill the entire doorway, like Goliath, like Samson. His eyes looked all green, not amber and flecked. His mouth, under the mustache, was tight and small.

"Lady," the sergeant's voice came again. "Hey, lady—"

I felt the receiver slip from my hand and knew vaguely that I was slipping with it. All the way down to the floor into unconsciousness, my eyes were tied to Ernie's. I took them with me into the blackness—his eyes—and the simple unadorned sound of the church bell tolling a single note.

For what seemed an eternity I tried to climb up a black velvet ladder which sagged. It was unutterably difficult, but I had to try. Somewhere at the top a voice insisted, commanded, cajoled. Then, flashingly, the velvet was torn, the voice was loud, and all was bright. Ernie's face was so close to mine I could see the pores of his tanned skin. His arms were locked around me, holding me tight against the bed.

Relief filled my chest and eyes, and tears rolled down my cheeks. "A nightmare," I babbled. "Just a bad dream. Oh, Ernie—honey—I dreamed that you—that you—" I looked at his eyes then. It was no nightmare.

"I never knew you to pass out like that before," he said thoughtfully, his hands urgent on my shouders. I felt the shudder begin where his fingers lay, and travel, secret and sick, all the way down my body to my toes.

"You're shivering. On a day like this." He got up. "You lie still. I'm going to call the doctor."

Let him, the voice inside said quickly. The doctor is somebody in the house.

I listened to his heavy footsteps go down the hall to the kitchen, pause, then start back.

Ernie came toward me again. "He's out, but I left a message."

The most awful of all thoughts of this horrible day came to me then, as Ernie walked slowly toward me, his big hands extended. I had left the clipping on the kitchen table, naked and revealing. If he had seen it, had read it, had picked up that receiver, had heard the voice of Sergeant Anderson—then Ernie would want me dead too!

Maybe not want—but most certainly need!

I began to talk fast. "How did you happen to come home?"

"Spray gun jammed. Jim said we needed a new one. We hopped in the truck—"

Hope was a beat in my throat. "Jim's here?"

He shook his head. "Dropped me off for lunch." He was beside me now, bending over.

More fear—if he kills me now, having already called the doctor, could he make it look natural— "Don't!"

He pulled his hands away.

"I—my head aches."

Steve called, "Mama."

I pushed myself up. Ernie pushed me down. "Tell you what. I'll dress the kids and take them to Eloise's."

It sounded fine. The children would be safe.

He paced out of the room.

I was out of bed instantly, tip-toeing to the kitchen, grateful that Ernie had removed my shoes. The receiver sat crosswise in its cradle. The clipping was still on the table beside my purse. Had it been moved?

I snatched up the clipping and grabbed my purse, tucked the paper into it, zipped it shut again and carried it back to the bedroom to stuff it under my pillow. Then I lay down, breathing hastily.

Outside a shrill horn bleated and Ernie hurried into the room.

I sat up. "You go along. I can take care of the kids. Honest."

"You look funny," he said slowly. "You act funny. You got something on your mind?"

Maybe, then, the hope bubbled, he hadn't seen the clipping. "You go, Ernie. Don't worry. I'll be here when you come back." It was a promise, strong and meant. I had to see what he would do. I had to know for sure, even if it killed me!

He said, "Reason I couldn't get a hamburg, kid, I'm broke."

I reached under the pillow and pulled out my purse.

"How did that get there? It wasn't there when I carried you in."

I swallowed a thick lumpiness. "Sure it was. You were—excited."

I reached up and tucked the money into his coverall pocket and forced a smile.

Jim's horn sounded twice, roughly. As the kitchen door closed behind Ernie, the phone rang. By the time I picked up the receiver, the rings had synchronized with the two bongs of the church bell.

"Yes?" I sounded brusque.

"Sergeant Anderson speaking. You all right, lady?"

"Of course I'm all right."

"You hung up. You said murder and hung up."

"Police? There must be some mistake."

"We traced the call."

"But I haven't used the phone."

ALFRED HITCHCOCK'S ANTHOLOGY

"Something's haywire here. There anybody else in your house?"

I laughed, high, strange. "Two small children."

He said something I could almost hear to somebody I couldn't see. Then, "Don't see how it could happen, lady. Sorry to bother you. Some crank maybe. With a psycho on the loose—"

"Yes." *Psycho*. That was the word I had been searching for all day! "Okay then."

I held the receiver for a long moment, listening to the remote hum.

So that was the way it was going to be. I couldn't turn the clipping, the slacks, and Ernie over to the police. Five years and two children—I couldn't point the finger.

Why couldn't I point the finger? It had to be proved. I had to be sure.

I called the doctor's office.

"Mrs. Cochran," the girl said in answer to my question, "there's no record of any call from your husband."

I hung up.

Ernie hadn't called the doctor. Why? If I thought the doctor was coming I would stay home. I would be there whenever he could fix an alibi and sneak out of the garage to come to me—and with a "psycho on the loose"—be safe.

Wait a minute, this is Ernie I'm thinking about, my Ernie. Please, the benefit of the doubt.

I called Eloise. "I have to get to the bank before it closes. The kids —could you—?"

"Love it."

"I'll be right over."

Eloise's house looked very safe. I could stay here. Yet I drove on to the neighborhood bank, withdrew all the money in our joint account and turned it into traveler's checks. There wasn't a great deal, but there was enough to get my children and me back to the white house twenty-five miles from Kansas City, within the sanctuary of my parents' circle. Then maybe I could point the finger.

If I were a detective where would I start? Where Ernie started last night?

I drove back toward the house and cruised to the end of the block. To the right was the movie theater. I stopped before the marquee.

Sandy, the ticket seller's name was.

"Sandy," I said quickly, "you know Mr. Cochran when you see him?"

She laughed. "Everybody around here knows Ernie."

"Sandy, last night—were you here last night?"

"Sure. You know me—Old Faithful."

"Did you see Ernie—Mr. Cochran? Did he come in here?" By the sudden ache in the pit of my stomach, I knew I had been hoping that Ernie had walked this far, been tired, had stepped inside and let the picture ride by until he was calm again.

"He didn't come in."

"He didn't come in?" I repeated sharply. "You mean you saw him?"

"Yeah, About nine-thirty, little earlier maybe. I give him a 'hi,' but he didn't seem to see me."

"Thank you." I went back to the car.

Sandy called. "He went that-a-way." She flipped a thumb to the left, and I followed its gesture.

Halfway down the block I stopped the car again. Sometimes Ernie brought me to Joe's Cafe for a sandwich and a glass of beer. Big deal.

It was dark inside after the glare of the sun. Joe's voice reached me before I saw him. "Be with you in a sec." His voice changed when he saw me. "Mrs. Cochran." He belched a hearty laugh. "You taken to drink in the daytime?"

"What I wanted to know—well—I don't want to be a prying wife, Joe, but Ernie—"

"You checkin' up on that man of yours, eh?"

For a moment I wanted to turn, to run. This thing I was doing to Ernie was as bad as pointing the finger, planting suspicion. Sandy now, would she remember Sara Cochran trying to find out where her husband had been? Would Joe add two and two when the paper was tossed on the bar?

No, Ernie was too different now. I alone remembered how he looked five years ago—and Ernie, himself.

"It's a joke," I said quickly. "But was he—last night—"

He nodded definitely. "Sure was."

A funny looseness came around my heart again, If he sat here and tied one on until all hours—it would be an alibi. "How long?"

The laugh bounced. "In again, out again—one quick glass."

This see-sawing. This up-and-down.

Joe reached to an intricately carved clock behind the bar. He began to wind it. "I remember," he said. "Ten o'clock on the nose by Oscar here." As if to seal it, a small bird popped quickly out above Joe's head. "Cuckoo, cuckoo, cuckoo," he crowed proudly, and snapped himself back inside.

I left the cafe and walked steadily toward the corner. Where next? Ernie left home about nine-thirty. Down the street, turn right by the movie, one beer at ten o'clock. . .

What time did he get home?

I stared at my sandals following each other. If they could have a nose, like a dog on the scent, they could pick up one clear scent, of Ernie Cochran, to lead me where Ernie walked—and keep him away, away, away, from the Arnaughton Golf Course—but, of course, they couldn't. Six blocks, seven, ten, steadily forward, until the stores were gone, then on to the sign, a wide brown board with worn gold words: ARNAUGHTON MUNICIPAL GOLF COURSE

I watched the doll-like figures tossed out over the course. Last night, when the Arnaughton Golf Course was black instead of green, a labyrinth to snare her feet, Marylee Adams, eighteen, was smashed down in the bushes by the sixteenth hole.

Suddenly I couldn't take any more. I couldn't walk onto that course and find the sixteenth hole. I wasn't a detective. I was the wife of Ernie Cochran, and had trusted him completely until today. I wanted him innocent with all my heart.

I ran, until there was pain in my side and a wild bumping in my chest, until I reached the jalopy. There I sat, blind haze before my eyes, my hand on the ignition key, and watched the rain begin.

When I could breathe I started the car and steered it carefully back home. I got the big suitcase from the top of the neat shelves Ernie had built in the garage. I gathered all the children's clean clothes, packed them in and clicked the case shut. I lugged it out to the back and shoved it into the trunk of the jalopy, avoiding the place where the jack should have been.

I stood still, knowing something was forgotten, something I would need.

I darted back into the house. They were still there, over the kitchen chair—the slacks I was supposed to clean, the little rusty spots.

I rolled them up tightly and wrapped them in brown paper. My hand was on the door when the front chimes rang.

Instinctively, the brown package still in my hand, I went to answer it. A tall man stood there. Black patches of rain were soaked on the shoulders of his coat and the rim of his hat.

"Yes?" I clutched the package.

"Mrs. Cochran?"

I nodded.

He did a sleight-of-hand and a badge appeared in his open palm. "Police. Sergeant Anderson. I'd like to talk to you."

"Me?" It came out a croak. "Come in." I stepped back.

The wedding clock on the mantel, Mama's wedding present ("To keep track of happy times, Dollie") pinged in its breathless way, one, two, three, four pings.

"Nice little house you have here."

Trying to throw me off the track? Trying to make me think everything's all right? Had he been to places I hadn't thought of? Because I'm a wife, you see; not a detective.

"Won't you sit down?"

"I don't intend to stay, ma'am."

Suddenly the weight of the package under my arm turned from wool to lead, and I set it down on the planter, feeling each rusty brown spot as a pound, a ton, in my conscience.

Sergeant Anderson watched me. "You look like a sensible woman," he said abruptly.

"I do?" The croak was back.

"You look like a woman who, if she had information the police needed, would be telling it."

I might have known. Somehow they'd traced Ernie. They'd come this close.

"Mrs. Cochran," the sergeant said quietly, "last night a young girl was beaten to death. Everybody knows that. She wasn't much, but nobody, good or bad, deserves to die like she did."

I asked sharply, "What has all this got to do with me? Do you think I killed her?"

He smiled. "Of course not. I'm here because of that phone call. Like I told you when I called you back, somebody mentions murder, we hop on it. First when we traced your call—"

Did I let the receiver slip when I fainted? Did I hang it up myself, the way it was when I went back into the kitchen?

"When I talked to you first, I thought, some mistake. You sounded calm. But operators don't make mistakes."

"Everybody make mistakes."

He nodded. "I think I made one. I got busy after I talked with you. Then, when I was going over the scene of the murder, your call came back to me."

"I didn't call."

"Okay. But somebody called. This woman said she wanted homicide. You remember what she said?"

I swallowed thickly. "Don't try to trick me. I didn't call."

He shrugged. "She said, 'I mean murder.' "

"So?"

"So, I came to the phone. You—she—said, 'I want—I want—' Then she shut up. The wire hummed a long time. Three, four minutes."

I said, anger bright in my voice, "What are you trying to prove?"

"That I'm a dope. You—she—could have been murdered, the way I loused around. Out on the course there, it came to me. When you—she—didn't hang up she sort of faded away. Then, after that hum, somebody picked up the receiver. I heard breathing."

"Breathing?"

"Yeah. Not a woman's. A man's—heavy, lower breathing."

Panic bit like teeth against the back of my throat. "Did he—say—anything? Ask who—"

The sergeant shook his head. "Not a word. You're okay, but you look me in the face and lie in your teeth. Why?"

I was wild with desire to tell Sergeant Anderson everything, before what he was afraid could have happened really did. Tell him, and not have to get in the packed jalopy with the brown package. I didn't even have to say it. I could just hand him the package and tell him, "These slacks were worn by my husband last night." He'd do the rest.

Then the pendulum swung again. I was equally wild with the desire to get him out of the house, and Liz and Steve out of the state, so I could run into my father's arms and ask him what to do.

"I'm so ashamed," I heard myself say. "I'm—a scaredy cat." It sounded coy. "Neither house beside us is occupied. The yard backs up to that orange grove."

Suddenly I was really scared. It was true. Ernie could come after me and I could scream my head off and not be heard.

I took a big breath. "Well, this morning I read all that. When I emptied the rubbish, I—I thought I heard a noise. I locked everything and called the police. When I heard your voice, so official, I nearly—fainted. If there was a man, it was the owner—"

Sergeant Anderson looked tired. "Okay. I'll just take a look around outside." He walked past me to the door.

I picked up the brown paper package and hurried to the bedroom. The phone rang as I tucked it on the top shelf of the closet.

"Honey," Eloise cried, "Ernie rolled along home with Jim to unload the case of beer. He's taking Jim's truck to bring the kids home."

"He's leaving?"

"He left."

She hung up.

Left. How long ago? There was a knock on the back door.

"Everything looks okay around here," Sergeant Anderson reported.

Go, I willed. Any minute Ernie will clank up in Jim's old truck and step out—the man in the picture, the face you have studied so hard that twenty extra pounds, a crewcut and a mustache wouldn't fool you a bit.

"I'm sorry I caused you so much trouble."

"That's all right." I started to close the door.

He turned. "Mrs. Cochran," he said. "When you're scared you sure freeze at the receiver. You sure breathe like a man." He walked quickly down the sidewalk to his car.

The start of his motor fitted itself with two other sounds: the church steeple bell striking the first of five strokes, and the clatter of Jim's old truck swinging into the back drive off the alley.

*Softy now, all things softly.* My hands gripped themselves together in a gesture that was both a wringing and a prayer.

Through the window Liz and Steve, being lifted from the truck by Ernie, made a pretty picture; Daddy and the kids, the sun just coming out after the rain, and all small human troubles drying up from the late afternoon heat. Seeing them, everything in me denied the events of the day and my mind. Then Ernie, with Liz on his shoulder, strode to the back door and we stood staring at each other.

236                 ALFRED HITCHCOCK'S ANTHOLOGY

Look at his eyes, I commanded myself. What is that hardness way in back, like a rock under soft water?

There was some of the hardness in his normally warm voice. "Whose car was that out front?"

I stammered, "Just a man, selling books for children."

"You must have let him go through his whole spiel. The car was here when I came down Jim's street. I saw it from the corner."

"He was quite a talker."

Ernie looked at the clock. "Ten after five. Time to do a couple jobs before we get dressed."

Dressed! The slacks I was supposed to clean! "Ernie," I said carefully, "you know those gray slacks you wore last night?"

Did his mouth tighten?

"I couldn't seem to get the—paint—out. I dropped them at the cleaners."

He was still silent.

"I'll press your brown ones."

He spoke then. "You feel better?"

"Fine."

"Eloise said you went to the bank. Why?"

I was the silent one.

"Was it to get money for the dress we talked about?"

I shook my head.

"It's your money too."

"Forget the dress. It's caused enough trouble. Forget last night." I fought the tears.

"I'd like to forget last night," Ernie said, very softly.

"I'll press your brown pants. But I—my head—I still feel a little rocky. Anyhow, I couldn't find a sitter—"

Ernie said flatly, "I won't go without you."

My moves, then, were like the ones in the hour I couldn't remember before the long terrible day began. When it was all done I knew I was going to Eloise's and Jim's with Ernie. It was a way of buying time, putting off the hour when I would be alone with the man in the drawing, while dark pulled itself down around the tract house and the orange groves, and grew blacker and thicker.

I saw it all. I watched, Gulliver-high above a doll house, while a doll man leaned over a doll woman's bed and lifted a car jack with infinite slowness. I found myself, normal size, out on the street, running and running. As I ran, I knew for the first time exactly what I would do.

I would get old Mrs. Callahan to stay with the children. I would get dressed and go with Ernie to Eloise's and Jim's to laugh and talk. When the men got into the poker game in the dining room, which couldn't be seen from the patio, I would excuse myself to check on the children. I would take the jalopy, get them—and go.

When I was back in the white house, when my father knew the whole story, I would mail the slacks to Sergeant Anderson with a slip of paper reading: "These belong to Ernie Cochran." It would be settled.

When Mrs. Callahan agreed to come right away, I said I'd drive over and pick her up. At the open door of the garage a tiny noise broke the stillness.

Ernie stood with his back to me, whistling between his teeth contentedly. His right arm moved rhythmically. A greasy rag flipped back and forth.

I stood very still, but as if he sensed me, he swung around slowly, his arms never stopping. I forced my eyes to go with equal slowness from his face to his shoulder, down the length of his powerful arm, to his hands. Rub-a-dub-dub, smooth and gleaming in the maw of Ernie's strong greasy hands lay the missing jack from the trunk of the old jalopy!

Suddenly the church bells rang, grew louder and louder, until each of the oranges in the grove seemed to have a clapper in it, ringing, ringing, the news that it was six o'clock.

Ernie's whistle stopped. "You look awful. Did the doctor come?"

"Did you call him?"

His eyelids flickered. "You know I did. No, wait." The rag fluttered. "The line was busy. I called from the garage."

"You told me you called him."

"I didn't want to worry you. Did he come?"

"I told him not to. Anyway, I'm going to get Mrs. Callahan. I don't want you to stay home because of me."

"Maybe we'd better. You look so—funny—"

I laughed. "You've been saying that all day. Where did that jack come from?" It sounded casual.

ALFRED HITCHCOCK'S ANTHOLOGY

Ernie came toward me suddenly. He put his hands on my shoulders and pulled me against him, hard. The greasy rag touched one of my arms and the jack felt long and cold and hard against the other. Ernie put his mouth against mine. I pursed my own lips, trying to keep them soft and responsive.

"That's better." He let me go and once again the rag began to slick its way along the jack. "It makes me feel—bad—when we quarrel."

*How bad, Ernie?* Miles beyond my numbness a sort of pity stirred impersonally. There must be thousands like Ernie—people who had, deep and hidden, maybe even from themselves, a sickening twist of mind that turned them from the normal into hideous places of darkness and terror. When? When they felt bad. I remembered Sergeant Anderson's voice. "Psycho."

"Ernie," I said as he started toward the back of the jalopy, "what are you doing?"

"Putting the jack back where it belongs, of course."

"No." I ran to him. Was the trunk locked? It must be or Sergeant Anderson would have noticed—

Ernie tugged at it. "Darn," he said mildly. "Where are your keys?"

I took his arm and smiled at him. "Later, friend. We're going to a party, remember?"

"I don't get you." He shrugged, walked back into the garage and laid the jack on the workbench. He seemed tired of the whole thing as we went into the house, he to the bedroom. When I heard the shower begin I picked up my purse from the kitchen shelf, took out the traveler's checks, put them into the zippered compartment along with the clipping. I bent to the lowest shelf and put the purse in the heavy Dutch oven, settling the cover on tightly. Ernie loved stew made in a Dutch oven.

"Let's go," Ernie said when Mrs. Callahan was in, briefed, and before the TV. "We'll take Jim's truck back."

I hadn't thought of that, and gratitude went through me. No matter how engrossing the poker game, if I took the jalopy from the party Ernie would hear. He knew each cough of the motor.

High in the truck, he drove slowly. Over the noise I said, "Funny, when I put the groceries in the trunk this morning, the jack—it wasn't there." I snapped a glance at him.

"Of course it wasn't."

"Why not?" I was afraid to ask but I had to find out.

"Because I took it out to clean it." He stared straight ahead.

"Do jacks get dirty, even when you don't use them?"

"Anything gets rusty."

"I didn't see it anywhere—"

He switched toward me. "You mean you looked?"

"I thought, what if I get a flat tire?"

His laugh was short. "You've never changed a tire in your life."

"Oh, what's the difference?" I tried to laugh. "Just making conversation is all."

He waited a moment. "I see."

We parked in Jim's drive and Ernie cut the motor. The sound of the patio party reached thinly out to us.

If Ernie was pondering about me the way I had about him, then he knew that I knew. He could be deciding what move he should make—when we were alone, when the time was right.

"Seeing as how you're so interested," Ernie said, opening the truck door, "the jack was on the top shelf above the workbench for the last three days."

We walked together through Jim's gate, and I could see the two of us, the Cochrans, Ernie and Sara, as nice a couple as you'd want to meet. Our feet made a matched scuffling, louder than the voices of greeting, louder than the church bells, sounding muffled this time, far away and muffled—seven o'clock in the evening.

Almost at once, though, it was better. There were all these people, these friends. They made a ring around me, as my father's house would make a ring if I could get there. They protected me, not only from Ernie—from actual physical Ernie—but for a little while from all of the thoughts that had tormented me. The things they said were so usual.

It was wonderful, like when a toothache stops. You know it will hurt again, and will have to be drilled and cleaned out and packed with something new to take the place of the diseased portion. But at the moment it doesn't ache, and that little respite is wonderful.

The toothache stayed away until I heard Jim's voice over supper. ". . . no clues yet. What kind of a monster would do a thing like that? And to think it's so close."

Eloise cried, "Oh, Jim—cut it out."

Ernie said, close, just the width of the redwood table away, "Sara?"

I kept my eyes down then. I pretended not to hear, and called to one of the girls.

We ate. We cleared the tables. We played records and danced on the uneven bricks. We drank beer. The dusk was gone. The spotlight beside the garage sent down a shaft of light that widened as it slanted, so that the movement, the rhythm, was light and dark, swift and shadowy. Ernie didn't come near me, not even to ask me to dance.

Then the men moved, as if on signal, into the dining room for poker. The women sat in the deep light chairs, feet high, heads back. I lay there, too, looking upward. It was as if I had never seen a sky before.

In these clothes, then, this yellow dress and this white stole, would I start the long ride home, two sleepy babies soft against my lap? From these friends, then, would I go up over the mountains, which had always frightened me, across the desert which always seemed unending, into the middle west country?

I thought suddenly, I could call Sergeant Anderson from the phone in Eloise's room. All these people would be around to protect me. Or I could tell Jim what I knew, let him carry the burden. But lying there, ankles crossed, my hands folded, too filled with tension to allow themselves the luxury of tenseness, I shook my head at the stars and I knew I could do neither.

I could run away from Ernie, even be caught by Ernie, but somehow, all day and now tonight, I could not stand up and tell these people, tell anybody, that Ernie Cochran was a monster—a murderer and a monster.

Eloise's hand came down on my shoulder. "Let's go make the girls some lemonade."

I pushed myself up out of the chair. After the bells, the sirens, the wedding clock, the cuckoo, had cut each hour off sharply with razorlike strokes, now, outdoors in the dark, cool, silvered night, I had been given this refreshment. Now, the time had come.

"I have to run home a minute," I whispered to Eloise. "Don't bother about me. Mrs. Callahan—"

She patted my shoulder. "Okay. Bring back some ice cubes, will you?"

I nodded and moved toward the gate. The clock seemed loud. I walked quickly, silently around the house. The street stretched before me. In all of the tract there were no lights.

This was the way, then, that the world looked to Ernie on those nights when he was troubled. This was the way it was for Ernie last night—the darkness, widespread, acres of it, eighteen holes of it—with a stopping place at the sixteenth hole where the bushes were darker than the greens, where anything could happen and nobody would see. Not until dawn came and revealed—

It was then I heard the footsteps. They were unhurried, wider than mine. They grew closer, heavy, steady, closing in.

I walked faster. I trotted. Then I began to run. The footsteps ran too. Light exploded behind my eyeballs. Then I was on my own porch. My hand was on the knob—and Ernie's hand crashed solid and tight against my shoulder.

I screamed. Ernie put his other hand against my mouth.

Mrs. Callahan opened the door. "Sakes' alive," she yelped, " you near scared the life out of me!"

Ernie said, breathlessly but quietly, "I'm sorry. My wife was giving me a race."

I pushed my heart down out of my throat. "Ernie'll walk you home," I managed. "Then he's going back to the party. Me—I'm going to bed."

Ernie said, "Me, I'm going to bed too." He slipped Mrs. Callahan's shawl over her shoulders. "Let's go, Mrs. Callahan."

I closed the door and leaned against it. Then I went, weak and shaky, into the kitchen and poured myself a glass of water. The jalopy sat in the drive, with its suitcase. "What will I do now?" I asked aloud.

The front door opened and shut, quietly. I could hear Ernie's breathing, the click of the night lock. I listened to his feet, the heavy feet that had chased me down the street, had caught me, too late, on our own front porch.

What if those feet had caught me on the middle of the first block? Or the second?

I looked down at my yellow dress. These are not the clothes I will run away in, I thought with deep hopelessness. These are the clothes I shall die in. The yellow all smudged and stained. The white turned red. And my hair—

Ernie was in the doorway. "That was a fool thing to do."

I nodded dumbly.

"Where did you think you were going?"

"How did you know I was gone?"

"I went to the kitchen—Eloise told me."

The silence closed in.

Ernie said, "You should have known better. After last night."

"What about last night?"

"A girl was killed on the golf course."

"I know."

"A man who can kill once can kill twice."

"I know."

Ernie moved. I gripped the slick tile of the sink, but he didn't come near me.

"I think we'd better settle this once and for all."

"Settle what?"

"What's on your mind. What's been on your mind all day."

The words were there to yell at him. Settle it, then, they screamed in my throat. Grab something. A knife, or get the jack. It's cleaned and ready again. Kill me. Go on. Murder me. But—get—it—over—with! But the words stayed inside me.

"I'm going to bed," Ernie announced surprisingly. "I'll wait for you."

In the dark then, like the doll house.

When he was gone, I walked weakly into the livingroom and sank down in the nearest chair. A reprieve. Maybe he would fall asleep. Maybe he was in no hurry. Maybe he wanted me to sleep first.

If he would sleep, I could call Sergeant Anderson. Or perhaps, by a miracle, by prayer, I could get the children out to the jalopy. I closed my eyes and let the prayer fill me.

After a while I leaned forward and switched on the TV, keeping it soft. The grayness came and the hum, and finally the eleven o'clock news face, its mouth moving quickly.

The words that tumbled from the fast mouth made no sense at first. Then they caught me like a tossed lariat.

". . . brilliant police work. The young man—he's just turned seventeen—was recently released from a mental institution. He admits having followed Marylee Adams for the past week. Last night he stole a car. He offered her a ride when she left work. He says she did not object to driving up the back road behind the Arnaughton Golf Course.

He became chaotic about the actual crime, but he took the police to the place where he threw away the murder weapon—a golf club given him by a man for whom he caddied, which he'd hidden in the back of the car. His reason? 'I don't like pretty girls.'

"And now to the weather picture for southern—"

*Seventeen!* I leaned forward and turned off the TV. My body felt as if warm milk flowed sleepily through my veins. I lay back in the chair and floated for a long long time.

The trip back to reality was short and brutal. I sat up, pain all through me.

In the bedroom was Ernie Cochran. He was waiting for his wife. He was wondering, and hurt, by her actions of the day. Good, kind Ernie Cochran.

The pain grew and spread. A murder had been committed. And Sara Cochran had committed it. By suspicion, by lack of faith, I had killed the goodness of Ernie, my husband. I had turned him from the man he was into a monster.

That was the reason I couldn't point a finger. A deep instinct had kept me from telling Sergeant Anderson or Jim or anybody. The knowledge that Ernie Cochran was good.

I began to cry then, the day's thousand tears streamed down my face and choked in my throat. Filled with them, I stumbled down the hall. I went directly to Ernie's bed and flung myself down.

"Forgive me," I heard myself murmur over and over. "Forgive me."

Then I was pulled into Ernie's arms. "Forgive you for what, darling?"

That moment was the worst of all the moments of the day. I couldn't tell him. I could never tell him. The shame and the guilt were mine to hold alone all the rest of our years together. What man could live with the thought that his wife believed him, even for one day, capable of brutal murder?

After a while my sobs slowed.

"All day," Ernie was saying, "I've felt awful. You looked at me so strangely. On the phone you were so cold. This noon—oh, honey, you scared me silly."

His kiss was long now, an interlude and a promise.

"Then I called this afternoon and you were gone. I saw the man— quite close. He looked smart, sure of himself. The suitcase was gone

ALFRED HITCHCOCK'S ANTHOLOGY

from the shelf—and you didn't want me to look in the trunk of the car—"

It was all there. Ernie had been puzzled too. He had added up the strangeness of my actions, words, looks, and had persuaded himself that his wife no longer loved him—was leaving him—was unfaithful.

Such tenderness filled me that it beat with an ache against my skin. I wanted to help, but if I eased his mind in one way I would kill him again in another. I kissed him instead.

I lay in the circle of Ernie's arm and listened to his contented breathing beside me. I closed my eyes and drew my breath easily through lungs that could now breathe without fear.

Far away, gentle, sweet, silver, the bells of the church steeple chimed slowly, the long count, from one to twelve.

I drifted with the chimes: Tomorrow I'll make Ernie a stew. He loves stew made all day in the Dutch oven—

In the Dutch oven. The traveler's checks—

I can take them back in the morning.

The long terrible day was over.

On the brink of sleep, on the very cliff, ready to fall softly into nothing, I sat bolt upright, awake, staring into the dark, the now familiar clawing of my heart tearing at my chest—the Dutch oven!

"Police Chief J. Hampton Jones remarked upon the similarity of this crime and that of the killing of one Sandra Hims, also 18, on a public golf course in Kansas City about five years ago. At that time the murder weapon was found, a heavy car jack.

The drawing (at right) was forwarded from that city, and is based on a witness' description of the suspect, the man with whom Miss Hims was last seen leaving a Kansas City bar."

# Cicero

## by Edward Wellen

**"K**now somethin'?" Cicero seemed almost shy confessing it, an alarming thing in a man of his bulk. "I got a itch in my trigger finger to do the rubbin' out by myself."

Brains didn't glance up from his chess problem, but Lefty dropped his scratch sheet and his jaw.

"Yourself?" Lefty finally said. "Now, Chief. You can't help bein' aware of the fact that you got where you are today by knowin' when and how to delegate responsibility."

"Yeah. Still and all, Herrin is my one big mistake. Who'd ever figure a guy like Herrin, a guy that seems to have nothin' on his mind but dressin' swell and keepin' his self neat, to have the gall to cross me, who give him his start, and set him up on his own?"

"Nobody'd figure that, Chief."

"Yeah, I just itch to do this one myself personal." He looked wistful. "Be like in the good old days when I was just startin' out myself and workin' my way up."

"I hear you sure had the gift, Chief."

"Yeah. The steady hand and the steely eye. And most important— the sense of timin'."

There was a moment of silence as Cicero gazed feelingly back across the years. A growing firmness of purpose showed on his face.

Lefty took alarm. "Now, listen, Chief."

"Yeah?"

"You ain't serious. I mean about doin' the rubbin' out yourself?"

"No?"

"You can't be. You know yourself you're kinda rusty now, Chief. You know that."

"Yeah?"

"Well, you know I wouldn't wanna wound your feelin's for the world, Chief, but—"

"No, go on. That's all right, Lefty. I ain't in the least bit touchy. You go on ahead and say it."

"Okay, let's face it, Chief. Your eye ain't what it used to be, and neither is your hand."

Lefty failed to get out of the way in time.

"Ow! I thought you said you wasn't touchy."

"I ain't. That's for negative thinkin'. Maybe my eye ain't what it used to be and maybe my hand ain't what it used to be—"

"The hell it ain't," Lefty said under his breath.

"But my sense of timin' is just as good as ever. And as long as my sense of timin' stays sound I ain't licked. Brains. Brains!"

Brains shoved the board back and got up with a sigh.

"Brains, I'm gonna rub Herrin out myself. But I got tobacco tremor and bum glims. To you I delegate the responsibility for figurin' out how I score a bull's eye."

Brains drew nourishment from something challenging. His eyes lit, but he didn't waste energy pacing. He leaned against the wall and walled his eyes in speculation.

Cicero and Lefty tensed like hawks when Brains cleared his throat.

"You know, it might not work out bad at all," Brains said. "You'll have the element of surprise going for you. They count you out. They know Lefty is a muscle man, but a torpedo he ain't. They know I'm no killer. And the rest of the bunch—I won't even waste my breath. Herrin will be expecting that if and when you make your move, it'll be in the shape of hiring a gun. Local talent is out. He'll be looking for out-of-town talent. He'll know the minute it blows in. Until he hears that word, he'll feel safe. He won't break routine. Lefty, what's Herrin's routine?"

Lefty closed his eyes and began to recite. "At ten on the nose, Herrin comes outa the hotel and crosses to the beanery. He could have room service breakfast in bed, but he has his eye on one of the waitresses at the beanery. After breakfast he—"

"That's enough. That does it."

The interruption discomfited Lefty for an instant; he could have gone on and on. Then he smiled. "I know. You figure to get to the dame and set Herrin up. The Chief'll be waitin' behind the door of her room and when Herrin and the dame walk in—. Sure, how can the Chief miss with the gun right in Herrin's ribs?"

Brains stepped over to his chess problem, picked up the red queen, grinned at it, then set it down. "No."

Lefty was hurt. "No?"

"Never trust a dame. No, what I have in mind is a whole lot safer and surer."

Lefty leaned forward. "I know. We clout a heap and drive past when Herrin starts to cross the street. The Chief blasts him when we're right alongside, just like that."

"No."

"No?"

"The car is out." Brains first made sure he was out of range of a possible punch from Cicero; then he said, "In the Chief's case we can't risk a moving triggerman. That would be compounding the difficulty. What I mean is, here we already got a moving target. No, the Chief has to be stationary. But we can't sit waiting in a car. Herrin would spot us."

"I know—"

"We gotta get a room overlooking the street, shoot Herrin from a window."

"But the Chief's eye, his hand—"

Brains raised an eyebrow and put up a hand of his own. Lefty subsided. Brains cleared his throat and the others held their breath.

"You know how they put 'X marks the spot' when they print the picture of the scene of the crime?"

"So?"

"So why not put the X in first? Before the crime. This X will be like cross-hairs in a sight. Only big. So big you can't miss it, Chief. See, we paint a big X on the crosswalk, clamp a high-powered rifle in the window, zero it in on the X, and when Herrin is crossing over it you pull the trigger. You don't have to worry about aiming or holding. You don't need a steely eye or a steady hand. All you need is a sense of timing to tell you when to squeeze the trigger. Then out the room, up the stairs, across the roofs."

Cicero smiled. "Sounds great." Then he frowned.

"What is it, Chief?"

"That X. Seems to me a bull's eye'd be more in keepin'."

"Anything you say, Chief. Be easy enough to lay out the circles with string and chalk." Brains' enthusiasm had begun to peter out now that he had the answer all cut-and-dried, and his voice took on a mocking tone. "Of course we want to get things like the circumferences of the circles all squared away. It'll take a bit of working out with pi—the three point fourteen sort—but we'll put your man on the spot."

"But to paint a big target on the street—"

"Don't fret about that, Chief. That's the easiest part."

It may have seemed easy to Brains, who whistled as he wielded his brush, but Lefty was sweating. Wooden horses detoured early morning traffic around the two men painting big bright-red concentric circles in the center of the crosswalk. Brains and Lefty had smeared their faces with paint to hide their identity and wore old coveralls for the same reason. The cop on the beat had given them a perfunctory glance as he went by. But under the makeup Lefty was pale.

Brains grinned one of his rare grins. "Take it easy, Lefty. Just go ahead and behave as though you know what you're doing and no one will ask questions."

Lefty grunted and went on painting. He painted mighty furiously.

"Boy, you're sloppy, Lefty. Look at mine, nice and neat."

Lefty grunted and went on painting.

They heard one passerby say to another, "What is it? Why, there's going to be a helicopter landing there. I think I read something about it."

Brains grinned.

They were getting there, working from the inside out.

Lefty paused and said in a whisper, "I can feel the Chief lookin' down at us."

Brains said deadpan, "Yeah, Lefty, we must be making a perfect target out of ourselves. Be a good joke on us if the Chief was thinking of wiping us out."

"Let's finish up and get outa here."

They worked silently and swiftly and soon Brains was straightening with a groan. He eyed their work.

"It's quick-drying paint, but we'll lay down these wet-paint signs to keep pedestrians from rubbing it out. Okay, Lefty, everything's in order, let's go. Ten minutes before Herrin comes out we return, take away the horses. . ."

Cicero had to tell himself to hold his horses, his trigger finger was itching that bad. Herrin was stepping out of the hotel. He was nearing the target, one foot over the rim.

Cicero was happy. He liked it now with the finger on the trigger, the squeeze of flesh and metal, and now the tightness of no more give, and the shock, and the hot metal.

Brains and Lefty were at Cicero's shoulder and they saw Herrin, at the last instant, dance his spotless white shoes away from the target. Cicero didn't see this. At the last instant, Cicero blinked, anticipating the noise and recoil of the shot.

When the blink was over, he saw Herrin still alive, still moving— moving fast for cover.

Cicero was numb, wholly numb. Lefty and Brains had to drag him to get him away before the police got there. They hauled him home, got him safe behind his steel doors and steel shutters.

Outside his bedroom they whispered.

"I know what it is. He's in shock. He thinks he's lost his sense of timin'."

"And he'll pine away into a pine box."

"You gonna stand by and let the Chief think he's a has-been?"

"I sure won't be the one to tell him Herrin sidestepped the target because we forgot to remove the wet-paint signs."

"Me neither."

Brains eyed Lefty shrewdly before making up his mind to say, "Before the word gets out Cicero is through, we'd better throw in with Herrin."

ALFRED HITCHCOCK'S ANTHOLOGY

# Winter Run

## by Edward D. Hoch

Johnny Kendell was first out of the squad car, first into the alley with his gun already drawn. The snow had drifted here, and it was easy to follow the prints of the running feet. He knew the neighborhood, knew that the alley dead-ended at a ten-foot board fence. The man he sought would be trapped there.

"This is the police!" he shouted. "Come out with your hands up!"

There was no answer except the whistle of wind through the alley, and something which might have been the desperate breathing of a trapped man. Behind him, Kendell could hear Sergeant Racin following, and knew that he too would have his gun drawn. The man they sought had broken the window of a liquor store down the street and had made off with an armload of gin bottles. Now he'd escaped to nowhere and had left a trail in the snow that couldn't be missed, long running steps.

Overhead, as suddenly as the flick of a light switch, the full moon passed from behind a cloud and bathed the alley in a blue-white glow. Twenty feet ahead of him, Johnny Kendell saw the man he tracked, saw the quick glisten of something in his upraised hand. Johnny squeezed the trigger of his police revolver.

Even after the targeted quarry had staggered backward, dying, into the fence that blocked the alley's end, Kendell kept firing. He didn't stop until Sergeant Racin, aghast, knocked the gun from his hand, kicked it out of reach.

Kendell didn't wait for the departmental investigation. Within forty-eight hours he had resigned from the force and was headed west with a girl named Sandy Brown whom he'd been planning to marry in a month. And it was not until the little car had burned up close to three hundred miles that he felt like talking about it, even to someone as close as Sandy.

"He was a bum, an old guy who just couldn't wait for the next drink. After he broke the window and stole that gin, he just went down the alley to drink it in peace. He was lifting a bottle to his lips when I saw him, and I don't know what I thought it was—a gun, maybe, or a knife. As soon as I fired the first shot I knew it was just a bottle, and I guess maybe in my rage at myself, or at the world, I kept pulling the trigger." He lit a cigarette with shaking hands. "If he hadn't been just a bum I'd probably be up before the grand jury!"

Sandy was a quiet girl who asked little from the man she loved. She was tall and angular, with a boyish cut to her dark brown hair, and a way of laughing that made men want to sell their souls. That laugh, and the subdued twinkle deep within her pale blue eyes, told anyone who cared that Sandy Brown was not always quiet, not really boyish.

Now, sitting beside Johnny Kendell, she said, "He was as good as dead anyway, Johnny. If he'd passed out in that alley they wouldn't have found him until he was frozen stiff."

He swerved the car a bit to avoid a stretch of highway where the snow had drifted over. "But I put three bullets in him, just to make sure. He stole some gin, and I killed him for it."

"You thought he had a weapon."

"I didn't think. I just didn't think about anything. Sergeant Racin had been talking about a cop he knew who was crippled by a holdup man's bullet, and I suppose if I was thinking about anything it was about that."

"I still wish you had stayed until after the hearing."

"So they could fire me nice and offical? No thanks!"

Johnny drove and smoked in silence for a time, opening the side window a bit to let the cold air whisper through his blond hair. He was handsome, not yet thirty, and until now there'd always been a ring of certainty about his every action. "I guess I just wasn't cut out to be a cop," he said finally.

"What *are* you cut out for, Johnny? Just running across the country like this? Running when nobody's chasing you?"

"We'll find a place to stop and I'll get a job and then we'll get married. You'll see."

"What can you do besides run?"

252                    ALFRED HITCHCOCK'S ANTHOLOGY

He stared out through the windshield at the passing banks of soot-stained snow. "I can kill a man," he answered.

The town was called Wagon Lake, a name which fitted its past better than its present. The obvious signs of that past were everywhere to be seen, the old cottages that lined the frozen lake front, and the deeply rutted dirt roads which here and there ran parallel to the modern highways. But Wagon Lake, once so far removed from everywhere, had reckoned without the coming of the automobile and the postwar boom which would convert it into a fashionable suburb less than an hour's drive from the largest city in the state.

The place was midwestern to its very roots, and perhaps there was something about the air that convinced Johnny Kendell. That, or perhaps he was only tired of running. "This is the place," he told Sandy while they were stopped at a gas station. "Let's stay a while."

"The lake's all frozen over," she retorted, looking dubious.

"We're not going swimming."

"No, but summer places like this always seem so cold in the winter, colder than regular cities."

But they could both see that the subdivisions had come to Wagon Lake along with the superhighways, and it was no longer just a summer place. They would stay.

For the time being they settled on adjoining rooms at a nearby motel, because Sandy refused to share an apartment with him until they were married. In the morning, Kendell left her the task of starting the apartment hunt while he went off in search of work. At the third place he tried, the man shook his head sadly. "Nobody around here hires in the winter," he told Kendell, "except maybe the sheriff. You're a husky fellow. Why don't you try him?"

"Thanks, maybe I will," Johnny Kendell said, but he tried two more local businesses before he found himself at the courthouse and the sheriff's office.

The sheriff's name was Quintin Dade, and he spoke from around a cheap cigar that never left the corner of his mouth. He was a politician and a smart one. Despite the cigar, it was obvious that the newly arrived wealth of Wagon Lake had elected him.

"Sure," he said, settling down behind a desk scattered casually with letters, reports, and wanted circulars. "I'm looking for a man. We always hire somebody in the winter, to patrol the lake road and keep an eye on the cottages. People leave some expensive stuff in those old places during the winter months. They expect it to be protected."

"You don't have a man yet?" Kendell asked.

"We had one, up until last week." Sheriff Dade offered no more. Instead, he asked, "Any experience in police work?"

"I was on the force for better than a year back East."

"Why'd you leave?"

"I wanted to travel."

"Married?"

"I will be, as soon as I land a job."

"This one just pays seventy-five a week, and it's nights. If you ˑ ˑˑ out, though, I'll keep you on come summer."

"What do I have to do?"

"Drive a patrol car around the lake every hour, check cottages, make sure the kids aren't busting them up—that sort of thing."

"Have you had much trouble?"

"Oh, nothing serious," the sheriff answered, looking quickly away. "Nothing you couldn't handle, a big guy like you."

"Would I have to carry a gun?"

"Well, sure!"

Johny Kendell thought about it. "All right," he said finally. "I'll give it a try."

"Good. Here are some applications to fill out. I'll be checking with the people back East, but that needn't delay your starting. I've got a gun here for you. I can show you the car and you can begin tonight."

Kendell accepted the .38 revolver with reluctance. It was a different make from the one he'd carried back East, but they were too similar. The very feel and weight and coldness of it against his palm brought back the memory of that night in the alley.

Later, when he went back to the motel and told Sandy about the job, she only sat cross-legged on her bed staring up at him. "It wasn't even a week ago, Johnny. How can you take another gun in your hand so soon?"

"I won't have it in my hand. I promise you I won't even draw it."

"What if you see some kids breaking into a cottage?"

"Sandy, it's a job! It's the only thing I know how to do. On seventy-five a week we can get married."

"We can get married anyway. I found a job myself, down at the supermarket."

Kendell stared out the window at a distant hill dotted here and there with snowy spots. "I told him I'd take the job, Sandy. I thought you were on my side."

"I am. I always have been. But you killed a man, Johnny. I don't want it to happen again, for any reason."

"It won't happen again."

He went over to the bed and kissed her, their lips barely brushing.

That night, Sheriff Dade took him out on the first run around the lake, pausing at a number of deserted cottages while instructing him in the art of checking for intruders. The evening was cold, but there was a moon which reflected brightly off the surface of the frozen lake. Kendell wore his own suit and topcoat, with only the badge and gun to show that he belonged in the sheriff's car. He knew at once that he would like the job, even the boredom of it, and he listened carefully to the sheriff's orders.

"About once an hour you take a swing around the lake. That takes you twenty minutes, plus stops. But don't fall into a pattern with your trips, so someone can predict when you'll be passing any given cottage. Vary it, and, of course, check these bars along here too. Especially on weekends we get a lot of underage drinkers. And they're the ones who usually get loaded and decide to break into a cottage."

"They even come here in the winter?"

"This isn't a summer town any more. But sometimes I have a time convincing the cottagers of that."

They rode in silence for a time, and the weight of the gun was heavy on Johnny Kendell's hip. Finally, he decided what had to be done. "Sheriff," he began, "there's something I want to tell you."

"What's that?"

"You'll find out anyway when you check on me back East. I killed a man while I was on duty. Just last week. He was a bum who broke into a liquor store and I thought he had a gun so I shot him. I resigned from the force because they were making a fuss about it."

Sheriff Dade scratched his balding head. "Well, I don't hold that against you. Glad you mentioned it, though. Just remember, out here the most dangerous thing you'll probably face will be a couple of beered-up teenagers. And they don't call for guns."

"I know."

"Right. Drop me back at the courthouse and you're on your own. Good luck."

An hour later, Kendell started his first solo swing around the lake, concentrating on the line of shuttered cottages which stood like sentinels against some invader from the frozen lake. Once he stopped the car to investigate four figures moving on the ice, but they were only children gingerly testing skates on the glossy surface.

On the far side of the lake he checked a couple of cottages at random. Then he pulled in and parked beside a bar called the Blue Zebra. It had more cars than the others, and there was a certain Friday night gaiety about the place even from outside. He went in, letting his topcoat hang loosely over the badge pinned to his suit lapel. The bar was crowded and all the tables were occupied, but he couldn't pinpoint any under-age group. They were young men self-consciously trying to please their dates, beer-drinking groups of men fresh from their weekly bowling, and the occasional women nearing middle age that one always finds sitting on bar stools.

Kendell chatted a few moments with the owner and then went back outside. There was nothing for him here. He'd turned down the inevitable offer of a drink because it was too early in the evening, and too soon on the job to be relaxing.

As he was climbing into his car, a voice called to him from the doorway of the Blue Zebra. "Hey, Deputy!"

"What's the trouble?"

The man was slim and tall, and not much older than Kendell. He came down the steps of the bar slowly, not speaking again until he was standing only inches away. "I just wanted to get a look at you, that's all. I had that job until last week."

"Oh?" Kendell said, because there was nothing else to say.

"Didn't old Dade tell you he fired me?"

"No."

"Well, he did. Ask him why sometime. Ask him why he fired Milt Woodman." He laughed and turned away, heading back to the bar.

Kendell shrugged and got into the car. It didn't really matter to him that a man named Milt Woodman was bitter about losing his job. His thoughts were on the future, and on Sandy, waiting back at the motel. . .

She was sleeping when he returned to their rooms. He went in quietly and sat on the edge of the bed, waiting until she awakened. Presently her blue eyes opened and she saw him. "Hi. How'd it go?"

"Fine. I think I'm going to like it. Get up and watch the sunrise with me."

"I have to go to work at the supermarket."

"Nuts to that! I'm never going to see you if we're both working."

"We need the money, Johnny. We can't afford this motel, or these two rooms, much longer."

"Let's talk about it later, huh?" He suddenly realized that he hadn't heard her laugh in days, and the thought of it made him sad. Sandy's laughter had always been an important part of her.

That night passed much as the previous one, with patrols around the lake and frequent checks at the crowded bars. He saw Milt Woodman again, watching him through the haze of cigarette smoke at the Blue Zebra, but this time the man did not speak. The following day, though, Kendell remembered to ask Sheriff Dade about him.

"I ran into somebody Friday night—fellow named Milt Woodman," he said.

Dade frowned. "He try to give you any trouble?"

"No, not really. He just said to ask you sometime why you fired him."

"*Are* you asking me?"

"No. It doesn't matter to me in the least."

Dade nodded. "It shouldn't. But let me know if he bothers you any more."

"Why should he?" Kendell asked, troubled by the remark.

"No reason. Just keep on your toes."

The following night, Monday, Johnny didn't have to work. He decided to celebrate with Sandy by taking her to a nearby drive-in where the management kept open all winter by supplying little heaters for each car.

Tuesday night, just after midnight, Kendell pulled into the parking lot at the Blue Zebra. The neoned juke box was playing something plaintive and the bar was almost empty. The owner offered him a drink again, and he decided he could risk it.

"Hello, Deputy," a voice said at his shoulder. He knew before he turned that it was Milt Woodman.

"The name's Johnny Kendell," he said, keeping it friendly.

"Nice name. You know mine." He chuckled a little. "That's a good-looking wife you got. Saw you together at the movie last night."

"Oh?" Kendell moved instinctively away.

Milt Woodman kept on smiling. "Did Dade ever tell you why he fired me?"

"I didn't ask him."

The chuckle became a laugh. "Good boy! Keep your nose clean. Protect that seventy-five a week." He turned and went toward the door. "See you around."

Kendell finished his drink and followed him out. There was a hint of snow in the air and tonight no moon could be seen. Ahead, on the road, the twin tail lights of Woodman's car glowed for a moment until they disappeared around a curve. Kendell gunned his car ahead with a sudden urge to follow the man, but when he'd reached the curve himself the road ahead was clear. Woodman had turned off somewhere.

The rest of the week was quiet, but on Friday he had a shock. It had always been difficult for him to sleep days, and he often awakened around noon after only four or five hours' slumber. This day he decided to meet Sandy at her job for lunch, and as he arrived at the supermarket he saw her chatting with someone at the checkout counter. It was Milt Woodman, and they were laughing together like old friends.

Kendell walked around the block, trying to tell himself that there was nothing to be concerned about. When he returned to the store, Woodman was gone and Sandy was ready for lunch.

"Who was your friend?" he asked casually.

"What friend?"

"I passed a few minutes ago and you were talking to some guy. Seemed to be having a great time."

"Oh, I don't know, a customer. He comes in a lot, loafs around."

Kendell didn't mention it again. But it struck him over the weekend that Sandy no longer harped on the need for a quick marriage. In fact, she no longer mentioned marriage at all.

On Monday evening, Kendell's night off, Sheriff Dade invited them for dinner at his house. It was a friendly gesture, and Sandy was eager to accept at once. Mrs. Dade proved to be a handsome blonde woman

258                                              ALFRED HITCHCOCK'S ANTHOLOGY

in her mid-thirties, and she handled the evening with the air of someone who knew all about living the good life at Wagon Lake.

After dinner, Kendell followed Dade to his basement workshop.
"Just a place to putter around in," the sheriff told him. He picked up a
power saw and handled it fondly. "Don't get as much time down here
as I'd like."

"You're kept pretty busy at work."

Dade nodded. "Too busy. But I like the job you're doing, Johnny. I
really do."

"Thanks." Kendell lit a cigarette and leaned against the workbench.
"Sheriff, there's something I want to ask you. I didn't ask it before."

"What's that?"

"Why did you fire Milt Woodman?"

"He been giving you trouble?"

"No. Not really. I guess I'm just curious."

"All right. There's no real reason for not telling you, I suppose. He
used to get down at the far end of the lake, beyond the Blue Zebra,
and park his car in the bushes. Then he'd take some girl into one of
the cottages and spend half the night there with her. I couldn't have
that sort of thing going on. The fool was supposed to be guarding the
cottages, not using them for his private parties."

"He's quite a man with the girls, huh?"

Dade nodded sourly. "He always was. He's just a no-good bum. I
should never have hired him in the first place."

They went upstairs to join the ladies. Nothing more was said about
Woodman's activities, but the next night while on patrol Kendell spotted him once again in the Blue Zebra. He waited down the road until
Woodman emerged, then followed him around the curve to the point
where he'd vanished the week before. Yes, he'd turned off into one of
the steep driveways that led down to the cottages at the water's edge.
There was a driveway between each pair of cottages, so Kendell had
the spot pretty much narrowed down to one of two places, both big
rambling houses built back when Wagon Lake was a summer retreat
for the very rich.

He smoked a cigarette and tried to decide what to do. It was his
duty to keep people away from the cottages, yet for some reason he
wasn't quite ready to challenge Milt Woodman. Perhaps he knew that
the man would never submit meekly to his orders. Perhaps he knew

he might once again have to use the gun on his hip.

So he did nothing that night about Milt Woodman.

The following day Sheriff Dade handed him a mimeographed list. "I made up a new directory of names and addresses around town. All the houses are listed, along with the phone numbers of the bars and some of the other places you check. Might want to leave it with your wife, in case she has to reach you during the night." Dade always referred to Sandy as Kendell's wife, though he must have known better. "You're still at that motel, aren't you?"

"For a little while longer," Kendell answered vaguely.

Dade grunted. "Seen Woodman around?"

"Caught a glimpse of him last night. Didn't talk to him."

The sheriff nodded and said no more.

The following evening, when Johnny was getting ready to go on duty, Sandy seemed more distant than ever.

"What's the matter?" he asked finally.

"Oh, just a hard day, I guess. All the weekend shopping starts on Thursday."

"Has that guy been in again? The one I saw you talking to?"

"I told you he comes in a lot. What of it?"

"Sandy—" He went to her, but she turned away.

"Johnny, you're different, changed. Ever since you killed that man you've been like a stranger. I thought you were really sorry about it, but now you've taken this job so you can carry a gun again."

"I haven't had it out of the holster!"

"Not yet."

"All right," he said finally. "I'm sorry you feel that way. I'll see you in the morning." He went out, conscious of the revolver's weight against his hip.

The night was cold, with a hint of snow again in the air. He drove faster than usual, making one circuit of the lake in fifteen minutes, and barely glancing at the crowded parking lots along the route. The words with Sandy had bothered him, more than he cared to admit. On the second trip around the lake, he tried to pick out Woodman's car, but it was nowhere to be seen. Or was his car hidden off the road down at one of those cottages?

He thought about Sandy some more.

Near midnight, with the moon playing through the clouds and reflecting off the frozen lake, Johnny drove into town, between his inspection trips. There wasn't much time, so he went directly to the motel. Sandy's room was empty, the bed smooth and undisturbed.

He drove back to the lake, this time seeking lights in the cottages he knew Woodman used. But all seemed dark and deserted. There were no familiar faces at the Blue Zebra, either. He accepted a drink from the manager and stood by the bar sipping it. His mood grew gradually worse, and when a college boy tried to buy a drink for his girl Kendell chased them out for being under age. It was something he had never done before.

Later, around two, while he was checking another couple parked down a side road, he saw Woodman's familiar car shoot past. There was a girl in the front seat with him, a concealing scarf wrapped around her hair. Kendell let out his breath slowly. If it was Sandy, he thought that he would kill her.

"Where were you last night?" he asked her in the morning, trying to keep his voice casual. "I stopped by around midnight."

"I went to a late movie."

"How come?"

She lit a cigarette, turning half away from him before she answered. "I just get tired of sitting around here alone every night. Can't you understand that?"

"I understand it all right," he said.

Late that afternoon, when the winter darkness had already descended over the town and the lake, he left his room early and drove out to the old cottages beyond the Blue Zebra. He parked off the road, in the hidden spot he knew Woodman used, and made his way to the nearer of the houses. There seemed nothing unusual about it, no signs of illegal entry, and he turned his attention to the cottage on the other side of the driveway. There, facing the lake, he found an unlatched window and climbed in.

The place was furnished like a country estate house, and great white sheets had been draped over the furniture to protect it from a winter's dust. He'd never seen so elaborate a summer home, but he hadn't come to look at furniture. In the bedroom upstairs he found what he sought. There had been some attempt to collect the beer bottles into a neat pile, but they hadn't bothered to smooth out the sheets.

He looked in the ash tray and saw Sandy's brand. All right, he tried to tell himself, that proved nothing. Not for sure. Then he saw on the floor a crumpled ball of paper, which she'd used to blot her lipstick. He smoothed it out, fearing, but already knowing. It was the mimeographed list Sheriff Dade had given him just two days before, the one Sandy had stuffed into her purse.

All right. Now he knew.

He left it all as he'd found it and went back out the window. Even Woodman would not have dared leave such a mess for any length of time. He was planning to come back, and soon—perhaps that night. And he wouldn't dare bring another girl, when he hadn't yet cleaned up the evidence of the last one. No, it would be Sandy again.

Kendell drove to the Blue Zebra and had two quick drinks before starting his tour of duty. Then, as he drove around the lake, he tried to keep a special eye out for Woodman's car. At midnight, back at the bar, he asked the manager, "Seen Milt around tonight?"

"Woodman? Yeah, he stopped by for some cigarettes and beer."

"Thanks."

Kendell stepped into the phone booth, and called the motel. Sandy was not in her room. He left the bar and drove down the road, past the cottage. There were no lights, but he caught a glimpse of Woodman's car in the usual spot. They were there, all right.

He parked further down the road, and for a long time just sat in the car, smoking. Presently he took the .38 revolver from his holster and checked to see that it was loaded. Then he drove back to the Blue Zebra for two more drinks.

When he returned to the cottage, Woodman's car was still there. Kendell made his way around to the front and silently worked the window open. He heard their muffled, whispering voices as he started up the stairs.

The bedroom door was open and he stood for a moment in the hallway, letting his eyes grow accustomed to the dark. They hadn't yet heard his approach.

"Woodman," he said.

The man started at the sound of his name, rising from the bed with a curse. "What the hell!"

262

Kendell fired once at the voice, heard the girl's scream of terror and fired again. He squeezed the trigger and kept squeezing it, because this time there was no Sergeant Racin to knock the pistol from his hand. This time there was nothing to stop him until all six shots had been blasted into the figures on the bed.

Then, letting the pistol fall to the floor, he walked over and struck a match. Milt Woodman was sprawled on the floor, his head in a gathering pool of blood. The girl's body was still under the sheet, and he approached it carefully.

It wasn't Sandy.

It was Mrs. Dade, the sheriff's wife.

This time he knew they wouldn't be far behind him. This time he knew there'd be no next town, no new life.

But he had to keep going. Running.

# You Can't Blame Me

## by Henry Slesar

Now it was Beggs' turn. A generation had grown to manhood since he went behind the gates, and now they were opening for him. As he stood in the Warden's office, his skin itching in civilian tweed, he thought, First twenty-year-old I see, I'll go up to him and say, kid, I'm one guy you never laid eyes on before, I'm one guy you can't blame for anything, because I've been sitting out your lifetime.

Twenty years!

"Fifty's not old," the Warden said. "Plenty of men get new careers at fifty, Beggs. Don't go getting discouraged, because you know what that leads to."

"What?" Beggs said dreamily, knowing the answer, only wanting to keep the talk going, to delay the moment.

"You know. Trouble. You wouldn't be the first I've said goodbye to one day and hello to the next."

He cleared his throat and shuffled papers. "I see you have a family."

"Had," Beggs said, not with bitterness.

"Your wife wasn't much for visiting, was she?"

"No."

"That money you stole—"

"What money?"

"All right," the Warden sighed. "I remember now. You're one of the innocent ones. Well, fine. That's the kind I like to see leave." His hand was out. "Good luck, Beggs. I hope you find what you want out there. Only wish I had some good advice for you."

"That's all right, Warden. Thanks just the same."

"I'll give you one tip." He smiled benignly. "Dye your hair."

"Thanks," Beggs said. . .

He was out. He knew Edith wouldn't be waiting on the other side of the wall, but he stopped and looked up and down and sat on a hydrant to smoke a cigarette within ten yards of the prison gates. He heard a guard chuckle on the catwalk overhead. Then he got up, and walked to the bus stop. He sat in the rear seat of the bus and watched his white-haired reflection all the way into town. I'm an old man, he thought. But that's all right.

He used up most of the rehabilitation money in two days. Some went for shelter, for new clothes, for food, and for train fare. When he stepped onto the platform at Purdy's Landing, a taxi man solicited his business. He said yes, and got into the front seat. "Do you know the Cobbin farm?" he said.

"Nope," the cabdriver said. "Never heard of it."

"Used to be on Edge Road?"

"Heard of Edge Road."

"That's where I want to go. I'll tell you where to stop."

He told him, within sight of a small housing development. He paid the man, but waited until he was driving off before he approached one of the houses. When the car was out of sight, he turned out of the driveway and started walking down the road. Nothing seemed familiar, but he wasn't worried. Everything changes. Latitudes remain. Stone endures.

He saw the jagged rim of the rocky slope ahead of him, and he knew he was in the right place. He slid down the small embankment, bracing himself against a fall. He had been nimbler twenty years ago. There was a steep woodland at the end of the slope, and he entered the thick of it. He stumbled around until he saw the rough circle of stacked stones, the old blackened tree stump, and the spot where he had hidden the money.

He began removing the stones. There were many of them. He had no fear that his hiding place had been discovered in his absence. His confidence was as strong as faith.

It was there, still in the leather suitcase, all in cash, neatly bundled up by denomination, slightly damp but still new-looking and spendable. He wiped off the suitcase—it had cost forty dollars, new—and clucked when he saw the mold damage on its edge. But it was sturdy still, and hefted well by its stout handle.

He returned to the road, carrying the suitcase. This time, he did stop at one of the houses, and knocked on the door. A woman answered, looked dubiously at his suitcase as if expecting a sales pitch, and then relaxed when she saw his snowy hair and heard his question. Could he have a drink of water? Of course. Could he please call a taxi? Go ahead, phone's right over there. She was a nice woman, not young. With a shock, Beggs remembered that Edith would be the same age now.

He reached the old neighborhood at dusk. The light dab of rouge on the tenements didn't improve their appearance; it was like makeup on a trollop. Not much change here, he thought, only for the worse. Dilapidation and decay, another twenty-year layer of dirt on the pavements and building stones. Then he saw the difference: an all-glass front on the corner drugstore; an empty lot where a candy warehouse had been; a change in nationality in the street urchins; a new sign, neon, in front of Mike's Bar and Grill. The sign read "Lucky's," and when it blinked, the "L" fizzled and crackled and seemed ready to burn out.

He went into the bar. He had spent plenty of hours there in his youth, even after his marriage. But only the latitude and longitude were the same. Mike's place had been rough-furnished, honestly lit, and the bartender had had sweat on his forearms. Lucky's was another sort of place altogether. It was dark, too dark for an old pair of eyes, jeweled up with chrome and colored glass, a lousy cocktail lounge. There were even women: he saw a black dress and a string of pearls and heard hard, feminine laughter. The bartender wore a white uniform and had a ferret's face. He played the cash register like a Hammond organ.

"Yes, sir?" the barman said.

"Phone?" Beggs said hoarsely.

Contempt. "Back there."

He stumbled on something, righted himself, found the phone booth. He searched clumsily through the directory, marveling at its thickness, the smell of alcohol around him almost strong enough to make his head spin; there hadn't been whiskey past his throat in two decades. He found her listing, BEGGS, EDITH, the number different but the address the same. He felt almost weepy with gratitude towards his wife for being stubborn and changeless.

He went into the booth, forcing the suitcase in between his legs, dug a nickel out of his pocket and then saw that rates were different. He found a dime, but he didn't deposit it. His hands were shaking too much. He couldn't face the moment, couldn't sit here in this glass cell and hear the voice from yesterday tinny and disembodied in the receiver. He came out of the booth, sweating.

At the bar, he sat on a plush stool and placed his elbows on the bar and rested his head in his hands. There was nobody drinking. The barman moved in on him like a bird of prey. "What'll it be?" he said seductively. "You look like you need one, friend."

Beggs looked up. "Whatever happened to Mike?" he said.

"Who?"

"I'll—I'll have a whiskey."

The glass was in front of him, paid for, easing the strain between them. The barman relaxed and said: "You mean Mike Duram? Used to be his bar once?"

"Yes."

"Six feet under," the man said, jerking his thumb downwards. "Maybe ten years ago. Place had four owners since then. You a friend of Mike's or something?"

"I knew him," Beggs said. "A long time ago." He downed the drink and it exploded in his head like a grenade. He coughed, choked, almost fell forward on the mahogany counter. The bartender cursed and got him water.

"What are you, a wise guy?" he said. "Tryin' to make out my whiskey's no good?"

"I'm sorry; it's been a long time."

"Yeah, don't give me that."

He walked off, injured. Beggs covered his face with his hand. Then he felt a touch in the middle of his back, and turned to see the cheap dead-white pearls and the slim throat severed by a low black neckline.

"Hello, Pop, you got a cold or something?"

"It's nothing," he said. She came and sat on the opposite stool, a young, pale, pretty girl, her skin even whiter than the fake necklace she wore. "I'm not used to it," he said. "Can't take the stuff anymore."

"You need practice," she smiled. Then he realized that this wasn't amateur cordiality; the girl worked there. He reached for the suitcase handle. "Stick around, Pop, you can't fly on one wing."

"I don't understand."

"Have another drink. It'll taste better this time."

"I don't think so."

"I'll tell you what. You buy one and try it; if you don't like it, I'll finish it for you. It's like a moneyback guarantee, only you don't get your money back." She laughed gaily.

He started to refuse, but he hated to see even the false smile disappear.

"All right," he said gruffly.

The bartender returned, all prepared. He set two shot glasses in front of them, and filled both to the rim. He placed the bottle in front of Beggs, turning it to display the brand name. Beggs, chastised, gave him a small grin. The girl's thin white fingers closed around her glass, and she lifted it.

"Here's to you," she said.

The second went down easier. It didn't relax him, but it made his depression easier to bear. It made him remember what a drink was for. He looked shyly at the girl, and she patted his shoulder. "Nice man," she said, cute, patronizing. "Such nice white hair."

"You're not drinking," he said.

"Come to think of it, I'd like mine with ginger ale. Couldn't we sit at a table?"

Beggs looked to the end of the bar; the bartender was wiping glasses and appeared contented.

"Sure, why not?" he said. He picked up the suitcase and climbed off the stool. His foot didn't feel the ground when he touched it, and he laughed. "Hey, what's going on here? My foot's asleep."

She giggled, and looked at the suitcase. Then she put her arm through his. "Gee, you're cute," she said. "I'm glad you came in."

He was in the prison shop, the machines roaring, his body stiff with fatigue, his head hurting. He rested it on the cool surface of the lathe, and the guard gripped his shoulder and shook it.

"Wake up, buddy."

"What?" Beggs said, lifting his head from the micarta tabletop. His hand was still around a glass, but the glass was empty. "What did you say?" he said.

"Wake up," the bartender grumbled. "This ain't a hotel. I got to close up."

268     

"What time is it?" He straightened and gongs rang in his ears. His fingertips were tingling and there was glue in his mouth. "I must have fallen asleep," he said.

"It's after one," the bartender said. "Go on home."

Beggs looked at the other side of the booth. It was empty. He reached down for the suitcase handle and clutched air. "My suitcase," he said calmly.

"Your what?"

"Suitcase. Maybe I left it at the bar . . ." He got up, stumbled toward the stools and started pushing them around. "It's got to be here someplace," he said. "Didn't you see it?"

"Look, buddy—"

"My suitcase," Beggs said distinctly, facing the man. "I want my suitcase, you understand?"

"I didn't see any suitcase. Listen, you accusing me of—"

"The girl I was with. The one who worked here."

"No girl works here, fella. You got the wrong idea about the kind of place I run."

Beggs put his hand on the man's lapel, not rough. "Please don't fool around," he said. He even smiled. "Look, don't joke. I'm an old man. See my white hair? What did you do with it? Where's the girl?"

"Mister, I'll tell you this once more." The barman plucked off his fingers. "I didn't see your lousy suitcase. And no girl works here. If you got rolled by somebody, that's your business, not mine."

"You *liar!*"

Beggs hurled himself forward. It wasn't an attack; his arms were spread out in pleading, not violence. He shouted at the man again and the man walked away, disdainful. He followed him, and the man turned and said nasty words. Then Beggs started to sob, and the bartender sighed wearily and said, "Oh, that did it, that's too much." He grabbed Beggs' arm and began propelling him to the doorway. He scooped up his overcoat from the rack and threw it at him. Beggs shouted, but he kept moving. At the door, the barman gave one final shove that sent him into the street. The door slammed shut and Beggs pounded it with his fist, only once.

Then he stood on the sidewalk, and put on his overcoat. There were cigarettes in the pocket, but they were crushed and worthless. He threw the crumpled pack into the gutter.

Then he walked off.

He remembered the stairs. There were three flights of them, easy to take when he had been young and newly married and Edith was waiting for him upstairs. Steeper when he had been drinking at Mike's after a jobless day. Now they were endless, a wooden Everest. He was puffing by the time he reached the apartment door.

He knocked, and in a little while a woman who could have been Edith's mother opened the door. But it was Edith. She stared at him, pushing back the limp yellow-gray strands from her face, a bony hand fumbling with the dangling button of a soiled housecoat. He wasn't sure if she recognized him, so he said, "It's Harry, Edith."

"Harry?"

"It's kind of late," he mumbled. "I'm sorry to come so late. They let me out today. Could I come in, maybe?"

"Oh, my God," Edith said, putting her hands flat over her eyes. She didn't move for almost thirty seconds. He didn't know whether to touch her or not. He shifted from one foot to another, and licked his lips dryly.

"I'm awful thirsty," he said. "Could I have a glass of water?"

She let him in. The room was in darkness; so his wife lit a table lamp. She went into the kitchen and came out with the water. She brought it to him, and he sat down before drinking it.

When he handed her the empty glass, he smiled shyly and said, "Thanks. I sure was thirsty."

"What do you want, Harry?"

"Nothing," he said quietly. "Only a glass of water. I couldn't expect nothing else from you, could I?"

She walked away from him, fooling with her hair. "My God, I look terrible. Why couldn't you give me some warning?"

"I'm sorry, Edith," he said. "I better get going."

"Where to?"

"I don't know," Beggs said. "I haven't thought about it."

"You got no place to go?"

"No."

She took the empty glass to the kitchen, and then came out. She remained in the doorway, folding her arms and leaning against the doorframe.

270                                    ALFRED HITCHCOCK'S ANTHOLOGY

"You could stay here," she said flatly. "I couldn't turn you out, without no place to go. You could sleep on the couch. Do you want to do that, Harry?"

He rubbed his palm over the cushion.

"This couch," he said slowly. "I'd rather sleep on this couch than in a palace." He looked at her, and she was crying. "Aw, Edith," he said. "Don't mind me—"

He got up and went to her side. He put his arms around her.

"Is it okay if I stay? I mean, not just tonight?"

She nodded.

Beggs held her tighter, the embrace of a young lover. Edith must have realized how foolish it looked, because she laughed brokenly and pushed a tear off her cheek with the heel of her hand.

"My God, what am I thinking of?" she said. "Harry, you know how old I am?"

"I don't care—"

"I'm a woman with a grown daughter. Harry, you never even saw your daughter." She freed herself and went to a closed bedroom door. She knocked, and her voice trembled. "Harry, you never saw Angela. She was only a baby when—Angela! Angela, wake up!"

A moment later the door opened. The blonde girl in the loose-fitting nightgown was yawning and blinking. She was pretty, but her expression was cross.

"What the heck's going on?" she said. "What's all the yellin' about?"

"Angela, I want you to meet somebody. Somebody special!"

Edith clasped her hands together and looked at Beggs. Beggs was looking at the girl, smiling foolishly, in embarrassment. The smile didn't last. Edith saw it go, and made a sound of disappointment. They looked at each other, the old man and the girl, and Angela tugged nervously at the strand of cheap dead-white pearls still around her throat.

# Death of a Derelict

## by Joseph Payne Brennan

One afternoon in early summer I sat sipping cold sarsaparilla in the Victorian livingroom of my investigator friend, Lucius Leffing. Shades were drawn against the sun; the room was cool and quiet. Leffing sprawled in his favorite chair.

As I glanced around at the gaslight fixtures, the mahogany furniture, and Leffing's favorite pieces of Victorian pressed glass, I smiled. "I suppose," I said, "that two gentlemen must have sat much like this in somebody's parlor back in the so-called Gay Nineties. If I should hear the clop of horses' hooves outside, it would not surprise me."

Just then the doorbell rang.

Leffing got up reluctantly. "I fear a little reminiscent trip backward into time must be delayed for a more propitious moment. The present seems to be intruding."

I heard conversation at the door and then Leffing ushered in an individual who was not conducive to moods of gentle nostalgia.

He was short, fat and fiftyish with a large-toothed smile which in the dimly lighted room seemed to switch on and off like a neon sign. A suit with a pattern of large checks did nothing to enhance his pot-bellied presence.

Leffing introduced him as Mr. Clarence Morenda and waved him to a chair.

Glancing around, Mr. Morenda favored us with another flashing grin. "Well, well, you gentlemen have got yourselves a cozy little hideaway here." He laughed uproariously.

"Mr. Morenda," Leffing informed me when the storm had subsided, "is manager of the entertainment concession at Frolic Beach. He is here on business."

Mr. Morenda, recalled to the purpose of his visit, scowled porten-

ALFRED HITCHCOCK'S ANTHOLOGY

tiously. "Crummy nuisance, that's what it is!" He cleared his throat. "But first you better tell me what this will cost."

"That depends on the particular circumstances, the time consumed, expenses and so on," Leffing told him. "But compensation can be decided later. I do not press my clients."

Mr. Morenda seemed momentarily confused by such an unbusinesslike attitude, but then he shrugged and grinned again. "Okay, Mr. Leffing, I like a man who don't make too much of money."

Leffing nodded. "Quite so. And now, what is your case?"

Morenda's shaggy eyebrows stitched together again. "About a month ago we found a stiff in an alley which runs alongside the Cyclone. Head all bashed in. Couldn't figure out whether he'd fallen off the Cyclone or got slugged. The coroner said he 'came to his death in a manner at present unknown'—or something like that. We'd seen this bum hangin' around for quite a while, but nobody knew his name or anything. They took pictures and then kept him on ice, but nothing turned up so finally they planted him in Potter's."

He paused, took out a large purple handkerchief and wiped the perspiration from his face. "Then a week ago this nutty dame shows up. Claims this stiff was her cousin, Joel Karvey, says he fell off the Cyclone. Claims it was our fault. Now she's gettin' ready to sue us for $100,000!" He snorted. "Imagine that! Why that bum wasn't worth two cents!"

"I appreciate your problem, Mr. Morenda," said Leffing, "but I fear you need an astute attorney, not a private investigator."

Morenda shook his head vigorously. "Those finky shysters! They'd keep the case goin' for five years. I want the suit thrown out before they start chewin' on it. That bum didn't fall at all—he was murdered! If I can prove that, the suit comes apart at the seams."

Leffing winced at the metaphor. "Mr. Morenda, is there any definite evidence to indicate that it was murder—or are you just engaged in wishful thinking?"

"Sure it was murder! The guy's head was all bashed in, but there wasn't another mark on him. If he'd fallen off the Cyclone, he'd be banged up all over."

"Perhaps he landed on his head," I suggested.

Morenda scowled at me impatiently. "It ain't likely. He'd have to take a real swan dive off the top of the Cyclone and drop directly into that little alley. If he fell off, he'd hit at every tier, bang into the railings and bounce around."

"Assuming you are correct," Leffing put in, "why should anyone murder a penniless drifter? Can you suggest a motive?"

Morenda hesitated. "Well, I ain't sure. Maybe somebody thought he had a few bills. You know how it is—they'll cosh you for a quarter these days. Or maybe he got in a fight with some drunk." He spread his hands. "Could be lots of things."

Leffing sat silently for a minute or two. "I will take the case," he said at length. "The motive intrigues me. We cannot at this point, of course, rule out the possibility that the drifter's death was an accident."

After assuring Mr. Morenda that he would start work on the case the next day, Leffing conducted his new client to the door.

"Well, Brennan, what do you think?" he asked as he settled back in his chair.

I set down my sarsaparilla glass. "The whole sordid business looks pretty obvious to me. This female cousin had the drifter murdered and left near the Cyclone so that she could bring a suit against the Frolic Beach. Some rat-trap lawyer is calling the plays for her."

"Well, well, you may already have solved the case!" Leffing replied with a touch of sarcasm. "However, your solution must bear up under investigation. Much remains to be done."

I did not see Leffing again until several days had passed. One evening I stopped in to ask how the case was coming along.

Leffing leaned back in his chair and put his fingertips together. "I am now convinced that the drifter, Joel Karvey, was murdered. I studied the morgue photographs and talked to the coroner, who, incidentally, does not agree with me. I believe Karvey was struck over the head by a lead pipe. The coroner thinks he struck his head against the iron railings which parallel the Cyclone's track along both sides of the structure."

"If Karvey fell," I asked, "wouldn't he have been seen?"

Leffing shook his head. "Quite possibly not. Not if he fell at night. The Cyclone is not too well lighted and the alley in which he was found is dark. There is also the possibility, as the coroner pointed out, that he climbed up on the Cyclone after closing hours—midnight—as a lark, or just to get a view of the harbor lights."

"Highly unlikely!"

"Where murder is suspected, or where $100,000 lawsuits are pending, one cannot dismiss possibilities."

I grunted.

"I can't believe a drifter would be riding around on the Cyclone or climbing up to see the harbor lights. I still think this female cousin had him killed."

"The female cousin," Leffing said, "is a charwoman living in Newbridge, a drab unimaginative creature with no criminal connections that I can discover. She mentioned to someone that the dead drifter was a distant relative; an opportunistic attorney learned the circumstances and descended upon her. He will obviously be rewarded only if he wins the case."

"You are convinced Karvey was murdered?"

"The head wounds indicate assault so far as I can judge from the photographs and autopsy descriptions. What baffles me is the motive. Why should anyone murder such a nondescript beggar?"

I had no further suggestions to offer but the case began to interest me and I made Leffing promise to keep me informed. When I stopped back a week later, he was restless and fretful.

"You have made no progress?"

He stopped pacing the floor and sat down. "The motive, Brennan! The motive! I am now more firmly convinced that the female cousin is innocent, but we have no other suspect."

"How about Morenda himself?"

"He had no reason to kill Karvey."

"Suppose," I said, "Karvey fell off the Cyclone, was found injured, but conscious, and threatened to bring suit? Maybe Morenda finished him off to avoid getting hauled to court."

Leffing frowned. "An unpleasant possibility I must admit I had not entertained. But if Morenda 'finished off' Karvey, as you say, why would he seek help to prove Karvey was murdered? Is he brash enough to risk his own life or freedom in order to nullify a lawsuit?"

I nodded. "I believe he may be bold and callous enough to take the risk. All he wants you to do is establish the fact that Karvey was murdered, in order to end the lawsuit. If he himself is guilty, he must be confident that you can never prove it. Probably he believes he would never be suspected."

"I intend to question him again, in any case," Leffing said. "We will see then what turns up."

"You have learned nothing more at all?" I asked presently.

"Only one minor thing, insignificant perhaps, yet puzzling. Karvey never did any work at the concessions and he was never seen panhandling, yet he always seemed to have a little money—enough for hamburgers, chips, soda and so forth. Morenda hoped to get him arrested for begging and thus get rid of him. He even had the Frolic Beach watchman, Henry Marnault, spy on him at intervals, but Marnault never caught him panhandling."

"He may have been a pickpocket."

"Doubtful. If he picked pockets, he must have been an accomplished professional. He'd never been arrested for anything except vagrancy. A professional of his age—he was about sixty—would certainly have a police record."

"What is your next move?"

"Tomorrow afternoon I am going to make another visit to Frolic Beach. I will see Morenda again and then perhaps just prowl about. Would you care to accompany me?"

Frolic Beach, south of New Haven along the Sound, is a cluster of carnival-like concessions, interspersed with hamburger stands, popcorn palaces, lemonade stalls, and several surprisingly good restaurants.

Early afternoon found Leffing and myself walking down Lavender Street, the main thoroughfare which bisects the beach area. Morenda's office was located in a dingy building behind the merry-go-round.

He glanced up from a sheaf of greasy-looking sales slips as Leffing and I entered. "You got any news for me, Mr. Leffing?"

Leffing shook his head. "Nothing fresh, Mr. Morenda. Can you take time out to stroll about a bit? Perhaps another visit to the scene of the crime might be helpful."

"Sure, sure. But we been there before." He left his sales slips with obvious reluctance to accompany us.

Screaming couples were rocketing about on the Cyclone's track when we arrived. The alley in which Karvey had been found ran along one side of it, a dim, narrow little lane empty except for candy wrappers, bottle caps and a piece of yellowed newspaper.

We followed Leffing inside. He poked about for a time and then stood looking up at the Cyclone. Suddenly he pointed. "A section of the railing up there was recently replaced, Mr. Morenda? Correct?"

Both Morenda and I squinted upward. Most of the iron-pipe railing looked old and rusty, but there was one small section which appeared shiny and bright.

Morenda nodded his head. "Yeah, a piece got loose up there, so we had a new section put in a couple months ago."

"Where was the old piece of railing left?" Leffing asked. "Was it by any chance discarded in this alley?"

Morenda scratched his chin. "Might be. I never paid any attention. You think that bum got bashed with it, Mr. Leffing?"

"I believe it highly possible. That may be why the coroner thinks Karvey fell. The wounds on his head would indicate that that pipe railing caused them, but in my opinion it was the discarded piece, left lying in the alley here, which did the job."

"If we could locate it, we might have fingerprints!" I exclaimed.

"Possibly. But the murderer probably walked a few yards down to the beach and hurled it into the breakers. We would have a herculean task recovering it, and any fingerprints would be scoured off by now."

Morenda shook his head. "You sure got all the answers, Mr. Leffing!" Suddenly he broke into a roar of laughter. "All except the big answer. Who killed Karvey?" He went on laughing like an hysterical hyena.

If Leffing was annoyed, he gave no sign. "You are right, Mr. Morenda," he said quietly when the raucous hee-hawing had subsided. "The big answer still eludes me."

As we walked back towards Morenda's office, Leffing inquired about Henry Marnault, the Frolic Beach watchman.

"We got a real bad worry about fire," Morenda explained. "After midnight, when we close, Henry checks up on all the rides and stands. You know how it is—a smouldering butt could bring down the works."

"That is the extent of Marnault's duties?" Leffing asked.

"His night tour takes about two hours. Then he goes off and doesn't come on again till four the next afternoon. He sweeps my office and does a few odd jobs, but mostly he just drifts around picking up soda bottles and stuff. Sometimes if a stand runs out of change, he'll bring a bill to my office. We don't push Henry. It's hard to get a man for that night tour."

"Where does he live?" Leffing asked.

"Lives in a barn down off the end of Lavender Street. We fixed it up for him and we don't charge any rent. He's got all he needs in there."

Leffing nodded. "Well, we may just have a chat with him, if you've no objection."

"Sure, sure. Leave no stone unturned, as they say, Mr. Leffing!"

We left Morenda and walked down Lavender Street, stopping for a lemonade along the way.

Henry Marnault's barn was situated in a salt meadow off the end of the street. It was not much more than an oversized shack, but the roof looked new and storm windows had been fitted into the front.

We walked around to the rear, but Marnault was not in sight. As we came back around to the front, we noticed someone walking down the near end of Lavender Street. He was hunched over with his head bent down, and for a moment we thought he was searching the road for something he had lost. As he turned in toward the barn, however, we saw that this was his habitual way of walking.

Marnault looked up at us suspiciously out of somewhat bloodshot eyes, but he became friendly enough when Leffing explained his errand.

"Karvey? Yeah, sure. I knew who he was. Mr. Morenda had me watchin' him for a while. We figured he was panhandlin', but I never did catch him at it. Slippery cuss. But I ain't got no information about him. He just hung around, never talked to nobody."

"You think he was murdered?"

Marnault ran a hand through his ragged hair. "Naw. Who'd want to kill him? He wasn't worth killin', a bum like that. But I don't think he *fell* off the Cyclone. I figure he just climbed up there one night and *jumped!*"

"What reason had he for suicide?" Leffing asked.

Marnault tapped his head.

"He was loose up here. Those kind of people get crazy urges like that."

Leffing nodded. "Well, you may be right, Mr. Marnault. You may be right."

He could tell us nothing more. Leffing thanked him and we started back up Lavender Street.

"If Karvey committed suicide," I pointed out, "we are wasting our time."

"Well, there are worse ways of wasting it, Brennan. We have the tang of sea air, and fresh lemonade is just at hand."

Leffing then began a series of inquiries which exasperated me and eventually left me exhausted. He stopped at every stand and stall along Lavender Street and inquired about Karvey. Did they remember him? Did he ever buy food or drink from that particular stand? How did he pay for it?

By the time I fell into my car for the drive back to New Haven, my legs were literally aching. Leffing, apparently immune to fatigue, was in an optimistic mood.

"Well, well, Brennan, I think the case is clearing."

"I can't recall that you learned anything of consequence from the various vendors along Lavender Street."

"You attach no significance to the fact that Karvey invariably paid for his food or drink with coins—usually nickels and dimes?"

"The only significance I attach to it," I replied, "is that he was an elusive and hard-working panhandler."

Leffing would say no more. He began humming an old English music hall ballad. This went on until we arrived back at Autumn Street.

He turned to me as I stopped the car in front of his small house. "Brennan, are you willing to drive me down to Frolic Beach tomorrow morning—about five o'clock?"

I groaned. "Good grief, are we going in pursuit of a murderous milkman?"

He laughed. "I think not, but we must have an early start."

"I'll be right here at five o'clock," I told him.

I knew it would be useless to question him. He loved being both melodramatic and secretive, and I had come to accept the irritating fact that apparently he could not be cured of this deplorable childishness.

I set my alarm for four-thirty and was still sleepy as I stopped in front of seven Autumn Street. It was just beginning to get light. A heavy fog filled the streets.

Moments after I pulled up, a disreputable-looking figure appeared out of nowhere, slouched up to the car and yanked open the door.

I turned in alarm. "What do you want?"

DEATH OF A DERELICT 279

The tramp leered at me. "I want a lift down to Frolic Beach. That's where you're headed, ain't it—Brennan?"

I stared at him for a full half minute before the import of his words came through. "Leffing! You've given me another gray hair!"

He got in the car. "Sorry, Brennan. Did my little disguise take you in?"

I shook my head. "I had no idea you were a master of makeup. Where did you learn the art?"

"In my distant youth I was identified with several amateur theatrical groups. At various times my early stage experience has proved invaluable."

Traffic was light, but the fog slowed us up considerably. Leffing chatted about everything except the case at hand. I remained completely mystified as to the reason for his disguise.

We parked a few blocks from the beginning of Lavender Street. Leffing peered cautiously through the fog. "No more talking, Brennan, and remain close to the buildings. We must not be seen."

We skulked down Lavender Street single file, like a pair of thieves. About halfway down, Leffing nudged me into a doorway.

"We will take our stand here," he whispered.

The light strengthened and the fog lifted a bit as we waited. Suddenly Leffing squeezed my arm and nodded.

Inching out, I looked down Lavender Street. At the far end a shambling figure came into sight. In the fog he looked like a wraith beginning to materialize. He kept his head bent forward and down. Twice, as we watched, he bent swiftly and seemed to pick something out of the street.

This weird behavior was repeated several more times as he approached. When he drew closer, Leffing edged slowly into the street and began to stroll toward him.

I watched, puzzled but fascinated, and now Leffing stooped and appeared to pick up something. He seemed to be entirely oblivious to the figure coming toward him from the other end of the street.

As the other figure slowly emerged from the fog, I finally recognized the features of Henry Marnault, the Frolic Beach watchman. He kept his head bent and his eyes on the ground most of the time, so he did not see the disguised form of Leffing until they were less than a block apart.

He stopped in his tracks and stared. Leffing continued shuffling forward. At intervals he bent to pluck something from the gutters.

Marnault watched him like a man bewitched. He seemed frozen into immobility. When he found his voice, it was high-pitched, frantic, filled with rising hysteria.

"Karvey! Get back! You're dead, you crazy bum, I killed you! Get away from me!" ·

As Leffing continued toward him, Marnault turned with a scream and began to run down Lavender Street. Leffing straightened up, drew something from a pocket and put it to his lips. The shrill blast of a police whistle cut through the foggy morning air. A moment later a blue-clad figure came pounding from somewhere out of the fog and collared the terrified Marnault.

Leffing called out in his own voice, "Splendid work, Sergeant Corliss! Arrest that man for the murder of Joel Karvey!"

Marnault signed a full confession later in the day, admitting that he had slugged Karvey over the head with a piece of pipe railing found in the alley next to the Cyclone. He had dragged Karvey into the alley, walked to the shore and thrown the murder weapon into the ocean. This had occurred just at daybreak, when the Frolic Beach area was still deserted.

He had killed Karvey, he explained, because Karvey, in spite of repeated threats, had continued to "muscle in" on his territory. Marnault had found that an early-morning inspection of the Frolic Beach streets, gutters and sidewalks almost invariably yielded a modest crop of coins. The area, which was open until midnight, was not well lighted; many coins dropped during the· evening remained waiting to be picked up on the following morning. Marnault had averaged enough to pay for his weekly bottle of gin.

Then Karvey had drifted in. One morning Marnault had run into him prowling the gutters in search of coins. The watchman had warned him to leave, but Karvey had remained. Morning after morning Marnault ran into the drifter, and the watchman's daily harvest of coins dwindled ever lower. The amount involved was small, but so was Marnault's salary, and the bottle of gin was important to him. At length his irritation had turned to murderous rage. Finally, one foggy morning, he had waited in the little alley next to the Cyclone, where he had picked up a length of pipe railing. Karvey's coin collecting had come to an abrupt end.

That evening I sat in Leffing's gaslit Victorian livingroom while he poured a generous portion of his choice, cask-mellowed brandy.

I sampled it with relish. "It certainly was a bizarre murder motive," I commented, "but two things still puzzle me. Why was Marnault so terrified when he saw you approaching in the fog? And how did you figure out the business in the first place?"

Leffing smiled. "Marnault was terrified," he replied, "because I had made up to resemble Karvey. I had studied the morgue pictures, you know. I made up my face to look like his and I had even scoured the secondhand shops to get some rags of clothing which resembled his own. It was a gamble, of course, but it worked."

He set down his glass. "From the beginning the motive interested me. It eluded me for some time. Then I began to speculate as to Karvey's source of money. He never worked and was never seen begging, yet he always seemed to have a few coins. I was still groping in the dark until that day when we went to see Marnault. When I saw him approaching, I immediately tagged him as a 'stooper'—a tramp term for a person who scrounges around looking for coins in the gutters and streets. Marnault had no physical deformity; the bent head and constantly downcast eyes, therefore, could mean only one of two things: atrocious posture arising out of sloth and indifference, or the habitual stance of a confirmed 'stooper.' I was not sure of myself at first, but when I canvassed the stall operators and found that Karvey almost invariably paid for his snacks with small coins, I felt that I had found the motive for his murder."

I shook my head. "It seems unbelievable to me that a man would murder for a few miserable coins snatched out of the gutter!"

Leffing shrugged. "Those 'miserable coins' meant a regular weekly bottle of gin. To a person such as Marnault, alcohol can become pretty important."

A whimsical grin touched his thin face, "Speaking of alcohol, Brennan, would you care for another brandy?"

I held out my glass.

# Present for Lona

## by Avram Davidson

There was sawdust—just like in a butcher shop—on the floor of the long room where Jack Clauson stood waiting for the man he was going to kill. Whatever the man had done, Clauson did not hate him for it. But he had to die, and Clauson had to kill him. Not out of hate, but for love—for love of Lona.

I won't be the only one, he kept telling himself. It won't just be me . . . And he has it coming to him anyway . . . But it was no use. He felt an unfamiliar rigidity in his throat, struggled against nausea.

Bright lights, terribly bright lights, bore down from overhead on the far end of the long room. The near end was dark. The men there shifted from foot to foot, coughing nervously. The coughing stopped abruptly as the door at the far end opened.

Clauson tensed, fighting against the impulse to drop what he held in his hands and run.

A group of people entered, but Clauson had his eyes only on the one in the open shirt. As he watched, the man—his face paper-white— blinked and ran the tip of his tongue along his lips. I can't do this . . . Clauson's thoughts darted around frantically, like rats cornered in a pit. I never saw him before . . . I won't do it; they can't hurt me if I refuse . . . The man walked steadily enough and his head was up and he didn't say anything. But there was suddenly the sharp fresh smell of his sweat; it was the odor of fear.

Clauson started to move. Then he remembered. I must. I have to. He'll die anyway. He deserves to die. He killed an innocent man.

The guards bound the arms of the man in the open shirt swiftly, tightly. The chaplain murmured from his little book. A target was pinned over the heart.

The man's head began to move from side to side. It was still moving when the bullets hit him.

Jack Clauson counted his money. Twenty-five dollars. Not a lot, not for killing a man. His hand jerked suddenly at the thought. Why, he could earn that much from his regular work in a single morning, and work six days a week—to say nothing of overtime. So what was twenty-five dollars?

Not much. Only a man's life. Only another man's marriage. Clauson loved his wife. Now he'd killed for her. This was the first money he'd made in over a month, and it was for just a few minutes' work too. He'd buy Lona something. Something nice. She loved to get presents. He'd make her smile; she'd come into his arms, and things would be all right between them again . . . Or would they?

He drove along the new road on his way back. It was really longer. There was a quicker route to reach the trailer camp, but he liked to ride along the new one. He'd helped build it. It was finished a month ago. He and Lona really should have been moving on long ago. She couldn't have much left out of the last of his earnings—the money he'd given her when everything was all right between them. But everything wasn't all right between them anymore. He was moody; she was moody; they quarreled and yelled at one another. *She* wanted to settle down and *he* wanted to keep moving; *that* was the trouble. And so they rubbed each other raw, and it had been sullen and ugly and apart that they'd spent the last week. They both knew that a split was coming, knew the other knew. It had been hell. Because he wanted her. Badly.

Jack knew he had to *do* something to show he wanted her. Words would no longer be enough. There had to be something from outside the two of them.

How the man's head had weaved from side to side! As if he was looking for an out—and knowing there wasn't any. Then the bullets, smashing into him—

Recalling it made Jack hunch over the wheel, drive faster and faster, sorry he'd taken the longer route, anxious to be back at the trailer camp, eager to show her his token of love—the present. Lona had always loved to get presents. He laughed—why, he hadn't even bought it yet! But it wouldn't take long; it was Late Closing Night at the stores

284          ALFRED HITCHCOCK'S ANTHOLOGY

in the little town. The neon signs beckoned to him as he carefully parked the car. They were mostly red. Red. The color of blood. Blood soaking into sawdust. When the bullets hit, the man didn't even yell. He just grunted. And then the blood . . .

Seeing the lights out in the trailer, Jack thought Lona might be asleep. If she was, he'd wake her up. He couldn't just turn in by himself, not *now*, not with *this* on his mind and heart. He'd done it for Lona and Lona alone could make it all right. He could forget, in her arms. . . . Maybe she was just lying awake in the dark as she sometimes did. Softly, he opened the door. "Lona?" he called, making his voice gentle. There was no answer, and his eyes, adjusting to the dark, saw she wasn't in bed. He grunted, flicked on the lights.

He jumped at the sudden flood of brightness, swore. For a moment he'd thought he'd seen a man under the lights, a man with bound arms and a bloody target on his chest. Badly frightened. Clauson stood still, waiting for his racing heart to slow down. He looked around him.

The place was a mess, clothes scattered all around, bed unmade, a paper bag of garbage spilling on the floor. Lipstick-smeared tissues and a scattering of face-powder told him that she'd gone somewhere she expected to meet people. But—he hastily checked—her things were still here. She'd be back—but he wasn't going to wait. Not alone.

"Why couldn't you be here?" he asked the empty trailer, aloud. "I wanted to give you the present I got for you." His face twisted in disappointment as he looked down at the fancy-wrapped package. The money had gone just far enough—two crisp tens and one new crisp five. Twenty for the present. A bottle of bourbon used up all but some loose change out of the remainder.

A man's life = a present + a bottle of bourbon = a happy couple and a saved marriage. *Or does it?* Because it was as close as that with them. It was as close at that . . .

There was an almost-empty half-pint on the table. That was something Lona had taken to again. She did that when things were bad between them. If only she'd drink *with* him—but she wouldn't, not with that black mood on her. And afterwards they were certain to quarrel, screaming at each other the empty threats that made no more sense than the rest of their quarreling.

"You like it so much here?" his own voice rang in his ears. "Then you can stay—all by your lonesome! I'm getting out!"

And her voice, shrill, "I'll kill you! I'll kill you!"

Each knowing the other didn't mean it . . . With a sigh, Jack went out and walked over to the Roanes' trailer. Ed and Betty Roane were the only friends they had left in the trailer camp; most of the construction workers had moved away as soon as work on the new road was over. Jack envied them; he longed for the feeling of freedom, the long trips across the state and even into a different part of the country, perhaps. But not Lona.

He sighed again.

There was a heavy weight on his chest. How much of it, he half-formed the question, was his wife—and how much of it was the man he'd helped kill?

The sounds of radio and TV, the smell of late suppers cooking, the murmur of conversation, children's voices . . . Maybe if they'd had children, but each had wanted to be modern and wait. Suddenly bitter, he muttered, "Wait for what?" and then he was at the Roanes' trailer, knocking.

And with each knock, he felt it was no use. It had all been for nothing. His heart sank, and he felt he was sinking with it. The gap between him and Lona was too wide by now for any gift to bridge. He'd done a terrible thing, and it was all for nothing.

Ed and Betty never fought. They were easy-going, and it was always "Yes, dear" and all that sort of thing.

Lona was there. She smiled briefly and tightly as she saw him. He was right: it *was* too late. No—she wouldn't snap or snarl if others were present, but neither would she pretend. And old Mrs. Cheener was there too: Mrs. Cheener who owned the camp, a tiny little woman with wild white hair. Her age and position made her a privileged character and she now at once proceeded to take advantage of it.

"Well, so you finally got here, did you?" she rattled away at him. "I suppose you were boozing it up while your poor little wife sets here with us. If she takes a notion to walk out on you, nobody'd be to blame but you there, Clauson, I'm speaking to you. The way you yell and threaten her!"

Jack asked, with a forced grin, "But what about the way she threatens *me*, Mrs. Cheener?"

Lona looked up. Jack noticed that she didn't appear to be taking his remark as an affront. Could it possibly be that it wasn't too late, after all?

Mrs. Cheener's bright eyes turned to the Roanes. The implication, that she didn't want to waste any more of her valuable time on Jack.

"Turn on the television," she directed, as if it were *her* place. "I want the news." Betty obeyed—reluctantly, it seemed to Jack. Ed avoided his eye.

The newscaster's face flowed into focus. "—the only State which allows such a choice or uses such a means of execution—" his voice boomed out. Betty, grimacing, hastened to soften it.

"There, we tuned in late and missed the beginning," the old lady fretted.

"—a target was pinned over the condemned man's heart and—"

"Ah, it's that no-good from down the state that killed his partner," the old woman remarked grimly.

"—the firing-squad was, as is customary, composed of paid civilian volunteers, who—"

Betty shuddered. "Oh, I'd rather not listen to this!" She screwed up her face and put her hands over her ears. She and Ed stared at each other. Mrs. Cheener gazed avidly at the screen, as if expecting it to reveal the death-event itself. Jack Clauson sat stiff, saying nothing. Then he reached across to where Lona was sitting and took her hand, held it though she did make an attempt to free it.

"Meanwhile, the death toll continues to mount in the California floods," the announcer was saying, in his smooth, rich voice, summing up the number of drownings as if he were lauding a hair tonic.

As soon as the news was over, Lona and Jack left.

They walked to their trailer without speaking. Just wait until she sees that present, Jack told himself. Just you wait.

As soon as they got inside, still without speaking, Lona started picking up some of the stuff that littered the place, not to make order but to be doing something, absently.

He got the box in its fancy wrappings, wanted to hand it to her, but didn't know how. That she might refuse to unwrap it bothered him. So he said, "Here's something for you," and started jerking off the ribbon and the paper. He got the nightgown out. "Take a look at this, would you," he said, holding it up. And the festive quality he'd put in his voice, he didn't feel.

Lona dropped what she had in her hand and moved toward Jack—toward the black lace nightgown—as though mesmerized.

"Oh, it's *beautiful!*" Lona's face—so like a child's, he thought, for all that she was almost thirty—was wide-eyed and delighted. Her eyes explored the nightgown avidly. She touched her cheek to its softness, virtually embraced it.

"Lovely," she said. "It's lovely . . ."

"Glad you like it, honey," Jack said, but he was aware that Lona was still so taken up with the beauty of her present that she hadn't heard him. He wanted to kiss her. But he couldn't let her think that he was buying her affection with the present. Slowly does it, he told himself.

"How about a drink?" he asked, louder this time. They'd celebrate the end of all bad feeling. And he, in addition, would celebrate the fact that his plan had worked—the end of his fear that it wouldn't. "How about a little drink?"

Then—as suddenly as if a curtain had been pulled—the smile left Lona's face. "Will one bottle be enough?" She didn't so much ask the question as throw it at him.

"I, ah, I guess so," he answered, uncertainly. He was confused. "What do you mean, doll?" he asked.

She stood there, stiff. Her face was cold, sullen. "This lovely nightie." There was a sneer in the way she said that. She pushed the nightgown from her, glowered at it. "All this lace. The woman in me must have been carried away by it. Take the thing back. Go on, get your twenty-five dollars. That—that ought to buy enough liquor to get you good and drunk. I know if I were you I'd never want to sober up again as long as I lived."

What *happened?* What made her change? Why had she—? Then, ringing like a bunch of jangly bells, the words—*Twenty-five dollars Twenty-five dollars Twenty-five*— He stared at her, swallowed. "How'd you know?" he asked, his voice thick. He poured whiskey into the glass, tossed it down.

"How'd I *know?*" Her voice rose shrilly. "Why, there won't be anybody around here tomorrow who won't know! Mrs. Cheener's son-in-law, the guard at the pen, called to give her the information. Did you forget about her son-in-law? He *saw* you there. Ugh!"

She looked at him with disgust and horror. He *had* forgotten. He never once thought of it. "How could you *do* it?" Lona asked, her face twisted.

"I did it for *you!*" He cried his outrage aloud. "*That's* how I could do it! For *us*—to buy some nice present for you—to make you happy . . ." He moved toward her, his face hurt and baffled, his hands groping. They found the nightgown she had dropped, held it out to her in one last offering.

Lona stepped away. She shook her head. "Oh, no," she said softly, almost in a whisper. "Not for me. I wouldn't touch it. What do you think I am?" And once again she cried, incredulously, "How could you do it? *Oh!*"

His head was buzzing. The straight whiskey, no supper, the whole horrible business at the penitentiary, now this. But he had to answer her question.

"Well, uh . . . he had it coming to him. He killed someone. If it wasn't me, it would of been someone in my place, so what's the difference? That's the law." And, pleased with this neat summation, he cocked his head on one side and looked at her. For a moment there was silence. Then Lona moved away, began to pick up her clothes and fold them up haphazardly. She pulled a suitcase from its place. Her mouth was tight-pressed.

Jack looked at her in anguish. Ten minutes ago he'd thought, hoped, that their marriage was saved. Now . . . He wiped his face. "Where're you—? Lona? Please!"

She spun around and screamed at him, "I'm packing up! I'm going to get out of here. And this—and this—" She pushed at the black lace nightgown which he continued to hold out to her in supplication. "Get it away from me!"

Jack dropped the frothy garment and held her shoulders.

"Oh, no, you've got to stay—you've got to wear it, Lona! I only did it for you—only for you. It was awful, horrible—and if you don't stay, then it was all for nothing. I'll have helped kill a man I never knew, never even saw before, and all for nothing. All—"

She struck away his hands from her shoulders, and—when he touched her again—she clawed at him, spitting out ugly words. Then he knew that it had indeed been all for nothing, and a fury he had never known in his life took him.

"I'll kill you!" he cried. "I'll kill you!" He hit her—once—twice. He lost count . . .

There were voices outside, old Mrs. Cheener's, the Roanes', others. What was he looking for? he asked himself. A towel. There wasn't any. He knelt slowly to the floor, picked up the black lace nightgown, wet it at the sink, knelt again, began to wipe the blood away. The voices were baying outside, people pounding at the door, while he sponged his wife's face. "Lona?" he said slowly. "Lona?"

There was sawdust on the floor of the long room, just like in a butcher shop. Bright lights, terribly bright, bore down from overhead on the far end. The near end was dark. The men there shifted from foot to foot, coughed nervously. The sound stopped abruptly as the door at the far end opened.

A group of people entered, but the men already waiting had eyes only for the one in the open shirt—the one who blinked, who ran the tip of his tongue along his lips. The man walked steadily enough and his head was up and he didn't say anything. But there was, suddenly, the sharp fresh smell of his sweat. It was the odor of fear. His face was paper-white.

The guards bound his arms, swiftly, tightly. One of them pinned a target over his heart. The chaplain murmured from his little book. These were the regular officials of the State and the State's justice and mercy. The men waiting at the far end of the room—the bright lights enabled them to see but not to be seen—were volunteers. They had driven up to the prison in their own cars. Later they would drive away, each one with twenty-five dollars in his pocket (two crisp tens and one crisp five); and many of them would drive away along the newly-built road. The road Jack Clauson had helped to build.

Jack Clauson blinked in the bright lights. The straps were very tight. His head moved from side to side—as if he was looking for an out—and knowing there wasn't any. He blinked and licked his lips and waited.

# Murderer #2

## by Jean Potts


It would never have occurred to Rolfe Jackson to kill his mother if it had not been absolutely necessary.

He was not a criminal. He was an artist. (True, there were those who held that the pictures Rolfe painted were crimes of a particularly brutal sort. They were fools, of course; he had not yet found himself, that was all.)

Besides, he was really quite fond of the old girl. He had her to thank for his name, for instance. She might so easily have called him Henry or Albert, both of which were traditional family names. Henry Jackson. Albert Jackson. Why, with such a name he might never have had the heart to embark on his artistic career at all! Certainly the identity he had created for himself as Rolfe J.—which was the way he chose to sign his pictures—would have been inconceivable.

He was quite a character, this Rolfe J. who had been built up with such care and who would someday come into his own. Hard-boiled. Dedicated. A Hemingway among painters. There was his stubby beard to prove it, and his lumberjack taste in clothes. Without them, he would have looked what he was—short and pudgy. With them he was impressively burly. Rolfe J. talked tough. He had choice unprintable phrases for the critics and for the work of other artists. He sneered at creature comforts. Publicly, that is. Very few people ever saw the inside of his apartment, and so very few people knew how much he loved luxury.

None of it—his whole beloved, outwardly rough-hewn, secretly luxurious life—would have been possible without Mother. Because it was Mother's father who had set up the trust fund, and the trust fund saved Rolfe J. from having to make a living.

Yet it was also the trust fund that made it absolutely necessary for him to kill Mother. The realization hit him, like a blow from a fist, while he and Mr. Webb were having their little talk. Mr. Webb was Mother's attorney, and a friend of many years' standing; he lived in an apartment just across the hall from hers. Rolfe was instantly wary when one night Mr. Webb asked him to come in. His own relations with the man had always been notable for their lack of cordiality. No open quarrels. Just a mutual case of low estimation. Mr. Webb looked like a Yankee farmer—stringy, lantern-jawed, granite-eyed. His study was just what you would expect. Rolfe had never in his life sat on a more uncomfortable chair.

"I've been meaning to have a little talk with you for some time," Mr. Webb began. "Ever since your mother had this stroke. How are things going with the nurse?"

Mr. Webb had found the nurse for Mother. An ugly, devoted woman named Stella, who came in every day. By now Mother could manage alone, at night. But she was never going to get beyond the wheelchair stage. Poor old girl. What a change after all the bustle and pressure of the job she had had for years with one of the ladies' magazines . . .

"Stella? She's a paragon," said Rolfe. He felt, as usual, an impulse to shock Mr. Webb, jolt him out of his flinty composure. "If she wasn't god-awful ugly I'd marry her, to save her salary."

Mr. Webb just looked at him. He had a talent for the unsettling silence. Finally he said, "That's what your mother's worried about. Money. She shouldn't be. But she is. So I thought we ought to get the whole thing straightened out."

"What's to straighten out? She's got the pension from her office—"

"Peanuts," said Mr. Webb curtly. "Hardly pays the rent. That's why she's worried. She knows she's going to have to dip into your trust fund to pay the nurse and the doctors' bills." He opened his brief case and spread some papers out on the desk in front of him. "I don't know how familiar you are with the terms of your grandfather's will. It might be well to review them. He left his money in trust for you, with the proviso that your mother may draw on it, in case of emergency. Now I don't believe anyone would question the fact that your mother's illness constitutes an emergency."

"Who's questioning it?" said Rolfe irritably. "Not me."

"I'm glad of that. It's only fair to warn you that the drain on your trust fund will be considerable. Very likely you will find it necessary to curtail your present and future expenses." Mr. Webb said this with relish. "Your living arrangements, for example, aren't exactly economical. My own suggestion would be that you move in with your mother. Why not? You're already living in the same apartment house. It would simply mean paying rent on one apartment, instead of two. As far as Stella's salary, and her appearance, are concerned"—he produced a wintry smile—"it's not necessary for you to marry her. Since you don't go out to work anyway, I don't see why you shouldn't take over some of the care of your mother. Combine art and nursing, say, two or three days a week. It would mean quite a saving."

It was Rolfe's turn to just look at Mr. Webb. For once in his life he had nothing whatever to say. Mr. Webb did not seem to notice. Having curtailed living expenses to his Yankee heart's content, he was now proceeding to "go over the figures."

They appalled Rolfe. He had not realized their true nature until now; it was like the moment when the dentist's drill touches a live nerve, sending out shoots of excruciating pain. He sat bolt upright (there was no other way to sit in that contemptible chair of Mr. Webb's), his eyes riveted on Mr. Webb's bony face, while he watched his beautiful trust fund trickle away day after day, year after year. The doctor had said Mother might live for years. Fifteen, even twenty. And every day of every one of those years meant ten dollars for Stella, at least another ten for food and medicine and miscellaneous expenses.

And Rolfe was supposed to stand for this without a murmur of protest; he was—yes, Mr. Webb was making it quite clear—he was supposed to stand for it *gladly*, just because Mother had gone out of her way to keep the trust fund intact, until now. As if that were Rolfe's fault! He hadn't asked her to pay for his education, the summers in France, all the rest of it, out of her own earnings. It was her business, how she chose to spend her salary. And yet, now that there was no more salary, he was to be penalized, his very life was to go down the drain!

Well, he *wouldn't* stand for it. They were dealing with a man, not a mouse. And no ordinary man, either; he would show them, once and for all, the caliber of Rolfe J. The dream, the vision of himself as a man among men, touched with genius, ruthlessly molding his own destiny, had never been more vivid. He would—

"As I say," Mr. Webb was concluding, as he shuffled his papers back into their folder, "I'm glad you're taking a sensible attitude about this. Even if you weren't, it wouldn't make any difference. There's not a thing you can do about it."

That was what Mr. Webb thought. Rolfe knew better. It had hit him in the second before Mr. Webb stopped speaking: the flash of crystal understanding, and the resolution.

Nothing he could do about it? Ah, but there was, there was. Something so obvious, so necessary and right (for why should Mother, simply by living, cheat him of what was rightfully his?) that even a fool like Mr. Webb ought to see it. He didn't though. There was a gleam of satisfaction in his granite eyes as he said good-night. He thought he had scored, in this little talk of theirs. He thought he had taken Rolfe down a notch or two.

Out in the hall, Rolfe paused a moment, waiting for his heart to stop pounding. Then he let himself into Mother's apartment and called cheerily, "Anybody home? How about a glass of sherry?"

Mother was in bed—Stella always got her settled for the night before she left—but bright-eyed, obviously brimming over with news. She was a fat little woman, with a halo of white curly hair. "You'll never guess what happened to me today," she began, while Rolfe poured the sherry. "I was approached by an ex-narcotics addict!"

"What? Now really, Mother—"

"Really. Oh, a strictly business approach. He wants me to help him write a book. 'I Was a Narcotics Addict'—that sort of thing. I must say, he doesn't look like a man with a lurid past. Quite presentable. I don't know why I— Maybe it was his missionary zeal that put me off. This project seems to be kind of a crusade with him."

"That's normal, isn't it?" said Rolfe. "Look at the reformed drunks that go around spreading the good word. I suppose it works the same with dope addicts."

"I suppose. Or maybe it was his name. It's Borden, and all I could think of was that little verse about Lizzie Borden taking an axe . . . It's awful to have a free-wheeling mind like mine."

They both laughed. Rolfe became aware of a prickle at the back of his neck, a tremor of obscure excitement. But he kept his voice casual. "You turned him down, then?"

"No, I told him I'd think it over and let him know tomorrow. It *would* be fun, you know." Just the thought made her look, for a moment, quite like her old busy, enthusiastic self. "And then supposing it turned out to be a best seller and we all got rich."

"I wasn't thinking of the money," said Rolfe truthfully. "Nice as it would be. I was just thinking how much you'd enjoy having something to do again."

"You think I'm being silly?" she asked wistfully. "You think I ought to do it?" She waited for his answer, and at once the illusion of vigor vanished. For in the old days she would not have needed Rolfe's advice, she would have known her own mind. Now uncertainty clouded her eyes. Her whole face sagged into lines of doubt, almost of fear. But it was the delicacy of her temple that fascinated Rolfe. Above her plump cheek it was slightly sunken and threaded with blue. It looked fragile as an egg shell.

"Good Lord, Mother, I've never seen the man, so how can I tell? And I've been wondering, how'd he happen to get in touch with you?"

"Well, he works in a bindery, a book bindery. Someone there suggested an editor, who in turn suggested me. So he looked me up in the phone book—"

"If you want me to look him over when he turns up again tomorrow," said Rolfe, "I'll be glad to . . ."

The deal was clinched next day, on the spot. Mother, now that Rolfe had disposed of her original vague doubts, was frankly delighted at the prospect. So was Borden.

Only Stella held out. She cornered Rolfe as he left; she had been lurking in the kitchen, waiting to speak her piece. Which she did, in an ominous whisper. "I don't like it, Mr. Jackson. I just think you and your mother are taking an awful chance, letting that dope fiend in here three evenings a week. Oh, I know. He claims he's cured. I've heard that one before. They're none of them ever cured. Not for sure. I don't like it. Not one little bit."

Good old Stella. Under her white nylon uniform she wore what appeared to be a suit of armor; it jutted out in ridges across her meaty shoulders and back. Lumpy wriggles of varicose veins showed through her white stockings. And she dyed her hair shoe-polish black. As ugly as ever, and yet Rolfe regarded her with something very like affection. Good old doubting Stella.

"*Sh,*" he whispered back. "The only reason I'm going along with it is that she needs something to keep her occupied. It's brightened her up already. Don't worry, I'll make sure she's never left alone with him. That's why I insisted on meeting the fellow, to make sure he seemed all right."

"All right!" Stella snorted. "With those gooseberry eyes of his, and those long twitchy hands? Gives me the shivers just to think of him."

But even Stella seemed to forget her doubts as two weeks, three weeks, went by, with no danger signals from Borden. Rolfe found it necessary to remind her now and then, in an unobtrusive way.

He himself was busy exploring. He had been quick to sense Borden's potentialities. But they would remain only potentialities until he had found the way to use them. To use them he must know his man, through and through.

He found the whole project almost alarmingly easy. No one could have been more cooperative than Borden, either in striking up a friendship or in promoting the exploration of his own character. The circumstances were favorable too. In his capacity as watchdog, Rolfe was always present on Borden evenings, for Stella—having first given Mother her early dinner and settled her in bed—left at seven thirty. Rolfe did not intrude on the book sessions, which were held in the bedroom; he lounged in the living room, pretending to read, waiting for Borden to emerge, ready with his suggestion—so natural—that they drop into the bar and grill next door for a sociable drink. Borden snapped at the invitation like a hungry dog at a bone. The drink or two often stretched out to dinner and beyond: a whole solid evening of analyzing Borden.

It was a subject that fascinated them both. Borden's experiences as a psychiatric patient had left him with an insatiable interest in his own mental processes. Sometimes he would work himself up into a transport of confession, like a religious convert glorying in the spectacle of his remembered sins. His prominent green eyes dilated even more than usual, and he would sway on his bar stool, making jerky gestures or running his hand through his lank blond hair.

At other times he was coldly objective. "It's a classic type," he would say. "The rejected child." And he would tick off the "classic" elements—the family-deserting father, the indifferent mother, the succession of even more indifferent substitute parents. The few friends

ALFRED HITCHCOCK'S ANTHOLOGY

he had managed to make always ended by sloughing him off—frightened away, probably, by the violence of his attachment to them. For he was violent. He was so famished for affection that he could not help it.

"You'll never know what it's meant to me, meeting you and your mother. You've always had friends, so you can't possibly understand—" He broke off with an embarrassed laugh, and went on more calmly. "You see, it's not just a question of getting cured of the dope habit. You've got to get cured of whatever it was that made you turn into a dope addict in the first place. That's where you can't ever be sure. I'm 'cured' now, and I can stay 'cured' as long as I've got my job at the bindery, and the book to work on, and most of all you and your mother. But let something go wrong, maybe the least little thing—"

It was the truth. When Rolfe tested it out a few nights later by breaking a dinner date they had made, Borden's face turned quite white and into his eyes flashed a look of desperate presentiment: here it was again, the pattern as before. Rolfe and his mother, like all the others, were going to cast him off. He wrote Rolfe a cringing, overwrought letter: What had he done to offend Rolfe? How could he make amends? It took Rolfe several days to quiet the fears he had set off with his trivial slight.

He was excited, even a little bit scared, at how easy it was going to be.

The crucial slight, he decided, must come from Mother, because the full force of Borden's devotion was focused on her rather than on Rolfe. It would have to be faked. Though Borden sometimes made Mother nervous ("He's so intense, poor fellow!") still she sympathized with him; she would stick with him as long as he behaved himself. Of course if she thought for one minute that he had gone back to drugs . . .

A little manipulation by Rolfe, and that was exactly what she thought. She couldn't understand it when Borden failed to turn up for three sessions in a row. (The doctor, Rolfe had explained to him, felt that Mother might be overdoing; she was showing signs of strain.) Why didn't Borden call? Why didn't he explain? ("Whatever you do, please don't call her," Rolfe had cautioned. "It would only upset her, and we're trying to keep her as quiet as possible.") She fretted. She hoped against hope—until Rolfe, commissioned to investigate, brought back a report that confirmed her worst fears.

Of course there was nothing to do but call the whole project off. They couldn't risk letting Borden come back now, under any circumstance. But Mother didn't know when she had been so disappointed in anyone. And just when she had thought he was doing so well! She had a good cry over it. Then—with Rolfe's help—she wrote the letter that had to be written to Borden.

It was all that was needed to push Borden over the edge. A prey, as always, to his own insecurity, he had been suspicious from the first. "You're not telling me the truth," he had raged to Rolfe. "It isn't doctor's orders. She hasn't been overdoing. I've offended her somehow, the way I always do, with everybody I've ever cared about. She wants to get rid of me. Doesn't she? Doesn't she? Why won't you admit it?" And Rolfe had been just kind enough, just evasive enough, to keep him simmering.

He had expected an immediate explosion after the letter. But it was several days before he heard from Borden. No letter this time. None of the frantic telephone calls he had grown used to. His doorbell rang very late one night, and there was Borden—an ominously different, glassy-eyed Borden who at first seemed to have nothing to say and then suddenly burst into a flood of abject pleading. He couldn't stand it, that was all. They had to give him another chance. It was true that he had lost his job and hocked most of his clothes (he was not even wearing a jacket, though the night was raw and windy) but only because he couldn't stand it, they couldn't do this to him, another chance and he would be all right again.

"But that's why I've been trying to get.hold of you!" Rolfe broke in—all sincerity, the distressed friend eager to help. "I've told Mother all along she was being unfair. Only I didn't know where to find you, and here she is, all but convinced that she ought to give you another chance—"

"Let me see her! Now! Right away!" Trembling with excitement, Borden jerked himself out of his chair. "I'll do anything, anything. Let me see her. You come with me, Rolfe, she'll listen to you—"

"Are you crazy?" said Rolfe coldly. "At this hour of the night? And you in the shape you're in? We wouldn't have a prayer. I'll tell you right now, I'm not doing one thing for you unless you pull yourself together. Is that understood? You've got until tomorrow night. Let's say tomorrow night at nine thirty. We can meet next door at the bar, and if you're okay I'll take you to see Mother and I'll do all I can for you. But remember, it's up to you."

"Anything, I told you I'll do anything—" Borden drew a long, shaky breath. "Can't we make it earlier?" he whispered. "It's so long to wait. Nine thirty. I don't know if I can wait."

"You'd damn well better," Rolfe told him. "I can't make it till then."

He thought he never was going to get rid of the fellow. Borden promised, over and over again. Agonized hope flared in his eyes; he knew that if he could just see Mother, speak to her for only a minute, he could convince her. He apologized, he explained, he all but licked Rolfe's hand in a transport of gratitude.

When he was leaving, as an afterthought, Rolfe lent him his own sports jacket. It seemed like the least he could do.

He may have slept some, during what was left of the night, but very little. Mostly, he paced the floor and planned. And as the hours of the next day slid by into afternoon, into evening, a mystical calm spread through him. Here was what he had waited for all his life—the moment (and of his own choosing, brought about by his own contrivance) that would change Rolfe J. in one incandescent flash from vision to reality. Soon, very soon. A bare half hour from now. He had only to slip down the fire escape and into Mother's bedroom through the window he had surreptitiously unlatched when he said goodnight to her, and then—and then—

It would take a very few minutes. He knew so well the exact location of the paperweight, on the desk beside her bed. He knew so well the way she would be lying, with the blanket pulled up to her chin and above it that egg-shell temple exposed, waiting for the blow. Asleep. She would be fast asleep. She would never know what hit her. Or who. Or why.

Back up the fire escape, because he could not afford the risk of being seen in the elevator. A few minutes later he would emerge from his own apartment quite openly, take the elevator to the street floor, and go into the bar next door. Most likely Borden would already be there, wild with anticipation. "Come on," Rolfe would say, "Mother's expecting us." And into the apartment house they would go, up in the elevator to Mother's door, where Rolfe would suddenly pause in the act of turning his key in the lock. "Oh, damn!" (slapping his pockets) "I forgot my pipe. I'll just run up to my place and get it. Go on in, I'll be right back." Opening the door, he would call in to Mother the business about the pipe, just as though she could hear. Up to his own place again. Five, ten minutes.

When he came back, Borden would have discovered what had happened in the bedroom. He might be standing there, stunned; he might—even better—have fled in panic. Rolfe's story to the police would fit, in any case. "I never trusted the guy," he would say. "Stella can tell you. I made a point of always being here, when he came for his sessions with Mother. But it never occurred to me— It couldn't have been ten minutes. Just while I went upstairs for my pipe. I shouldn't have left him there. God, if only I hadn't!" As for what Borden would try to tell the police— Well, who was going to take the word of a hophead? He didn't have a prayer. Like as not, before it was all over, Borden, along with everybody else, would become convinced of his guilt.

It had been snowing lightly, Rolfe found when he stepped noiselessly through his window. The fire escape steps looked ghostly under the thin white coat. The windows of the two floors between him and Mother's apartment were dark. So was the church next door. No one to see or hear him. Everything was just as he had planned: the swift, silent descent, Mother's window opening smoothly under his hands, his leg thrusting inside, feeling for the floor, avoiding the little chintz chair . . .

He was inside. And suddenly nothing was as he had planned: the paperweight was not there on the desk. He stumbled into the medicine table, setting off a nervous clash of silver against glass, and still there was no stir or sound from the hump in the bed. His own rapid breathing unnerved him; he could not make it slow down. He became aware of a smell in the room, and that too was wrong because it was unfamiliar—pervasive, yet not like Mother's medicine; sweetish, yet not like her dusting powder. The smell of fear? Might Mother, having heard the intruder, be lying there frozen with terror? It could not be that Rolfe himself was afraid.

It was just that he could not see to find the paperweight. But to turn on the lamp would be to meet Mother's eyes . . . Again he groped over the desk; for a moment he thought he had it, his fingers closed

300                                          ALFRED HITCHCOCK'S ANTHOLOGY

convulsively, and at once a snatch of wistful music tinkled out. Horrified, he clapped the lid back on the damned-fool contraption: one of those musical cigarette boxes. Mother loved such trinkets. He braced himself for what must surely come now—some movement, some sound from the bed. It did not come. He held his own breath, listening for hers. It was not there.

He turned on the lamp.

The shock came not so much from what had been done to Mother—after all, he himself had planned it—as from the fact that it had been done without his realizing it. For his first nightmarish conviction was that his memory had betrayed him, tricked him by blanking out. How could I have done it, he thought, and I have absolutely no recollection of it? Why, there I was, fumbling around for the paperweight, when all the time I had already . . .

The paperweight was on the bed, where it had been dropped once it had served its purpose. Mother's smashed-in head lay sideways on the pillow. She had put up quite a struggle for her poor life; one fat dimpled hand reached vainly toward the telephone, and her eyes, glazed and terrible with knowledge, stared up at him. She had known who hit her, and why.

It could not have been Rolfe. At last his mind grasped the truth. Memory was not playing tricks on him. Someone else had beaten him to it, had carried out his plan for him. A glance around the room, and he had the answer. The someone else was Borden. There across the chintz chair was Rolfe's jacket, the one Borden had borrowed last night. Maybe he had left it here on impulse—simply shucking off anything connected with Rolfe or his mother—or maybe on purpose in the hope (the dirty little rat) of implicating Rolfe. Well, Rolfe wasn't having any of that. He had come down in his shirt sleeves. With a feeling of triumph he slipped into the jacket. The comfortable set of it on his shoulders seemed to steady him.

Not that he was really shaken, of course. Not Rolfe J. Naturally it was a jolt, to find that Borden had come barging in ahead of time. But only a minor jolt, only momentary.

How had the fellow gotten in? The open fire-escape window? No, Rolfe remembered. There had been a key to Mother's apartment, an extra one, in his jacket pocket. Finding it must have been the spark that set Borden off. There right in his hands was the means of cutting short the agony of waiting; he could not resist using it. And Mother—taken by surprise, unaware that she was supposed to be on the verge of giving Borden another chance—would not have minced words. A flat, harsh turndown. What followed was inevitable.

Yes, there was the key on the desk, where Borden must have tossed it when he came in. Rolfe reached for it. And hesitated.

Supposing the police didn't believe him? He had never doubted that he could convince them of a lie. But now, in a chilling flash, he saw the situation as it would look, for example, to someone walking in on him at that moment. Standing there with the weapon in his hand (hastily, he slipped it into his pocket), the open fire-escape window behind him . . .

But of course nothing like that was going to happen. It wouldn't take them long to catch up with Borden, and he would crack. He had none of Rolfe's stamina; he was sure to crack. Guilty as he was, he might already be turning himself in. He would spill everything—the jacket borrowed from Rolfe, the extra key accidentally left in the pocket.

So it was a mistake to wear the jacket away. He must leave everything just as it was. And it would be a mistake to call the police quite yet. Because the other key to Mother's apartment was upstairs, on his chest of drawers; and it would be hard to explain why, with it lying there, Rolfe had chosen to come down the fire escape. Thank God he had thought of it in time! He drew a breath of relief at the simplicity of what he had to do—another trip up the fire escape for his key, down again in the elevator, back here to the bedroom (he must remember to lock the fire-escape window) and then the distraught call to the police. He had it made.

All the same, he had one leg through the window when he realized he was still wearing the jacket. The near-blunder shook him; it gave him a grim glimpse of how treacherous his mind could be. But must not be. Would not be.

The trouble was that everything happened at once: he discovered in his hurry to shed the jacket why Borden had left it behind. There was blood on the sleeve; it was already beginning to stiffen. And he heard the voice and the footsteps. His whole body locked in a paralysis of listening. Someone was in the apartment. Someone who was moving through the living room, on toward the bedroom. That fool Borden must have left the door ajar, simply walked out and . . .

302                                    ALFRED HITCHCOCK'S ANTHOLOGY

Move. Get out of here. But get out of the jacket too, the damning jacket, because the footsteps were appallingly close now! At the last moment his arms and legs unlocked, but only to a flurry of witless jerks that neither got him through the window nor out of the jacket. And it was all too late. He was lost. Ignominiously straddling the window sill, with one arm still trying to fumble its way out of the jacket, he looked into the granite eyes of Mr. Webb and knew that disaster was upon him.

Complete disaster. He felt Rolfe J.—the masterful man of destiny— disintegrate, once and for all, into the reality of what Mr. Webb saw—a pudgy, guilty wretch, caught red-handed and babbling (somehow that was the worst of all, that he could not stop babbling) an incoherent story that no one was going to believe.

"Tell it to the police," said Mr. Webb, and reached for the telephone.

So Rolfe went on babbling to the police that they must find Borden, all they had to do was find Borden. He babbled on and on.

They found Borden. What was left of him. He had either fallen or jumped from the window of his room to the alley below. Nobody knew exactly when. Or why. As the police said, who knew what made hopheads do any of the screwball things they did?

Luck had been with Borden—until he went out the window, of course. Nobody had seen him entering or leaving Mother's apartment. Nobody had seen him wearing Rolfe's jacket; there was only Rolfe's word that he had ever borrowed it. Only Rolfe's word, which nobody believed.

Yet there was nothing else for Rolfe to do but to go on hopelessly telling the truth. At the very end, while he was waiting in the death cell, he said, "I am guilty. I did not do it, but I am guilty."

A garbled sort of confession? Or just some more crazy babbling? No one recognized it for what it was. The deepest truth of all.

# The Third Call

## by Jack Ritchie

At 1:20 in the afternoon I phoned Stevenson High School and got through to Principal Morrison.

I spoke through the handkerchief over the mouthpiece. "This is no joke. A bomb is going to explode in your school in fifteen minutes."

There were a few seconds of silence on the other end of the line and then Morrison's angry voice demanded, "Who is this?"

"Never mind that. I'm not fooling this time. A bomb is going off in fifteen minutes."

And then I hung up.

I left the gas station, crossed the street, and returned to the main police station. I took the elevator to the third floor.

My partner, Pete Torgeson, was on the phone when I entered the squad room.

He looked up. "Stevenson High School just got another one of those calls, Jim. Morrison is having the school evacuated again."

"Did you get the bomb squad?"

"I'm doing that right now." He dialed and completed the call to Room 121, giving them details.

The enrollment at Stevenson was 1800 and all the students were out of the building by the time we arrived. Their teachers, following the instructions we had given them the last two times the school had received phone calls, were keeping them at least two hundred feet away from the building.

Principal Morrison was a large graying man wearing rimless glasses. He left the group of teachers at the curb and came forward. "The call came at exactly 1:20," he said.

The bomb unit truck and two squad cars pulled up behind our car.

ALFRED HITCHCOCK'S ANTHOLOGY

My son Dave lounged against the wire fence with a half a dozen of his buddies. He waved. "What is it, Dad? Another bomb scare?"

I nodded. "And let's hope it's nothing more than a scare this time too."

Dave grinned. "I don't mind a bit. We were just going to have a history exam."

Morrison shook his head. "I'm afraid that most of the students regard this as nothing more than a welcome break in the routine."

Several more details of men arrived from headquarters and we began searching the building. We finished the job at 2:30 and I went back to Morrison. "It was another hoax. We didn't find a thing."

Morrison ordered the students back to their classes and then took Torgeson and me to his office.

"Did you recognize the voice?" Torgeson asked.

Morrison sat down at his desk. "No. It was muffled and indistinct, just as before. But it was a male voice. That much I'm certain about." He sighed. "I'm having the attendance records checked right away. Are you sure it's one of the students?"

"In cases like this, it usually is," Pete said. "A boy decides he hates one of the teachers or the whole school because he's getting bad marks. So he uses this way to get what he thinks is revenge. Or maybe he just thinks the whole thing is a roaring joke."

The attendance records were brought to Morrison. He glanced at them and then passed them over to us. "Ninety-one absences. About average."

Pete and I went over the names of the absent students. I knew that Bob Fletcher would be there, but that didn't matter. I hoped that Lester Baines had come back to school in the afternoon.

"Fletcher's here," Pete said. "But he's out, of course." His eyes went back to the list. "And Lester Baines was absent." He ran down the rest of the names and then looked up and smiled. "Just Lester Baines. He's our boy."

Morrison had Lester's records brought in. He shook his head as he read. "He's seventeen. No disciplinary problem at all, but he's absent a lot. His grades are pretty bad. He failed in two subjects last semester."

Pete was looking over Morrison's shoulder. "Do you know him?"

Morrison smiled wanly. "No. A principal knows fewer of the students than any teacher."

Torgeson lit a cigar. "This looks like the end of this one, Jim. You should look more cheerful."

I got to my feet. "I just don't like to see any boy get into trouble."

We drove to the Baines home. It was a medium-sized two-story house much like any of the others in the block.

Mr. Baines was tall and blue-eyed. The smile left his face when he opened the door. "You here again?"

"We'd like to talk to your son," Pete said. "Lester wasn't at school today. Is he sick?"

Baines' eyes flickered and then he said, "Why?"

Pete smiled faintly. "The same thing we were here for before."

Baines let us in reluctantly. "Lester's at the drug store. He'll be back in a few minutes."

Torgeson sat down on the davenport. "He isn't sick?"

Baines watched us narrowly. "He had a cold. I thought that it was best to keep him home today. But it wasn't so bad that he couldn't go down to the drug store for a coke."

Pete's face was bland. "Where was your boy at ten-thirty this morning?"

"He was right here," Baines snapped. "And he didn't make any phone calls."

"How do you know that?"

"This is my day off. I was with Lester all day."

"Where is your wife?"

"She's out shopping now. But she was here at ten-thirty. Lester didn't make any phone calls."

Pete smiled. "I hope so. And where was Lester at 1:20?"

"Right here," Baines said again. "My wife and I will swear to it." He frowned. "Were there two calls today?"

Pete nodded.

We sat in the living room waiting. Baines fidgeted nervously in his chair and then got up. "I'll be right back. I've got to check some of the upstairs screens."

Pete watched him leave the room and then turned to me. "You're letting me do all the talking, Jim."

"It doesn't take two for something like this, Pete."

He lit a cigar. "Well, everything turned out all right. We won't have to lose sleep on this one." He picked up the phone on a table at his elbow and listened. After awhile he put his hand over the mouthpiece. "Baines is on the upstairs extension. He's calling around. He doesn't know where his son is."

Pete kept listening and after awhile he smiled. "Now he's talking to his wife. She's at the supermarket. He's telling her about us. She's supposed to say that Lester was at home all day and made no phone calls."

I was looking out of the picture window, when a blond teenage boy turned up the walk and came toward the house.

Torgeson saw him too and put down the phone. "There's Lester now. We'll try to have a few fast words with him before his father comes down."

Lester Baines had a new sunburn and he carried a rolled-up towel under his arm. His normally cheerful face sobered when he stepped into the house and saw us.

"Where were you today, Lester?" Pete asked. "We know you weren't at school."

Lester swallowed. "I felt pretty rotten this morning and so I stayed home."

Pete indicated the towel under his arm. "Is there a wet pair of swimming trunks in there?"

Color came to Lester's face. "Well—around nine this morning everything seemed okay again. Maybe I didn't have a cold. I mean, maybe it was just an allergy or something and it cleared up." He took a deep breath. "So I decided to go swimming, get some sun."

"All day? Didn't you get hungry?"

"I took along a few sandwiches."

"Who did you go with?"

"Nobody. Just me." He shifted uneasily. "Was there another one of those phone calls?"

Pete smiled. "If you were feeling so fit, why didn't you go to school in the afternoon?"

Lester's hands worked on the towel. "I was going to. But the next thing I knew it was after one o'clock and I couldn't have got back in time anyway." He went on lamely, "So I just decided to swim some more."

"If you were just going to be away for the morning, why did you take the sandwiches along?"

Lester's color deepened and he finally decided to tell the whole truth. "I didn't have a cold today. I just stayed away from school. Mom and Dad don't know that. There was going to be a civics test this morning and a history test in the afternoon, and I knew I'd flunk them both. I figured that if I studied tonight I'd be able to pass make-up tests tomorrow."

We heard the footsteps coming down the stairs and waited.

Baines stopped when he saw us with his son. "Don't tell them anything, Lester. Let me do the talking."

"I'm afraid it's too late for that now," Pete said. "Your boy admitted that he wasn't in this house today."

Lester's voice showed panic. "I didn't make any of those calls. Honest, I didn't!"

Baines moved beside his son. "Why keep picking on Lester?"

"We're not picking on Lester," Pete said. "But we're reasonably certain that one of the students did the phoning. However, all of the calls came during times when classes were in session. And that means that only a student who was absent could have made them."

Baines wasn't impressed. "I'm sure that Lester wasn't the only student absent today."

Pete conceded that but went on. "The first of the three phone calls came eighteen days ago. We checked the attendance records at Stevenson at that time and found that ninety-six students had been absent at the time it was made. Sixty-two of those were boys and we talked to all of them—including your son. Your boy was home at that time with a cold . . . and alone. You were at work and your wife was attending the birthday party of a friend. However, your son denied making the call and we had to accept his word for that."

Lester appealed to his father. "I *didn't* make that bomb call, Dad. I wouldn't do such a thing."

Baines met his eyes for a moment and then turned back to us, his face expressionless.

Pete continued. "The second phone call came this morning at tenthirty. We went over the attendance records again and discovered that only three boys had been absent on both this morning and on the day of the first phone call."

Baines' face showed a faint hope. "Are you checking the other two boys?"

"We were about to do that, but then another bomb scare call was made this afternoon and we were saved the trouble. We went back to the attendance records. One of our three suspects had returned for the afternoon session and therefore could not have phoned."

"What about the other boy?" Baines demanded.

"He's in a hospital."

Baines grasped at that. "Hospitals have phones."

Torgeson smiled faintly. "The boy caught scarlet fever while he was out of the state with his parents last weekend. He's in a hospital five hundred miles away from here—and the phone calls were all local."

Baines turned to his son.

Lester paled. "You know I never lie to you, Dad."

"Of course you don't, son." But there was doubt on Baines' face.

The front door opened and an auburn-haired woman stepped inside. Her face was pale, but determined, and it took her a moment to get her breath.

"I just stepped out for a moment to go shopping. Otherwise I was here all day. I'm sure I can account for every moment of Lester's time."

"Mom," Lester said miserably. "It's no use. I played hookey all day today and they know it."

Pete reached for his hat. "I'd like both of you to talk to your son tonight. I'm sure you can do that much better than we can." He put one of our cards on the table. "We'd like to see all three of you tomorrow morning at ten."

Outside, when he pulled our car away from the curb, Pete said, "We might find ourselves in for a hard time, if they decide to keep lying for their son."

"Suppose it wasn't somebody from the school?"

"I hope it wasn't. But you and I know that the chances are ninety-nine out of a hundred that it was." Pete sighed. "I don't like to see things like this. The bomb scare is bad enough, but what's happening to that family now is a lot worse."

I checked out of the station at five and got home a little after five-thirty.

My wife, Nora, was in the kitchen. "I read in the paper that there was another bomb scare at Stevenson this morning."

I kissed her. "And one this afternoon. That one happened too late to get into the paper."

She lifted the cover off the pot roast. "Did you find out who made the calls?"

I hesitated a moment. "Yes. I think we have."

"Who was it?"

"One of the students. A Lester Baines."

Her face showed pity. "What would make him do something like that?"

"I don't know. He hasn't admitted making the calls yet."

She studied me. "You look tired, Jim. Is something like this a little worse than usual?"

"Yes. A lot worse."

Her eyes showed worry, but she smiled. "Supper's just about ready. Why don't you call Dave? He's out in the garage trying to get that car of his to run."

Dave had the carburetor on the work bench. He looked up. "Hi, Dad. You look beat with the heat."

"It was a hard day."

"Find the fiend?"

"I hope so."

Dave had the gray eyes of his mother. He frowned. "Who was it?"

"A boy named Lester Baines. Do you know him?"

Dave peered down at the parts before him. "Sure."

"What kind of a boy is he?"

Dave shrugged. "I just know him to talk to. Seems like he's all right." He still frowned. "Did he admit making the calls?"

"No."

Dave picked up a screwdriver. "How did you narrow it down to him?"

I told him the method we had used.

Dave seemed to have trouble with an adjustment. "Is he in a lot of trouble?"

"It might turn out that way."

"What do you think will happen to him?"

"I don't know. He's never been in trouble before. He might get probation."

Dave thought about that. "Maybe he did it as a joke. I mean nobody

ALFRED HITCHCOCK'S ANTHOLOGY

got hurt. All he did was stop school for awhile."

"A lot of people could have gotten hurt," I said. "It wouldn't have been a joke if there had been a panic."

Dave's face seemed slightly stubborn. "We have fire drills all the time. Everything goes off okay."

Yes, and that was what I had counted on when I called. I didn't want anyone to get hurt.

Dave put down his screwdriver. "Do *you* think Lester did it?"

"He could have."

Yes, Lester Baines could have made those first two phone calls. And I had made the third.

Dave was silent for awhile. "Dad, when the school got the first phone call, did you talk to all the boys who were absent?"

"Not myself. But the department got around to seeing all of them."

Dave had a faint wry smile. "I was absent that day, Dad. Nobody talked to me."

"I didn't think it was necessary, son."

And I hadn't. Other men's boys might have done such a thing, but not my boy. But now I waited.

Dave spoke reluctantly. "I was absent this morning too."

"Yes," I said.

He met my eyes. "And that narrowed it down to how many boys?"

"Three," I said. "But we discovered that one of them couldn't possibly have made the call. He was in a hospital out of the state." I watched Dave. "And that left us with just two suspects. Lester Baines—and you."

Dave had trouble manufacturing a grin. "Some luck, huh? I was at school this afternoon when the third phone call came and so that left just poor Lester."

"That's right. Poor Lester."

Dave licked his lips. "Is Lester's dad standing by him?"

"Of course. That's the way dads are supposed to be."

Dave seemed to be perspiring slightly. He worked silently at the carburetor for a minute or two. Then he sighed and met my eyes. "Dad, I think you'd better take me down to headquarters. Lester didn't make those bomb calls. I did." He took a deep breath. "I did it as a joke. I just wanted to pep things up. I didn't mean anything wrong."

I hadn't wanted to hear those words, and yet now I felt a pride that I had a son who wouldn't let someone else suffer for his own mistakes.

"But, Dad, I just made the first two calls. Not the one this afternoon."

"I know. I made that particular call myself."

His eyes widened. And then he understood. "You tried to cover up for me?"

I smiled tiredly. "It was something I shouldn't have done, but a father doesn't always think too clearly when it involves his son. And I was hoping that it might turn out to be Lester after all."

Dave wiped his hands on a rag and there were a few moments of silence.

"I guess I ought to tell them I made all of the calls, Dad," Dave said. "There's no sense in all of us getting into trouble."

I shook my head. "Thanks, son. I'll tell them what I did."

And now when Dave looked at me, I had the feeling that somehow he was proud of me too.

"We'll have supper first," I said. "And then we'll phone Lester's father. A half an hour won't make much difference."

Dave smiled wryly. "It will to Lester and his dad."

I made the phone call as soon as we got back to the house.

ALFRED HITCHCOCK'S ANTHOLOGY

# A Home Away from Home

## by Robert Bloch

The train was late, and it must have been past nine o'clock when Natalie found herself standing, all alone, on the platform before Hightower Station.

The station itself was obviously closed for the night—it was only a way-stop, really, for there was no town here—and Natalie wasn't quite sure what to do. She had taken it for granted that Dr. Bracegirdle would be on hand to meet her. Before leaving London, she'd sent her uncle a wire giving him the time of her arrival. But since the train had been delayed, perhaps he'd come and gone.

Natalie glanced around uncertainly, then noticed the phonebooth which provided her with a solution. Dr. Bracegirdle's last letter was in her purse, and it contained both his address and his phone-number. She had fumbled through her bag and found it by the time she walked over to the booth.

Ringing him up proved a bit of a problem; there seemed to be an interminable delay before the operator made the connection, and there was a great deal of buzzing on the line. A glimpse of the hills beyond the station, through the glass wall of the booth, suggested the reason for the difficulty. After all, Natalie reminded herself, this was West Country. Conditions might be a bit primitive—

"Hello, hello!"

The woman's voice came over the line, fairly shouting above the din. There was no buzzing noise now, and the sound in the background suggested a babble of voices all intermingled. Natalie bent forward and spoke directly and distinctly into the mouthpiece.

"This is Natalie Rivers," she said. "Is Dr. Bracegirdle there?"

"Whom did you say was calling?"

"Natalie Rivers. I'm his niece."

"His what, Miss?"

"Niece," Natalie repeated. "May I speak to him, please?"

"Just a moment."

There was a pause, during which the sound of voices in the background seemed amplified, and then Natalie heard the resonant masculine tones, so much easier to separate from the indistinct murmuring.

"Dr. Bracegirdle here. My dear Natalie, this is an unexpected pleasure!"

"Unexpected? But I sent you a 'gram from London this afternoon." Natalie checked herself as she realized the slight edge of impatience which had crept into her voice. "Didn't it arrive?"

"I'm afraid service is not of the best around here," Dr. Bracegirdle told her, with an apologetic chuckle. "No, your wire didn't arrive. But apparently you did." He chuckled again. "Where are you, my dear?"

"At Hightower Station."

"Oh, dear. It's in exactly the opposite direction."

"Opposite direction?"

"From Peterby's. They rang me up just before you called. Some silly nonsense about an appendix—probably nothing but an upset stomach. But I promised to stop round directly, just in case."

"Don't tell me they still call you for general practise?"

"Emergencies, my dear. There aren't many physicians in these parts. Fortunately, there aren't many patients either." Dr. Bracegirdle started to chuckle, then sobered. "Look now. You say you're at the station. I'll just send Miss Plummer down to fetch you in the wagon. Have you much luggage?"

"Only my travel-case. The rest is coming with the household goods, by boat."

"Boat?"

"Didn't I mention it when I wrote?"

"Yes, that's right, you did. Well, no matter. Miss Plummer will be along for you directly."

"I'll be waiting in front of the platform."

"What was that? Speak up, I can hardly hear you."

"I said I'll be waiting in front of the platform."

"Oh." Dr. Bracegirdle chuckled again. "Bit of a party going on here."

"Shan't I be intruding? I mean, since you weren't expecting me—"

"Not at all! They'll be leaving before long. You wait for Plummer."

The phone clicked off and Natalie returned to the platform. In a surprisingly short time, the station-wagon appeared and skidded off the road to halt at the very edge of the tracks. A tall, thin, gray-haired woman, wearing a somewhat rumpled white uniform, emerged and beckoned to Natalie.

"Come along, my dear," she called. "Here, I'll just pop this in back." Scooping up the bag, she tossed it into the rear of the wagon. "Now, in with you—and off we go!"

Scarcely waiting for Natalie to close the door after her, Miss Plummer gunned the motor and the car plunged back onto the road.

The speedometer immediately shot up to seventy, and Natalie flinched. Miss Plummer noticed her agitation at once.

"Sorry," she said. "With Doctor out on call, I can't be away too long."

"Oh yes, the house-guests. He told me."

"Did he now?" Miss Plummer took a sharp turn at a crossroads and the tires screeched in protest, but to no avail. Natalie decided to drown apprehension in conversation.

"What sort of a man is my uncle?" she asked.

"Have you never met him?"

"No. My parents moved to Australia when I was quite young. This is my first trip to England. In fact, it's the first time I've left Canberra."

"Folks with you?"

"They were in a motor smashup two months ago," Natalie said. "Didn't the Doctor tell you?"

"I'm afraid not—you see, I haven't been with him very long." Miss Plummer uttered a short bark and the car swerved wildly across the road. "Motor smashup, eh? Some people have no business behind the wheel. That's what Doctor says."

She turned and peered at Natalie. "I take it you've come to stay, then?"

"Yes, of course. He wrote me when he was appointed my guardian. That's why I was wondering what he might be like. It's so hard to tell from letters." The thin-faced woman nodded silently, but Natalie had an urge to confide. "To tell the truth, I'm just a little bit edgy. I mean, I've never met a psychiatrist before."

"Haven't you, now?" Miss Plummer shrugged. "You're quite fortunate. I've seen a few in my time. A bit on the know-it-all side, if you ask me. Though I must say, Dr. Bracegirdle is one of the best. Permissive, you know."

"I understand he has quite a practise."

"There's no lack of patients for *that* sort of thing," Miss Plummer observed. "Particularly amongst the well-to-do. I'd say your uncle has done himself handsomely. The house and all—but you'll see." Once again the wagon whirled into a sickening swerve and sped forward between the imposing gates of a huge driveway which led towards an enormous house set amidst a grove of trees in the distance. Through the shuttered windows Natalie caught sight of a faint beam of light—just enough to help reveal the ornate facade of her uncle's home.

"Oh, dear," she muttered, half to herself.

"What is it?"

"The guests—and it's Saturday night. And here I am, all mussed from travel."

"Don't give it another thought," Miss Plummer assured her. "There's no formality here. That's what Doctor told me when I came. It's a home away from home."

Miss Plummer barked and braked simultaneously, and the station-wagon came to an abrupt stop just behind an imposing black limousine.

"Out with you now!" With brisk efficiency, Miss Plummer lifted the bag from the rear seat and carried it up the steps, beckoning Natalie forward with a nod over her shoulder. She halted at the door and fumbled for a key.

"No sense knocking," she said. "They'd never hear me." As the door swung open her observation was amply confirmed. The background noise which Natalie had noted over the telephone now formed a formidable foreground. She stood there, hesitant, as Miss Plummer swept forward across the threshold.

"Come along, come along!"

Obediently, Natalie entered, and as Miss Plummer shut the door behind her, she blinked with eyes unaccustomed to the brightness of the interior.

She found herself standing in a long, somewhat bare hallway. Directly ahead of her was a large staircase; at an angle between the railing and the wall was a desk and chair. To her left was a dark panelled

316                    ALFRED HITCHCOCK'S ANTHOLOGY

door—evidently leading to Dr. Bracegirdle's private office, for a small brass plate was affixed to it, bearing his name. To her right was a huge open parlor, its windows heavily curtained and shuttered against the night. It was from here that the sounds of sociability echoed.

Natalie started down the hall toward the stairs. As she did so, she caught a glimpse of the parlor. Fully a dozen guests eddied about a large table, talking and gesturing with the animation of close acquaintance—with one another, and with the contents of the lavish array of bottles gracing the tabletop. A sudden whoop of laughter indicated that at least one guest had abused the Doctor's hospitality.

Natalie passed the entry hastily, so as not to be observed, then glanced behind her to make sure that Miss Plummer was following with her bag. Miss Plummer was indeed following, but her hands were empty. And as Natalie reached the stairs, Miss Plummer shook her head.

"You didn't mean to go up now, did you?" she murmured. "Come in and introduce yourself."

"I thought I might freshen up a bit first."

"Let me go on ahead and get your room in order. Doctor didn't give me notice, you know."

"Really, it's not necessary. I could do with a wash—"

"Doctor should be back any moment now. Do wait for him." Miss Plummer grasped Natalie's arm, and with the same speed and expedition she had bestowed on driving, she steered the girl forward into the lighted room.

"Here's Doctor's niece," she announced. "Miss Natalie Rivers, from Australia."

Several heads turned in Natalie's direction, though Miss Plummer's voice had scarely penetrated the general conversational din. A short, jolly-looking fat man bobbed toward Natalie, waving a half-empty glass.

"All the way from Australia, eh?" He extended his goblet. "You must be thirsty. Here, take this, I'll get another." And before Natalie could reply, he turned and plunged back into the group around the table.

"Major Hamilton," Miss Plummer whispered. "A dear soul, really. Though I'm afraid he's just a wee bit squiffy."

As Miss Plummer moved away, Natalie glanced uncertainly at the glass in her hand. She was not quite sure where to dispose of it.

"Allow me." A tall, gray-haired and quite distinguished-looking man with a black mustache moved forward and took the stemware from between her fingers.

"Thank you."

"Not at all. I'm afraid you'll have to excuse the Major. The party spirit, you know." He nodded, indicating a woman in extreme décolletage chattering animatedly to a group of three laughing men. "But since it's by way of being a farewell celebration—"

"Ah, there you are!" The short man whom Miss Plummer had identified as Major Hamilton bounced back into orbit around Natalie, a fresh drink in his hand and a fresh smile on his ruddy face. "I'm back again," he announced. "Just like a boomerang, eh?"

He laughed explosively, then paused. "I say, you *do* have boomerangs in Australia? Saw quite of bit of you Aussies at Gallipoli. Of course that was some time ago, before *your* time, I daresay—"

"Please, Major." The tall man smiled at Natalie. There was something reassuring about his presence, and something oddly familiar too. Natalie wondered where she might have seen him before. She watched while he moved over to the Major and removed the drink from his hand.

"Now see here—" the Major sputtered.

"You've had enough, old boy. And it's almost time for you to go."

"One for the road—" The Major glanced around, his hands waving in appeal. "Everyone *else* is drinking!" He made a lunge for his glass, but the tall man evaded him. Smiling at Natalie over his shoulder, he drew the Major to one side and began to mutter to him earnestly in low tones. The Major nodded exaggeratedly, drunkenly.

Natalie looked around the room. Nobody was paying the least attention to her except one elderly woman who sat quite alone on a stool before the piano. She regarded Natalie with a fixed stare that made her feel like an intruder on a gala scene. Natalie turned away hastily and again caught sight of the woman in décolletage. She suddenly remembered her own desire to change her clothing and peered at the doorway, seeking Miss Plummer. But Miss Plummer was nowhere to be seen.

Walking back into the hall, she peered up the staircase.

"Miss Plummer!" she called.

There was no response.

Then from out of the corner of her eye, she noted that the door of

318                    ALFRED HITCHCOCK'S ANTHOLOGY

the room across the hallway was ajar. In fact, it was opening now, quite rapidly, and as Natalie stared, Miss Plummer came backing out of the room, carrying a pair of scissors in her hand. Before Natalie could call out again and attract her attention, Miss Plummer had scurried off in the other direction.

The people here, Natalie told herself, certainly seemed odd. But wasn't that always the case with people at parties? She crossed before the stairs, meaning to follow Miss Plummer, but found herself halting before the open doorway.

She gazed in curiously at what was obviously her uncle's consultation room. It was a cozy, book-lined study with heavy, leather-covered furniture grouped before the shelves. The psychiatric couch rested in one corner near the wall and near it was a large mahogany desk. The top of the desk was quite bare, save for a cradle telephone, and a thin brown loop snaking out from it.

Something about the loop disturbed Natalie and before she was conscious of her movement she was inside the room looking down at the desk-top and the brown cord from the phone.

And then she realized what had bothered her. The end of the cord had been neatly severed from its connection in the wall.

"Miss Plummer!" Natalie murmured, remembering the pair of scissors she'd seen her holding. *But why would she have cut the phone cord?*

Natalie turned just in time to observe the tall, distinguished-looking man enter the doorway behind her.

"The phone won't be needed," he said, as if he'd read her thoughts. "After all, I *did* tell you it was a farewell celebration." And he gave a little chuckle.

Again Natalie sensed something strangely familiar about him, and this time it came to her. She'd heard the same chuckle over the phone, when she'd called from the station.

"You must be playing a joke!" she exclaimed. "You're Dr. Brace-girdle, aren't you?"

"No, my dear." He shook his head as he moved past her across the room. "It's just that no one expected you. We were about to leave when your call came. So we had to say *some*thing."

There was a moment of silence. Then, "Where *is* my uncle?" Natalie asked at last.

"Over here."

Natalie found herself standing beside the tall man, gazing down at what lay in a space between the couch and the wall. An instant was all she could bear.

"Messy," the tall man nodded. "Of course it was all so sudden, the opportunity, I mean. And then they *would* get into the liquor—"

His voice echoed hollowly in the room and Natalie realized the sounds of the party had died away. She glanced up to see them all standing there in the doorway, watching.

Then their ranks parted and Miss Plummer came quickly into the room, wearing an incongruous fur wrap over the rumpled, ill-fitting uniform.

"Oh, my!" she gasped. "So you found him!"

Natalie nodded and took a step forward. "You've got to do something," she said. "Please!"

"Of course, you didn't see the others," Miss Plummer said, "since they're upstairs. The Doctor's staff. Gruesome sight."

The men and women had crowded into the room behind Miss Plummer, staring silently.

Natalie turned to them in appeal. "Why, it's the work of a madman!" she cried. "He belongs in an asylum!"

"My dear child," murmured Miss Plummer, as she quickly closed and locked the door and the silent starers moved forward. "This *is* an asylum . . ."

ALFRED HITCHCOCK'S ANTHOLOGY

# The Handyman

## by Clayton Matthews

The man in the witness chair twisted the stained, broad-brimmed hat in big-knuckled hands. His weathered features took on a pale hue. "Well, sir, it was pretty bad. About the worst I've ever seen, I reckon, in all my years lawing."

The prosecutor asked, "Bad in what way, Sheriff?"

"Why, the blood. Blood on the bed, even on the walls . . ."

At the defense table the defendant shuddered, drew a deep breath, and shuddered again. He leaned over and whispered to his attorney, "I remember."

The defense attorney swiveled his head. "You remember? Everything?"

"It was his mention of blood that brought it all back."

The lawyer shot to his feet. "Your Honor! I beg the court's pardon for this interruption, but I would like a short recess. My client is . . . uh, feeling ill."

There was a brief silence, then the gavel fell. "Very well. Court will stand in recess for fifteen minutes."

Quickly the lawyer hustled his client into the anteroom off the courtroom. When the door was locked behind them, he said, "Then this amnesia, or whatever it is, was real? You haven't been faking?"

"I haven't been faking."

"All right. Then talk. But if you're lying to me—"

"I'm not lying. I remember everything. I wish to God I didn't!"

Spring weather in north central Texas is deceptively mild. The days of March can be quite warm, but a blue norther can boil up any time and send the temperature plummeting thirty degrees within an hour.

On such a day it was that Cliff Dandoy first saw the Ledbetter place. He had left the main highway, as he liked to do, some miles back and was hiking down a gravel road, khaki shirt open at the throat, shoulders loose under the warm sun, knapsack strapped to his back, canvas-cased guitar slung over one shoulder.

Cliff was slender, quick, rawhide-tough, with eyes a deep blue and hair as blond as harvest wheat, and was just short of thirty. By many he was considered a transient farm worker. To Texas folk, he was a handyman, an extra hand hired to do seasonal farm labor. Cliff thought of himself as a troubadour, an unfettered soul, going where the wild goose goes.

At the last farmhouse where he had inquired about a job they hadn't needed a hand, but the woman had provided him with a lunch of cold fried chicken, cold biscuits and a slab of peach pie. He sat under a tree beside the road and ate the lunch. Finished, he smoked his pipe and dozed for a little while. When he awoke, he saw the norther, stretching from horizon to horizon, a solid blue cloud moving fast like smoke billowing in advance of a prairie fire.

Cliff knew what a norther could do. He had wintered in the Rio Grande Valley where winter clothes were rarely ever needed. One of his traveling-on moods had seized him, and he had walked north early. He had no warm clothes with which to weather a norther. He had to find shelter before nightfall or risk freezing to death, but there wasn't a farmhouse in sight.

He started walking. After an hour he rounded a bend in the road and saw the Ledbetter place. The house, he learned later, was close to a hundred years old. It looked it. It hadn't been painted recently, if ever. A porch ran the length of the house, with a rain cistern at the east end. Fifty yards behind the house was a steep-roofed red barn not over a year old. Involuntarily he glanced up at the parallel-bar patterns of wires overhead, leading both to the house and the barn. At least the place was electrified, and there was a new, rubber-tired tractor standing before the barn.

Cliff, wise from experience, went around back. At this hour of the afternoon, a rap on the front door would most likely be considered a peddler's knock and be ignored. He knocked on the kitchen door, waited a moment and knocked again.

The door swung open, and he saw the heat-flushed face of Kate Ledbetter for the first time. She was tiny, lithe, with long blonde hair and eyes the color of wood smoke. She wore a shapeless housedress that nonetheless revealed a figure adequately curved. She couldn't have been much more than twenty.

She pushed a strand of moist hair out of her eyes, saying, "Yes?"

"Ma'am, I was wondering if you'd be needing a hand around the place?"

"You'd have to speak to Troy about that. Troy's my husband." Then, as though fearful she had somehow discouraged him, she added quickly, "We did let a man . . . go, just last week."

She smiled shyly, and it seemed to Cliff that the smile cost her an effort, as though she hadn't smiled for some time.

"I reckon your husband's out in the fields?"

"He's somewhere on the place, but I can't say just where." She shivered suddenly, hugging herself, and Cliff realized that the front of the norther had struck. The sun had disappeared, and a cold wind was pushing against the house.

She stepped back inside. "It's going to be freezing out there soon. Why don't you come into the kitchen and wait? Maybe you'd like a bite?"

Cliff never turned down food, no matter how recently he'd eaten, the involuntary omission of meals being commonplace in his life. Her pecan pie was delicious, the glass of milk cold and foaming fresh.

The kitchen, while sparkling clean, had a primitive air about it. There was an ancient refrigerator that, when on, thumped like a jukebox; it was the only electrical appliance in sight. The cookstove was a huge wood range, and in the sink was a hand pump, not faucets. On the stove a tub of water heated. The splintery floor was slightly damp, and Cliff surmised she had been scrubbing it, hence her heat-flushed features when she answered the door.

Apparently she spoke only when spoken to and, since reticence was a normal condition with Cliff, they waited mostly in silence. Yet it wasn't at all uncomfortable. Cliff fired his pipe and smoked while she worked about the kitchen. Once or twice he heard her sigh and looked up to find her standing at the window over the sink, gazing out. The full fury of the norther worked on the old house now, setting up ghostly creakings and groanings.

Then, again at the window, she said, "He's coming. Troy's coming."

Troy Ledbetter wasn't at all what Cliff had been expecting. He was a slight, wiry man, an inch shorter than his wife, and, it was Cliff's guess, perhaps twenty years older. His features were pale. Most men who spent their working days in the fields under the scald of the Texas sun had skin a dark red, the backs of their necks also red and cracking like baked earth. Ledbetter's expression was mild, and gentle brown eyes peered out at Cliff from under the bill of a baseball cap.

When his wife had explained Cliff's purpose, Ledbetter said, in a voice as mild as his manner, "I reckon I still do the hiring, Kate."

Her hands fluttered. "I know, Troy, I know. But I just thought you'd—"

"You just thought," Ledbetter said tonelessly. He switched his gaze to Cliff. "It so happens I do need a man. Handle an axe?"

"I've used one."

"Not much field work this time of the year, reckon you know, but I'm clearing timber off thirty acres by the river for fall planting. If you want to work the timber, I might keep you on until fall harvest time, which means you have a job until winter sets in, you care to stay that long."

Cliff didn't take offense. A transient farm hand was expected to move on whenever a whim struck him. He said, "All right, you've hired a hand."

Ledbetter's nod was meager. "There's a spare room down the hall you can use, and you'll take your meals with us. Supper soon ready, Kate?"

His wife, at the stove with her back to them, said in a muffled voice, "Yes, Troy." There was a fear in her. It didn't show in the way she spoke or acted but in a certain tenseness that had come over her the moment her husband had entered the kitchen.

As Cliff picked up his knapsack and guitar case, she faced him. "You play and sing, Mr. Dandoy?"

"A little of both." He smiled. "Dogs howl and cats scamper, but I manage to entertain myself."

He felt certain she wanted to return the smile, but her husband was watching, and she didn't.

Cliff awoke sometime in the night. The norther had blown itself out, and the old house was still. He thought a cry had awakened him. He dismissed it as the residue of a dream, and yet, just before he drifted into sleep again, he thought he heard muffled weeping.

Kate Ledbetter was an excellent cook. Breakfast was a stack of wheatcakes and thick slabs of smokehouse ham. Ledbetter ate with his eyes cast down, rarely speaking. Kate didn't sit with them. She moved back and forth from the table to the stove, serving them. Cliff knew this wasn't a cruelty practiced by Ledbetter; it was customary. She would eat later, when they were gone.

He wanted to ask her to sit and eat with them, but he knew it wouldn't do. He did say, leaving the table, "Best-tasting breakfast I've had in a while, Mrs. Ledbetter."

She didn't blush coyly and look away. She met his gaze levelly, searching for mockery. Finding none, she did, then, glance away with a flutter of hands.

To ease her embarrassment Cliff turned aside, fumbling for his pipe, and saw Ledbetter watching them, a slight smile curving his thin lips.

The day was clear, the sky scoured clean of clouds, and a little crisp. Cliff was given two sharpened axes by Ledbetter and shown the area to be cleared of timber, an S-shaped section of river bottom. The river was a narrow, deep-running stream. The timber was live oak, black oak, a scattering of mesquite and a snarl of underbrush. It took Cliff a couple of hours to settle into a working rhythm. By mid-morning he had warmed up enough to remove his shirt.

At noon Kate came out with a hot lunch. She stared at the smooth skin of his heaving chest, then quickly averted her gaze.

Cliff accepted the lunch with a grave, "Thank you . . . Kate."

She nodded, smiled briefly and fled. He stared after her for a moment, shrugged, and sat down to eat.

The Ledbetters baffled Cliff more and more as the days passed. They didn't speak a dozen words to one another during the day, at least not in his hearing, and Cliff very much doubted they were more loquacious when he wasn't around.

Their evenings were spent in the parlor, Kate with a lap piled high with mending, Ledbetter poring over farm journals or equipment catalogs. They didn't have a television set, not even a radio. Cliff owned a transistor radio and he brought it into the parlor on the third evening. At the sound of music Kate glanced up from her mending with an anticipatory smile, a smile that quickly died as she looked at her husband. Cliff was stubborn: he stayed for an hour. Ledbetter didn't say a word; as near as Cliff could ascertain he never once glanced up from his journal perusal, but Cliff felt his disapproval as powerfully as if the man had shouted it at him.

Cliff never carried the transistor into the parlor again. In fact, he never went into the parlor again. He remained in his room, listening to the radio or idly strumming on the guitar and singing softly to himself.

The morning after that particular evening, he managed a moment alone with Kate. He said, "Would you like to listen to my radio here during the day?"

Eagerness swept her face, was instantly gone. "No, Mr. Dandoy. It's nice of you to offer, but I have too much to do to bother with such things."

Most farmers Cliff had worked for had possessed a radio to catch weather reports and crop prices; even those too stingy or too poor to own a TV had that, at least. Then he discovered that Ledbetter had a radio on his tractor on which, apparently, he received all the reports he deemed necessary.

That, of course, was only another bafflement. Ledbetter owned the latest in farm equipment: two tractors, disk plow, row-top planter, hay baler, and others, but the very few appliances in the house were falling apart and the furniture was ancient and worn thin with repeated polishings. Kate housecleaned with a broom, dust mop and dust cloth. And their only means of transportation was a ten-year-old pickup.

Cliff's first conclusion was that Ledbetter was of some religion that frowned upon electrical appliances and electronic entertainment. But his first Sunday there disabused him of that notion. The Ledbetters didn't go to church. After breakfast Ledbetter went to the fields and Kate worked around the house. Their only concession to the Sabbath was Ledbetter's gruff remark, "It's Sunday, Dandoy. You don't need to work today."

It was on the tip of Cliff's tongue to say, "Well, thanks a *heap*," but he doubted it would be received in the proper spirit.

It wasn't a household he would ordinarily be happy in, and he would, ordinarily, have taken his leave after the first week. Yet he remained, angry with himself for doing so, and even more furious because of the reason. He was in love with Kate Ledbetter. It was

326                                    ALFRED HITCHCOCK'S ANTHOLOGY

ridiculous, idiotic, insane. She hadn't given him the slightest encouragement, yet he sensed she somehow knew.

By June the weather had warmed sufficiently for Cliff to sit on the porch evenings, and play and sing. He knew Kate was listening. He halfway expected Ledbetter to object, but the man said nothing.

It was a week before Kate ventured out to sit on the porch and listen, hands folded in her lap. The light was out in the parlor. Ledbetter had gone to bed, which he did early seven nights a week.

This also puzzled Cliff—that Ledbetter would go off to bed and leave Kate alone with the hired hand—but he didn't question his good fortune.

Kate said nothing at all during those first few evenings. Then one night Cliff stopped playing and leaned back to gaze dreamily at the full moon, and Kate said softly, "Play another sad song for me, Cliff."

It was the first time she had called him by his first name. Cliff turned to her and said urgently, "Ah-h, Kate, Kate!"

He half-started to his feet, but she was gone with a pale flutter of hands, vanishing into the dark innards of the house like a wraith.

Weeks passed. The weather heated steadily, and then it was summer. Cliff's axe flashed in the sun, and trees fell like columns of soldiers shot down one by one. Crops grew toward the sun. Thirty acres of alfalfa Ledbetter had planted on the river-bottom land would soon be ready for mowing and baling.

Evenings, Cliff played and sang on the porch, but to himself. Kate didn't join him again, and didn't call him Cliff again. Always "Mr. Dandoy."

Cliff wanted to leave. He stayed on, cursing himself for a fool.

One unusually hot day, Kate was a little late bringing his lunch. He had been burning piled underbrush near the river and was sweaty, covered with a dusting of ash. The water looked cool and inviting. Every night now he swam awhile in the river before going up to the house.

On an impulse he stepped out of his shoes and socks and dived into the water. The trousers didn't matter; they would dry within a matter of minutes in the sun. He came up snorting, blowing water. He heard clear, ringing laughter. He saw Kate on the river bank. It was the first time he'd heard her laugh.

She said, "You look like a little boy caught playing hooky."

It was never quite clear in his mind what prompted him to say what he did next, but something told him this was the right time, the right moment for them. He said, "Come play hooky with me, Kate, dress and all. The sun'll dry it before you get back to the house."

Without hesitation she set the lunch pail down, unlaced and removed her sneakers, then cut the water in a perfect dive.

For a time they frolicked like children. Kate was good in the water. Cliff was sure she forgot everything but that moment in that little time. She laughed and yelped and splashed.

Finally they staggered up the slippery bank. Her hair clung to her head like seaweed. Her dress was plastered to her figure. She was a mess.

She was the loveliest thing Cliff had ever seen.

With a groan he reached for her. "Kate, Kate, I love you. You *must* know that!"

She came into his arms willingly, her mouth raised, seeking. Then she tore away with a strangled cry. "No, no! I won't be responsible for another death!"

He stared at her, blinking. "Kate . . . What in God's name are you talking about?"

She stood with her face turned away. "There was another man before you came . . ."

"I know that. You told me your husband let him go."

"That's what I told you," she whispered, "but I think Troy killed him!"

"Killed . . ." Cliff caught her chin and forced her face around. Her eyes were clenched shut. "What are you talking about? Why would he do a thing like that?"

"Troy caught us laughing together. That was all it was, Cliff. I swear there was nothing else!"

"All right, I believe you. Go on."

"Well, the next morning Joel was gone. Troy told me he had left in the middle of the night."

"How do you know he didn't?"

"He left a suitcase full of his things."

"That could well be, if your husband scared him enough. Why do you think Ledbetter killed him?"

328                    ALFRED HITCHCOCK'S ANTHOLOGY

"Because . . ." She shivered. "I just know!"

"That's only a woman's reason, Kate."

"He was a drifter. No folks, nobody. No one would ever miss him."

"Kate, I don't like Troy Ledbetter, but that could be because of the way I feel about you. Even so, I can't see him killing a man."

"You don't know him, that's why. He's stingy and mean, all knotted inside like a fist!"

"Why did you marry him, Kate?"

Orphaned and left penniless when her parents were killed in an automobile accident four years ago, Kate had looked upon Troy Ledbetter's proposal of marriage as her salvation. At seventeen, in her last year of high school, she hadn't known which way to turn. Troy was well thought of, a prosperous farmer; he was clean, frugal, and seemed a kind and gentle man. She hadn't loved him, but maybe love was for the storybooks and the movies. Four years of marriage had taught her that the frugality was stinginess, the gentle manner a façade concealing an infinite capacity for small, subtle cruelties. For instance, they lived seven miles from town; twice a year Troy drove her into town and allowed her to buy a few clothes. He did all the other shopping, and all spare money went for machinery and farm improvements. Too, of late he had become unreasonably jealous.

It was a story as old as time and as such was suspect. Cliff couldn't keep the skepticism out of his voice. "If he's like you say, why didn't you leave him? Run away, if nothing else?"

"I've thought of it many times, but he swore he'd find me and kill me. I believe him."

Cliff knew that she did believe this. Whether it was true or not really didn't matter. She was just as frightened.

"Kate, you haven't yet said. Do you love me?"

"I . . ." She gazed up at him, eyes suddenly enormous. "I don't . . . It's wrong, Cliff!"

"It's no more wrong than you being married to him," he said soberly, "not loving him and believing the things you do about him. Look, I'll go to Ledbetter and tell him about us, then I'll take you away."

Her hands fluttered wildly. "No! He'll kill you, Cliff!"

"Kate, listen to me now," he said gently. "I've been a drifter too. I've had no reason to settle. Now I do."

Apparantly those were the words she needed to hear. Her resistance crumpled. In his arms she still trembled, and he knew she hadn't overcome her fear of Ledbetter, but she obeyed him without question when he told her to put on her sneakers, and she snuggled her hand trustingly in his as they walked back to the house.

They didn't have to look for Ledbetter. He had started baling hay that morning. Cliff didn't hear the tractor motor as they walked to the house; evidently Ledbetter had gone in for lunch. He came out of the kitchen to meet them as they approached.

Kate's hand leaped like a frightened bird, and Cliff's closed tightly over it. "Ledbetter, Kate and I love each other . . ."

"Just like those songs you sing, eh, singer?" Ledbetter said mildly. The man's eyes had the glassy, bottomless look of marbles, and Cliff knew that Kate had reason to fear him.

Cliff said, "We're leaving together. This afternoon."

"That so?"

Cliff stood away from Kate, stood loosely, ready to meet Ledbetter's attack. He was confident he could defeat the man in a fair fight.

But Ledbetter was looking at Kate. "You're my wife, Kate. You belong to me, just like this farm and everything on it. I'll kill the man who tries to take anything of mine."

"You can't stop us, Ledbetter, with threats or anything else." Cliff glanced at Kate. "He's just trying to scare us, Kate."

Ledbetter still didn't look at him. "Kate, you know I mean what I say."

Kate's hands fluttered. One went to her mouth. She gnawed on her knuckles. She stared at Cliff, her eyes alive with fear. "Cliff . . . I'm sorry! I can't! I just can't!" Her breath caught in a sob. She broke toward the house, running awkwardly.

Cliff took a step after her, then turned toward Ledbetter.

The man's features were void of triumph. He could have been discussing the weather. "I'll expect you gone, singer, when I come in tonight. You have a month's salary coming. Why don't you try singing for it?" He wheeled and started off, never once looking back.

Cliff gazed after him for a moment, then plunged into the house. Kate had barricaded herself in the bedroom. Through the door he pleaded, cajoled and threatened.

Over and over she said the same thing, "Go away, Cliff! Please go away!"

330                                    ALFRED HITCHCOCK'S ANTHOLOGY

Finally he knew he had lost. Maybe she had never intended going away with him at all. He trudged to his room, packed his knapsack and left.

As he walked up the road, he heard the tractor chugging down by the river.

After an hour's walking, he began to think more clearly. Slowly the realization came to him that Kate's fear had been more for his safety than her own. He should have known that all along. His anger had blinded him.

He turned and started back. He would take her away with him even if he had to carry her.

He had been gone over two hours by the time he saw the house again. He heard the stutter of the tractor in the field long before he glimpsed the house.

The back door was open, but Kate wasn't in the kitchen. He went through the house calling her name.

There was no answer.

He found her in the bedroom, almost cut in half by a shotgun blast.

Cliff groped his way outside and was violently ill. The distant whine of the tractor motor, rising and falling, rasped across his raw nerves. He knew Ledbetter had killed her. He would come home tonight, pretend to find Kate dead and blame it on his hired hand who had fled.

But why? Why had he killed her?

Cliff started toward the field, staggering at first but gaining strength as he went.

The tractor pulling the hay baler was at the end of a windrow and was executing a wide turn to start on a new one. At the sight of Cliff, Ledbetter halted the tractor, but didn't shut off the motor. As a result the baler, connected to the tractor drive shaft, continued to run, the auger flashing in the late afternoon sun.

Ledbetter said calmly, "I didn't expect to see you again, singer."

"Why? Why did you do it, Ledbetter?" Cliff had to shout to be heard over the tractor motor and the baler. "She wasn't going to leave you!"

"Oh, but she was. She was packing to leave when I went back to the house for a minute." For one of the rare times Cliff saw the man grin. "She waited until she was sure you'd gone. Didn't want you hurt, she said. She was going off by herself."

Through a shimmering haze of fury Cliff reached up and caught Ledbetter by the shirt front and hauled him down off the tractor seat.

His lawyer said, "Then you killed him?"

"Yes, I killed him," Cliff said. "Oh yes, I killed him."

"But the body? It was never found. The sheriff looked everywhere. You're being tried for killing Kate, I guess you know now. Since you wouldn't, or couldn't, tell us what happened, the sheriff figured you also killed Ledbetter and buried him somewhere."

"The baler? Is it still in the field?"

"No, the tractor and the baler were driven into the barn the next day. But the hay's still there. It rained that same night and ruined the hay."

"The rain," Cliff mused. "I guess it rinsed away the blood."

"The blood?"

"Ledbetter loved his machinery, you know, more than he ever did Kate." Cliff looked at his lawyer without expression. "When I pulled him off the tractor, I hit him once, knocking him into the hay baler. I could have saved him, I guess, but I didn't try. Tell the sheriff he'll find what's left of Troy Ledbetter in the last two bales of hay from his machine."

# Nothing But Human Nature

## by Hillary Waugh

Captain of Detectives Mike Galton, or "the old man" as he was known to his underlings, looked down at the woman's body. It was dressed in a nightgown and a blue flannel robe and lay on the kitchen floor in a crumpled heap. The woman was a brunette, thirty-three years old, and perhaps twenty pounds overweight. Whether she was pretty or not was hard to tell from the way her head was smashed. The instrument that did the damage, a length of lead pipe, lay beside her. There was a bag of groceries on the kitchen table, and the back door was open.

"Photo been called?" the old man asked William Dennis, the young detective beside him.

"Yes, sir, and the M.E."

The old man turned and went back to the little front parlor where Joseph Eldridge, the dead woman's husband, sat twisting his hands between his knees. A policeman stood nearby, trying to look invisible.

"That piece of pipe," the old man said to the husband. "Did that come from somewhere in the house?"

Joseph Eldridge focused on the detective's face. He was a lean, handsome man in his mid-thirties though now he looked harrowed and white. "No," he said, shaking his head. "I never saw it before."

"You want to tell it again—exactly what happened this A.M.?"

"I went to do the marketing, same as every Saturday morning—"

"You do the marketing?"

"My wife teaches school all week. I want—wanted her to relax on weekends."

"You work, Mr. Eldridge?"

"Me?" He looked startled. "Yeah. I sell insurance." Then he said, "I didn't touch her money, if that's what you mean. We lived on what I make."

"But she taught?"

Joseph Eldridge nodded. "She taught because she loved teaching. She didn't want to give it up when we married, and I didn't make her." He sighed deeply.

Mike Galton nodded. "And you do the marketing Saturday mornings. Tell me about this morning."

Eldridge shrugged and looked down at the floor. He spoke in a choked voice. "There's nothing to tell, really. I went to the supermarket, I bought the week's groceries, I drove home, came in the back door and—and found her."

"Any idea who did it?"

He shook his head slowly. "I can't imagine."

Detective Dennis said, "Did you go into the bedroom?"

Eldridge nodded. "When I called you. The phone's in there."

"You touch anything?"

"No."

Dennis said to the old man, "The bedroom's been ransacked, Captain. The bureau drawers, the closets."

Galton said, "You have valuables in the house, Mr. Eldridge?"

"Not anything much. A few dollars maybe, and May had a couple of rings that might have been worth a little—a hundred bucks or so."

The photographer arrived and Galton and Dennis took him out to the kitchen. Then the medical examiner came and was also shown the scene.

Galton returned to the husband. "What time did you go to the store, Mr. Eldridge, and what time did you get back?"

"I left the house around nine o'clock, give or take ten minutes. I wasn't noticing the time."

"Somewhere between eight-fifty and nine-ten, then?"

"That sounds about right."

"And you got home?"

"I didn't notice. I came in. I saw her. I guess after that I just stopped thinking."

"Can you give me a rough idea what the time was?"

Eldridge tried to think. "About half an hour ago, I suppose. I phoned the police, and then—" He looked up. "Wait, I do remember. The clock in the store said twenty of eleven when I was checking out. Five minutes to load the car and five minutes to get home here— Call it

ALFRED HITCHCOCK'S ANTHOLOGY

about ten minutes of eleven when I found her."

"How long have you been married, Mr. Eldridge?"

"Ten years in June."

"No children?"

"No."

"Did she have any enemies that you know of?"

"She couldn't have. Everybody loved her."

"Any relatives?"

"Her mother, two brothers and a sister. But they live on the west coast."

The old man went back to the kitchen. The medical examiner told him the woman had been beaten to death with the pipe. The photographer said he'd got his pictures and did the captain want him to dust for fingerprints?

"See if you can get anything off the pipe," the old man said. "And the drawers in the bedroom. I understand the bureaus have been ransacked."

Dennis said, "Do you believe the burglar theory?"

The old man shrugged. "It's possible there was a burglar. It's possible Eldridge killed her and faked the burglary. It's possible someone else killed her and faked the burglary." He said to the doctor, "Do you think she was beaten unnecessarily—by someone who hated her rather than someone who wanted to rob her?"

The doctor said he couldn't venture an opinion. He sat down at the kitchen table to fill out his papers.

The body was lying face up now, and Captain Galton said to Dennis, "See if you can find a sheet or something and cover her."

Policewoman Jenny Galton came through from the livingroom. She was a young and pretty redhead, but poised and experienced despite her youth, for she was Mike Galton's daughter.

"Hi, Pops," she said. "I hear I'm to search a body." Then she saw the dead woman and she sobered. "That's not very pretty," she said. "It's a homicide, then?"

Galton said, "It's a homicide, pet, and a nasty one."

While Jenny searched the apparel on the body, Galton went outside for a look around. The house was a tiny brick bungalow in an area of tiny brick bungalows, packed together on midget lots with one-car garages in back and just room for a driveway between. Joseph Eldridge's station wagon was standing in front of the garage and two steps from the stoop. In the back were two more bags of groceries like the one on the kitchen table.

Detective Dennis came out to join him. "No fingerprints on the pipe," he said, "and it doesn't look like there's going to be anything on the bureau knobs either." He smiled wryly. "We aren't left with much."

"We never are when there are no witnesses." Galton sighed and turned to the porch steps. "Well, I guess the next step is to canvass the neighborhood, see if there've been any strangers around—salesmen, vagrants, and the like—and see if anybody can tell us anything about the Eldridges. I'd like to know whether his grief is as real as it looks."

A sheet was over the body when they came back in, and Jenny told them the woman was missing her wedding and engagement rings. Otherwise there was nothing to report.

"You get any ideas when you examined the body, kitten? Any female intuition?"

She said, "If you mean do I think Mr. Eldridge is telling the truth, I don't know. Nothing I found is inconsistent with his story. It could have happened like that."

The captain went on into the little bedroom. The police photographer was putting away his fingerprint equipment and shaking his head. "Just smudges," he said. "One partial on the bureau top but it looks like the woman's."

The old man and Dennis brought Mr. Eldridge into the bedroom then to make a search. He looked through the drawers and his wife's purse. He found there was no money in the purse and her jewelry box was missing from the drawers.

"You got any insurance on the jewelry?" Dennis asked him.

Eldridge shook his head. "It wasn't worth that much."

The old man showed him a note on the telephone pad. It said: "Membership comm. Tues. at 4:00."

"May wrote that," Eldridge told him. "They usually meet at the church on Mondays. I guess it got changed."

"Do you know when she received the call?"

"I don't have any idea. It wasn't when I was around."

"Do you know who would have made the call?"

Eldridge said it was probably the committee chairman. Her name was Mrs. Bertha Crump, and the old man found her number in the address book on the phone table.

Dennis took Eldridge back to the livingroom while Galton got the woman on the line. Yes, she told him, she was the one who called May Eldridge about the change. She'd called her just that morning, in fact.

"Do you know what time this morning, Mrs. Crump?"

"About quarter past nine. Why, is something the matter?"

"Yes, something is the matter. But can you say for sure that you made the call at quarter past nine?"

"Well," Mrs. Crump said hesitantly, "I wouldn't want to swear to it. But I do know that I don't make phone calls before nine o'clock, and Mrs. Eldridge was the fourth person I talked to about the change. It couldn't have been before quarter past nine. Of that I'm sure."

"It was Mrs. Eldridge who answered the phone?" Galton said.

"Yes."

"How long did the two of you talk?"

"Oh, perhaps two minutes. Usually I'd talk longer, but I had five others to call so I didn't want to dally."

"Did she mention her husband at all?"

Mrs. Crump said no, and asked again what the trouble was.

Galton told her, helped her over her shock, and questioned her some more, but the answers didn't change.

When he hung up, Galton went back to Eldridge and had him tell the story over again two more times. It came out the same way, but with two additions. He knew nothing of Mrs. Crump's phone call, for he had already left. He knew of nobody who could support his alibi.

The hearse pulled into the drive and two morgue attendants came through the back door with a stretcher. Galton watched them lift the body onto it with practiced precision and take it out. He sent the patrolman back to his beat and, with Detective Dennis, started a canvass of the neighborhood to see what they could learn.

The brick bungalow abutting the Eldridges' driveway was their first stop and the door was answered by a trim young bottled blonde in shorts and halter. Galton showed his badge, apologized for the intrusion, and explained about the death next door.

"Yeah," the woman said. "I saw the hearse. You say she was killed, huh? Gee, that's terrible."

"Did you know them well, Mrs.—ah—"

"Jenks. Mimi Jenks. No, I didn't know them except to say hello to."

"What about Mr. Jenks?"

The woman laughed. "Mr. Jenks sends me an alimony check once a month. That's all I know about him or care."

Galton said, "Oh." Then he said, "Can you tell me anything about this morning? Did you see anybody or hear anything next door?"

Mrs. Jenks frowned in thought. Then she said, "I heard their car go out at nine o'clock. I can't think of anything else."

"Did you say nine o'clock?"

She shrugged. "Well, it might not have been exactly nine o'clock. It might have been two or three minutes after."

"How do you remember the time so well?"

She laughed. "That's easy. I got up at nine. I looked at the clock. And I had just got out of bed when I heard their car start up."

"And you saw or heard nothing else?"

"Nothing else. Until the hearse."

"You didn't hear his car return?"

She shook her head. "I only heard it go out because the bedroom's on that side of the house and the window was open."

"I see." Galton pursed his lips. "One more question. You know anything about what kind of a marriage they had? Did they get along or fight, or what?"

Mrs. Jenks said she didn't have any idea. All she knew was she never heard them fight. She never heard anything from them at all.

"I see. Now, one last thing. It's very important. Are you absolutely sure it was nine o'clock when he drove away?"

"Absolutely, because I looked at the clock when I got up and then I did my exercises by the window for fifteen minutes and I remember the car wasn't there. Why is that so important?"

"Because it supports his own story that that's when he went shopping."

"I see. I'm his alibi, in other words?"

"Yes, you could call it that."

"I'm glad I can help."

"So are we. You'll be asked to testify, of course."

She smiled. "Any time."

Galton and Dennis tried the family on the other side of the El-

ALFRED HITCHCOCK'S ANTHOLOGY

dridges' but they could not help at all, nor could anyone else in the neighborhood. No one had noticed suspicious strangers around. No one had seen Eldridge go to the supermarket.

The old man and his youthful companion returned to police headquarters at half past twelve. The chief was there and so was Jenny.

"We're up a tree," Dennis told the chief. "Absolutely no clues." He went on to explain the problem. Mr. Eldridge left the house between nine and nine-five. Mrs. Eldridge received a phone call from Mrs. Crump between nine-fifteen and nine-twenty, between nine-twenty, when she hung up, and ten-fifty, when Mr. Eldridge returned, someone came in the back door, beat Mrs. Eldridge to death with a pipe, ransacked the bureaus in the bedroom, and made off with a box of inexpensive jewelry and the few dollars in Mrs. Eldridge's purse.

The chief said, "Is that how you see it?" to the old man, but Galton's attention was on his daughter.

"You're a right pretty girl, kitten," he said. "Now that I notice, I'm struck by that fact."

She laughed and told him he was dotty.

"No, I'm not dotty, I'm serious. What are your measurements, thirty-eight, twenty-three, thirty-six?"

"That's reasonably close. Why?"

"Because when you go home for lunch, you're going to change into your prettiest dress. Then we're going to see what kind of an actress you are."

Jenny, the chief, and William Dennis all were curious, but the old man merely said very mysteriously, "Wait and see."

At half past two that afternoon, the old man rang Mrs. Jenks' doorbell again. He smiled and said he was sorry to trouble her but could she come down to headquarters so they could take her statement? She said she'd be glad to oblige and got her coat.

On the way he told her how much he appreciated her cooperation and she said she was only doing her duty. As an innocent man's only alibi, she had to testify.

"Yes," the old man said, "except, you will be pleased to learn, the burden is no longer solely on your own shoulders. We've found someone else to verify his alibi."

"Oh?" she said, and turned to look at him. "Who?"

"A young woman he knows. She's come forward to testify that she saw him enter the supermarket at ten minutes past nine."

Mrs. Jenks said, "Oh," again, in a strange voice.

The chief and William Dennis were in the squad room when the old man brought Mrs. Jenks in. He introduced her and told her that they'd take her statement in just a few minutes, and if she'd wait in the other room . . . He took her to the door and there was Jenny, sitting on the couch in her prettiest dress, her hair just so, looking as luscious as chocolate cake. "This is Miss Murphy, Mrs. Jenks," the old man said. "She's the one I was telling you about, the one who saw Mr. Eldridge in the supermarket. Isn't that right, Miss Murphy?"

Mrs. Jenks stopped dead in the doorway but "Miss Murphy" didn't seem to notice. "That's right," she said brightly. "Joe came in at exactly ten minutes past nine. I know because I was looking at my watch."

Captain Galton smiled with approval, but Mrs. Jenks didn't smile at all. "She's a liar," she said.

Miss Murphy put her nose in the air. "I ought to know when Joe came in," she said. "I'm the one who was looking at my watch."

"She's a liar," Mrs. Jenks repeated in a louder voice. "Because Joe Eldridge didn't leave his house until half past nine."

"Half past nine?" the captain said.

"Half past nine," she told him. "Because that's how long it took that two-timing cheat to bash in his wife's head. And he didn't go to the store for five more minutes after that because he got blood on his shirt and had to change it. I know, because the bloody one is in the bottom of my laundry bag, wrapped around her jewelry box."

Captain Galton said, "Is that right?" but Mrs. Jenks wasn't paying any attention to him.

She was pointing at "Miss Murphy" and saying, "So if you think you're going to run off with him to the Virgin Islands while I'm left holding the bag, forget it. He's going to jail. And I'm going to put him there."

She told it all to the detectives and a tape recorder, how Eldridge promised her marriage and a life of Caribbean luxury in return for a murder alibi. Then they got the district attorney in and she went over it again. After that, they sent two policemen out with a warrant for Mr. Eldridge's arrest.

In the squad room, Detective William Dennis and the chief of police looked at Captain Galton and shook their heads. "Absolutely amazing," they said.

"It's nothing but human nature," the old man replied. "I figured the moment she thought a younger and prettier girl was also lying to save Eldridge's neck, she'd blow his alibi to kingdom come."

Dennis said, "That, I understand. But how did you know she and Eldridge were a twosome to begin with? That's what amazes me. What tipped you off?"

The old man said, "Human nature again, Bill. Put a sexy young grass widow next door to a handsome free-lance insurance agent whose wife is away at work all day and you can expect there's going to be a situation. And when the wife has ten years' worth of teaching salary lying around unspent, you know the answer to that situation isn't going to be divorce, it's going to be murder.

"We had the murder, so one look at the woman next door was all I needed to know the whole story. It wasn't the piece of pipe or the missing jewelry or the stories they told that gave it away. It was her shorts, her halter, and her bleached hair."

# Murder, 1990

## by C. B. Gilford

The case of Paul 2473 really began when he discovered the old book. He recognized it instantly for what it was, because he had once been through the Micro-filing Section where they were recording some old-fashioned but worthy volumes on genetics before destroying them. But the sight of this book, obviously an uninspected relic of the dim past, provoked a simultaneous curiosity and dread in him.

He'd been marching with the Thursday Exercise Platoon over a country back road, and now they were enjoying their ten-minute rest period, lying by the roadside among the grass-strewn brick ruins of some ancient building. Paul was bored—Thursdays always bored him intensely—and both his mind and eye were casting about for something of interest to focus upon.

Which was why his gaze had roamed over the crumbling, disintegrating wall beside him. He saw the aperture almost immediately. At this particular spot, the bricks seemed to have fallen down against a still standing portion of the wall so as to make a small igloo or cave. A tiny, cozy, rain-proof den, he thought, for some small wild thing. A few of the little beasts always seemed to survive the best efforts of the decontamination squads which constantly scoured vacant areas.

Paul turned over and lay on his stomach so that he could peer into the dark hole, and saw the book. He knew instantly, of course, what the proper procedure was. He should take the thing, not open it, but hand it over instead to the Platoon Leader. He'd been taught that all such objects pertaining to the former civilization could be either valuable or dangerous. He had no more right to destroy the book than he had to look at it.

Half-intending deceit but not fully decided, he checked first to see if he was being observed. The Leader was nowhere in sight. The mem-

     ALFRED HITCHCOCK'S ANTHOLOGY

bers of the Platoon were all prone, none of them close to Paul, and none of them paying the least attention to him. Tentatively, still not committed to disobedience, Paul reached into the hole, grasped the book and drew it out.

It was small, light, and seemed ready to fall apart at his touch. Trembling, but overwhelmed by curiosity, he lifted the cover and glanced at the fly leaf. *The Logic of Murder,* he read.

For a moment, he experienced a dismal disappointment. The word "logic" had some meaning for him, though vague. The last word, "murder," was completely and totally mysterious. The book was useless if he knew absolutely nothing of its subject matter. But as he pondered it, he was not so sure. The book might teach him what "murder" was. And "murder" might be something vastly entertaining.

"Everybody up!" The Platoon Leader's shrill bark of command came from far away through the trees.

In the instant before the somnolent members of the Platoon could rouse themselves and stir from the matted grass, Paul 2473 came to a momentous decision. He thrust the little book inside his shirt. Then he got up, stretched, and walked back to the road where the files were forming.

In his cubicle, Paul 2473 re-invented the ancient stratagem of schoolboys. Every evening during the few minutes he had to himself, he held the little book behind the afternoon edition of *The News of Progress*, and thus, while seeming to be immersed in the sort of reading that was his duty, he was actually engaged in a forbidden pastime. He practiced this little deception in case the wall television screen chose at any time to look in on him.

As he read, though more and more conscious of the dangers involved, he grew more and more fascinated by what he found in the little book. Gradually, by piecing together scattered references, he began to arrive at some conclusions.

Murder, he discovered with something of a shock, was the taking of a human life. It was a completely new and hitherto undreamed-of idea to him. He knew that life did not go on forever. He knew that elderly people sometimes got sick, were carted off to some medical building or physiology laboratory or clinic, and then were never seen again. Death, he also knew, was usually painless—unless there was a specific, scientific reason for the authorities to decree it should not be—and so he had neither considered death much nor feared it.

But murder had apparently been a phenomenon of the previous civilization in which the authorities not only did not arrange human death, but were actually opposed to individuals who took such matters into their own hands. Yet the practice, though accompanied by danger, seemed to have been amazingly popular. Paul 2473 shuddered at the barbarism of it, but could not stop reading.

But as he came to understand the title of the book, he discovered that although murder was hideous, it had been in its own past environment rather understandable. In a society where people had chosen their own mates at random, murders had been committed out of sexual jealousy or revenge. In a society where the authorities had not provided sustenance for the population, murders had been committed to acquire wealth.

As he read on, Paul was treated to the full panorama of homicidal motivations, both sane and insane. There was a chapter on methods of murder. There were sections on the detection, apprehension, and punishment of murderers.

But the conclusions of the book were the most amazing part. "Murder," it was stated emphatically, "is a much more widespread crime than statistics indicate. Many murders are committed without premeditation, in the heat of emotion. Those who commit such murders are quite often brought to justice. Much more successful at evasion, however, are the murderers who plan their crimes beforehand. The bulging files of unsolved murders are predominantly of this variety. In the battle of wits between murderer and policeman, the former has all the advantage. Although the findings of various statistical studies have varied somewhat, they all point inescapably in one direction. Most murders go unsolved. Most murderers live out their natural lives in peace and safety and the enjoyment of the fruits of their efforts."

Paul 2473 was thoughtful for a long time after he finished the book. He recognized the peril of his own position more than ever. The new civilization simply could not afford to let this book be disseminated, to allow humanity to realize how recently it had emerged from primitive savagery. He himself had therefore broken an important rule in reading the book, and he saw now why it was an important rule. If he were found out, he would surely be reprimanded, demoted, perhaps even publicly disgraced.

344

But he did not destroy the book. Instead he hid it inside his mattress. The notion of murder, like some inventor's dream, intrigued him, and he devoted all his spare time to thinking of it.

He even considered mentioning it to Carol 7427. He saw Carol 7427 almost every evening at Recreation, and on many occasions had gone into the Caressing Booths with her, more often than with any other girl. He had taken Compatibility Tests with Carol 7427, and was hoping for a Three-Year Assignment with her, a Five-Year if he could get it.

That first evening after he had finished the book, he came very close to confiding in her. She came into the Recreation Center still in her work slacks, but they fitted her so neatly and snugly that he did not mind. He gazed at her close-cropped blonde hair, at her bright blue eyes and clear skin, and he thought about the Mating Assignment. It would be very nice to share a double cubicle with someone, to have someone to talk to, really talk to, someone to whisper to, out of reach of the microphones, someone with whom to discuss strange and fascinating and bizarre ideas, such as murder and what civilization must have been like when individuals dared to murder one another.

He maneuvered her over into a corner, away from the Group Conversation on Radiation Agriculture. "Would you like to know a real secret, Carol?" he asked her.

Her long lashes blinked at him, and her color heightened prettily. "A secret, Paul?" she breathed. "What kind of a secret?"

"I've broken a rule."

"Really!"

"A serious rule."

"Really!" She was enthralled.

"And I've discovered something that's terribly interesting."

"Tell me!" She leaned closer to him. She had taken a perfume tablet, and her exhalations enchanted him.

"If I told you, you'd either have to report me, or you'd be in the same dangerous position I'm in."

"I'd never report you, Paul."

"But I wouldn't want to get you into trouble."

She looked disappointed and began to pout. But her reaction pleased him. They shared the same spirit of adventure and curiosity. He wouldn't tell her now. But when the Mating Assignments came out—next week for sure—when they shared a cubicle, then he would give her the book to read, and they could discuss the wonders of homicide for hours and hours.

That was the day that Paul 2473 definitely decided he was compatible with Carol 7427. And surely the Tests, scientific as they were, would bear him out.

But the Tests didn't. He saw the results on a Thursday, as he came back from Exercise. The enormous poster almost covered the bulletin board, and it read, "Five-Year Mating Assignments for Members of Complex 55." Confidently he raced down the list. But it was with horror that he made two discoveries. Carol 7427 was paired with Richard 3833, and he had drawn Laura 6356.

Laura 6356 for five years! A simpering, dumpy little thing with mouse-colored hair. Was she the sort with whom they thought he was compatible? And Richard 3833, who was to have exclusive possession of Carol for five years, was a beast, a swaggering, arrogant beast.

Paul contemplated his future with indignation. He was now in the age group to which the Caressing Booths were no longer allowed. The authorities had found that at this age a worker would be more productive if he had a settled and well-defined social pattern. Therefore, the Mating Assignment meant that he would be tied exclusively to Laura 6356, while Carol would be just as exclusively the companion of Richard 3833.

He and Carol would scarcely see each other! There would be no cozy cubicle for them. No stealthy little discussions after hours about his wonderful book.

The book!!!

It was by no devious, hesitant line of reasoning that Paul 2473 came to a conclusion about committing murder. It posed itself instantly as the solution to his problem. His mind traveled briskly through the check list—motives, methods, risks.

Certainly the motive was there. He was to be mated with an incompatible person, while his compatible person was to be mated with someone else. As he referred to his handbook for possible variations to remedy this situation, he perceived that a purely emotional murderer might choose to eliminate Carol to prevent Richard's getting her. But that line of action would not obtain Carol for himself, and it would leave him with Laura.

346                          ALFRED HITCHCOCK'S ANTHOLOGY

A double murder was necessary then. Richard and Laura. A bit more complicated in the execution, but the only procedure that would guarantee satisfaction.

The details of the method he left for later. But he did choose a weapon. Or rather, necessity chose it for him. He had no gun, nor means of obtaining one. He had no knowledge of poisons, nor access to any. Richard 3833 was bigger and stronger than he, and Laura 6356 was hardly a frail creature, so strangulation and all such feats of overpowering violence were impossible to him. But he could get a knife, and he could sharpen it adequately. And he knew enough physiology to know how a knife should be used against the human body.

Finally, he tried to calculate the risks. Would they catch him? And if they did, what would they do to him?

It was then that something really amazing occurred to him. As far as he knew, there was no crime called murder in the statutes. If there were, he surely would have been aware of it. They were lectured often enough on things they should do and things they shouldn't do. At the head of the list, of course, was treason to the state. This included such things as sabotage, insurrection, and subversive activities of all sorts. Below treason on the list were the crimes of sloth, failure to fulfill work quotas, failure to attend meetings, failure to maintain mental and physical health.

And that was it. Murder wasn't listed, nor any of the other crimes often connected with murder—no fraud, none of the old attempts to gain material wealth by violence. Paul realized that he lived in an ideal civilization, where there was an absolute minimum of motivation for crime. Except the one that he had found—when some official made an obvious error in grading the Compatibility Tests.

Now the amazing thing then was simply this. Without the crime of murder even mentioned in the law books, the state simply possessed no apparatus for dealing with murder. There was no organization, no experienced detectives, no laboratory scientists trained in sifting clues, none of the things or people that the book had said existed in the old civilization. With just a little reasonable caution and planning then, the murderer of this new, enlightened age could take the authorities completely by surprise, catch them utterly unprepared. And he could commit his crime in absolute safety!

This realization set Paul's heart to beating fast, and set his mind to scheming. The Mating Assignments would go into effect just as soon as the plan for the shifting of cubicle occupancy could be drawn up. This would, he knew, take a week. As it turned out, he had plenty of time. He was ready to begin operations in two days.

His job gave him an initial advantage. As an air filtration maintenance engineer, he was free to rove throughout the entire area of Complex 55. No one would question his presence in one place or his absence from another. All he needed was a work schedule that would take him on a route in the vicinity of first one of his victims and then the other.

Thursday came, and he had to waste a whole afternoon trudging about with the Exercise Platoon. On Friday, however, luck turned in his favor. As he glanced at the sheet which listed the air filtration trouble spots he was to visit that morning, he knew the time had come.

He carried his sharp steel blade tucked into his belt under his shirt. In his soft-soled, non-conductive shoes he padded noiselessly along the antiseptic corridors. His work schedule was tight, but the route was perfect. He could spare a minute here and there.

He arrived first in the vicinity of Richard 3833. The latter worked in Virus Chemistry, had his own private corner where he could work more efficiently out of sound and view of his fellows. Paul found him there, absorbed in peering through a microscope. "Richard," Paul greeted him softly, "congratulations on your Mating Assignment. Carol's a fine girl."

There was always a chance, of course—perhaps one in fifty, or a hundred—that a microphone would be eavesdropping or a television screen peeking in on them. But Richard—and Laura too, for that matter—had never caused any trouble. So they would not be under special surveillance. And very seldom did the guards monitor anyone during working hours. The small risk had to be taken. He would conduct his business as quickly as possible though.

"Thanks," Richard said. But his mind wasn't on Carol. "Say, while you're here, take a look at this little beast on this slide." He climbed off his stool and offered his place to Paul.

Paul took an obliging look, and managed surreptitiously to turn a couple of adjustment knobs while he was doing it. "I can't see a thing," he said.

Richard patiently went back to re-adjusting the knobs. His broad

348

back was turned to Paul, all of his attention concentrated on the microscope.

Paul slipped the knife from under his shirt, chose the exact point to aim at, and struck hard.

Richard's reaction was a startled grunt. His hands clutched at the counter top. Before he sagged, Paul withdrew the blade, then stood and watched as his victim slumped into an inert heap on the floor. Then very carefully he wiped the bloody knife on Richard's shirt, and left the laboratory immediately afterward. No one saw him go.

Within four minutes from the time he stabbed Richard 3833, Paul arrived at the Mathematical Calculation Section where Laura 6356 tended one of the huge machines. As in the case of Richard, Laura worked practically alone, out of contact with the other girls who did similar work on similar machines. Her only companion was the monster itself, an enormous panel of switches, buttons, dials, and blinking lights of all colors.

Laura saw her visitor out of the corner of her eye, but her fingers continued to type out information for the machine. She was a very conscientious worker.

"Hello there, Paul," she said with a little giggle. She had scarcely noticed him before the Mating Assignments came out, but since that time she had grown very feminine. "Don't tell me our cubicle's ready to move into!"

Did she imagine that he would make a special trip to bring her news like that? He maneuvered to a position behind her and groped under his shirt for the knife.

Possibly she imagined he was going to caress her, despite the fact that such things were strictly forbidden during working hours. Her chubby shoulders trembled expectantly, awaiting his touch. He plunged the knife in quickly.

She did not sag to the floor as Richard had done, but instead fell forward over her keyboard. The machine continued to hum, its lights continued to flash, as Laura's dead weight pressed down upon the keys.

The machine will be giving some inaccurate answers, Paul thought with grim amusement as he withdrew the knife and wiped it on the sleeve of Laura's blouse.

But then as he went away and back to his own work, another, pleasanter thought occupied his mind. Carol 7427 and Paul 2473 now had no mates. Surely it would be logical—and the easiest thing to do in view of the compatibility scores—for the Committee to assign these two orphans to the same cubicle. For five years, subject to renewal, of course.

He had not known what to expect. He could not predict how the rulers of Complex 55 would react. The book was an inadequate guide in this respect, since it dealt with the phenomenon of murder in the old civilization.

Murder always had the power to excite interest, the book said. Especially if the victim was well known, if the method of murder was particularly gruesome, or if there was some sensational, scandalous element involved. The newspapers featured detailed description of the crime, then followed along as it unraveled, and finally—if the murderer was caught—reported on the trial. The whole thing could drag on for weeks, months, even years.

But in Complex 55, *The News of Progress* was circulated that afternoon without containing any mention of an unusual happening. At Recreation that evening, nothing seemed amiss, except that Richard 3833 and Laura 6356 were missing.

Paul saw Carol there, and realized he had not spoken to her since the Mating Assignments were published. He managed to detach her from her companions, and carefully asked her:

"Where's Richard?"

She shrugged.

"I don't know. I haven't seen him."

He was overjoyed at her attitude. Richard was missing and she didn't seem in the least concerned, as if she had never read the Mating Assignments. Probably she didn't care for him at all. When this was all straightened out, she'd be quite willing to accept a new arrangement without mourning for Richard.

He stayed with her most of the evening, in a happy, languorous state. He was even beginning to believe that the authorities, confronted with a new problem outside the realm of their rules and experience, might even decide to hush the matter up, pretend it never happened, in the hope that the rank and file, if kept ignorant of the idea of murder, would never think of indulging in it.

350                                ALFRED HITCHCOCK'S ANTHOLOGY

By the time he retired that night, Paul had convinced himself of the soundness of this theory.

Reveille on Saturday morning shattered his illusions. In fact, he wasn't even certain it was reveille because the high-pitched buzzer seemed to sound louder and more insistent. And also at an earlier hour. It was still dark outside his single window.

He climbed into his clothes quickly and joined the others out in the corridor. They were all as startled as he was, very meek, slightly uneasy.

"Forward . . .march!"

They tramped in long files to the end of the corridor, plunged down the iron stairs on the double, emerged into the courtyard where light awaited him. All the floodlights on the roofs and the high walls had suddenly been turned on. In their harsh glare platoons and companies formed quickly and stood at stiff attention. There was no talking in the ranks, no complaining at being routed out at this early hour. An atmosphere of fear and foreboding settled over the whole place.

Paul felt it. Even if he had known of no reason to be afraid, the others' fear would have communicated itself to him. Nothing quite like this had ever happened before. Surely nothing pleasant was in store.

What were they going to do? There would be an announcement probably, stating that two people had been killed. And what then? Would they ask the guilty party to identify himself? Or ask if anyone could volunteer any information?

Then quite strangely, he felt calm. If they had brought everybody out here, that meant they didn't know who was responsible, didn't it? That was encouraging. Of course it appeared now that there would be an investigation of some sort. Questions asked. Whereabouts checked. He would have to be careful. But the main thing to remember was that the authorities did not yet know who the murderer was. And if he could keep his wits about him, they need never know.

But there was no announcement from the loudspeakers. The long ranks of silent men were left to contemplate the unknown, to nurse their fears. Perhaps the authorities had planned it this way, to let those fears wreak their psychological mischief for a little while before the questions began.

Half an hour went by, and still the dawn did not appear. Yet no one broke ranks. No one coughed or shuffled his feet. The only sound was the moan of the night wind over the high walls.

What bothered Paul the most was the floodlights. They seemed to be shining directly into his eyes. He could blink against the glare, but he discovered that if he tried to close his eyes for a few seconds, his body had a tendency to sway. He didn't dare call attention to himself by falling down or even by swaying too much. So he tried to endure the glare, tried to think of the pleasant things that would happen when this ordeal was over.

And it had to be over sometime. The whole machinery of Complex 55 with its hundred thousand members could not be halted and disrupted indefinitely because two of those members had been murdered. People were taken off to die every day, and their places were filled with recruits from the Youth Farms. There would be some excitement and tension for awhile, but sooner or later things would have to return to normal.

Normal . . . a mating cubicle with Carol . . . somebody to talk to . . . talk to privately . . .an end to the deadly aloneness . . .even with the microphones and the television screens, he knew that mated couples could manage a certain degree of privacy.

"Company Number One! Right face! Forward march!"

A sound of trampling feet, and a hundred men left the courtyard.

By listening to the shouted commands that followed, Paul could estimate where they had gone. To the Recreation Hall adjoining the Dormitory. Whatever was happening to them, whatever processing they were going through, was being done in the Rec. That didn't sound too ominous. If they had marched out the gate, he might have felt more uneasy.

A few more minutes passed. Possibly a quarter of an hour. The lights were becoming unbearable, and there was still no sign of dawn. But Paul was in the second company. Perhaps he could manage. But there were pains shooting up and down his legs. A slight dizziness attacked him momentarily. The floodlights danced before him. He closed his eyes tightly, but they could not be shut out. The dance became weird.

"Company Number Two!"

He marched, fawningly grateful for the exquisite feeling of being able to move again. Yes, they were going to the Rec. Two guards held

352                    ALFRED HITCHCOCK'S ANTHOLOGY

the doors ajar, and the entire company tramped into the big place.

More lights, but no longer painful. A buzz of human voices pitched low. The company was taken to the far end, then formed in a single file. They were held at attention no longer, but still the men could not relax. Their fears had been worked on too long. They were silent, refusing to speculate among themselves.

Finally, the single file became a queue, and began moving through the small door. Paul was perhaps the twentieth man in line. It seemed to him that the men ahead of him moved through the door at a rate of one every thirty seconds or so. He awaited his turn, still calm, confident that the huge scale of this maneuver indicated desperation and helplessness on the part of the authorities.

Then he saw around the shoulders of the man ahead of him, saw through the door into the room beyond. There was no one and nothing there, but a nurse with a tableful of hypodermic needles beside her.

He could have either laughed or cried with relief. They were only giving shots. Oh, of course, it perhaps meant a plague scare. Or a test of some new serum. Or even a possibility of bacteriological warfare—and they were being given a precautionary antidote. It had nothing at all to do with his two insignificant little murders.

When his turn came for the needle, he endured the small sting with supercilious disdain. After the long ordeal in the courtyard and his occasional uneasy imaginings, this was a small enough price for reassurance.

Yet the effect of the shot was rather strange. There was scarcely any pain in his arm, but there was an odd lightness in his head. Surely, he thought, he wasn't going to faint in this moment of triumph.

But then he lost all awareness of himself as self. He did as a guard told him. He walked into the next room. There a man in a white coat and a very penetrating stare confronted him.

"Did you stab two people to death yesterday?" the man asked.

Somehow there didn't seem to be any choice, but to answer with the truth. Perhaps it had been the shot.

"Yes," he said.

There was a big trial. He was dazed throughout most of it. But it wasn't for his benefit anyway. It was rather for the edification of all the members of Complex 55.

Then afterward they put him in a glass cage at one end of the court-yard. He was strapped there in an upright position. More than a hundred wires were inserted into various portions of his body, and ran down through the floor and thence out into a control box where there was a button for each wire. His torturers were the members of Complex 55 themselves, who were expected to display their devotion to civilization by pausing in front of the cage whenever they had a moment and pushing a few of the buttons. The result was exquisite pain, which made him scream and writhe inside his bonds, but which was never fatal.

Once a day, of course, the loudspeaker reminded him and all the others why he was there. "Paul 2473," it would intone, "in wantonly and wilfully destroying two pieces of valuable state property, Richard 3833 and Laura 6356, committed sabotage, and is a traitor to the state."

But his miscalculations had not ended there. One of the most frequent visitors to the cage, and one of the most enthusiastic button-pushers, was Carol 7427.

# Panther, Panther in the Night

## by Paul W. Fairman

If this final account—the end of the Cozenka story—satisfies you, you're an exceptional person. It didn't come anywhere near satisfying me. But then, I'm a pretty ordinary person. I like things neatly tied up and rounded off at the corners.

And I don't like murder.

Or at least I keep telling myself that I don't. But the fact remains—I'm a writer. I make my dubious living reporting on extraordinary people and places and things. So perhaps I was subconsciously conditioned to stand back and let it all happen.

I hope not, but I can't be sure.

I was even witness to the tragedy in a professional capacity. I'd interviewed Cozenka in New York on her arrival from Africa and had been invited to drop out to "their little hideaway," as she termed it, to look over the animals she'd brought back.

She and Peter Wyndham.

And I certainly had no reason to suspect that I was being invited for any other reason.

I was getting the story for a top magazine and had a liberal expense account, so the trip into the Southwest, halfway across the country, was no problem—merely a pleasant excursion on someone else's money.

Thus, a week later, I was picked up at a lonely whistle stop and driven twenty miles to Ken Bender's place by a chauffeur in a custom-built station wagon, a pith helmet, and what appeared to be the hiking uniform of an African scoutmaster.

Of course, Cozenka is no stranger to you, her picture having appeared in every important magazine and newspaper in the nation, the sultry Eurasian beauty's romance with Ken Bender holding the national spotlight strictly upon its own merits.

A glamour natural; the merging of oriental loveliness with Texas oil millions; east is east and west is west and the twain met head on to make a fool out of Kipling.

There was plenty of post-marriage ammunition too. Cozenka's love of Africa, the safari, and all the noble beasties of jungle and veldt. Ken Bender's apparent acceptance of handsome Peter Wyndham as Cozenka's guide and companion both here and abroad. The money he poured out like water at her slightest whim, turning a portion of his endless lands into an African replica as a sanctuary for the animals she brought back and couldn't bear to part with.

A colorful background with ever-potent possibilities news-wise.

So the three of them were in the papers as often as Khrushchev and that was the situation when the knobby-kneed chauffeur dropped me off in front of Bender's twenty-room lodge.

Bender himself was waiting for me and there was nothing stiff about our meeting because I'd interviewed him several times before and we'd gotten on well together.

A big, shapeless man without veneer or polish; no touch of the sophistication one would expect in the man Cozenka chose as a husband.

He seized my bag and crushed my hand and bellowed, "Marty, you old wrangler! Great to see you. Zenka's down at the sheds with Pete. A sick monkey or something. How about a brandy? And by the way, you've never seen this place before. How do you like it? Great place, isn't it?"

That was Ken Bender; a man who seemed always to be tumbling eagerly forward through life; a study in clumsiness, physical and otherwise. But honest, open, and as friendly as a stray pup.

"Nice of you to let me come," I said. "I'm finishing up a piece on Cozenka's latest trip and I'm out here to check on the deer and the antelope, African style."

"Great," he boomed. "Stay a month. Stay a year. But now, how about that brandy?"

So we had a couple of Texas-sized snifters and then—because it never occurred to Bender that anyone ever got tired—we headed for the sheds.

The trip was a five-minute drive into the heart of the Dark Continent—a million-dollar never-never land carefully recreated out there in the middle of nowhere.

And there were animals to go with it. I saw a pair of sullen water buffalo, a giraffe nibbling its mate's ear way up there in the stratosphere, a rhino in its own private puddle, and a zebra that looked completely bored with the whole impossible business.

Cozenka and Wyndham were not in the monkey house, but in a shed further on where we found them standing very close together in front of a cage that housed a gorgeous black leopard.

Very close indeed, I thought. But Bender took no notice at all and I couldn't help wondering about his blindness. I couldn't help thinking also what the scandal sheets would do with an eyewitness account of this situation.

Not that I'd ever had any dealings with such outfits. I merely wondered about the true relationship between Bender and the woman he'd married.

Nor did Cozenka react from guilt. As we approached, she dazzled us with her famous smile and flowed into Bender's arms and when he kissed her I envied him.

There was something about Cozenka that conjured up visions in a man's mind—in my mind at any rate; thoughts of Javanese dancing girls, ancient temples, orange-robed Buddhist monks, and fragrant tropical nights. Arrestingly attractive, she still symbolized beauty rather than radiated it; a beauty so fragile I was loath to reach for it even with my mind for fear it would shatter like a Ming vase.

Moreover, Cozenka needed no atmospheric background. She could produce this illusion in riding britches, a cocktail gown, or—so I suspected—even an old flour sack.

She turned from Bender's kiss to give me her hand and say, "How wonderful of you to find us way out here, Marty darling. You must stay a long, long time. You know Peter of course."

I knew him mainly as Cozenka's eternal shadow. He was a striking brute of a man who'd proved it wasn't necessary to look like Gregory Peck in order to fill the white hunter role to perfection. He was blond and made the most of it; a shock of carelessly perfect sunbleached hair conspired with bushy, overhanging eyebrows to give him just the correct touch of masculine ruggedness. Yet he would have been at home in a dinner jacket at the Savoy.

He took a bulldog pipe from his mouth just long enough to say, "Payne, old fellow—delighted to see you looking so fit," and put it back again.

I replied in kind and we turned our attention back to Cozenka. She was gripping Bender's arm and staring into the leopard's cage as though hypnotized. "Darling," she said, "if I'd lived in pagan times I'm sure I would have worshipped the cat god. Just look at him crouching there in all his savage black symmetry! What murderous thoughts he must be thinking. How he must hate us!"

Bender smiled, more at Cozenka than at the cat, and said, "I sure wouldn't want to meet him on a dark night with a gun in my—"

"Watch it, Payne! Stand away! Have a care, man!"

The warning came from Wyndham—rapped out sharply—and I jumped as though bee-stung.

"Sorry," he went on. "Didn't mean to frighten you, but those cats are the soul of treachery—that one in particular. A little closer and you could have lost an arm. You certainly could have."

"Sorry," I mumbled, still shaken.

"Not the right kind of cage for his breed. He should really be paneled off with steel netting."

I viewed the beast with new respect. It lay facing us, satiny black except for the white star on the sleek head that rested gracefully between its barbed front paws, looking more classically beautiful than dangerous.

But I saw that Wyndham could well have been right. The animal's eyes, though motionless, were pools of living green flame and I was able to read into them all the hatred and treachery of which Cozenka and Wyndham had spoken.

Cozenka broke the silence with a laugh.

"Come, darlings," she said, "Marty will give us a bad press— bringing him here to be scared to death by our lovely Demon. We must try now to be good hosts and perhaps he will forgive us."

"Right you are," Bender said heartily.

"Quite," Wyndham intoned and put a match to his pipe.

And good hosts they were, with a dinner few cosmopolitan restaurants could have hoped to match; with coffee and brandy on the screened patio later, where Bender—boring and voluble—told of his pre-millionaire struggles; where Wyndham's manner implied he was graciously contributing his presence; and Cozenka, without effort, overshadowed everyone and everything with her electric aura.

It was either a trio that represented rarely achieved compatibility, or a lot of color and personality wasted on the desert air—I couldn't tell which.

But late the following afternoon, a new insight into the picture was furnished by Bender himself. He and I had ridden out together, Bender acting as guide so that I might get some idea of how much land he owned.

We each had a canteen strapped to our saddles and gradually it dawned on me that Bender's had been filled with brandy, most of it having gone into the big man by the time we started.

I realized this when he began swaying in his saddle and we were drawn down to a walk. Then he stopped his horse and got off and sat down on a rock and said, "They're going to kill me, Marty old pal. They're going to kill me as sure as—"

He stopped and rubbed a big hand over his face as I got off my own horse and sat down on the rock beside him.

"I think maybe you've had a little too much sun and brandy," I said.

"Sure, I'm drunk—as drunk as I ever get—but I always keep my head." He shook it groggily as though to prove it hadn't gone anywhere, and said, "Were you ever in love, Marty?"

"A couple of times. But I was always too busy to follow it up."

"There's love," he said, "and then again—there's love."

"I don't quite follow you."

"The kind that's a good thing and the kind that's dope, a drug—all the drugs on earth rolled into one. And when this second kind hits you, you're done, man—finished—all washed up but good."

It was beginning to be a little embarrassing, but I could hardly ride away and leave him there; at least, that was the excuse I gave myself for sitting tight with both ears wide open. "You were pretty lucky in that particular department," I said.

"You're crazier than a spooked herd." And there seemed to be more weariness in his voice than drunkenness. "I got cursed the day I set eyes on her and I've been cursed ever since."

I measured my next question carefully. On one side, I put the wisdom of minding my own business; on the other, the fact that he'd opened the subject, not I, and I asked, "Is it Wyndham?"

He thought that over, giving the impression of a bewildered man trying to penetrate the logic behind a swarm of flies. "No. He's incidental. It's me—the way I feel about her—because if I didn't feel the way I do, I'd throw him right out and kick him clear back to Africa."

"Exactly how *do* you feel about her?"

"Like I said—she's dope to me. I want her so bad it makes me sick—so bad I ain't been the same man since I met her. She's so damned important to me that I'm afraid to open my mouth about Wyndham or that idiotic zoo or traipsing off to Africa or anything else. Scared for fear she'll walk out on me. The way it is now I'm willing to settle for whatever little bit of affection she'll give me."

"I'd say that's a pretty dangerous attitude. Aren't you afraid it's just the kind of thing that might kill her love for you altogether? I don't think a woman like Cozenka could care a great deal for a spineless man."

He looked at me in disgust, for being so stupid. "Her love for me? Why, you fool—there isn't any. There never was. She told me that when I chased her all over the world, begging her to marry me. But I was willing to settle for any scraps she was willing to kick my way, so long as she'd give me a chance to make a fool of myself on a permanent basis."

"I don't think that's the situation at all. I think that somehow you've completely lost your perspective. What actual proof do you have that she doesn't love you?"

"Are you blind? Look at me. I know what I am. A big loudmouthed slob—not her kind at all. The only excuse for me being in the same county with her is that I've made a lot of money and Cozenka needs money like she needs God's breath."

I raised a hand in protest. "Now wait a minute—"

But he rushed on. "I know how she looks to you, Marty. The way she looks to all the men she isn't married to—a woman of beauty and warmth—but that's only on the outside. Actually, she takes everything she can get and gives nothing in return."

"Then why don't you face up to what you've got to do. Get her out of your system. Divorce her. Pay her off. You can afford to make it worth her while."

"Sure I can—financially, but that's not how it is. In plain words, I can't. If I sent her away, I'd be on her heels begging her to come back before she'd gone no more than a mile."

So this was the reason for his blindness where Wyndham was concerned. Not blindness at all, but a fear of accusing Cozenka of anything lest she walk out on him.

I could partially understand his position, having been around Cozenka's beauty enough to realize it would be dangerous to fall in love with her. I said, "Look here, Bender. You've got to take hold of yourself. Because one thing is certain, the answer doesn't lie in the direction you're going. In fact, I think you're distorting the whole situation."

He was a man who needed reassurance and he snatched pathetically at what I was offering.

"Do you really think so?"

"It's obvious. Give things a little more time. Then, if you can't see that you're wrong, go away alone somewhere and think it all out. You'll land on your feet, believe me."

"That's a good idea."

"And forget this nonsense about your life being in danger. You're way off base with that kind of thinking."

He jerked suddenly to his feet and said, "Sure—sure. Sorry, Marty—putting my problems on you this way."

I wanted to make him understand that I thought none the less of him for it; that I saw the outburst for what it was, not the maudlin whining of a weak man, but rather, the blowing of a strong man's safety valve. "You needed to get it off your chest," I said.

"We can forget it then?"

"Of course."

He scowled. "Look—if you've got any idea of putting this little talk into the piece you're writing about my wife—"

"Now you know I wouldn't do that."

Again he was abjectly sorry. "Sure you wouldn't. Forget I said that too."

He grinned now. "I really do things up right, don't I? When I sound off, I pick a writer out here for a story—"

"You did nothing of the kind. You picked a friend."

"Thanks, Marty. And now we'd better get back to the lodge. You'll be plenty saddle sore tomorrow, I bet."

We headed back and I was glad he'd blown off. I was sure it had done him some good, especially getting that murder fantasy out of his system.

But it wasn't fantasy at all.

They killed him that night.

They killed him right under my nose.

The evening began pleasantly enough. We had as fine a dinner as the night before and another session on the patio with Bender having sprung back to his old self. The way he felt about Cozenka was quite obvious.

Cozenka fairly outdid herself as the gracious hostess and showed Bender such marked affection that I felt he had to be wrong in his doubts of her love.

"Darling, shall I change? Shall I look beautiful for you and our guest in an exquisitely beautiful evening gown?"

"You look just fine in that riding outfit, honey, and I know Marty feels the same way about it."

That sort of thing, with Wyndham sitting back—as he had the night before—and generously lending his presence and its continental glamour.

It was Bender who suggested the movie, an hour-long affair that we watched in his den; the color-film record of Cozenka's last trip; a dazzling parade of lions, tigers, zebras, monkeys, and ton after ton of elephant with Cozenka and Wyndham always showing off to good pictorial advantage.

Cozenka tiptoed out before the film ended. The three of us watched it to the finish, then went back to the patio to wait for her.

I visualized her returning in some ravishing Parisian creation and looked forward to it with anticipation. But I was disappointed. When she came back, a little while later, she was still wearing the riding habit.

Then, some ten minutes later, the curtain came up on the heart of the drama.

It was raised by a running man, a man in coveralls, who rushed into the patio breathing heavily, his voice reflecting unrehearsed fear.

"The leopard, Mrs. Bender! The black cat! It got loose! It ain't in its cage!"

Cozenka stiffened and Wyndham sprang to his feet.

She asked, "You mean he's out and running around in the shed?"

"He's running around loose on the grounds—anywhere. I came by on my midnight check and—"

"You went into the shed and baited him!" Cozenka shrilled, and it was the first time I had ever heard her speak in other than throaty, liquid tones. "You disobeyed orders, you stupid, senseless clod!"

"I didn't—"

"You angered him."

"No. No. Why should I?"

"Because you are a fool! You know Mr. Wyndham and I are the only ones who tend him. All others are ordered away. He was quiet as a lamb when we left him at five o'clock."

The man wouldn't be cornered into any damaging admissions. He shook his head stubbornly. "I just did like I always do—opened the shed door and flashed my light—no more. And the first thing I saw was the cage door open. I stayed just long enough to make sure he wasn't anywhere in the shed. Then I ran up here to tell you."

Wyndham's eyes met Cozenka's. "The cat could have broken out," Wyndham said.

"Not unless he was annoyed. This fool—"

"I'm not so sure. We debated putting a heavier lock on the cage—don't you recall? And the upper windows were open. Fifteen feet would have been no problem to Demon."

"This oaf is to blame," Cozenka insisted.

Wyndham turned to the man. "Go around to the kitchen and wait there until you're sent for. We don't want anyone roaming the grounds until something's done."

The man left, obviously hurt by Cozenka's ill-treatment, and Wyndham tried to smooth her down.

"It doesn't really make any difference who's to blame," he said. "We both know what has to be done now. We'd better get at it."

He didn't have to draw her a picture, for her anger flared even higher.

"No! I refuse. I will not see him destroyed—shot down like a common alley cat. He is the royalty of his kind. It would be a sacrilege."

Wyndham's face was grim. "I agree. It's a bloody shame. But better the cat than—"

"Not so fast," Bender cut in. He'd remained silent, leaving decisions to the experts, but as Cozenka's shoulders drooped he put his arms around her and scowled at Wyndham. "Zenka loves that cat. We aren't going to just walk out and kill it simply because you think that—"

"But Peter is right, my love. Demon is a killer. It is his nature to kill. We must think of the helpless human life at stake. We have no other choice."

Wyndham knocked the ashes from his pipe. "You people stay as you are. I'll go out and get a wind on him. It shouldn't take very long to do that."

But Cozenka objected. "Alone? You would leave me here to wait and suffer? Peter, sometimes you have no regard for how—"

"But this is a man's job."

"When have I not done as well as a man? I am as capable as you."

Wyndham shrugged, appealing silently to Bender as the latter said, "You and I will handle it, Pete. Zenka stays here with Marty."

Cozenka brightened as she kissed Bender. "No, you and I, my love. We two—together. We will find our beautiful Demon. Our bullets alone will destroy him."

She appeared to be throwing this as a challenge at Wyndham. The Englishman shrugged again. "Very well. Let's get about it. No telling what deviltry that killer is up to. I'll swing to the west of the sheds. You two take the eastern side. We should turn him up in fairly short order."

So they trekked off into the night with lights and rifles. I stayed behind, happy to agree that my experience with an air gun at the age of ten hardly qualified me for a job Wyndham wouldn't even allow the animal handler to attempt.

I saw them off, three flashlights bobbing in the gloom, and then sat back to wait.

But no finishing shots broke the heavy silence and it grew lonely there on the patio. I waited awhile longer and then got up and went back into the den where we'd left the brandy.

It was more comfortable there—and safer, with four stout walls around me instead of the patio screening. Much safer, until I raised my eyes and looked straight into those of the black leopard.

It had come in the window; the soft thud of its four paws on the thick carpeting and there it was, death in a satiny black skin.

364

I dropped my brandy and my first thought—when my brain functioned again—was why had the beast sought me out? There must have been others far more conveniently located.

Then a lot of thoughts skittered through my head: disgust with myself for not having had the sense to close the window; resentment at my hosts for not realizing I wouldn't have the sense and had to be reminded; anger at the leopard for looking so incredibly evil as it squatted there obviously understanding my predicament and enjoying it.

There was no chance to reach the door even if I'd had the strength to get up out of my chair. There was nothing in my favor except a faint hope—something I'd heard somewhere—that certain animals ignore you if you remain motionless.

I remained motionless, but the cat did not ignore me. It came up on its four sturdy legs and stretched fore and aft as it contemplated the coming slaughter. It opened its maw and showed me its fine white teeth.

It moved toward me, slowly, gracefully.

Then, as its whiskers practically brushed my paralyzed knees, a suspicion was born in my mind. It was soon quite clear to me that the ape-jawed expression was only a grin, that the menacing rumble in its throat was not a snarl, but a purr.

And immediately the cat verified my dawning doubt as to its ferocity by rolling over on its back to make kittenish passes at me with open paws.

ı The animal was as tame as a house cat. Lonely out there in the dark, it had seen my open window and come in search of company. It quite obviously wished misfortune to no one.

Reaction drained me of what little strength I had left, and I was on the verge of a nervous giggle as I extended a timid hand of friendship and actually patted the beast's head.

But we were given little time to cement relations because a few moments later a shot sounded somewhere out on the grounds—a sharp report that brought the cat to its feet, and sent it back to the window where it crouched, a black bundle of uneasiness.

Then scream upon scream from the same direction as the gunfire sent the leopard back out the window into the protecting night.

I left also, through the patio, guided by the continuing screams, until I saw a light to the east of the sheds. I ran hard and came finally upon Cozenka crouching over the still body of Ken Bender. They were both within range of a flashlight that lay on the ground nearby, its beam marking the bloody wound in Bender's chest.

It took no medical experience—only common sense—to know that Bender was dead.

Cozenka had stopped screaming. Her face was empty, her eyes stared and she swayed rhythmically back and forth.

"I killed my love. Oh! Oh, God forgive me, I killed him."

I knelt down. "How did it happen?"

She stared at me as though not comprehending. I shook her, rather roughly, by the shoulder. "How did it happen?"

"We were hunting separately. I was not using my light—watching for the glow of Demon's eyes. My darling must have veered over—gotten in front of me. But Demon was here. I swear it—I swear it. I saw the green of his eyes. I was sure he charged me as I fired. But of course it was—"

A pounding of feet cut off her flow of words and Wyndham arrived. He took in the scene like a white hunter should—no panic, no shock. "What's happened here?"

"Cozenka shot Ken. She thought he was Demon. She thought he had green eyes."

If Wyndham found my tone sarcastic, he gave no sign as he turned away to sweep his light in a circle. "The cat isn't here now," he said. "Go to the sheds. Bring a blanket to cover the body and someone to stay with it. Leave him one of the guns. Then you take Cozenka back to the lodge. I've got to keep going until I find that bloody cat."

"It shouldn't be too difficult," I retorted. "Just sit by an open—" But he'd trotted off into the night and I went about obeying orders.

Ten minutes later, leaving a stunned guard with the body, I led the now-silent Cozenka back to the lodge. As we entered the patio, we heard the bark of Wyndham's gun from beyond the lodge. A few minutes later, he returned to find us waiting for him in the den.

He knocked off a stout shot of brandy before saying, "What a mess! What a bloody mess!"

Both Cozenka and I asked the obvious question silently, with our eyes, and Wyndham nodded. "I found him in that brush patch, out away from the house—on the den side. I got in a good, clean shot. He's dead."

Cozenka had recovered somewhat, to just the extent that would be expected after what she'd been through. I paid her unspoken tribute as an actress when she said, "My love is dead. My beautiful, beautiful love."

"Are you referring to your husband, or the cat?" They both looked at me sharply. I wondered suddenly about my own chances of surviving the night, and pondered the wisdom of keeping silent.

But my sense of outrage was too great. "I should have paid more attention to what Ken told me this afternoon," I said.

Wyndham waited.

Cozenka asked, "What did my darling tell you?"

"Your darling said you two were planning to kill him. I think he was indirectly asking me for help, but I was too thick to understand. And by the way, I don't like to seem pickishly technical, but shouldn't someone call the police?"

"I took care of that on the way in," Wyndham said. "The County Sheriff. He comes from Kenton—a small village. A half hour's drive."

"You were speaking of Ken," Cozenka said. "But you're lying, of course. What sort of nonsense are you—"

"I took it for that, but I was wrong. I thought he was a little drunk and emotionally upset. But he obviously knew more than I let him tell me."

At this point, Wyndham won my respect as a cool operator if not as a human being. He sat back, masking the concern he must have felt, listening, saying nothing.

Excitement intensified Cozenka's foreign way of speaking. "Marty, darling—has this terrible tragedy shocked away your reason? What madness in heaven's name is this—what delirium?"

"Stop it. Your whole murder plot went down the drain. The cat that Wyndham was so desperate to shoot just now paid me a visit earlier—just before you shot Ken Bender down in the coldest kind of blood. The cat was lonely. It wanted to be petted and played with. It was as tame as a kitten."

"What utter insanity. If Demon was here, you're fortunate to be alive!"

"Perhaps I am. But I was never in any danger from the cat. The soul of treachery Wyndham spoke of out in the shed lies elsewhere—the cat never possessed it."

Wyndham was still content to let me do the talking, and Cozenka had assumed the role of a cruelly persecuted innocent. "But why, Marty? Why? What motive could I have had? Why would I kill the man who gave me everything?"

"He did give you everything. But all his love and money couldn't change the fact that he was a crashing bore—a big, clumsy, childlike man with only one qualification for your exquisite attentions. He was rich as Croesus. He, in short, had plenty of dough—you know, money. So you were quite willing to take everything he had except the one thing he wanted you most to accept. Himself."

"Marty—please—"

"So you figured out a foolproof way to kill him and have it called an accident. So foolproof it almost worked."

Wyndham had exhibited only one sign of uneasiness. He'd let his pipe go cold. He took it out of his mouth, now, and said, "Do you plan to tell all this to the sheriff, old man?"

"I do. That is, unless you feel you can explain away two corpses as easily as one. There's a rifle standing two feet from your hand."

Wyndham smiled a thin smile.

"Good heavens, no. In fact with things as they are now, it will be deuced difficult to explain away one."

Cozenka had no doubt been frightened, but she drew courage from Wyndham's refusal to panic. "Marty, you're being very, very foolish."

"That's right, old fellow," Wyndham added. "I don't think you'll get very far with the constable—not with that silly yarn."

"I see no reason why he shouldn't be interested."

"Oh, no doubt he will be, but the cat's dead. And the law likes witnesses to such startling bits of revelation."

He was right, of course.

I began to realize how right, when I talked to the sheriff. He was a small man with a hat and boots that appeared too large for him. He came to the lodge in an officially marked station wagon, and the first thing he did after looking at the body was to go to the phone and call the coroner.

He talked to Cozenka privately, then to Wyndham. I had no opportunity to learn what they'd said, although I was inclined to think they would both stick to their original story.

He questioned me last, in the den, alone also, and I told him the whole miserable story, beginning with Bender's fears and ending with my accusations before he'd arrived.

He listened politely, putting in a question here and there. Then, when I'd finished, he said, "Those are pretty grave charges, Mr. Payne."

"I'm aware of that."

"And are you aware that you have nothing with which to support any of it?"

"There's my word as a reasonably honest citizen."

He'd spent a great deal of time outdoors and there were skeins of tiny wrinkles at the corners of his clear blue eyes. These made him appear to be looking into a high wind as he studied me and said, "A newspaperman too."

"I beg your pardon?"

"I said you are a newspaperman."

Not quite that, but I saw no point in explaining the difference. "What's that got to do with it?" I asked.

"Nothing, maybe. But you *are* out here looking for a story. These poor people haven't been left alone ten minutes since they got married. Writers and newshawks snooping around—snooping in their business—practically peeking in their bedroom windows."

I could have explained also that the publicity they gave her was very important to Cozenka, but the sheriff was too close to antagonism as things now stood. "I don't see what that's got to do with the case. I really don't."

"Well, you might find it real easy to exaggerate—make yourself a sensational story. The leopard, for instance. Are you sure it was tame? Are you dead certain you know the difference between a purr and a snarl?"

"If it wasn't tame, why didn't it attack me?"

"Conceding it was there in the first place, I can't say. Maybe it was blinded by the light and didn't see you. Or maybe it was more interested in hiding than in killing someone at that particular time."

"All right. Suppose we concede that it was vicious and I was just lucky. That still puts the cat in the den with me when Cozenka claims she saw it out by the sheds."

The sheriff shook his head. "She didn't tell me that. She said she *thought* she saw it. She's making no claim that it was actually there."

I began to heat up under the collar. "Sheriff, tell me. Are you on their side?"

"I'm not on anybody's side. I'm interested only in the facts. But you don't have to worry about that. You'll get a chance to tell your story at the inquest tomorrow—that is, if you still think it's a good idea."

"Why shouldn't I tell the truth?"

"You should, by all means. But in matters of this kind, the truth has to be supported by a little tangible evidence and I don't think you've got much."

"It seems to be my word against theirs."

"And I'd give a little thought to the libel laws, Mr. Payne. You can be certain Mrs. Bender's legal battery will know all about them. They might take a dim view of unsupported accusations. You could get into serious trouble."

"I'll think it over."

"In the meantime, it's Mrs. Bender's wish this tragedy doesn't leak out—at least until after the inquest tomorrow."

"And you're cooperating with her?"

"Why not? She has a right to privacy. So don't try to use a telephone tonight. If a mob of reporters flood down on us, I'll know who to blame."

I was angry with him even while knowing I had no right to be. Actually, I'd given him nothing to sink his teeth into. The "word of a decent citizen" bit wouldn't hold water in court. I'd suspected that even before talking to the sheriff. But to let those two icy-veined killers get away with it—

I boiled over that for awhile and then remembered what he'd said about the inquest.

Put up or shut up.

He was right. If I went ahead with my accusations, I could get myself into a serious jam.

I retired to my room before the coroner arrived and no one bothered me any more that night. Only my conscience, as I pondered the advisability of keeping my mouth shut.

Ken Bender, a fine man who hadn't deserved it, had been murdered by two calculating killers. I knew it. Yet there was absolutely nothing I could do.

Nothing except pace the floor all night thinking about the old chestnut—*there is no perfect plan for murder.* The killer always makes a small mistake—one that gets him convicted and hung.

But where was the mistake here? This one was so good, they could get away with it even when luck turned against them. Certainly it was only their bad luck that had sent that black cat into the den.

And yet their plan hadn't been seriously damaged.

I knew now the reason for Wyndham's almost casual attitude when I'd accused them. A much faster thinker than I was, he knew instantly that things would work out as they'd planned.

Of course, he hadn't threatened my life. There was no need for him to.

And I realized that the perfect murder was not only a possibility, but a fact. The fallacy in the old saying was that the perfect ones were never uncovered.

Fuming and fretting, I finally got to sleep—so late I didn't wake up until ten the next morning. I showered and shaved and went downstairs to find the sheriff alone in the dining room with a cup of coffee and a notebook.

He was neither friendly nor hostile as he looked up. Simply impersonal.

"Good morning, Mr. Payne. Sleep well?"

"Not very, but that's beside the point. Do you still think the death of Ken Bender was nothing more than an accident?"

"Nothing's happened to change my mind."

"By the way, I didn't get your name last night. You do have a name, don't you?"

"Henderson—Milt Henderson."

His answer was annoyingly mild, and I was fully aware that I was deliberately trying to irritate him—using him as a target for my own frustrations.

And the keen-eyed little lawman sensed the same thing because he said, "I don't want you to misunderstand what I said last night, Mr. Payne."

"Misunderstand? Why should you care one way or the other?"

"For two reasons. I do my job and I don't want anyone to think otherwise."

"And the other?"

"This case is going to cause a national stir when it breaks. As a reporter on the scene, your copy will be in demand and you could easily make me the goat. You could make it look like I covered up for Mrs. Bender—that her money and position made me tip my hat and say yes, ma'am, and no, ma'am. Do you see?"

"And that isn't true?"

He scowled for the first time since I'd known him. "You're damned right it isn't. Mrs. Bender and Wyndham get no more from me than any other resident of my county. You know yourself you've got nothing that will stand up. So go find something that will hold up in court, Mr. Payne. You do that and I'll back you to the limit. But don't expect me to accuse people of murder when it isn't proved."

He was right, of course, and maybe what he said was just what I needed. At any rate, it started me thinking along positive lines instead of sitting around feeling sorry for myself because nobody would believe me.

Not that it reaped any immediate harvest. With Sheriff Henderson's parting instructions to be on hand for the inquest that had been scheduled for two o'clock, I wandered out toward the sheds trying to figure out a way to back my story with some proof the law would recognize as such.

There had to be a hole in their scheme somewhere.

I think now my anger was centered mainly around having been played for a fool. Cozenka's invitation, putting me on the scene at the time of the murder, had not been coincidental. I'd been carefully chosen as an amiable, not-too-bright slob who would automatically back up their play and give it the prestige of a witness whose copy appeared nationally in top magazines. An accessory, in essence, to bolster the vicious plot with blindly sympathetic testimony after the fact.

This made me mad. Together with the sheriff's prodding, it forced my mind to labor mightily and bring forth a hunch, one that sent me rushing back to the lodge and up to Cozenka's room.

She answered my knock, incredibly beautiful in a black lace gown. She'd done something to her eyes to make them appear red from weeping, and the sight of her—even with what I knew—was a strain on my determination. Could this sorrowing creature be anything but a grieving wife? I had to bring in a quick image of her as she must have looked with her rifle aimed at Bender's chest.

"You have come to apologize, Marty dear? Then I will accept your sorrow. I will forgive you. Do come in."

I went in and found Wyndham sitting on the edge of the window seat with a scotch in his hand. The streaming sun turned his blond thatch into a halo. He looked like a good friend for one to have in time of grief.

He said, "Hello, Payne," and then knocked off the rest of his drink.

With what I had in mind, I didn't want their antagonism. All I wanted was a little time alone in Cozenka's room. Not that I was sure I would find what I hoped to, but it was the logical place to look and the sooner the better.

So I smiled engagingly at Wyndham and patted Cozenka's hand. "I guess I was a little cruel last night, but Ken was my friend. Perhaps we can—"

Wyndham, pipe in hand, suddenly turned grimly serious, the first hint of hostility that he'd shown. "I'm afraid it isn't quite as simple as that, Payne."

"I don't understand."

"Good lord, man! You aren't so stupid as to believe you can throw vicious charges all around the place and walk off scot-free, are you?"

"But we were all upset last night. I—"

"You called us murderers to our face. You also gave the same ridiculous story to the sheriff. That means it will get around. Your ugly accusations are no doubt on every tongue in the place right this minute. Do you think we can just stand by under such circumstances?"

"What do you plan to do?"

"Drag you into court. Sue you to the limit. Any other course would indicate fear of your charges on our part. Therefore, in countering, we must strike deep, so the magazine you're representing must also be named as a defendant."

Wyndham took a baleful puff on his bulldog.

"I wouldn't be surprised if when we get through with you, you'll not only be a pauper, but you'll be blackballed in every editorial office in the country."

Obviously, Wyndham had considered all aspects and decided they had nothing to fear from me. That made his sudden turn to the offensive entirely logical. An attack of the sort he'd outlined would block me off permanently from gaining any official sympathy. I would become a persecutor of upstanding manhood and the defamer of a woman crushed by tragedy.

I wondered who the executive of this team was—Wyndham or Cozenka? The turnabout could have been advocated by either of them. I turned to Cozenka.

"Do you really think I deserve this?"

She chose to pout. "But, Marty darling, you said cruel things to Pete and me. We have our good names to think of. And the world must know how deeply I loved the man I married."

"I think I know. And there's something else. I think you loved Demon. I think you truly grieved for the animal when he had to be sacrificed."

"I did love him because I love beauty. And Ken loved him too. I loved Demon, yet I did not flinch from turning my rifle on him to save human life."

"And the fact that you hit Ken only added to your grief."

"Marty—you are so cruelly sarcastic."

She was right. I was doing a bum job of placating them and I knew I had to get out of the room or there would be fists flying. "I'm sorry it sounds that way."

"You are cruel—cruel—"

Then my clumsy approach worked inadvertently in my favor and Cozenka flared into sudden resentment. "We were waiting here for a visit from Mr. Henderson. He has been so kind—so thoughtful. But we will not wait. We will go to him. I cannot stand your presence a moment longer."

"She's telling you to get out, Payne. That should be clear, even to you."

I got out, hoping Cozenka meant what she said about going to the sheriff. I was in trouble—with only the slimmest chance of clearing myself, and very little time left for even that.

I went back to my own room at the end of the hall where I could watch Cozenka's door through the keyhole. And a few moments later, she and Wyndham emerged and went downstairs.

The moment they vanished, I was out of my own room. And before they reached the bottom of the stairs, I was snooping through Cozenka's personal belongings like any other common sneak thief. I didn't enjoy it.

374                    ALFRED HITCHCOCK'S ANTHOLOGY

It was a big room and there was a lot to go through and I spent the most uncomfortable fifteen minutes of my life. I heard them back at the door every time I opened a fresh closet, but I kept right on, reconciled to being caught in the midst of things if it should happen that way.

They didn't return and I found what I was looking for—or hoped I had. There was no way of really telling. I didn't have enough time, because my discovery, like the hunch it had sprung from, came too late to give an opportunity for complete investigation. I could only sneak out of the bedroom and trot downstairs with my find in my pocket—before they came hunting for me—to attend the inquest.

I only had time enough to say a small prayer and hope I had what I needed to trip up Cozenka, Wyndham and Company.

There were six men on the coroner's jury—all recruited on the premises from among the help—the coroner himself being a Doctor Wendell whom—I later learned—hadn't even told his wife what had happened there at the Bender lodge.

Such was the prestige and power of Bender's millions. The same millions, I thought nervously, that might soon be turned like cannon in my direction.

Doctor Wendell was a man in his sixties, quietly efficient, with something of a judicial bearing. He was admirably suited to the job of presiding. He'd obviously been briefed by the sheriff as to my contribution to the general confusion, because he regarded me with marked interest as I entered and took my seat.

But there was no over-leaping of routine procedure. He questioned Cozenka first, and she did very well, so well that every man in the room wanted to come forward and comfort her personally. Not that they were callous and unmindful of Bender's tragic taking off, but he was dead and absent and Cozenka was very much alive and present.

And she was Cozenka.

Wyndham came next and he also handled himself beautifully. They both stuck to the story as it was originally laid out in their plan. Cozenka tearfully admitted her carelessness in acting hastily—admitted it most convincingly—and they lied with sincerity about the exceptional viciousness of the cat, giving justification to Cozenka's nervousness and fatal mistake.

In short, they stuck to their story right down the line.

Then the slightest of chinks appeared in their armor, the first one since Cozenka's shot had rung out the night before. This when Wyndham leaned casually forward and placed his lips close to my ear.

He said, "A deal, old man. You can only hurt yourself with that fool yarn about a tame cat, so let's call it a stalemate. Forget the nonsense and I'll forget what I said upstairs. No point in our flailing each other."

"You're scared," I whispered.

"Not scared. Just sensible. And you should follow suit, because you know damned well that if you open your mouth I'll crucify you."

With that cheerful reminder, I was called to the stand.

Doctor Wendell, possibly from a keen sense of the dramatic, worked backwards in his questioning. He started with my hearing the shot and the screams and running out to investigate. I verified everything Wyndham and Cozenka and the watchman had told him of the actual tragedy, a girl—recruited from the late Mr. Bender's small office force—taking down every word meticulously. Then Doctor Wendell jumped clear over to the arrival of the sheriff and the removal of the body.

After that, he fired a question that was the business, the showdown. "I understand that shortly after Mr. and Mrs. Bender and Mr. Wyndham left the lodge to hunt down the leopard, you had an extraordinary experience. I'd like to hear about it."

This was my last chance to back down.

And I won't deny that I was frightened for my career and future as I agreed with Doctor Wendell that it had been most extraordinary and gave it out, for the record, exactly as it had happened.

There was a time of silence after I'd finished, probably longer to me than anyone else. I used the time to steal glances at Cozenka and Wyndham. Cozenka was crying softly into her handkerchief, crying in a way that made the coroner's jury hate me and my story—I was sure of that.

Wyndham took it with perfect aplomb, tamping tobacco into his pipe as though he had been indirectly accused of nothing more than swatting a troublesome fly.

Finally Doctor Wendell spoke. "Mr. Payne, do you have any proof whatever, other than your unsupported word, that the incident in the den, the coming and going of the leopard, actually occurred?"

376                                      ALFRED HITCHCOCK'S ANTHOLOGY

"I hope so, but at the moment I can't be sure."

"That's a pretty ambiguous statement."

"I realize that, but it's all I can tell you at the moment."

"When do you expect to be able to tell us more?"

"When we run this off and see what's on it," I said, and took from my pocket the reel of sixteen-millimeter film I'd found on a shelf in one of Cozenka's closets.

"You don't know what's on it?"

"No. I haven't had time to check."

"How did you happen to come into possession of this film?"

"As a result of what I hope will turn out to be logical thinking on my part. From observation, I believed that Mrs. Bender entertained a definite affection for the black leopard named Demon, that she was sincerely sad when the cat had to be sacrificed as a part of her plan.

"So it seemed strange to me that the leopard did not appear anywhere in the hour-long film covering her last trip to Africa. I viewed the film last night, and saw enough to convince me that Mrs. Bender considered motion pictures of her activities over there and the animals she captured as being very important.

"So why no pictures of the animal she obviously regarded more highly than any of the others?

"From that point I proceeded on the belief that such films or stills actually existed and went about hunting for them. This is what I found and only viewing them will prove me right or wrong."

But I knew I was right. Cozenka went pale as death and while Wyndham didn't jump up and break any windows, he tightened up in a manner that was almost the equivalent for a man of his self-control.

Cozenka did spring to her feet.

"No! No! He is wrong. He is deliberately torturing me. That film is most personal. I beg you not to run it off. You have no right to shame me!"

She was making a desperate all-out effort and Doctor Wendell was most polite in his ruling. "I'm very sorry, Mrs. Bender, but this is an investigation into a man's death and as such takes precedence over any personal feelings. Grave charges have been raised. Is there a film projector available?"

It was all there: highlights in the taming of a black leopard named Demon; shots mainly of Wyndham and the cat that could probably

have been used in a course of instruction on how to take the viciousness out of jungle cats; a record from the time Wyndham first entered
Demon's cage, somewhere in Africa, to the high point where Cozenka
frolicked with the happy and gentle beast on the sylvan meadow.

There was a sound track, too, and during the final sequence I
couldn't resist turning to Sheriff Henderson to say, "I think you will
agree, Sheriff, that the cat is purring, not snarling."

I was instantly regretful. After all, Henderson hadn't been against
me. He'd only been doing a difficult job as well as he could.

The verdict said nothing about accidental death. It merely stated
that Kenneth Bender had died of a gunshot wound under circumstances that warranted further investigation, and it enjoined Sheriff
Henderson to continue with that investigation.

I wish I could report that the film did the trick—confounded two vicious murderers and that full payment was demanded.

But I can't. That wasn't how it finally worked out.

I left the lodge, of course, but I stayed on a few days in the sheriff's
town. Some disturbing rumors made me seek him out.

He was busy in his office and so I got right to the point. "What's this
I hear about charges being dropped against Mrs. Bender and Wyndham?"

"Nothing was dropped. Charges were never made. The grand jury,
upon advice of the County Attorney, refused to indict."

"And how did that gross miscarriage of justice come about?"

"Through orderly, logical thinking."

I was thoroughly disgusted.

"Then we'd better have more disorderly and illogical thinking. It's an
outrage."

"I can understand your point of view," Henderson said, "but let's
look at facts as they really are."

"I've looked at them."

"But you haven't seen them as they are. What was there, really, that
would have a chance of getting a guilty verdict from twelve jurors?"

"Proof that their vicious cat was as tame as a kitten."

"Sure, but that isn't proof. It's merely a point for argument in court.
Bender and Wyndham would have had a battery of the country's finest
defense attorneys, but even a mediocre one would have thrown doubt

378                                ALFRED HITCHCOCK'S ANTHOLOGY

upon whether a black leopard, regardless of the evidence, is ever really tame.

"And their reason for hiding the fact could have been any of several that would have nothing to do with murder. Mrs. Bender could admit not being the hunter she claimed to be; that she wanted the prestige of owning a vicious cat without the danger."

He stopped to light a cigarette and then added, "Do you see my logic?"

"I'm beginning to."

"And your story about Bender's fear of death probably wouldn't even be admitted as evidence."

"I see."

"And one last point. Would you care to go before a jury made up principally of men and try to get Cozenka Bender convicted on the evidence we have?"

I thought it over for a moment. "No, but just the same they're both guilty."

"I think you're right," he agreed. "And now, how about a drink? I'll buy."

Perhaps there is some consolation in the fact that Cozenka and Wyndham gained nothing but tragedy from the tragedy they instigated. So it seemed.

They were both dead within six months after Cozenka fired her fatal bullet.

Wyndham, in Africa where he was pounded into the mud by a water buffalo after he missed a hundred-foot shot and had no time for a second.

He went back there, alone, two months after Bender's death. And three months later, Cozenka was killed when her sports car rocketed off the road one dark night.

It would be nice to think that she did away with herself because she couldn't face the guilt of her crime. But if her death was other than an accident, it was probably because Wyndham refused to step into Bender's shoes, and she realized that his clinging to her had been for the money she no doubt settled on him, not for love of her.

I think she truly loved Wyndham; ironically, in the same hopeless way Bender had loved her. And perhaps realization that Wyndham was the one man in this world that she couldn't have was sufficient grounds for suicide.

Then too, there's another possibility. Could I have been wrong from the beginning?

As Sheriff Henderson said, my conversation with Bender probably wouldn't have been allowed in court, and there were many reasons why Cozenka could have covered the true situation relative to Demon.

One thing is certain. Even though I was sure of their guilt, I wouldn't have wanted to pull the switch personally on either of them. Not on the evidence that I actually had.

So, in the final summing up, I was sure of only one thing.

The cat was tame.

ALFRED HITCHCOCK'S ANTHOLOGY